G000162183

Pilgrimage on the Path of Love, a spiritual odyssey, delivers the richness and complexity of life in India, and brims over with convincing, memorable characters, not the least of which is her narrator/protagonist Shantila, a seeker after something we too seldom see in literary fiction – spiritual awakening and liberation. Through many suspenseful twists and turns of fortune, a reader follows Shantila's journey with the certainty that the outcome of her story will enrich his or her own meditations on the timeless question of why we are here, and how we can follow a spiritual path in a world so stained by suffering. This is a book I would recommend for everyone who loves wisdom and wishes to live an examined life.

Dr Charles Johnson, Ph.D, Professor Emeritus, University of Washington, MacArthur Fellow, Recipient of an American Academy of Arts and Letters Award for Literature, and National Book Award for his novel *Middle Passage*

Reading through *Pilgrimage on the Path of Love* by Barbara Ann Briggs gave me the feeling of moving gently on a canoe in a beautiful lake on a bright sunny evening when the approaching twilight leaves you nostalgic to see the day coming to an end. Making lucid use of the confessional mode of expression, her debut novel remarkably captures the spirit of the times. The quest that Shantila, the chief protagonist, undertakes on the path of love unveils to her not only the agony of pain and suffering implicit in meetings and partings but also the ecstasy of understanding and appreciating the intrinsic beauty of the landscape of the soul, the true nature of life as we live it. Her rumination at the end of the journey: "The pilgrimage I sought to complete has been completed, not to the temples of Rishikesh, Haridwar, Badrinath or Gangotri, but to the omnipresent God, to the temple hidden within every human heart" – comes as a potent antidote to growing intolerance bordering on clash of cultures and civilizations that characterizes a world in individual as well as collective distress. The charm of the novel lies in its ability to capture the attention of the reader from beginning to the end as it takes us over picturesque rivers, dales and hills to experience a kind of peace that defies understanding. I wish her maiden venture all success!

Dr Nibir K. Ghosh, Ph.D, UGC Emeritus Professor, Dept of English Studies & Research, Agra college, Agra, (India); Senior Fulbright Fellow, University of Washington, USA & Chief Editor, Re-Markings Journal

Pilgrimage on the Path of Love by Barbara Ann Briggs is a loving account of a woman's quest for spiritual fulfillment. At heart is a palpable undeniable love for the country of her adoption, its multitudinous life, its minor duplicities and wider generosities are so fondly captured with a liveliness, both authentic and amusing, that I felt fresh love gushing for this crazy country of mine. In the book, we travel from Dubai to Delhi to Manali and Leh with its far flung monasteries and brooding temples, and with each ascent, the protagonist is symbolically nearing that state which neither gains nor wanes, where plenitude and beautitude are suffused. These visitations are presented with gossamer delicacy, the author's luminous prose spreading its lacy veil over creation till creation becomes a salutation and a benediction. The inherent discipline encourages emulation. The devotion which the author brings to her enterprise and the serenity that follows are an inspiration.

Dr Shernavaz Buhariwalla, Ph.D, retired Professor of English Literature, Nagpur University, Nagpur, Madya Pradesh (India)

Reminiscent of Irina Tweedie's Daughter of Fire, Herman Hesse's Siddhartha, and Teresa of Avila's Interior Castle, *Pilgrimage on the Path of Love* is a tale of human love transformed into divine love, of desperation into exaltation, of darkness into enlightenment. Barbara Briggs writes with a poignant, transcendent grace that enables us to experience the story, not merely read it. And this is an experience to treasure.

William T. Hathaway, author of *Wellsprings: A Fable of Consciousness*, Cosmic Egg Books

Pilgrimage on the Path of Love

Pilgrimage on the Path of Love

Barbara Ann Briggs

Winchester, UK
Washington, USA

First published by Roundfire Books, 2016
Roundfire Books is an imprint of John Hunt Publishing Ltd., Laurel House, Station Approach,
Alresford, Hants, SO24 9JH, UK
office1@jhpbooks.net
www.johnhuntpublishing.com
www.roundfire-books.com

For distributor details and how to order please visit the 'Ordering' section on our website.

Text copyright: Barbara Ann Briggs 2015

ISBN: 978 1 78535 201 0
Library of Congress Control Number: 2016934232

A CIP catalogue record for this book is available from the British Library.

Design: Stuart Davies

Printed and bound by CPI Group (UK) Ltd, Croydon, CR0 4YY, UK

We operate a distinctive and ethical publishing philosophy in all
areas of our business, from our global network of authors to
production and worldwide distribution.

CONTENTS

Acknowledgments

The author wishes to thank Janneke Segaar for her editorial advice.

desiring union
i returned yet again
molding a form
out of ether air fire water and
this my beloved wayward earth
desiring to find You
i returned
wandering through a maze
of interminable veils
peeling away
layer after layer of illusion
until i could stand before You
illumined by Love alone

Chapter One

The plane landed in Dubai on its way to New Delhi. I wheeled my luggage carrier up the long passageway, enjoying the exercise after the eight-hour flight from London. I was hungry. Since the food served on airplanes is not my favorite, I had had nothing but raisins and almonds on the way. My stomach grumbled but I ignored it. In five more hours, I would be in India.

As I moved slowly toward the waiting room, I was conscious of heads turning as I passed. I glanced hurriedly at my yellow and pink summer dress to see if the thin cotton fabric revealed too much. I tossed the matching shawl over my shoulder and let it fall gracefully down the middle of my back. Then finding an inconspicuous corner by the door, I took the comb from my handbag and proceeded to comb back my thick black curly hair. When I took out my mirror, I was not entirely displeased, but I rummaged through the red cosmetic bag until I found the lip pencil. I turned to face the door and as discreetly as possible applied a fresh layer of coral to the natural brown hue of my mouth. Perched on top of the luggage carrier was a gold-colored wide-brimmed hat with a peach silk scarf. As I replaced the cosmetics, it tottered and fell onto the floor with a soft swishing sound. In a circular motion, I swooped down and retrieved it, putting it on, and tying the silk scarf under my chin.

Then I glanced around. It was a modern airport with clean, sleek and polished floors. I wanted to sit down as my feet ached. However, Indian men who were fast asleep occupied all the seats in the waiting area. They sat slouching with curved backs or bent forward with their head hanging down on their chest. The Indian women were awake, tending to the babies they carried in their arms, or rocked gently backwards and forwards in their strollers. The women were all well adorned with colorful gold-trimmed saris trailing regally on the floor, and sparkling 22-carat gold earrings dangling from their small delicately sculptured heads.

I smiled to myself as I wistfully inhaled the scene spread out before me.

So this – India – is to be my home for the next... How long? – I do not know... Will he meet me at the airport? What will he be like? I sighed inwardly.

The boarding area was already full. I had to leave the airport luggage carrier outside before entering. It was a long queue. The unshaven man standing in front of me with matted hair down to his waist and torn brown trousers smelled as if he had not taken a bath in a month. I held my breath and turned in the opposite direction with my back to the door leading to the plane. My arm ached from carrying the blue vinyl bag. Although not unusually big, it was full of hardcover notebooks.

"Tickets! Passports! Please have them ready!" An Air India attendant shouted at the amorphous mass of people moving like a horde of humming bees toward the entrance to the plane. I was pushed forward.

"Free seating! Just be seated. Madam, there is an empty seat just here." The attendant pointed to a seat to my right next to a man who was obviously Indian. He was wearing tight blue jeans and a black T-shirt that accentuated his well-developed chest and muscular biceps. The T-shirt had "FLORIDA" written on it in blaring orange and yellow letters that simulated dancing flames. He was tall, agile and his strong regular features were framed by a mass of smooth black hair.

He smiled, his eyes perusing my figure as I passed him to sit in the window seat. Then he tugged at his jeans on the upper part of his legs as if to lessen their discomfort. I looked away embarrassed.

"What is your country?" he asked.

"America – I was born in New York," I answered. "How many more hours to Delhi?"

"Three," he answered. "How long you will stay in India?" he

asked, looking directly into my eyes. His sleek strong body exuded the feline grace of a leopard stalking his prey, but he had a sweet gentle quality, which made his manner less obtrusive.

"I have a one-year visa." I stared straight ahead, as if peering into a vast open space, which contained the secret of my future. I felt a slight shiver go down my spine.

"Have you been to India before?"

"Oh yes, twice. I was in Simla in the foothills of the Himalayas and I lived in Varanasi for almost six months. I was studying music." My mind drifted back to Varanasi. "In Varanasi, I lived near the Ganges. I used to go to bathe in the river at dawn. Watching the sun rise on the Ganges was the best part of the trip."

"Oh? You liked it. It is a holy river." He paused. "What's your name?" he asked, turning in his seat to face me.

"Shantila."

"Mine is Yogesh," he said.

"Sounds like yogi," I replied, smiling. "You should be a yogi with a name like that."

"My mother chose the name. I think my mother hoped I would be religious – I mean more than I am."

"You're not?" I asked.

"Oh I used to be, but I don't have time now. I work for Air India. I'm a manager. I just returned from a ski trip in Aspen, Colorado. Nice place. Do you ski?"

"No," I answered, "but once I tried cross country..."

"Fasten seat belts!" the loudspeaker blared out.

As the plane lifted into the sky, I leaned back in the seat and closed my eyes. I remembered those early-morning walks in Varanasi down the dirt road leading to the shore. As the plane soared ever-higher into the sky, the picture of the Ganges unraveled on the canvas of my memory: *India, India... I saw again the wide expanse of the river spreading out before me. The pale blue waters of the river had stirred my soul with such peace. Those waters* had whispered to me of a world without end or beginning where love wove the garment of life – a love eternal which reigned supreme over all.

The river seemed to open her eyelids at dawn, her veil fluttering in the morning air. Her veil, of pale blue silk, made of undulating waves and woven by the hands of God rippled in the shimmering light of dawn. Her voice, like a caress, sang in silence of a world born before time. Her voice seemed to call to me as I boarded the simple wooden boat...I remember even now how the oars of the boat kissed the surface of the water, and then sank momentarily into the translucent folds of soft blue silk. The divine Ganga did not mind the touch of the wood upon her body. Like a woman who willingly bears all burdens, the waters yielded to the slow rhythmic pressure of the oars as the boatman plied his way forward toward the rising sun.

The voices of prayer coming from the ardent devotees who lined the bank of the river rose and fell like the gentle waves murmuring in the unbounded ocean of silence which pervaded everything.

I drifted in and out of sleep as these images arose in my mind:

I saw again the straight-backed women carrying puja pots of brass bend low before the waters. They pressed their foreheads to the sand before their holy Mother Ganga.

The pink sky breathed its ambiance into the air and black crows pierced the white haze in the distance with their large black wings. The wild crows cawed loudly as they circled the stone steps of the temples and flew above the waters in a dance to music, which only they could hear.

The iron temple bells rang out. I heard again their sound inside. The Ganges, the bells, the sky aglow with the light of dawn – they summoned me, called me forth from my room each morning and I knew that I had to come to the shores of the river to offer obeisance and to bathe...

The plane suddenly dipped down and I felt as if the seat had fallen out from under me. My stomach bounced up with a jolt as I lurched forward.

"We will be in Delhi in fifteen minutes," Yogesh said. "You are fine? Were you sleeping?"

"No – not really... Yes I'm fine," I said, leaning back in the seat and tightening the seat belt around my waist.

The wheels hit the runway with a loud thump as the plane skidded forward into the space reserved for it. Before the seatbelt signs were switched off, the aisles were filled with Muslim men, tall, heavyset, cramming to get to the overhead luggage compartments. The men looked aggressive, almost ominous in their demeanour, as they filed out with their bulging bags, one after another. The women wearing black headdresses and skirts which covered their ankles, followed.

I tugged unsuccessfully at the vinyl bag in front of me. Yogesh, touching my arm, reached down and with a quick flick of his wrist tossed its handles over his shoulder.

"Let me have it," he said, moving into the aisle with an agile twist of his body.

With a quiet sigh of relief, I followed him down the long narrow aisle with only my tanpura, the Indian musical instrument I played. A wave of exhilaration arose as I thought, *"India! I'm here at last!"*

The crowd shoved past me, eager to get to the checkout counter. The exhilaration faded fast. When I arrived, Indira Gandhi Airport was a nondescript arena containing only the most basic amenities. It had a gray pallor, like an aging woman, wearing faded garments.

I had to struggle to keep up with Yogesh. He took long rhythmic strides and as an Air India official, he knew everyone at all the checkout counters, and we walked to the front of every queue.

Before long, we stood in front of the large revolving wheel which groaned under the weight of all the baggage emerging from the circular tunnel. I marvelled at the huge round bundles wrapped in different colors of cloth and tied round and round with rope. These bulging bundles swayed precariously back and forth on the rotating wheel. Four men were required to roll it off the luggage wheel. It was quite a substitute for a suitcase! Equally unwieldy were some of the huge cardboard boxes and old battered metal trunks.

Yogesh already had his suitcase. "I'm going to duty-free. I'll be back," he said and sauntered off. I took my blue suitcase off the wheel and waited anxiously for the green one. The revolving wheel finally stopped. There was no sign of my green cloth suitcase with the brown leather trim.

About half an hour later, Yogesh returned, dangling a large plastic bag containing several boxes of duty-free cigarettes.

"One of my suitcases is missing," I said wearily.

"Don't worry. Just wait. I'll find it," Yogesh said, striding off to a place behind the revolving wheel. After a few minutes he returned swinging my green suitcase deftly from his left hand.

"Is this it?" he asked. "It has Shantila Martin written on it, so it must be, right? Unusual name – Shantila. I like it," he murmured, placing the case on the luggage carrier. "Is someone meeting you?" he asked, lighting a cigarette.

"I hope so," I replied, looking around as we headed toward the taxi stand. It was still very dark outside.

Several thin old men dressed in dirty shabby clothes stood huddled together smoking. Their dark sunken eyes framed by rough haggard faces streaked with weather-beaten lines looked wild. Their hollow cheekbones accentuated the poverty that hung like broken wings from lean and pointed bones. The windless air around the taxi stand was thick with black smoke which was constantly being belched from the rusted exhaust pipes of the three-wheel auto rickshaws and ramshackle buses desperately in need of repair.

"Baksheesh, madam – one rupee, madam."

I looked down into a tiny face with large hungry eyes. She was about five years old with pockmarked skin and uncombed hair. Her dress had once been yellow. She held out her cupped palms and looked up at me. Then she very shyly reached out and tugged gently at the bottom of my cotton dress.

Yogesh reached into the pocket of his jeans, took out a coin and gave it to her. She smiled and ran to her mother who stood looking on some distance away.

I stood at the edge of the sidewalk and nervously glanced at my watch. It was four in the morning.

Brahma muhurta – the first breath of dawn, the hour of the awakening of the gods – a good time to arrive. "I just hope someone comes to collect me." I sighed.

"Any sign of your friend?" Yogesh asked, puffing amiably on his cigarette.

"No, I, uh...maybe I should phone him. I sent him an email telling him I was coming. I don't have any rupees. I haven't changed any money yet."

"Give me his number. I'll call – just wait here and watch your bags."

Searching in my shoulder bag, I found my address book. I scribbled the telephone number on a scrap of paper and then watched until Yogesh disappeared down the long passageway leading to the main lounge of the airport.

I started to feel uneasy.

"Taxi, madam! Taxi! Where you want to go?" A young Indian man in flashy trousers strode up to me, pointing to his shiny Ambassador.

I shook my head from side to side indicating that I was not interested. I moved further away from the rickshaw drivers who stood coughing and spitting into the gutter. *Why isn't he here to meet me? I told him what time I would be arriving – I don't like standing here among all these men in the dark!* I felt so vulnerable. After what seemed like a very long time, Yogesh appeared.

"He had no idea you were coming to India. He was fast asleep. I woke him up; he was not pleased at being disturbed in the middle of the night. He said he'll come to get you in about an hour or so." Yogesh's voice trailed off. There was a glimmer of concern in his expression.

"One hour!" I shouted. "One hour! I have to wait here all alone for an hour! It doesn't feel right to be here alone. I don't feel safe," I said wearily in a low voice. *Oh God, he didn't get the email. Why, oh why didn't I phone him to confirm the date? How stupid of me!* I covered my face with my hands, as my mind raced forwards: *Oh, Shantila, you've done it again! You've never been very worldly and I know you feel more comfortable in the realm of abstract ideas than in the harsh realities of day-to-day life, but now you'll have to face the consequences!*

"Well, he said he just woke up. He needed a little time, and he had just returned from a trip. Take it easy, Shantila, I'll take you to the waiting room. I told him you would wait there."

Yogesh swiftly wheeled the cart with my suitcases piled on it across the street and up a ramp. We entered a large, rather bleak hall. It was empty except for an old man with a woolen cap sitting on a wooden bench near the door. I went and sat on the other side of the bench.

"You wait here. You are fine?" Yogesh asked.

"Yes, I, uh, I'll be alright," I said, but I was thinking: *If he doesn't come then what will I do?*

Yogesh reached into his pocket. "Here take this." He handed me five rupees. "Here is my telephone number. If you need me, just call. I'll come and help you."

"Thank you," I murmured. "Thank you very much for your help."

Yogesh swiveled around on his heels and left the hall.

I fumbled in my bag for my mirror. I looked tired – no, exhausted! *He invited me to come! This is such a special time in my life. Oh, why did this have to happen? He did not get the email!* A raucous sound behind me shook the air like a bolt of lightning. I whipped my neck around.

That poor man... I saw his body bend forward like a broken twig. Again, without any warning, the air was bombarded with a similar blast of thunder. The cough seemed to erupt like a volcano. I shuddered and moved away to the end of the bench.

I was starving. *You're entering India starving, Shantila,* I heard an inner voice say in the tone of a warning. *Not a good omen, is it?* I remembered the time in Varanasi when I was without a single rupee. I had arranged to receive bank transfers from England, and then tension flared up between the Hindus and Muslims because of a dispute over a temple in Ayodhya. To avoid a riot in Varanasi, they imposed a curfew over the whole town. All the banks were closed for weeks, and there were days when no one was even allowed to come out of their houses.

The waiting room was hot, too hot. My clothes were already sticking to my body. The old man was still coughing. I shivered involuntarily. *When will he come?* I looked down at my watch.

I shifted my position on the bench. My stomach began to grumble. I was too tired to mind. Suddenly the door swung open. I sat bolt upright, staring at the entrance. A stout fair-skinned man with a bright red jogging suit strode in. He was wearing blue tennis shoes. He held out his right hand as he approached the bench.

"Shantila. Nice to meet you," he said, looking me straight in the eyes.

"Mr. Rao," I said, extending my hand. He was an attractive well-built man in his late forties or early fifties.

"Why didn't you tell me you were coming? You woke me up in the middle of the night and came without letting me know! I might not even have been in Delhi. I was in the Punjab until yesterday."

I sat still, watching as he gesticulated with his pudgy hands waving around in the air.

"I sent you an email," I whispered weakly. "Didn't you get it?"

"An email!" he trumpeted. "An email!" He laughed wryly. "Why didn't you phone me? You always telephoned me all the other times. The email system in India is not very sophisticated yet. It broke down last week. This is India, not America. It's still a new technology here." He gazed at me, and seemed to just be beginning to become aware of the effect his words were having on me. "Well, you're here. Let's go. My car is outside. Come on." He hopped briskly up from the bench and headed for the door while I followed with my luggage piled high up on the squeaky metal luggage carrier. The wheels screeched as I twisted them around toward the curving ramp. He did not turn around even once.

Chapter Two

A black wrought-iron gate gave way to a clean, fashionable entrance with cream-colored cement pillars on either side of the door. The wooden door shaped in an arch, had a small shiny brass bell. On either side of it were large clay pots containing sacred tulsi plants, or basil, as they are known in the West. Along the wall of the house were rose bushes with small red buds waiting to bloom.

This will be a nice place to stay... I thought to myself.

"Leave your bags in the car," Mr. Rao said. "Someone will bring them in later." Then he muttered to himself just loud enough for me to hear: "We are in the middle of whitewashing the house; very inconvenient time for you to arrive..."

He slipped a silver key into the lock. The heavy wooden door opened quietly, revealing a series of arches repeated in the hallway leading into the interior. The house appeared grand and spacious. It looked like a comfortable dwelling of a well-to-do Indian family. *Oh what a relief! At last, I will be able to rest.*

"Come in," Mr. Rao said.

He removed his tennis shoes in the hall by the entrance swiftly, without unlacing them. I stepped out of my leather sandals, feeling a slight quiver as my bare feet met the smooth white marble floor. Passing under the first arch, we were greeted by a large oil painting of an elderly man resembling Mr. Rao. He wore a wiser, more benevolent expression. I stopped in front of it, admiring the portrait.

"My father," Mr. Rao said, stopping beside me. "He was a great man."

A bronze statue of Lord Ganesh stood regally on a mahogany table. Ganesh is the elephant-headed deity, which Hindus traditionally pray to for success at the start of any important event. He is regarded as the remover of obstacles and is revered by writers and poets as their patron deity. From the vast pantheon of gods and goddesses prayed to in India, Lord Ganesh had come to occupy a special place in my heart. The face of the elephant-headed deity was imbued with a beautiful quality of love and devotion; it was undoubtedly the work of a spiritually minded artist.

After Mr. Rao had given orders to his servants in Hindi, he said: "Come in, Shantila. I'd like you to meet my mother."

I knew that this was an important occasion, for the mother is traditionally revered in an Indian family. She is the unspoken ruler of the family with regard to affairs within the home. I was also aware that a fundamental aspect of the Hindu way of life is that one should "See the mother as God. See the father as God. See the Guru (or teacher) as God. See the guest as God." In Varanasi, I learned that the guest referred to the "unexpected" guest.

I adjusted my scarf carefully over my shoulder and followed Mr. Rao as he walked down the hallway into a small sitting room filled with soft gray shadows of morning light. From the open door of the bedroom, a frail figure swathed in white silk emerged. Her fair skin was still smooth in spite of her advanced age. Her eyes were sunk deep within a series of finely chiseled concentric circles. Her visage was imbued with serenity.

"My mother doesn't speak any English," Mr. Rao said in a low voice.

His mother moved towards me with unpretentious grace. She was barefoot, walking with slow well-placed steps. She greeted me with a nod of her head. Her silver-white hair was partially covered by her sari. An air of silence surrounded her like a white mist. The weightless fabric of the white silk sari added to my impression of her as a very spiritual person. Widows traditionally wear white in India. She was also not adorned with any jewelry. It is the custom for a devoted Indian wife to remove all her jewelry when her husband has died because during their marriage, her adornments are worn mainly to give joy to her husband, the man whom she serves. She said something in Hindi to Mr. Rao, who nodded deferentially and smiled.

"I always take tea with my mother in the morning. I spend the first part of every day with her; half an hour every day before going to the office."

A young dark-skinned boy entered, carrying a silver tray with tiny white cups and saucers and a tin box, gaily decorated with a flowery design. Mr. Rao's mother removed the lid of the tin revealing an assortment of chocolate-covered biscuits.

"Will you take tea?" Mr. Rao asked, pouring the tea into his mother's cup first. "Sugar?"

"Yes, please," I replied.

"So how are things in England?" asked Mr. Rao, as he relaxed into the round white cushions of the low divan.

"Oh very well," I answered. "I live in a community where many people meditate together. I learned to meditate during a visit to England many years ago and became close to a group of people who meditate together there. I've recently been working on a book about my previous trip to India."

"What kind of book will it be?"

"A novel," I said. "Would you be interested?"

Mr. Rao ran a medium-sized publishing house in the center of New Delhi for which he was the managing director. He had agreed to publish a book I had written, my first book.

"I'm sorry," he answered, "we do not publish novels. But tell me, how else do you spend your time?"

"Well, I write in the morning. After lunch, I go for a short walk and I practice on my instrument in the afternoon."

"What kind of instrument do you play?"

"I play the sitar. I learned to play in Simla."

"I thought I saw an instrument with your luggage. Was that your sitar?"

"No, that is my tanpura. I use it for accompaniment when I

give poetry recitals. I have also played tanpura in many classical Indian music concerts in England. I love Indian music."

"Good, good. Now let me tell you something about my life: I am an early riser. I get up between five and six o'clock, take a morning walk, and then work until seven at night." He stopped, leaning forward to sip his tea and help himself to another biscuit.

"I'm very tired from the flight. Would it be possible to rest now?" I asked in a quiet voice.

"Of course. I'll arrange to have a room prepared upstairs."

I smiled at Mr. Rao's mother, bowed my head slightly, and placed my palms together as we in the West do while praying. In India, it is a form of greeting. As a sign of respect, I raised my palms to my forehead. "Thank you for the tea," I said.

"Breakfast will be in about half an hour. Would you like to wash? There is a bathroom in there," Mr. Rao said, pointing to a room. Then he got up to go.

I opened the door of the bathroom and found the room filled with wet clothes hanging up to dry in every available space. Gingerly I stepped up to the sink and turning on the tap, splashed cold water on my face, and brushed my teeth. I was too exhausted to undress and wade through the colorful menagerie in order to find a corner in which to bathe using the red bucket under the sink.

Opening my handbag, I found the white handkerchief in which lay a garland of small pink roses brought from England. As I unfolded the handkerchief, a faint fragrance of roses wafted through the air. I remembered the joy I had experienced while making it. I intended to offer it to the first statue of Ganesh I saw. I walked to the hallway and placed the roses at the feet of the benevolent-faced deity with a prayer: *Grant that the launch of my first book will be a success and that I will be able to tour India to promote the book, and that I will be able to visit many holy places while I am here.*

Moving as if in slow motion after the long flight, I returned through the cream-colored archway. The sitting room was empty and leaning back on the divan, I fell fast asleep. In my dream, I heard a voice calling to me: *Remember, remember, remember.* The echo reverberated in the mountain air like the sound of a distant drumbeat – calling, calling, calling to a child hidden deep within.

Remember the dawn on the Ganges, the rose-colored sunrise, the fiery heat of the sun, the cooling iridescent rays of moonlight, the whirling dance of the stars, remember the sparkling eyes of the river and remember the ageless mountains. Ah, the Himalayan heights, and the sweet fragrance of the cedar trees rising like silent sentinels beneath the vast temple of the sky. Remember, Shantila; remember the transparent mirror of silence in which your face, the face of the whole world, shines as in a lake. And see in the lake, Shantila, your smiling eyes, eternally laughing.

But how can I know that which I cannot see? How can I believe in that which is transparent? How can I surrender the dreaming, rippling breathing world for a world of timeless stillness without losing everything? How can I lose all I know and feel and believe and yet live – continue to live on this earth?

I sat alone in the forest. Before me, the Himalayan mountain range, like a cloak of dark green velvet covered the vast ethereal arms of the sky. The snow-covered mountains resembled the white fleece collar of the cloak and the thick cedars, which zigzagged downwards towards the valley, looked like a wide belt wrapped around the long flowing cloak. So vast was He.

The graceful boughs of the towering trees hung suspended like wings, quivering in the sunlit air. They whispered prayer songs to the mountain deities that inhabited the forest glades.

The trip had been arduous. It had taken a long, long time and the road had been jagged and steep, with many landslides, precipices and deep pits into which I had almost fallen, almost died. Yet each time, somehow, I don't know how – I arose, covered with dirt, blood, and tears. Like a lone eagle circling ever-higher into the blue abyss, I rose up, lifting my wings, heavy-laden with memories, until I soared on the breath of the wind and rested in the woven wisps of the clouds, until I could glide free, tracing endless pathways through the invisible sanctuary of His Being. Only now did I taste the nectar. Only now did the aching longing of my heart find rest – only now was the gnawing emptiness filled with undying LOVE.

Slowly, I opened my eyes. The dream lingered. I had the feeling that it was more than just a dream. *Is it the past? The steep, jagged roads? The landslides? Or is it the future that I saw?*

I was only half-awake when I heard footsteps. Hurriedly sitting up, adjusting my crumpled dress and feeling very self-conscious, I looked up and saw Mr. Rao.

"Will you join us upstairs for breakfast?" he asked.

"Yes."

As we passed the statue of Ganesh, Mr. Rao smiled.

"Your offering?" he asked, motioning to the garland of small pink rosebuds.

"Yes."

"Good, you will enjoy India," he said, leading the way up the carved staircase.

Mr. Rao's wife was waiting for us at the table. She wore a dark blue and brown cotton Punjabi suit, consisting of a long dress with matching trousers and shawl. Her auburn-colored hair revealed a hint of gray. It was parted in the middle and tied tightly behind her head.

"Why did she come here without calling us first?" she asked abruptly in Hindi while staring straight ahead. She had broad high cheekbones, a slim aquiline nose, a wide mouth and very narrow lips. She was, without any makeup, rather stern in her appearance. She sat as silent and still as a statue.

"She sent an email," Mr. Rao answered, coming to sit beside her. I saw him glance at her profile, and for a moment, his face betrayed a sign of weary resignation. Neither of them was aware that I understood a little Hindi.

Mr. Rao then motioned to the cook who stood silently at the doorway to the kitchen, peering in. Gesturing with his hands, Mr. Rao indicated that the breakfast should be ample.

Then there was a shuffle along the corridor. A small boy wobbled in on bare feet. He was a handsome boy with large bright eyes. He darted forward to Mrs. Rao. Immediately her face brightened. Then he gazed eagerly from one person to another until he stopped and stared at me. A tall, stately woman entered the room, moving slowly, almost as if gliding. Touching joined palms to her forehead, she reverently bowed her head to Mr. and Mrs. Rao, her father and mother-in-law, as she stood before them.

"Didn't he sleep last night?" Mr. Rao asked.

"No, Babaji," she said, adding the "ji' to the Indian word for father to indicate respect. "He was awake until dawn."

She sat down opposite Mrs. Rao.

"How is the fever?" Mr. Rao asked, with obvious concern.

"Fine. The doctor said the fever was nothing serious. He is going to the playgroup in the afternoon as usual."

The small boy scrambled playfully into Mr. Rao's lap, then sat on his knees as Mr.Rao bounced him up and down. Mr. Rao began to laugh and his whole body shook.

"What a pair!" said a man who walked in. Mr. Rao's son was tall and dark with a thin mustache and horn-rimmed spectacles. He had a big bundle of loose papers under his arm.

"Namaste," he said softly, greeting his parents with a slight nod of his head.

I saw Mr. Rao smile.

"My son," Mr. Rao said looking at me. "This is Shantila Martin from England."

"Very nice to meet you," his son said, glancing at me.

"Rajan manages all the finances in the company."

I could see that he was proud of his son. He had probably married a woman from a good family and she had fulfilled her responsibility by bearing a son which he loved.

Rajan spread the papers out on the polished surface of the mahogany table. He removed his glasses and rubbed his eyes. "So you wrote the book we are about to print," Rajan said.

"What is your book about?" Mrs. Rao asked, turning her head slightly to look at me. She sat on the far end of the table, beside Mr. Rao. Her expression seemed to say: "He's mine – so keep your distance."

"It's about the relationship between creativity and perception in the West and the East, and how art reflects our beliefs and ideals and also influences them."

"Oh, really? In India, the study of art requires great discipline and self-sacrifice. One has to find a Guru and all that. Have you read Anand Coomaraswamy's books? He is an authority on Indian art."

"Yes, I have. In one of his books, he mentions that the success of the creative act is based on the artist's ability to see inside what he has to create outside. His inner vision must be very clear, so the artist has to purify himself first. He says that Valmiki, who composed the *Ramayana*, saw the entire story within himself as clearly as a fruit on the palm of his hand. Then he began to write it down."

"Valmiki was one of our greatest sages," Rajan said quietly. "This kind of cognition was possible in ancient India, but things are very different now."

"How long do you plan to stay in India?" Mrs. Rao interjected.

"I would like to go on a tour around India to promote my book," I said.

Rajan, the financial expert at the publishing company, looked startled.

"Well, I said that we would discuss this when you came. We didn't plan to – I mean – I wasn't even sure you were coming," Mr. Rao said, shifting in his seat.

"But you wrote to me about the launch of the book. I'm really looking forward to celebrating the publication of my first book."

Just then, the cook arrived with our meal. The parathas were thick, square pancakes which had spinach inside and were served with fresh cream. I was so hungry I ate three. After breakfast, Rajan's family said goodbye and left the room.

"Do you like parathas?" Mr. Rao seemed to enjoy my appetite.

"Yes, I love them." I smiled. "I make them myself at home. I love Indian food."

Mrs. Rao watched me out of the corner of her eye without saying anything, and then she spoke to Mr. Rao in Hindi. I knew something was going on. She did not like me. Mr. Rao had written to me, saying that while I was in Delhi, I would be his guest. Outwardly, I browsed through a pamphlet about the upcoming events in the Art Center in New Delhi. However, I was already aware that there was some disagreement over where I should stay. Finally, the conversation came to an abrupt end. Mr. Rao picked up the telephone and began dialing one number, then another and another, without any luck. He looked annoyed. Finally, he managed to get through to someone. They exchanged a few words, and then he replaced the receiver and gave his wife the answer she wanted. Her stone-like stare relaxed and she got up to leave.

I asked Mr. Rao if it would be all right if I went to a room to rest.

"They are preparing a room for you at a guest house nearby. It will be ready in a few hours," he said in a dry, matter-of-fact tone of voice.

"A guest house? I, uh, a few hours? But you said that when I came to Delhi I would be your guest."

"My guest? Well, I, um, you will be my guest. I am a friend of the owner of the guest house. You will be her guest for five days there. I will pay for your stay there..." He shifted as if preparing to go. "You can rest downstairs in the bedroom next door to my mother's room until my driver returns. He will take you to the guest house." He turned back to me as he walked down the corridor leading to the stairs. "Don't worry. I have taken care of everything. The woman there owes me a favor. They don't usually take guests without prior reservations but she has made an exception for you," Mr. Rao said, before he left for his office.

Mr. Rao's driver was tall, dark and lean with jet-black hair. He grinned when he saw me.

"You – from England? Come with me. I take your bags." He briskly collected my bags from the sitting room and stacked them in the white minibus parked outside. He held the back door open as I climbed in.

It was spring: the sun was high in the sky. The white minibus zipped through the teeming traffic, which would have measured at least six lanes in width if there had been any lanes. However, there were none, nor were there traffic lights – only horns, blaring, screeching, trumpeting at each other. Painted in a large scrawling script on the back of nearly every bus, truck and rickshaw were signs in big, block letters, which read – BLOW HORN PLEASE and KEEP YOUR DISTANCE PLEASE! And blow their horns is exactly what everyone did, at every opportunity.

Mr. Rao's driver acted like the king of the road. Whenever he saw a three-wheel rickshaw, he nearly knocked it off the road by zooming so close to it that it had virtually nowhere to go. He was only slightly more polite with motorbikes on which helmeted men zigzagged through endless roads of traffic with their dainty wives, and sometimes even small children poised haphazardly on the seat behind them.

New Delhi was a morass of diverse cultures, colors, and smells, all candid expressions of a surging ocean of life. Everywhere one looked, there were people! As our minibus whizzed through the street, I craned my neck forward in the backseat and yelled, "Watch out for the cow!"

A large white cow was sitting with her newborn calf in the middle of the road. It gazed nonchalantly at the cars as they veered off to the right and left to avoid hitting her and the calf.

The driver merely laughed, and turning his head to face me, he said, "Don't worry."

How silly of me, I thought, *he probably goes through this every day.*

The city sprawled like a huge patchwork quilt containing the rich and poor, the satiated and the starving, the able bodied and the crippled, the saintly and the crooked, bunched together in one interwoven swarming mass, like a buzzing beehive. In the middle of the street, beggars with one arm or one leg missing roamed with peddlers selling incense, newspapers, magazines, or anything that could be sold quickly, before the traffic moved on. On the pavement, vendors spread their merchandise, adding their own flavor to the fast-flowing current in which everything moved onward, rising and falling, swept forward by an invisible force that was invincible in its might.

We reached what could be likened to a bustling business district. The driver made a sharp turn and sped down a narrow dusty alleyway. After driving for five or ten more minutes, and searching one long lane after another, he pulled up in front of a large red square building with an array of flowering plants and palm trees outside.

Without a moment's hesitation, he jumped out, and had a few words with the guard who stood by the high iron gate posted outside the south entrance. The guard unlocked the gate and the nimble-footed driver hopped back into the car and drove up to the front door. Then he got out and opened the rear door for me.

"I'll get the bags," he said with a smile. His broad grin revealed straight, very white teeth. There was a very efficient air about him. He obviously took his job seriously. He swung my two heavy suitcases out of the rear of the car and proceeded up the dark, gray stone slabs leading to the glass doors.

A teenage boy greeted us as we stepped inside. "I'm Harish. Your room is upstairs," he said in a soft voice.

Harish led the way through another glass door, which led to

an outer staircase made of concrete outside the building. I followed the driver as he ascended one flight of steps after another. I could not help noticing that as we got further up, the concrete steps were crumbling more and more until finally at the top of the staircase, there was only a vague resemblance of a step left on which to place one's foot.

Harish took a bunch of jingling keys from his trouser pocket and unlocked the heavy wooden door to my room. The driver whose face was dripping wet with perspiration nonchalantly entered the room, leaving my luggage by the nearest wall. As I stepped inside, my heart sank.

The "room" was one vast empty space with a plastic cot, like the ones used to sun oneself on the beach, in the middle of it. The walls were naked red bricks and the large windows had long, black iron bars in front of them. Only one window was open because the pane of glass was missing. From the open window, I could hear a cacophony of traffic noise in the street down below.

I walked in, numb with disappointment. The driver nodded his head to me and before I could speak, he was gone.

"Chai, madam?" Harish asked, gazing at me with unconcealed curiosity. "Tea?"

"No – uh – yes – um – alright."

I opened the door to my bathroom. A torn dirty rag hung on a rusting nail and the white tiled walls were smeared with grime. On the floor under two taps stood a dirty red plastic bucket. There was no sign of a shower or a bath.

"Bathroom – not clean! Look at this!" I shouted at Harish. "What is this?" The frustration, fatigue and disappointment of my first day in India surfaced all at once, spilling over into my voice.

Harish jumped back, his eyes widening. "Yes, madam. I clean for you, madam – one minute. I back." He backed hurriedly out the door.

Harish returned about one hour later and scrubbed the walls

22

of the bathroom. I was too exhausted to think. I lay stretched out on the plastic cot and stared at the ceiling.

Thank God I have a room where I can rest – at last. Sleep, I need sleep. I do not believe this! But I am too tired to call Mr. Rao now. But I'll definitely tell him about the state of this room!

When I finally got through to Mr. Rao, he apologized and assured me that he would have his driver bring me a blanket and a pillow. He also told me that he had arranged for me to eat in the restaurant downstairs. He knew the Sikh who was the manager.

The Sikh manager greeted me as I entered the restaurant. As is the custom with all male Sikhs, he wore a turban on his head to cover his long hair. The Sikh religion prohibits men from cutting their hair. He told me he was from the Punjab near the border of Pakistan.

The restaurant was a small and cozy place, and the food was good. They had three vegetarian dishes, which I sampled while I was there. The restaurant was only open for lunch. At night, Harish brought me tea and two slices of bread. Harish cooked his own meals on a one-ring gas burner in the alleyway outside the building.

Harish and I became friends. He was from the Himalayas. He was "in service" here as he called it, but he wanted to move on to another job. He did not like the woman in charge here. He hoped to go to Kuwait for two years and get a well-paid job, but it was difficult to get a passport and visa.

I decided to explore the place. In the lobby of the guest house was an art gallery. The paintings were garish red, black and orange expressions of what I can only describe as FURY. This one emotion blared forth from one oil painting after another. They depicted a woman consumed by anger. It was as if the artist had evoked a modern version of the wrathful goddess Kali, the goddess of destruction. Some of the canvasses actually showed a woman screaming, with her hair streaming out in long fiery waves behind her. I shuddered involuntarily as I stared at the paintings. I was shocked by what I saw.

Is this an expression of woman's liberation? Are the women of India demanding their freedom? I asked myself. An image of New York City in the early seventies flashed through my mind. I saw Harlem, the ghetto where I grew up. I remembered the African-American women there asserting their right to work in good jobs, to have a decent education for themselves and their children. I remembered their vociferous demand for power and the anger in their eyes as they marched through the streets, waving flags and carrying banners. The eyes of the woman in these paintings seemed to tell a similar story. I wondered who the artist was.

"She is in charge here," the Sikh manager of the restaurant told me as he took my order for lunch. "She is like that." He sighed in resignation.

One morning, Harish knocked on my door very early. I did not answer for a long time as I was meditating. When I finally heeded his incessant knocking, my eyes were only half-open.

"Madam asks you to come to breakfast with her," Harish said flatly.

"Tell madam that I'm sorry I cannot come. I'm meditating now. Please do not disturb me. Thank you," I said, closing the door.

A few minutes later, there was another knock. I decided to ignore it.

In the evening, Harish brought me burnt toast and tea.

"Would it be possible to have chapati and milk instead?" I asked.

"No chapati possible," Harish said. "Madam said toast and chai – this all." He put the tray with the toast and the glass of tea down on the board near the window and left.

Now that I was over my jet lag, I was eager to discuss with Mr. Rao his plans for the launch of my book.

I entered the library in the guest house. A few women were sitting inside in a circle, talking. I picked up the receiver of the old-fashioned telephone and dialed the number.

"Hello, may I speak to Mr. Rao please? Yes. Mr. Rao? This is Shantila Martin."

"How are you?"

"I'm fine. I want to come to talk to you about the launch. When do you think you'll print the book?" I asked him eagerly.

"Soon. These things take time. I'll let you know. I have to speak to the printers. I'm thinking about where in Delhi to have the launch." He spoke slowly.

"I can contact the British Embassy again. I received a fax from them before I came to India, and they mentioned that a tour of the major cities might be possible."

"If they are willing to pay for it, you can do it – by all means, do it." Mr. Rao sounded very pleased with the idea.

Finally, things were beginning to flow. I felt elated by the prospect of traveling through India to promote my book! If only the food situation here could be improved. I mentioned to him that the food I was receiving in the evening was not enough. He said he would contact the woman in charge of the guest house and see what could be done. I hung up the phone.

A woman draped in a dark red woolen shawl, whose back had been turned to me, stood up to face me.

"Get out! Tonight! Pack your bags and leave immediately!" she shouted in a voice which cut through the air like the serrated blade of a knife.

My body started to tremble as I realized that this was the woman in charge, the fleshly embodiment of the image in the paintings, only older.

"You're leaving now – tonight!" she repeated in the same grating tone.

"But why? What have I done?" I blurted out, still shaking. "I don't understand."

"I called you for breakfast and you didn't come! You could see we were having a meeting in here. How can you dare make a call while we are meeting and to complain!" Her voice was rising.

"But I wasn't talking very loud. Please excuse me..." I said, backing away from her.

The other women, still sitting in the circle, just listened, without moving or saying anything. Madam just grinned; her hard crooked teeth matched the heartless glint in her eyes.

"You will pack your bags and get out immediately." Then she turned to the circle, and returned to her chair as if nothing had happened.

I stood riveted in the spot where I stood; my mind was bombarded by a wordless despair. For a few minutes, my mind raced back and forth, grappling for a solution. As she was a friend of my publisher, I did not want to offend her or make a scene in front of the other women there. I decided to let Mr. Rao sort out the situation.

I pulled my spine up straight and my neck erect with an expression of utter defiance. Turning my back to her, I resolutely picked up the receiver and dialed the same number.

"Hello? Mr. Rao? She asked me to leave the guest house. I must be out immediately, tonight. Please can you tell me where I should go? What did you say? Yes, tonight. I do not know. I'll tell you later. You'll be here. When? In forty-five minutes? All right. Thank you very much."

The Sikh manager of the restaurant met me as I was on my way upstairs to pack.

"I am leaving tonight," I said simply, my body still shaking internally.

"I heard everything. Don't worry," he said softly. "She treats everyone like this. You should write to the President. Everyone should know. Otherwise, when will it end? How will it ever change?" He looked at me with compassion. "Where will you go now?"

"I don't know – yet," I answered wearily, turning to go.

"Wait."

I heard him rustling around with the plastic bag he was holding.

"Take this paw-paw. It is perfectly ripe. You will enjoy." He took out a very large orange papaya and handed it to me.

I smiled. I did not know what to say; I was so touched by his simple act of kindness. "Thank you very much. I really enjoyed my meals in the restaurant. Namaste." I placed my palms together and bowed my head slightly as our eyes met.

Mr. Rao was not at all pleased when he arrived. Although he tried to hide his feelings, I could see that he blamed me for not accepting Madam's invitations. He told me that I had jeopardized his prestige by my behavior.

"I know of one other place. A Japanese monk runs it but he will make you pay. It costs twelve hundred rupees per night to stay there. It is vegetarian and clean and safe."

"Twelve hundred rupees per night?" I gasped. "But you said that when I came to Delhi I would be your guest!"

"You have been, for the last four days. I paid; or rather, you did not have to pay anything. From now on, you are on your own. How long did you expect me to take care of you?"

Chapter Three

The car sped down the empty stretch of road leading to South Delhi. It was cool and the night breeze blew the white silk scarf I was wearing up into my face. The smooth feather-soft fabric glided over my eyes, nose and cheeks like a wistful caress. I pulled it down gently over my nose as the acrid smell of petrol fumes from the creaking bus roaring past filled the air. Quickly I rolled up the window.

It was a long drive. Mr. Rao sat in the front seat with the driver. I tried to calculate how much 1200 rupees was in dollars ($16). At that price, I knew I would not be able to stay there very long. Soon the launch would be organized and hopefully, the tour...

"Mr. Rao, when should we meet about the launch?" I asked him, leaning forward in my seat so he could hear me.

"Next week. I should know about the publication date by then."

The car slid to a halt in front of an ornate white oriental-style structure. As I opened the door of the car, I drew in my breath in awe. A huge golden Buddha in lotus posture with his right arm upraised in a gesture of blessing sat poised at the entrance.

Mr. Rao came up and standing behind me, said, "You will like it here in the Buddhist Center. You must speak softly inside."

As we crossed the threshold from the street, the outer environment gave way to an atmosphere permeated by silence and serenity. We left our shoes by the door before ascending the polished mahogany staircase to the sitting room. The inner sanctum of silence was deftly woven with straw mats and silk flower arrangements amid small bronze statues of Buddhas carefully placed on glass tabletops. There were also pastel paintings of snow-capped mountains, gently flowing rivers bathed in sunlight, and green flowering meadows surrounding white stupas, triangular structures sacred to the Buddhist faith. It breathed a stillness, which we all responded to noticeably. No one spoke as we followed Mr. Rao past the sitting room to the heavy wooden door of the office of the Japanese monk in charge. Mr. Rao tapped lightly and then waited several minutes.

A bald-headed man with wide cheekbones in a white kimono opened the door, bowing his head with joined palms and smiling.

"Come in. Please come in. Welcome." He led the way into a wood-paneled office. When he was comfortably seated behind his desk in his leather armchair, and had moved his computer to one side so that he could see our faces, he began in a low voice. "So nice to see you again, Mr. Rao. And you have brought a guest?" He examined my face.

"Yes. She would like to stay for a few days. She is from America. She teaches meditation in England," Mr. Rao said, leaning forward slightly as he spoke.

"How long she wants to stay?" the monk asked, still peering at me.

"One or two weeks?" Mr. Rao asked, with a questioning expression. "How much will she have to pay?"

"Twelve hundred rupees a day, the same as everyone," the monk said. "This includes breakfast, lunch and dinner. It contributes to maintaining this facility. It is very expensive to maintain." He looked slightly apologetic.

I was frustrated because of the price, but I thought to myself, *What option do I have? I can't travel around New Delhi with all my luggage to look for a cheaper place. Besides, it's safe here and the tranquility of the place appeals to me.*

"I will consider it a donation," I said quietly.

Then the monk pressed a buzzer on the wall. The door opened and a wizened old man in simple Western dress appeared, nodding his head humbly as he awaited his orders.

"Kalsang, take her to the room upstairs on the first floor – number three," the monk said in a tone of voice one might reserve for one's servants.

The old man bowed his head and turned to me.

"Your luggage?" he said, pointing to the suitcases outside the door.

"Yes," I answered.

"I take them for you. Your room this way," he said softly.

He led the way up the smooth, polished staircase inlaid with mahogany tiles arranged in an alternating pattern of light and dark. On the walls were silk-screens of gaily colored birds perched in the branches of trees.

As we entered the long, open hall on the first floor, I saw an arched stained-glass window depicting a Buddha in deep meditation sitting beside a lake with tall reeds, yellow flowers and lavender hills in the distance. His orange robes flowed around him in a graceful circular design, and a yellow halo framed his head. In lotus pose, on a deep lavender-colored lotus, the Buddha sat motionless, eyes closed, a smile of detached poise on his lips. Blue circles, in varying shades, unfolded like a flower blossoming around his body in a soft spiraling motion.

Beneath the arched window were two sculptures of the Buddha on a low table. One was gold plated with a crown and four arms upraised in a blessing, while the other was a simple white stone carving depicting the Buddha as a monk with a rosary of rudraksha beads around his neck. In front of each sculpture was a long, thin candle: gold before the gold statue and white before the monk. Beside each of the Buddhas, a porcelain vase of pink silk lilies had been placed. The table itself was covered with a black and gold cloth embroidered with a design of dragons; draped over it was a bright yellow cloth.

As I stepped barefoot from the polished mahogany landing onto the soft straw matting, the inner silence of the shrine enveloped me. Immediately next to the table was a door to which the old man pointed. Unlocking the door, he stood to one side allowing me to enter.

"This – your room," the old man said.

The room was simply decorated in browns, maroon and beige. A small table with a telephone on it separated two single beds. I walked past a long desk with a mirror above it to a window leading out onto a small balcony. Then I opened the doors to the bathroom and the tall wooden wardrobe. Everything looked neat and clean.

"What would you like? Chai – tea, coffee? Dinner?" the man asked with his head bowed.

"A cup of tea and toast. Is that alright?"

"Yes. I will bring for you. Anything else? You like some jam?"

"Yes, that would be nice."

I sat down on the bed, letting my fingers glide over the geometrical design of the cotton quilt. My thoughts drifted slowly like leaves falling gently to the earth from the branches of a tall tree. A feather-light stillness embraced me as I stretched out on my back and closed my eyes. "Thank you, God", I whispered.

The first rays of the morning sun filtered through the slit in the heavy maroon curtains, but I could not move. My body felt heavy, too heavy to stir. I was on the verge of falling asleep again when I heard a loud noise like the beat of a drum. The sound repeated itself in a rhythmic pattern, which reverberated through the walls of my room. I sat up in bed with a start, attempting to discover the source of the hollow bellowing sound. *Construction down below? Oh no, I won't be able to meditate. It feels as if it's in this building. But what on earth can it be?* I was at a total loss as to the origin of the repetitive bellowing which continued in a set rhythm for an hour. Then suddenly it was over, still, silent.

My head ached. I tried to sit up and meditate, but fell asleep.

It took some time before I had bathed and was ready to begin my morning meditation. I crossed my legs in lotus position and closed my eyes. Gradually, the outer world faded away as my breathing settled down. As the body relaxed, breathing became as if suspended and the thoughts loosened their grip, spreading out into a formless, amorphous mass like clouds blown apart by the wind. The faint almost imperceptible impulse of the mantra appeared and disappeared like a fine golden thread weaving the rippling fabric of the mind into a more integrated pattern of inner clarity and peace.

My heart seemed to melt into an ocean of silence, which erased all sense of time and space. As the rippling fabric of the mind became more and more transparent, the light of the inner sun shone through, igniting the fibers of awareness with light. Then the clouds passed, covering the sun and flickering images like flocks of wild birds flew across the canvas of the mind shadowing the light with their wings.

After an hour, I lay down and rested for a short time. In the stillness that followed, I heard my inner voice: *Remember there is nothing you have to do, nowhere you have to go, no one you have to become. You are already THERE. You are already ALL. It is already DONE. Just let go and feel – FEEL – and you will experience the truth of that reality that is, was and ever will be the same, here, now and always.*

I could almost touch that truth and then it was gone and I asked myself, *How much longer? It has been twenty years since I started meditating. When will God extend His arms...?* I banished the thought with vexation. *How can I ask such a question? The Divine Beloved comes when one is ready to receive Him – only then...*

There was a knock at the door.

When I opened it, I saw the old man who had helped me with my luggage. "It is time for lunch. Would you like me to bring it up for you?"

"Yes, thank you. I didn't realize it was so late."

I hurriedly tidied up my room, unpacking some of the things I needed. Then I went out and stood on the balcony. It was a warm day. The sunlight played on the whitewashed roofs of the houses, which were painted pink and blue. It seemed to skip between the leafy branches of the trees growing in the small courtyard down below. It lit up the faces of the women hanging out their washing on the line, it shone alike on the fruit and vegetable stands along the avenue.

The second knock on the door was eagerly answered. I greeted the old man as he placed the tray with my lunch on the desk.

"What is your country?" he asked me.

"I live in England," I replied. "Are you from Japan?"

"Oh no, no. Not Japanese. Me – Ladakhi. I'm from Ladakh," he said emphatically.

"Ladakh. Where is that?" I asked a bit embarrassed.

"In the Himalayas – eleven thousand feet up. Very high up. You don't know it? It is in Jammu Kashmir district. It was Tibetan, but now it is part of India."

"How long have you been here?"

"I have been in service here for fifteen years. I'm not a monk but before coming here, I was in service in a temple in Ladakh for about five years," he said quietly, looking intently at me. His face was deeply lined; the lines revealed a story of simplicity and humility – a life of service.

He had short-cropped hair, sprinkled with gray near the temples and sideburns. His straight mustache was almost entirely gray. He had brown eyes and a pointed nose. His features could have been Western, but his mannerisms and gentle speech were unique to his culture.

"You are visiting India for some time?"

"I came because my first book is scheduled to be published soon."

"You are married? You have children?" he asked.

"No," I answered, looking down. There was a pause.

"Then you are free," he said smiling warmly.

"What name should I call you?" I asked him as he turned to go. I had heard the name the Japanese monk used.

"Kalsang," he answered. "It may be difficult for you – Ladakhi name."

"Kalsang. It has a nice sound," I said.

He bowed and left, closing the door softly behind him.

Later that afternoon, I ventured downstairs. I was greeted by two lean young men of about twenty years, with shaved heads and wearing orange shirts and maroon dhotis tied like long skirts around their waists. They smiled at me and brought me to the dining room.

The dining area contained a long low table carved of dark wood. Around it were placed matching chairs without legs. On the walls surrounding the table were embroidered cloth tapestries of the Buddha and bodhisattvas in ornately intricate designs.

We sat down on the seats that were a perfect height for the table so that one could sit cross-legged with a back support. They told me they were monks or lamas and that they were from Ladakh. I also learned that there were five monks in this center. One of the lamas went to the kitchen and returned with a tray of tea and biscuits.

"Please take." He offered me the tray of biscuits. "These for you."

They wanted to know why I had come to India and what my country was like. I tried to find the simplest words, as they did not understand English very well. They gazed at me with such warmth and sweetness that I almost felt like crying. The sound of bare feet on the wooden floor announced the arrival of someone. A monk entered the room. He looked much older.

"Tashi!" one of the monks called to him with a smile. Their eyes lit up with happiness. Like the other monks, Tashi wore a dhoti, a long maroon skirt and an orange T-shirt. However, he was heavier, handsomer and taller than the others. His skin was light brown, almost the same shade as mine. The most appealing aspect of his body was his broad chest and long muscular arms. Tashi entered, walking like a king, his head erect and chest held high, and his presence immediately filled the room. He took a seat on my side of the table but kept some distance.

"Namaste," he said in a low deep voice, glancing at me.

His shaved head was nicely rounded with a wide forehead above high cheekbones. His nose was small and pointed and his mouth thin, but attractive. His slanted eyes made him appear a bit Chinese.

He started talking in Ladakhi to the other two, who obviously enjoyed his company. I listened to their language, which was so very different from any language I had ever heard. It flowed in soft, resonant syllables; the pronunciation was smooth and round like rolling waves, or the rise and fall of mountains and valleys. It was very easy to listen to for it had a soothing influence on the ear.

As the evening light filled the room, a sense of timelessness pervaded the air. I felt that it was unnecessary to do or say anything. It was enough just to sit still, listening – just to be there.

From time to time, I glanced at Tashi. He had an unmistakable quality of deep, inner silence that made one feel peaceful in his presence. One could almost hear the silence in his voice which was tender and yet deep and sonorous. It was a loving voice, yet he appeared much more detached, more indrawn than the others. He had the aura of a monk around him; yet I felt strangely drawn to him as a man.

At five o'clock, I excused myself and returned to my room. I picked up a diary from the small table by my bed and wrote: *Buddhist Center, a world apart... another dimension. I had tea with three monks who were like images of the Buddha: the Buddha as a child, a smiling youthful Buddha and the Buddha as a monk. In them, there is joy, peace and a sense of giving.*

After meditating, I wandered downstairs. When I reached the foot of the stairs, I heard the loud beat of a drum. Hesitatingly, I slid open a wooden door inlaid with glass mirrors, and peeked inside. It was a temple! Monks draped in orange shawls sat cross-legged on the floor. One of them nodded, inviting me to enter.

Shyly, I tiptoed in and sat down on the wooden floor behind him.

The temple had five golden Buddhas arranged in a semi-circle on a high pedestal. In front of the Buddhas was a colorful display of silk flowers amid silver trays piled high with boxes of sweets and biscuits. Along the front of the altar were round silver bowls filled with water. In the wood-paneled temple were pillars decorated with embroidered silk cloths of many varied patterns and colors. When Tashi saw me, he stood up, went into an adjacent room, and brought a broad, flat cushion with a pink silk cover, which he offered to me to sit on.

A young monk hit the large drum with a wooden stick. I found the sound much too loud, but I was determined not to leave. It hurt my ears but when I focused on the rhythm, the pain subsided. I noticed the regular 1-2, 1-2-3, 1-2, 1-2-3 of the beats. Then one of the monks started to chant; it was as if the sound issued forth from a deep hollow cave in the earth. His voice rose like a wave, ascending slowly in a melodious pattern of notes. Then another one of the monks joined him, and his voice wove in and out of the previous melody, augmenting and enriching the sound with the contrasting pitch of his voice. One by one, their voices formed an interwoven tapestry of rich, sonorous tones.

I felt transported. Never before had I witnessed a Buddhist ceremony or heard the chanting of Buddhists monks. I felt very much at home here! It was almost as if the unusual sound was calling awake an aspect of my own nature which had been asleep for a long time. My body began to sway unselfconsciously back and forth in harmony with the melody. Even the constant rhythm of the drumbeat in the background now seemed natural, and the loudness of the sound was not disturbing to me anymore.

The time passed too quickly. After one hour, Tashi stood up and tapped lightly on a very large earthen bowl, which made a sound like a bell. The ritual ended with a few quietly spoken prayers and then all the monks bowed their heads, touching the floor in front of the altar with their foreheads. The monks then removed their orange shawls, which were draped around their shoulders, and took them to the small room where the cushions were kept.

That evening, when we were in the sitting room together, I mentioned to Tashi how much I had enjoyed the chanting. "How long did it take to learn to chant like that?"

"Learn? It is not learned. We just do it. It is not learned," Tashi repeated, looking surprised.

I was in awe of them. The melodious pattern was so intricate. When they sang together, their voices spontaneously blended into wholeness. I had imagined that it would take years to perfect.

"How long have you been a monk?" I asked him.

Tashi hesitated, and then he said, "Well – twenty years – no, longer than that. I was ten years old when my mother and father gave me to the monastery." He paused, then added, "There are two types of monks: some choose to become monks and others are given to the monastery."

I detected a shadow of sadness in his eyes.

"They GAVE you to the monastery?" I could not conceal my surprise.

"Yes, it is a custom, especially in Tibet, to give one or two sons to become monks."

"But how can one give away one's own child? I don't understand. Do you have many brothers and sisters?" I asked.

"Yes, six brothers and four sisters."

"I am also from a big family: I have four sisters and two brothers. One of my brothers spent a year in a Buddhist monastery in Thailand after serving in the Vietnam War. I think he needed to recover from the experience. He learned woodcarving there."

"In a Buddhist monastery? Your brother?" Tashi was obviously pleased.

"Yes," I answered. As I looked at him, I realized that he

resembled the sculptures of the Tibetan Buddhas. He had a marked air of detachment about him and yet he was manlier, earthier than the other lamas were. "It must have been hard for you to leave your parents," I remarked quietly.

"Yes, it was very difficult."

"It must have been..." I repeated very softly.

We sat in stillness. The air was filled with a newborn softness, as if it had been made sacred by the touching of two hearts. "How long have you been here?" I asked, looking at him.

"Five years."

"And before this, where were you?"

"I was in Manali in the Himalayas for seven years, and before that, I was in a monastery in Karnataka for ten years."

"Karnataka? In the South? Did you enjoy living in South India?"

"It was alright. There were about one thousand monks from Ladakh and Tibet in that place. There, we did much study during the day and some monks took their exams at the university and some became geshes."

"Geshes? What's that?" I asked puzzled.

"That is doctor of Buddhism – most advanced level. I tried but it was very difficult. We had to study ten hours a day, until late at night. It was not for me, too much difficult."

"As a monk, can you choose which monastery you want to go to?"

"Yes we can choose. I wanted to come to Delhi. We can choose to go to a different place. The monastery outside Bangalore in Karnataka was very far from everything else – very alone." He paused, as if recollecting his life there. Then he said, "I want to travel to other places – foreign countries."

"Which countries? Where do you want to go?"

"I want to go – to America. It is the most advanced country. Some of the top monks in the Tibetan Monastery in the South, the geshes, they went to teach in a monastery in America, in Atlanta.

They told us stories about it when they returned. I want to go to Buddhist monastery in America. I want to live there, in America, for many years, many, many years." He spoke quietly as if he was revealing his secret thoughts and desires. Every once in a while, he glanced furtively around to see if anyone was coming. Then he said, "Don't tell to anyone please. I don't want any of the others to know."

"I won't tell anyone," I said.

"How long you will be in India?" he asked me in a gentler tone of voice.

"I don't know. I want to go on a tour and see some of the holy places. I want to make a kind of pilgrimage. You know what I mean?"

"Yes, I've been to the Buddhist places: Varanasi, Sarnath, Bodgaya..." He stared into the distance. Suddenly his face brightened. "Your family is in America?" he asked, looking straight at me.

"Yes, I've not seen them for many years, almost nine years."

"Nine years? Your mother and father – you don't visit them?" he asked.

"They have passed away," I answered.

"Both?"

"Yes, both."

The night fell quietly, imperceptibly around us, like the unraveling of a dark, purple silk curtain awash with the flickering light of the stars.

"OK. It is enough." Tashi stood up abruptly and turned to go.

I watched him walk away. It was as if he had entered a world forbidden to monks. I could feel him draw the line between my world and his, firmly though invisibly. Beyond it, as a fully ordained lama, he would not allow himself to go. Nevertheless, our hearts had touched.

Chapter Four

Time at the Buddhist Center seemed almost non-existent. The intervals between the chanting of the prayers at dawn and dusk flowed by quietly like a lake with hardly any ripples on its surface. Sometimes I awoke early and watched the sunrise from the balcony. First, a tiny speck of light above the rooftops in the distance, then as the rose-colored sky faded, the glowing golden ball would rear its head, hanging suspended like a pearl in an azure sea of light. The teeming river of life rose with the sun in a wave of song, a streaming forth of energy, of resurgence and renewal. A thrill vibrated through me as I watched the sky grow in brilliance and I was glad to be alive. As the horizon was washed with light, the drumbeat in the temple resounded in the air. Tum-tum, tum-tum-tum. First softly, then louder and louder – a call to prayer. Between the sounds, weaving a thread of melody, the monks chanted: "Na Mu Myo Ho Ren Ge Kyo." The sound of their prayers ascended and filled the building with peace.

The day began with a floodtide of sounds from the streets down below: the barking of dogs, meowing of stray cats, the cawing of crows as their dark wings sailed through the air, beating out the rhythm of the pulse of time. From the rickshaws parked across the street, one could hear the coughing of engines and the sputter of motors and the sound of vendors' voices bellowing out in the morning air.

I showered, meditated and then jotted down notes in my hardcover notebooks for my second book. As I walked downstairs to refill my thermos with purified water, Kalsang entered the kitchen for his usual cup of tea. As the steam rose from the kettle, we sat together on wooden stools. The aroma of the strong black tea filled my nostrils, making me feel warm and content just to be there.

This simple old man's entire being emanated the sweet fragrance of humility, deference and the joy of giving. He never raised his voice, and whenever he came to my door, he expressed a genuine desire to ensure I had everything he could provide to make my stay both pleasant and comfortable. I regarded him as a friend and was eager to learn more about his native land. I asked him about his family.

"My mother and father work on the land. My wife, she too, works on the land. Most of the people are farmers, but I am not. I only finished ninth grade in school, then I served in the Ladakhi army for twenty years. I patrolled the border between Ladakh and Pakistan."

"Ladakhi army?" I asked surprised. "But Ladakh is part of India, isn't it?"

"Yes, that's true, but it is a separate state. It has its own army. However, I had to leave the army. A bomb fell near me and hit me in the head. See, I still have scar here." He parted his hair on the left side of his head with his bony fingers and leaned toward me. I saw a wiry line like stitches four or five centimeters long. Although he was Ladakhi, his features were unlike the lamas. Rather than round, the shape of his head was long and thin and his skin fair, almost white, in contrast to the brown complexions of the lamas.

"I retired after that and they gave me pension. When this job came up, I quickly took it. It is service. It is middle-class; I will keep it. I only want that the people who come should be happy. My desire is for your happiness. However, I have language problem. Sometimes I make mistake." His eyes clouded over; he lowered his head.

"You haven't made any mistakes," I said. "Can you tell me more about your country?"

"In Ladakh, there is not much businessmen because they sin. If they buy a cloth for two rupees, they sell it for two-fifty or three rupees. This is a sin. So people do not become businesspersons.

41

In Ladakh, if we buy it for one price, we think we should sell it for the same price. It should be equal otherwise it is a sin." Kalsang focused strongly as he spoke. "In Ladakh, if you go shopping and leave your bag in a public place and come back later, it will still be there. No one will take it. No one ever steals from anyone."

A man poked his head into the kitchen. He had long white hair down to his shoulders. "A cup of tea," he said.

"Mr. Stanley. Welcome. It is good to see you again! I will bring to you – at the table. One minute." Kalsang took the kettle and poured steaming-hot tea into a cup. Then he took a pack of biscuits from the shelf and arranged them on a plate. "Very good man; he comes to make films. He is from Alaska," Kalsang whispered to me as he went out of the kitchen.

I joined them at the table.

"Kalsang, how are things with you?" Mr. Stanley asked with genuine concern, pushing aside the newspaper he had been reading.

"I am satisfied," Kalsang said quietly.

Mr. Stanley looked very robust, and with his ruddy complexion and bright blue eyes, he radiated vitality and good health.

"I'm in New Delhi this time to film the students' hunger strike in the colony where the Tibetan refugees are living."

"Oh, very sad," Kalsang said. "The world should know. This is a very sad time for all of us."

Mr. Stanley continued, "Yes – such young lads. They have vowed to fast until death. Noble deed. I will publicize it to the world. The world should know what the Chinese have done to the Tibetan people."

"You're right," Kalsang said.

Mr. Stanley turned to me and said, "Did you know that the Chinese invasion in 1959 resulted in the destruction of six thousand monasteries and the death of over one million

Tibetans? I was shocked when I first found out about it." Mr. Stanley's eyes were filled with indignation.

Kalsang nodded his head sadly and said, "In Ladakh, we pray: 'Thank you God that we are not dead.' We pray because we know death is always with us. It could be anytime, by fire, by accident, by wind, on the road, in the house – anytime, anywhere. We pray at least three times a day – maybe four times. We pray also before sleep. We ask forgiveness if we have made a mistake during the day with our speech, with our mind or with our heart. Each time we make a mistake, we start again. We are renewed each day."

Kalsang picked up the *Times of India* and showed us the headline, which read: Tornado in Orissa Kills 105. 1000 Lose Their Homes.

"Orissa." Mr. Stanley shook his head knowingly. "Off the Gulf of Bengal. I know the area. Hurricanes there can be terrible."

Then Kalsang spoke, framing his words with care. "In Ladakh, if we eat meat or fish, then we pray to God to forgive us for we know it is a sin. There is much fishing there. Anything that has blood, if we kill it, it is a sin." Kalsang said it kindly, yet emphatically. His deep-set eyes peered into Mr. Stanley's. "If we sin, then it comes back to us."

"Right you are," Mr. Stanley replied, nodding his head. "I believe in karma and reincarnation. What you give is what you get back. What you give is what you receive. This is the law of life. It's mentioned in the Bible too. As you sow, so shall you reap."

Kalsang sighed in agreement.

"And life doesn't end when the body drops off," Mr Stanley continued. "We keep returning in a new body again and again until we not only know the truth, but also LIVE it! Everything operates in cycles, day and night, work and rest, life and death. There is no end to it.

But the most important thing we have to learn is that we are all ONE! There is no difference between us or at least, the differences do not matter. Cultures, races, religions should not separate us. They really shouldn't! LOVE is all that matters, love and respect for one another. That's ALL one needs to know! Christ taught us to LOVE one another. He said, 'Love Thy Neighbor as Thyself.' These are the only fundamentals of my life." He paused, and then added with flashing eyes, "The rest is bullshit! All these holy wars between religions in the name of religion!! The church changed what Christ said so that they could manipulate us."

Two lamas came in to set the table for the meal. I marveled at Mr. Stanley. He exuded such forthrightness and obvious integrity.

"How long will you be here?" I asked him.

"Only today. Tomorrow I'm off to Nepal. And you?"

"A little longer. I'm not sure yet. The price is more than I can afford."

The aroma of hot chapatis filled the room. A guest came in and joined us at the table. All the lamas in the center knew him because he was sponsoring the building of a stupa next to an affiliated Buddhist Center in Manali. He must have been in his early forties. His name was Mr. Negi. He told us that he had come to visit his son who was studying at a university in New Delhi. Whenever he came to Delhi, he was welcome to stay at the Buddhist Center without any charge.

"Where are you from?" I asked him.

"From Manali. It's a hill station in the Himalayas, in the state of Himachal Pradesh."

A large copper pot of steaming-hot vegetable soup containing Ladakhi homemade noodles was carried to the table. The lamas chanted a short Tibetan grace before meals. Then we passed our bowls to the lama sitting at the head of the table and he served each of us in turn. We ate in silence except for a few words quietly spoken between the lamas. The lamas sipped their soup loudly. I could not help smiling as I thought of how the English would react to the sound. For me, though, it was such a relief to be free of such conventions, which I had always found a burden and a bore.

After supper, Mr. Negi said reflectively, "Sometimes I wonder why I was chosen to provide the land for the stupa. Why me? Why on my land? It was a blessing. I am happy to be able to give the land. There is much land around my home in Manali."

"Have you always been able to help the Buddhist Center?" I asked.

"Oh no. Not really." He paused. "A few years ago, I had almost nothing. I was worried about money all the time. There had been floods for three years in Manali and we farmers depend on the weather for our money. Because of the floods, I lost all my apples. The harvest was almost nothing. In Manali, the apple trees provide us with most of the money. The apples and the tourists – hotels and trees – that's all. I lost everything because of the floods. Then I thought of opening a hotel but I could not finish it because of lack of money. I have four brothers. They all got angry with me and even my father was angry. I wanted to leave India. I felt so ashamed, so bad because of it. Then I went to Japan; I took some souvenirs with me. I had hardly any money, but the Japanese people helped me a lot. I stayed there for almost two years and gradually I was able to earn back most of the money I had lost. Then I donated the land for the stupa. You should come to Manali and see it."

Tashi, who was sitting opposite me, said quietly, "You'll like it in Manali. You will like the forest. Many monks meditating in the forest. You'll like that." Then he was silent.

"Do you like meditation?" Mr. Negi asked me.

"Yes, I've been meditating for a very long time, over twenty years. I learned meditation in England."

"Over twenty years?" he said, surprised. "Meditation, it's a good thing. You will have good meditation in Manali; many holy places are there." Then he added, "Why you meditate?"

I hesitated for several minutes while I tried to decide how to explain the supreme goal of my life in as few words as possible. "Because I want moksha – liberation – to be able to live in perfect harmony with the will of God – to make no mistakes, to do no harm to anyone."

"No mistakes? That is not possible for the human being, is it?"

"I think it may be, but first the heart has to become pure. Pure heart, pure mind. To live in tune with the will of God, purification is necessary. All religions aim for the same goal: harmony with the Divine will."

Tashi, who had been listening to our conversation, looked up and said slowly, "The goal is the same for all. Some people go by different path. Some take cart, some take boat, some a car but all reach the same place. Buddhism teaches us to meditate in stages. We must go through each stage like the Buddha did. Only after much study can we practice meditation, otherwise it is too much difficult." Turning to me, he said, "How much time you meditate every day?" he asked.

"About two hours: one hour in the morning and one hour in the evening. I also do levitation, I mean, a flying technique."

"Flying technique?" Tashi smiled, his eyes lighting up with interest.

"Yes, the body lifts up slightly from the ground." I gestured, lifting my open palms up from the table. "Not very high, but we're only in the first stage of flying. It looks something like a frog hopping. A few people have also had experiences of floating."

Tashi interrupted and in a very serious tone of voice, he said, "In Ladakh, there are monks who can fly. They do not sleep during the night. They remain awake or sit up sleeping. They pray. They pray for six years, six months and six days and then, a few can fly. There is a round hole in the window in their room and they fly up through that hole."

"Have you seen it?" I asked, the hair on my neck standing on end. I leaned forward, my spine erect. This had been my secret desire for years.

"No, but I believe it. In Ladakh, there are monks who can fly."

Monks who can fly! I repeated his words in awe to myself. *Monks who can fly!*

One of the younger lamas switched on the television. We watched the news together. There was a long broadcast about some problems in the Indian parliament and then they showed images of the tornado. As I sat there, I felt the same warm feeling permeating my chest that I had felt earlier. I looked across at Tashi and our eyes met. For a few minutes, it was as if neither of us could pull our gaze away. I was momentarily overwhelmed by an upsurge of emotion; I closed my eyes and lowered my head. He aimlessly rustled the pages of the newspaper, which lay open before him. With my eyes still closed, I saw a vision of a lotus blooming between our hearts. The lotus unfolded on a ray of light, which ran like a golden thread between his heart and mine. A sensation of unspeakable inner peace washed through me, a peace that made the body feel as if it was melting...

We continued sitting at the table after everyone else had retired to their rooms. Finally, he spoke, "What is your age?"

I looked up, a bit disconcerted by the suddenness of his question. "I'm older than I look," I answered, not wishing to reveal my age to him.

"I think thirty-seven, thirty-eight," he said with a mischievous smile.

I did not respond to his mistake. The silence lengthened.

"You never thought of marriage?" he asked quietly.

"Yes – I have, but it – I – it, I mean, the right person didn't come..."

He looked at me and his eyes seemed to delve deep into my soul. It was a gentle look filled with silent understanding. I felt as if I was momentarily held in his embrace. A delicious warmth suffused my whole being, making my body tingle with delight.

"You would like?" he asked me simply.

My eyes filled with tears, but I did not answer. I only nodded my head once, then I looked down. My lips were parted in an irrepressible smile.

Night had fallen. The building breathed soundlessly, in stillness. The darkness seemed to glow. The light of the moon filtered in through the open curtains. It seemed to spread its radiance over us, uniting us in a shining circle of light. Tashi leaned forward toward me. He reached out to touch my hand resting on the table, palm down. Just as he was about to touch me, he pulled himself back with a jerk and slowly his whole body retreated until he was leaning far back in his chair, farther back than before.

"There are four rules for a lama: he must not tell a lie. Sometimes small lie is OK if it does not harm anyone, but a big lie, then he is no more a lama. He must not steal. He must not kill. And," he paused, "he must not marry. I am not allowed to marry." His voice fell. His eyes could not hide the sorrow in them. "I have taken my vows." He added in a lower voice.

"How long ago did you take your vows?" I asked, feeling as if I was drowning slowly.

"Eight years, no, nine years ago."

"And the vows – the vows are for life?" My voice quivered as I spoke. I was trying hard not to cry.

He did not respond. Instead he leaned toward me again, as if to comfort me and again he pulled himself slowly back. Then again, his body, as if involuntarily surged forward, impelled by an overwhelming inner wave of emotion, and slowly he pulled himself back. It was as if the reins of his intellect held him in check. Finally he spoke. "I must decide. This I must decide. I know I want to live in a foreign country – in America. I want to go there, either in the monastery or outside. This is my choice." He waited. We looked into each other's eyes. My heart began to pound with renewed vigor. A sudden flame of hope was re-ignited and its light flickered in the distance.

"Shantila, please can you ask your brother in America if he can get address of Buddhist monasteries in America? Then I write to them and see if I can come. I must have invitation letter from there so visa will be firm. After I go there, then I can decide. I decide after coming there."

"Yes, I'll write to him. I'll write tomorrow. You want it to be a Tibetan monastery?" I asked.

"Tibetan monastery is only for Tibetans. It will be difficult for me to go there. Any Buddhist monastery – please – thank you. Anything, Korean, anything is alright."

"I will help you. My brother is very good. He will send addresses. But why do you want to leave India?"

"I no like India. I want to go America. It is more advanced country. Lama from my village lived in New York for thirty years. He donated ten lakh rupees to monastery in Ladakh. He said life was very good there. I no can stay here. My friends in Ladakh write me. They ask, you are studying and doing pujas? What can I say? Here, no study, no puja – nothing. Here head lama is Japanese. We are Ladakhis. We are not even allowed to wear our robes – only this." He tugged ruefully at his yellow T-shirt. "Language problem, so we do no study, nothing. All day we're just cleaning the building, cooking meals, watching television – no good. How can I stay here?"

"But the prayers downstairs in the temple—"

He interrupted me. "All Japanese prayers, not our tradition. In Ladakh, we pray deeper, different, very different. You should hear it in Ladakh…"

He seemed totally convinced of the futility of the time spent in the Buddhist Center in Delhi.

"I understand," I said quietly. "You don't need to explain. I was only wondering if…" I paused, and then added, "…if you are happy as a lama?"

"Yes," he said without hesitation. He stood up. "OK. It is enough for now. I sleep now. You go rest. We will speak again."

He turned to go out. I followed him out to the top of the stairs, then he descended the steps to the monks' quarters and I returned to my room upstairs.

As I undressed for bed, my mind was at peace. I could feel his presence in the room. Perhaps it was the strength of his thoughts, I do not know. Although our bodies had parted, our common thoughts and feelings united us in an invisible bond. I chose to wear a simple white gossamer nightdress which I reserved for special occasions. It was embroidered with white lace at the bodice and a small satin bow with a tiny white pearl was sewn on each shoulder. As I slipped it over my head, I imagined that I was wearing it for him. In my imagination, I saw him smile as it fell in soft folds around my long thin limbs. I washed my face with warm water and rolled back the smooth white silk sheet I used to sleep on whenever I was away from home.

Lying in bed, I saw him beside me, touching me, caressing me. With each flourish of my imagination, his presence became more real, more vivid. As his mouth found my breasts, my whole body was flooded with bliss. We made love and for a few minutes, I transcended all the boundaries of time and space and floated in a light-filled ocean of eternal love.

Suddenly, there was a bright rush of light and my spine curved into an arch lifting the body off the bed into the air; it fluttered weightless like an undulating wave of pure energy and then resumed its supine position on the bed. The experience occurred in a flash. Without warning, I realized that I had slipped outside the limitations of the physical realm of life. My heart rejoiced.

My dearest Love, how I adore you... My heart framed its message in silence. *You have filled me with the calm splendor of your being and I am blessed, blessed by your touch, so divine, bathed in wonder at its depth and strength to move me so much. I give myself to you, my love, with all I am. I offer you my love now and forever.*

Sleep came sweetly, deeply, pouring over me, covering me

softly like the white wings of a bird, like a swan – gliding, gliding, gliding down to the still surface of a clear lake at dawn. In the mirror of the lake, a dream unfolded:

The summons came in the middle of the night. The call was heard and heeded by all who were awake inside. No one tarried. Everyone who heard it had waited long for the call and had prayed that it would come. Some had performed many years of austerities in order to be ready. In order to be capable of hearing it, they knew that subtle levels of the body, mind and heart had first to be purified so that the ears could hear the unmanifest sound, the eyes could see the inner light ever-aflame within the manifest world, the body could become light as the wind, as the very air, transparent, buoyant, weightless!

We rose into the air as one cosmic body, soaring into space, all in lotus pose, sailing free, like wild geese, flying in formation, up – up – up into the sky. We flew over the Atlantic Ocean, over the continent of Europe, down through Spain, over the Pyrenees, over the Adriatic Sea and the Sea of Galilee, then up, up, up toward the peaks of the Himalayas.

It was a gathering of perfected beings. We were all destined to meet there, in the hidden jungles of the deodar forests, high above the Rohtang Pass, near the Manasarovar Lake on the border of Tibet.

In the deep silence of the jungle, we received a secret teaching. And we chanted mantras, invoked the deities, and prayed for the release from suffering of all living beings. Above all, we experienced the quintessential joy of total unity, for all who were gathered there saw all beings as one, One Self. It was a fellowship of perfect union: one mind, one heart. A divine wholeness of inexpressible love joined us to each other.

When I awoke, it took several minutes to re-orient myself to the physical world; the dream was so vivid. My awareness seemed to have expanded. It encompassed the whole room at once and even beyond it. Beyond the walls, it seemed to breathe outwards into space and beyond it. Sunlight flooded the room. Its fiery brilliance danced in circles before me. I drew the sheets up over my eyes to protect them from the glare.

Chapter Five

The oldest of the monks in the Buddhist Center joined me while I was reading the newspaper in the sitting room. He moved slowly, with even measured steps, his head and back slightly bowed. He was shorter than Tashi, and the sprinkling of white hair on his oval-shaped head indicated a mature age. He sat down across from me.

"You are comfortable? Your room is fine?" he asked me in a gentle voice.

"Yes, it is fine. I really like it here. It is so peaceful," I said, smiling.

"It is a good place. I have been here for four years. Soon I will go to a new place."

"What's your name?" I asked him.

"Kunchen Lama."

"Have you been a monk for a long time?"

"Yes, yes." He smiled nodding his head. "A long time – since I was eight years old. I'm forty-five now." He paused. "It was my choice. I wanted to become a monk. When I was a boy, in Ladakh, my family – I have two brothers and two sisters – we used to visit the big monastery in my village at festival times. In the festivals, the lamas would be dancing. Many people came to our village for the festivals because they were so beautiful. When I was a small boy, I asked my mother and father to let me become a monk. They were very happy. In Ladakh, having a monk in the family brings honor to the whole family." His eyes radiated inner contentment. "It is considered a great blessing." He closed his eyes.

I felt like he was seeing his life before him. It was clear that it had been a good life, a dedicated life, one with few regrets. He seemed to be at peace with himself.

On my way up the stairs to my room, I remembered Tashi's words: *There are two types of monks: some choose to be monks and others are given to the monastery.*

Oh, Tashi, my dearest! I just want you to be happy in your life! my heart whispered fervently.

I was writing notes for the novel when I heard a knock on the door. I opened it and saw Tashi standing outside.

"Package for you," he said in a matter-of-fact tone.

"Come in, Tashi. A package? I wonder what it could be." I took the bulky square, which was wrapped in brown paper. "It's from my publisher..." Suddenly I jumped up in the air. "Tashi!" I exclaimed with excitement. "Tashi, I know what it is! Scissors! I need some scissors!" I ran into the bathroom and returned with some scissors. "It's my book! My first book! Wait, don't go!"

"Your book?" Tashi asked, laughing at me. "What book?"

"My book! It has just been printed! I'll show it to you. Here, help me get the string off."

"Give me the scissors. I'll do it." Tashi took the small scissors and deftly cut the taut, rough string. Then he gave me the package with a smile.

Quickly, I unfolded the layers of brown paper. Then I saw the books. There were six in all. I was delighted with the cover and flicking it over, I showed Tashi my photo on the back cover.

Tashi took a book and fondled it, turning it over and over in his strong hands. "You wrote this? Very beautiful book. I would like to read your book," he said, looking into my eyes.

"Yes, you can," I answered quietly. My heart had been pounding with excitement but when I looked into his eyes, I felt calmer immediately.

"What will you do today?" Tashi asked, moving toward the door.

"I have to go to see Mr. Rao, my publisher, then I must go to the tailor to have a blouse made for my white and gold sari."

"Will the blouse be gold color?" Tashi asked, his hand on the knob of the door.

"Yes."

"Good. I like gold color the best. See you later."

The traffic was especially heavy this morning, but my rickshaw raced forward. I covered my mouth and nose with a crumpled handkerchief as black smoke issued forth from the clanging exhaust of an old bus in front of us. We chortled and careered down the main road, inadvertently propelled forward by the mass of cars surrounding our small three-wheeler.

Suddenly, the rickshaw broke down in the middle of the road. Cars veered sharply to the right and left of us. The driver did not seem the least bit vexed by it all. He merely opened his metal seat, and took out a few tools. But then he decided that the ramshackle contraption just needed to cool off. He dragged the rickshaw with me in it to the side of the road and we sat together, watching the traffic zoom past.

It was getting progressively hotter: April in New Delhi. The brightness of the sun's rays bit into my forehead, making my head ache. I had forgotten to bring sunglasses; I shielded my eyes with my hands and wrapped my scarf around my head. Then I saw a child, very thin and dark, standing beside the rickshaw with her hand outstretched.

"Rupee, madam," she murmured, putting her fingers to her mouth to indicate that she was hungry. She was around twelve years old. She looked healthy; only her long dark hair was uncombed and she was wearing a Punjabi suit, which was badly in need of washing. Her eyes were clear and intelligent and her face finely chiseled.

The rickshaw driver looked annoyed. He motioned with abrupt gestures for her to move on. She hesitated then walked to the next car with her open palm outstretched.

"It is better not to give to them. They should go to school. With education, they have a chance to get some money. Otherwise, all their life they live in the street, with nothing to do but only beg." He pushed his foot down hard on the pedal and the motor of the rickshaw sputtered and coughed, but remained where it was. We waited ten minutes more.

At last, the rickshaw had cooled off enough. It reared its head, belching black smoke from the engine as we raced down the motorway toward Green Park. The road was quickly swallowed up beneath the wheels of the three-wheeler.

I finally arrived at Mr. Rao's office, ten minutes late. Even so, I had to wait. His secretary told me Mr. Rao was busy with an important client. Half an hour later, he stepped out.

"Shantila Martin. Please come in," he said, extending his hand. I followed him into the medium-sized office. Opposite me was a bookcase, which I thought probably contained some of the books his company had published. I wondered if my book would be placed among them. Mr. Rao took a seat behind his large wooden desk and motioned to me to sit in one of the chairs facing him. I sat down. To Mr. Rao's left were three telephones, a calculator and a buzzer to call his secretary. I recognized a photo of his deceased father on the desk. There was also a plaque with a quotation which said: Every Obstacle Is an Opportunity. Do not Waste Time. Transform It to Fulfill Your Desires.

"You received the book?" Mr. Rao asked. "How do you like it?"

"It's beautiful. The photograph on the cover came out perfect. I'm happy with it."

"Good, good. I like the cover too." Mr. Rao shifted a few papers around on his desk. I got the impression that he wanted me to leave soon. We had not even discussed the main topic yet.

"What about the launch? Have you fixed the date?" I asked, perplexed by his behavior.

"Haven't you heard the news? The parliament is hung." He placed his palms down squarely on the table as if to say that the subject was closed.

"Parliament hung? What is that? What does that mean?" I asked in bewilderment.

"It means that this is the worst possible time to launch a book. No one will be interested. It would be a waste of money," he replied flatly.

"What about the tour?" I whispered weakly.

"We never said we would finance a tour." He paused. "It's hot. In summer, everyone goes on holidays. I have to get to work now. I have an important meeting today. The board is going to decide about the Italian contract." He started adding up figures on his calculator.

I stood up, stunned with disappointment, and walked slowly out the door. *No launch,* I thought. *My book – who will read my book? Who will even know it exists?*

I got into a rickshaw that was parked outside and half-heartedly directed him to Lajpat Nagar, the market where the tailor's shop was situated. As he drove through the streets, I wondered what to do. How could I promote the book?

When I arrived at the shop, the shopkeeper asked me what the matter was. She was a rotund, motherly woman who naturally took an avid interest in all her client's personal affairs. I told her the story.

"Problem? No problem. I know someone who can help you. Mr. Patel! You get Mr. Patel to write about your book and everyone will buy it! Everyone in India reads his column!" She smiled broadly, as she measured the width of my shoulders.

"Mr. Patel?" I asked. "Who is he?"

"He writes for the newspaper, a weekly column. He is famous all over India. My God! The things he says!" She chuckled, shaking her head. "You must call him. He'll write about your book."

I felt better by the time I left the shop. I decided to telephone Mr. Rao about it.

The streets were crowded with the traffic of people returning home from work. Rickshaws carelessly squeezed between cars, shifting from lane to lane, barely avoiding being crushed between antiquated buses, which poured gaseous fumes into the searing heat of the thick, dry air. I said a silent prayer as my driver pushed harder and harder on the accelerator, the front wheels nearly lifting off the ground after every red light. Then I saw the cows: tranquil, regal, uninvolved witnesses of the madness unraveling all around. Unshaken, two large white cows stood, side by side, in the middle of the busy traffic. Cars, buses and rickshaws curved sharply to the side to avoid hitting them. Like a venomous serpent darting after his prey, the traffic lanes wriggled wildly forward. For a moment, I saw in a flash the whole of New Delhi as a huge web in which everyone was entangled, fighting for survival, trapped by his or her own doing. I wondered whether these drivers were immensely courageous or foolishly reckless. After all, I knew that Hindus believed that they lived one life after another...

I was catapulted out of my reverie when the wheels of the rickshaw banged against a massive bulge in the road. The top of my head hit the metal roof with a thud.

"Chelo! No, I mean, asta, asta, slower over the bumps please!" I shouted to the driver. My spoken Hindi had not improved much since my last visit and at first, I had said "chelo" which meant faster when all I desperately wanted was for him to slow down.

Everything in sight was moving at top speed, moving in tune with the racing heartbeat of New Delhi. It was a hard, rhythmic, pulsating beat, a constant throbbing that kept time with the distant intonation of the sun, from sunrise until sunset. The beat continued unweariedly urging one on, urging the city to keep to the beat or die.

When I arrived at the gate of the Buddhist Center, I realized that the rickshaw driver had not even turned on his meter. He quoted a price for the trip which I knew he reserved only for gullible foreigners.

I was anxious to call Mr. Rao to ask him about getting in touch with Mr. Patel. I phoned him as soon as I arrived at the Center.

Luckily, he was still in his office.

"It's a very good idea. However, it will be difficult. He has never done an article on any of my books."

"But we can at least try, can't we?" I asked pleadingly.

"Of course. Why not send him a card, and see what happens? I have his address."

"Mr. Rao, I must tell you something: I can't afford to stay in this place much longer. It is too expensive." I paused, and then added, "Can you pay me an advance for the book?"

"We pay only when the book is sold," he said firmly.

"But how will it sell if it isn't promoted?"

"Well, this is not a good time for the launch. In the fall, we can organize something."

"In September?" I asked.

"Yes, after the hot weather is over. It will be a better time," he said.

"Four months. I have to stay in India for four more months. I don't have enough money."

"You will be alright," Mr. Rao answered hurriedly.

I could hear a note of impatience rising in his voice.

"Would it be alright if I leave and go somewhere like – um, the Himalayas, where I can work on my novel?"

"Yes, of course. Just let me know where you are. Keep in touch in case something comes up." He hung up.

September! I was astounded. *He does not even care what happens to me! I thought he would be much more helpful. I thought I would be his guest! Now this! What am I going to do? Maybe I should go on a pilgrimage. I've always wanted to visit the holy places like Rishikesh, Haridwar, Badrinath and Gangotri.*

I walked slowly up the stairs to my room. My mind was in a whirlpool. *I have to find a place to stay. Where should I go? I did not expect this to happen. I'm on my own now.* I glanced vacantly at the stained-glass window with the smiling Buddha, and then opened the door to my room. As I entered the room, I suddenly caught myself in the middle of an onrushing tide of thoughts: *But Shantila – no one is ever ALONE! You should know that by now! WHO is doing this, creating this experience, this very situation, this place, this time! WHO is the author of ABSOLUTELY EVERYTHING we see, hear, feel, imagine we are achieving all the time? There is only ONE AUTHOR, one omnipresent AUTHOR of Everything! This – HE, SHE or It – can write or unwrite the script of life at any time. Do you think you are Alone? No, Shantila, you are immersed in THAT ocean of Being. You cannot step outside this fullness because it is omnipresent.*

You, even you, will find HIM one day everywhere, in everything and in everyone. Then whether or not Mr. Rao helps you or whether you are with Tashi, or whether you are in a deep forest, you will feel eternally embraced, loved and cared for – for ALL SENSE OF SEPARATENESS WILL HAVE VANISHED FOREVER!

I knew that my inner voice was the voice of truth.

It was time to begin my journey. It could be forestalled no longer; no more lingering in the comfort zone. I had to say goodbye to my newfound friends.

I decided not to join the others for supper; I was too exhausted. Kalsang brought the meal to my room. When he saw me, he immediately knew something was the matter.

"Shantila, you are not feeling well?" he asked, placing the tray on the desk.

"I, uh, I have to leave soon, but I don't know where to go," I answered in a low voice.

"Don't worry. You will find the right place. In Leh, I have a house. If you ever want to visit Leh, the capital of Ladakh, you can go to my house. My wife and two daughters live there. You can visit. My older daughter is called Ani; she is coming to Delhi in a few days. My house is near the Shanti Stupa. The Japanese monk in charge here built the stupa in Leh. I worked for the Japanese there too. When you come to Leh, just ask for 'Japanese Kalsang's' house."

At lunch the next day, we discussed where I would go. Mr. Negi asked me, "How long you will stay here?"

"I don't know – I'm not sure..." I replied, wishing he hadn't asked. "I can't afford to stay much longer. You see, when I came to Delhi, I expected to be my publisher's guest."

"Don't worry about the money. You are comfortable. Is the food alright?" He paused. "You are vegetarian?"

"Yes, I am. Everything is fine, but I must leave soon. I want to find a place in the Himalayas where I can live simply and write."

"Himalayas? You want to come there? Then you should come to Manali. You can live there. It's a beautiful place. I can find a place for you – very cheap. When you want to come? I'm returning tomorrow." He smiled warmly. "I'm telling you," Mr. Negi continued, "you will be all right in Manali. Just wait, and don't worry. Stay in India and you'll be all right. I'll help you."

I looked at his face. He was married and had one son and one daughter. He wanted to help me. I had only just met him, yet I trusted him completely. This was a new experience for me.

Tashi lifted his head up from the newspaper he was leafing through and gazed steadily at me for several minutes. Then he returned to the paper but he did not appear to be interested at all in what he was reading. Every few minutes he glanced at me curiously. I pretended not to notice but I felt a tingling sensation in my chest and then a warmth began to spread through my whole body. I could feel the power of his feelings. Spontaneously my heart responded in kind. *There is a thread between us,* I thought.

"Manali – good place," Tashi said with conviction. "Bus leaves from New Tibetan Colony. I can get you the ticket. I am going to visit the colony today. Some lamas are praying there for the students on the hunger strike. Everyone there is feeling very bad. Very terrible situation is there now. When you want to leave?"

"In a few days. I have a dentist appointment in Delhi on Monday morning," I said.

On Monday afternoon, I packed my bags quickly. Then I posted a letter to Mr. Patel, describing the topic of my book. I also called Mr. Rao to tell him I was leaving.

"Yes, you can go to Manali. I will let you know when you should return to Delhi. In a few months, the weather will be cooler, and then we will talk. Then you can return."

A few days passed. The bus was scheduled to depart from the New Tibetan Colony on the outskirts of Delhi that night. I was meditating in the temple downstairs when I heard Tashi's voice.

"Please come. I'll accompany you to the bus to see that you arrive safely. We must leave now."

I slowly opened my eyes. Tashi stood at the entrance to the temple, dressed in a gray khaki pants suit. It was the first time I had seen him without his dhoti, the long skirt he usually wore. He was tall and despite his shaved head, handsome in a simple, unpretentious way.

Before we left the Buddhist Center, I handed him a copy of my book.

"I want you to have this," I said.

"But – I – it's very expensive. Better you keep your books..." Tashi looked at me; he didn't know what to say.

"I want you to have it. Please, it's for you," I said softly.

"Thank you, Shantila. Now we must hurry or we'll miss the bus!"

He negotiated the price for the trip with the rickshaw driver. Then we set off together. I was overjoyed to have his company.

Chapter Six

The New Tibetan Colony consisted of a tattered-looking collection of cement buildings on the edge of nowhere. The streets wore a sad, haggard expression; garbage lay strewn in mounting piles along the pavement and in the gutters. Packs of wild dogs roamed the streets, sniffing at the rotting garbage and glaring at the people passing by. The place had the air of a refugee camp. Tibetan prayer flags, once gaily-colored, now faded and torn, waved limply in the hot, still air.

An extra weight of sorrow hung like a menacing black cloud over the community because the lives of the Tibetan youths who were in the third week of their hunger strike dangled on a thin, taut string which all their friends knew could snap at any time.

As the engine of the rickshaw churned to a halt on a deserted street in the New Tibetan Colony, I breathed a silent sigh of relief that Tashi was with me. He skillfully lifted my heavy case out of the rickshaw and placed it on the pavement.

We stood side by side without saying anything. It was our first time alone outside the Buddhist Center. I was, strangely enough, the only person waiting for the bus to Manali.

"Are you sure the bus will stop here?" I asked Tashi.

"Yes, this is the place. It stops here," he replied. He rubbed his palms over his shaved head a few times. "Sometimes I get headaches from the heat."

"Oh, what do you take for it?" I asked in a concerned tone.

"It's better now. I took Tibetan medicine for three months. Now I don't get them so much – only occasionally."

"Tibetan medicine? Where did you get it?"

"In Dharmsala. When I went there, I got from Tibetan doctor. In Ladakh, we use traditional medicine. Especially in my village, we mostly use our own medicine."

"That's good. That's much better than Western medicine

which has so many bad side effects. I also use traditional medicine, usually Ayurvedic herbs. Have you heard of Ayurveda?"

"Yes, I've heard of it." He glanced at his wristwatch. Then, he said, "You wait here. I will go across the street to see one of my friends who lives here. I'll be back." He walked toward the street leaving me with my luggage. I thought that perhaps he was feeling a bit uncomfortable being alone with a woman. I watched him cross the street. He had a noble bearing and his steps were firm and steady. He held his broad chest high and his neck and back straight while his long, muscular arms moved slowly, gracefully at his sides.

As he disappeared through a gate in a gray, cement wall encircling the colony, I felt my throat constrict. Moving closer to my suitcase, I gazed anxiously around. A lone dog ran out of an alleyway. It was being chased by a pack of dogs, all equally dirty and lean. They gazed in my direction, started toward me, then turned and ran away. My body tightened, then relaxed in a spasmodic jerk.

The white sky had already lost all its brightness. The dim pallor of dusk brushed the air with an even denser gray hue. As the light diminished, the laws ruling the day seemed to decrease in vitality while the laws of the darkness grew stronger. I heard a pack of dogs howling in the distance, and I imagined all virtuous people taking shelter in their homes. I waited nervously for Tashi to return. However, there was no sign of him.

Then a tawny figure in torn clothes, with the zipper of his trousers undone emerged from the shadows. He weaved back and forth towards me with a lurid grin on his face. His eyes were wide open, fixed in a glassy stare.

"Oh my God!" I watched him coming closer. With each step he took, my chest throbbed more painfully and my head felt so hot and tight, it was as if a rubber band had been twisted around it. I glanced furtively around, pleading inwardly for Tashi to return.

Then, suddenly, I saw him. He was standing across the street talking to another lama.

"Tashi! Tashi!" I called out in a frantic tone. "Come, come, please come!"

The other lama heard my voice first and alerted Tashi. Then Tashi turned round and saw me. Although there were many cars speeding past on the road, he darted between them. Tashi walked straight up to the drunk and stood between him and me with his legs astride and his arms folded squarely across his chest. He said something to him in Hindi, which I could not hear, just one or two words, and then he stood there in total silence, like a column of steel. The other lama, who had followed when the traffic died down, yelled at the drunk and waved him away with his arms. The tawny figure lingered for a while, then weaving back and forth, he slid away into the folds of night and disappeared, a figure of darkness covered by darkness.

I was shaking when Tashi came and stood beside me.

"Shantila, it's over. It's all right. I am with you. Don't be afraid." He stood as close to me as he could without touching me.

The nearness of his presence served to still the rapid throbbing of my pulse and immediately the calm equanimity, which I sensed to be the essence of his nature, flowed into me. It was like having a blood transfusion, bringing a renewal of energy and joy. "Thank you, Tashi," I whispered.

I looked at him. He was staring straight ahead, on guard again lest he become too emotionally involved.

Finally, he spoke, and in a very gentle, quiet tone, said, "Shantila, you please be careful on your journey. If someone offers you tea on the road, you must never take it. I had a friend who took chai from someone and they put something, some drug in it, and he became very dizzy, then he fell asleep and they stole all his things, his prayer beads, his money, everything. I mean it. You must be careful. Many thieves are there on the road and they carry drugs with them. Then they offer chai and steal money. Do not take anything to drink on the road." He looked at me then and his eyes were filled with love. For a moment, it felt as if we were intertwined, not our bodies as in an embrace but on a more subtle level of our being we became one, and then unraveled again, leaving us in freedom, but in a greater wholeness than before.

"I won't take anything from anyone on the road," I said. It was nearly eight-fifteen, over an hour later than the time the bus was supposed to have arrived. My legs ached from standing up for so long and my body felt limp, like a rag, which had been recently wrung out. Tashi squatted on his heels in the characteristic Indian way and I meekly tried to follow his example. At first, I could not get my ankles in the right position and it felt very uncomfortable. However, after I adjusted the width of my knees to take the strain off my ankles, I was fine. As we sat squatting together side by side on the pavement, time rolled backwards like the rewinding of a film on a reel, and I saw Tashi and me together in India as husband and wife in a past life. We lived on a farm high up in the Himalayas and we were sitting together, resting in the exact same position after a long day of working in the fields. We were very devoted to each other and lived a simple life with only the bare necessities, but we were happy.

"Shantila, your brother will send addresses of Buddhist monasteries in America? Do you think he will send reply letter to you?"

"Yes, Tashi, my brother is very good. He will send it. I will write to him again as soon as I get to Manali. I will ask him to send it to me there. Then I'll let you know."

I felt as if we were still married and yet "my husband" Tashi was a monk in this lifetime and my allotted duty was to help him find a Buddhist monastery to go to in America. I wanted the sweetness of our union in the past to be repeated again in this lifetime. I wished with all my heart that he would come with me to Manali. I did not want to be separated from him – not now, not ever.

Tashi looked up at the sky. "You do not see many stars here," he said. "In Ladakh, there, you can see so many stars."

At eight-thirty, the rattling of an engine in the distance caught our attention. Tashi stood up quickly.

"The bus! It's the bus!" he said enthusiastically. He waved his arms over his head, signaling the driver to stop. The bus roared to an unsteady halt. It was jammed full of people. The baggage on the roof of the bus tottered uneasily from one side to the other as it chortled and lurched forward on its old and rusted haunches. The door of the bus flew open and before I knew what was happening, Tashi had lifted up my case and tossed it in. The driver yelled, "Chelo, chelo, chelo!" at the top of his voice. I had no alternative but to leap onto the bus as it roared forward into the dark night.

I turned back to look over the person's head in the front seat, to look for his – Tashi's – face, but all I could see was an empty street. Soon many unknown streets were sweeping past me as I left New Delhi far behind.

Tashi had booked my ticket on the least-expensive bus available en route to Manali. Unfortunately, my seat was in the rear of the rickety bus, the bumpiest part. I sat next to a very old man who was curled up with his head practically in his lap sound asleep.

The bus ride out of Delhi into the state of Haryana and up and up and up into the hills was like a ride through purgatory. The seat rose and fell continuously like the seat of a rollercoaster, and the thin, tired tires skidded and screeched as we maneuvered our way through endless lanes of traffic. At one especially long halt, a group of men and boys carrying trays of fresh fruit and plastic bottles of mineral water appeared as if out of nowhere. They yelled out to us, holding their wares up to the open windows of our stiflingly hot bus. Arms waved, dangling oranges, apples and bananas, and high-pitched voices rang out, haggling about prices at ten o'clock at night. The journey to Manali was to take twenty-two hours. I was not sure whether or not this was our last chance for any food, and when I saw a thin, dark arm hold up a tray of oranges outside my window, my mouth began to water. I got hungrier and hungrier with every morsel of food they displayed. I knew that the bus could start up again at any moment and then the food would be but a memory, easy to recall but impossible to taste or to touch. I searched frantically for my purse in the dark, and dug out a ten-rupee note and bought three oranges. As soon as the bus pulled out, I wished I had also bought some bananas and another bottle of water.

We were immersed in a sea of darkness. Gazing across the aisle, I saw a young Indian couple resting against each other, her head on his shoulder. Her long, green embroidered shawl covered their bodies. They appeared to be sleeping. Time seemed to drag on. I could not sleep. I glanced at my watch; it was nearly midnight. I twisted and turned in the seat, trying to find a position that did not make my backache any worse. Each position had its own peculiar pitfalls. Finally, I sat cross-legged with my knees pointing upwards, leaned my head back against the soiled fabric seat cover and closed my eyes. I had just dozed off when I heard the bus grind to a stop. Half-dazed with fatigue, I peered out the window.

"Dinner! One-hour stop!" the bus driver shouted.

Everyone piled out and entered the outdoor makeshift cafe. I dragged myself out of the bus, bedraggled, disheveled and totally exhausted, taking the plastic bottle of mineral water with me. Finding my way to a metal water pump, I followed the example of the other Indian women, and sprinkled cold water on my face. Then filling my mouth with tepid water from the bottle, I swished it around for a while, and spat into the tall grass growing across the path from the pump.

A cup of tea; I'll order chai, I thought wearily. As soon as I had collapsed onto a red plastic chair, a young waiter began buzzing noisily around me.

"Chapatis? Paratha? Dinner? Thali?" he asked eagerly, staring curiously at my thick, curly hair and colorful Punjabi suit.

"Nay. Nay. Chai – and one chapati, please. That's all." All I really wanted was a comfortable bed to lie down on so I could go to sleep. I gazed around. Steaming-hot plates filled with rice, dhal and vegetables were served to many of the other passengers. Although I was very hungry, my mind told me it was too late to eat. How could I digest a meal so late at night? It was already long past midnight. Furthermore, I wasn't sure how clean the kitchen was. More than one hour later, we were herded back on the bus.

I closed my eyes, fell asleep and dreamed: *I saw my life like an endless series of windows in a house made of glass. And in each window was a face: the face of a man, a man who had vanished, or whom I had loved and lost in my life.*

Looking up at the open windows of the house, I saw them. Each of them was smiling and waving at me. In the bottom window was the face of my father, dark-complexioned and lean with his Africanesque features. He was tall, proud and graceful. He was the first man to disappear. I was only five years old when he receded into the distance, never to return. Then in the window above him was the face of August, a rabbi from Morocco, who had decided to devote his life to art. He was a prolific poet and painter, but most of all, a mystic who could spontaneously see into the inner life of things. He was the first one I met who saw beyond the veil. He had recognized something in me that I did not recognize in myself. He saw THAT SELF that is never born and never dies and in the rapture of that vision, he offered me his love.

It was summer; books and a table. I was twenty years old. The place: New York. I was sitting alone in a candlelit cafe, purposely avoiding the crowd, when he came and sat beside me. After gazing at me for some time, he asked the unanswerable question. "Where are you from? I mean, how did you come to be on this earth? You, who are so beautiful?"

I did not want to be disturbed. I shifted my eyes without answering. I felt embarrassed. I was wearing a turban on my head. I had no idea what he was seeing or what he meant by his words. Veils of illusion, veils of sadness, fear and uncertainty, shrouded my heart. I walked the streets of Manhattan, a stranger to everyone I met, even to myself. Yes, I was seeking answers, even then, to WHO I really was, WHAT I was, WHAT it truly meant to have been born as a human being, but when August arrived, I was without any answers.

His face was bright, his hair thick and dark, his eyes deep. His small, round lips held a tender smile and when he really laughed, his whole body shook. It was like a cascading river. One had to get wet in its fast-flowing current. Ah, the days and nights...like poetry, like a song... distilled red wine.

In the dream, he was laughing as he waved to me and the sheer white curtains on the window blew softly in the wind. There was his face that I had loved until he too disappeared, so long ago. Yet, had I not desired, in the quiet of my heart, that we not meet again until the veil had been lifted, until I had crossed the threshold beyond the world of illusion forever?

Then there was Andrew, quiet, gentle, conventional, and very British – a man who always needed to conform to the social norm. With a wistful smile, he waved to me, his right hand moving slowly above his head, palm open, moving from side to side as if to say, "I'm sorry." However, it had to end; after wavering like a dry reed in the wind for too many years to count, he had to finally let me go. I was glad to be free. Yes, Andrew, hello and goodbye, goodbye again. You loved me but there were too many shadows, too many veils of illusion that shrouded your love so that you saw my nationality, the contrasting color of my skin, my place on the social ladder before you touched me... Goodbye, Andrew. May you be happy always.

The next window was brighter and through it, the rays of the sun cast a golden glow. Framed by a halo of light, Ramesh stood, a jewel among men. He was a close disciple of a great spiritual teacher and a former Kathakali dancer. His broad, brown forehead gleamed and his large, dark eyes smiled as he stood, bare chested before me, his palms together as if in prayer. His wave was a bow. He nodded his head as if to express his acceptance of the will of God. "Thy will be done." His gesture spoke in silence and yet it was clearer than words. I smiled as his face vanished, called away by a will greater than his own. His marriage had been arranged by his parents before we met.

Goodbye, Ramesh, goodbye, my heart spoke in a whisper as a solitary tear trickled down from my right eye. "All is as it should be...all is right, well-ordered as it is and perfect as Thou art, my God." My wounded heart surrendered as the vision faded into the distance.

The glass shone brighter now like a prism of many colors lit from within by a rainbow of heavenly lights for the next window held a fair face, but even as I gazed at him, his face became soft and blurred and the sharp outline of his features was lost. This was a momentary dance, just a whirl around a blooming meadow at eventide and then the river rose and carried him away at high noon on a raft made of clay. He was pious but afraid to love, to let go of the tightly harnessed reins around his heart, afraid to risk falling into the vast unknown, to enter a world foreign to him from birth for his parents had hidden their feelings, and taught him to do the same, behind a veil of fear. Beneath the calm lake in his eyes, a fire burned in his heart, raging in sore distress, so much did he yearn for the freedom to express his deepest needs. But by then it was too late, too late for us. He waved and turned away quickly, to hide his shame.

And as each face faded, my body became lighter for the weight of those memories was lifted, one by one, as the images receded. Then the dream rippled; it breathed a last, long sigh and like a transparent wave of energy, melted into the ocean of air all around it. Then it too was gone. And I sailed like a lone eagle through the spacious temple of the sky – free, free, free.

When I awoke and looked out the window of the bus, it was as if the gates of heaven had been flung open. There, in all their unequaled grandeur, rose the towering mountains of the

Himalayas. Higher, higher and higher like mighty waves, they rose, hailing the glory of the indestructible power of life. In the heaving lap of the mountains, lush green valleys rolled, valleys with coursing rivers running in undulating curves round smooth, gray stones like a woman in the throes of love in the arms of a strong, silent lover. The lavender hues of sunrise blended in soft tones with the misty gray-brown mountains. The deep green of the soaring deodar trees heightened the beauty of the rushing silver streams and the youthful verdant shade of the leaves on the blossoming apple trees. It was a painting the like of which I had never seen. The last vestiges of the dream faded into nothingness as I sat upright in my seat, peering as if spellbound out of the window.

The bus crawled slowly upward along the narrow labyrinthine road. Sometimes it skirted the edges of precipices of deep gorges, sometimes it bent and swayed along roads swimming in mud, sometimes it ground its wheels into fallen rock and debris, the remnants of landslides, and monsoon storms. Yet it was as if the very air was glittering with joy. The trees, mountains, and valleys sang a song exulting in the sheer beauty of creation: the far-flung bursting melody ran unhindered issuing forth from every cascading mountain stream, and gushing from between the crevices of rocks. Beneath the tidal waves of song, an ageless silence stirred...

Upon steeply rising cliffs, the trees grew wild and free, their leaves glistening as the sun spread its golden radiance in the sky. And along the dirt road, wooden shacks perched haphazardly, their corrugated iron roofs pitched like a crooked cap on houses lined with clay. There were warm, brown earth houses painted a light shade of pink, yellow, or even bright blue to match the color of the sky at noon. Outside the houses, somnolent cows sat nibbling grass or grazed in the dipping valley drinking morning dew from sparkling fields awash with light, contented cows of dark brown or a pale golden hue, with cream-colored calves beside them. There were also square-shaped dwellings made of cement, often crumbling at the seams. Sometimes we saw houses made of firm, gray stone with dark wooden porches carved in elaborate designs. Sometimes the porches had carved arches inlaid with intricate patterns and sharply pitched roofs so that the raindrops could slide easily to the earth during the monsoon season. Most of the inhabitants were still indoors as the bus wormed its way forward, up, up, up, into the hills and beyond into the towering heights of the Himalayas.

Like a row of colorful caterpillars, the line of buses rolled along, a chain of clanking metal on rubber tires, half a kilometer long. We passed many lorries, painted orange with signs on the front, which read: Haryana, Punjab, Himachal Pradesh Goods Carrier. Each lorry had a painted picture of a Vedic god or goddess above the front window. Most carried the picture of Durga, the deliverer, borne aloft on her regal lion. It was She who was believed to be capable of subduing the enemies of her devotees; She, fierce yet benevolent, could overcome difficulties, and was a powerful protector on a road studded with danger at every turn. On these steep mountain paths from which the Angel of Death could step forth at any moment and snatch one away, one had to propitiate a mighty deity. In addition, many "goods carriers" bore the image of another Vedic deity, Lord Shiva, with snakes curled around his blue-colored throat. Lord Shiva signified the almighty power of eternal silence, immovable like the mountain kingdom. He was reputed to have His immortal abode on Mount Kailash in the hidden regions of the Himalayas. Lord Shiva symbolized the supreme yogi, who has attained total mastery over the senses and is unshakably established in the state of eternal peace and freedom beyond the ever-changing field of life, a mighty god. These were the mountain deities, which raised their invisible banner of protection as the lorries steered clear of oncoming vehicles, falling rocks and deep jagged ruts in the road.

As morning unfurled its multi-colored wings, gaily-attired

men, women and children walking barefoot along the path accentuated the brightness of the hills. Most of the women wore bandannas tied around their heads, and a large checked woolen cloth tied at their shoulders and worn like a dress. The men wore cheerful square hats, and gray woolen jackets with brown or black trousers. The girls had long braids dangling behind their ears and smooth brown skin. Their eyes were large and their smiles open and innocent. They may have had but little on the material level, but their faces glowed with an inner spring of happiness.

Quaint white temples growing out of the rocky steppes, perched on cliffs or blossoming on the shores of fast-flowing rivers, knelt beneath the sky with bowed heads and the wings of their souls outspread. Other temples were painted in bright colors, beckoning without words, with large brass bells at the entrance, and in the inner sanctum, an elaborately decorated image of the deity, calling, calling, calling, in silence, to the devotee.

My heart leaped forward whenever I saw a temple, as if it could confer a blessing, a taste of the otherworldly domain. I longed to catch a glimpse of the god hidden deep within it. It would have made the taste that much sweeter. But, from the window of the bus, it was rarely possible. Therefore, I feasted my eyes on the sunlight scattered over the landscape, the massive grandeur of the mountains and the silver streams. Though I felt full, I never tired of drinking in their beauty. I wondered what treasure might be hidden among these ancient mountains, and whether I was destined to find it:

This journey, high up into the Himalayas, would it bear the fruit of my life? Would I drink of the nectar of immortality in this divine abode? Would the deep silence of the Himalayas call awake the deity hidden deep within the cave of my own heart and would the flaming light of the sun ignite the pyre at the altar within the inner shrine? Would the pure truths that were etched in the rock cut gorges along the way and which scintillated through the lacy fibers of the firs unfold its golden petals in me, never to be shrouded by darkness again? How many unnamed saints and sages had climbed the steep and sloping cliffs of these mountains in search, not of gold, but in search of their own inner wealth? How many ascetics had performed arduous penances here as an offering to Thee? Now I had come, far-flung from the shores of New York and the greening hills of England, to lay my thirsting heart at Thy feet. Would I return to England or even America alone, empty-handed, or would I carry the transparent dignity of the Infinite, fully awakened, within me?

These questions rose and sank as the bus plied its way through the Parvati Valley, up to Mandi and through Kullu, on the last stretch of the journey to Manali.

And in the most silent, secret recesses of the heart, in a faint almost inaudible whisper, one more question surfaced: *Would I meet someone to share the newborn fullness of my life? Had I already met him?* And for a moment, Tashi's face floated on the rippling lake of my mind, and then disappeared into the flowing waves.

Chapter Seven

As the bus pulled into Manali late that afternoon, the town gave the impression of a happy place, bustling with energy and vitality. On either side of the busy thoroughfare, was the forest. Like ancient gatekeepers, the deodars, tall Himalayan cedar trees, stood guarding the town.

I saw a group of dark-skinned, unshaven, rough-looking men with heavy brown ropes slung over their shoulders. They stared greedily at us as we climbed out of the bus.

"Coolie! Coolie!" someone behind me shouted, gesturing to one of the men.

"Coolie, madam?" one of the younger men asked, looking at me and reaching for my suitcase. His skin was baked brown from the sun and the stubble on his chin looked coarse. He had a thin mustache and short hair, which was mostly covered by a long, brown piece of torn cloth, tied in a turban around his forehead.

I didn't know what to do. Would he run off with my case or could I trust him to carry it up the steep hills without damaging its contents?

"Yes, OK," I said rather warily, handing him the heavy case and watching as he deftly lifted it, and strapped it securely to his back with the thick brown ropes. He bent his neck forward to adjust the thirty-kilogram weight of the case. "Buddhist Temple," I said. I knew it was close to Mr. Negi's house where I had been invited to stay temporarily. He nodded, and then, with back bent almost double, headed up the forest path.

Walking up the mountain road in my open-toe sandals was virtually impossible. The dirt path was steep and covered in rocks. I kept slipping and stubbing my toes and was horrified at the thought of breaking my sandals, the only shoes I had brought. If they broke, I would have to walk the rest of the way in my bare feet. We had been walking for almost half an hour. It seemed as if we would never arrive. The coolie took such long strides that I found it difficult to keep up with him. Soon I was panting for air. Feeling hungry and exhausted after the lengthy journey, I paused for a while to catch my breath.

When I looked up, the coolie was gone; he was completely out of sight. Alarmed, and feeling weak with fatigue, I simply gave up and collapsed on a grassy patch of earth by the side of the road. My breath was labored, my forehead dripping wet, my Punjabi suit sticking to my skin like wet newspaper.

Oh what should I do? What should I do, I thought in desperation as I held my hand to my aching head. I was so tired I started weeping. Lowering my head onto my knapsack, I covered my face with my hands letting the tears gush forth unhindered.

A huge wave of depression threatened to engulf me when suddenly I heard a rustling of leaves close by and the sound of footsteps. Lifting my head, I saw the rustic face of the coolie peering at me from between the leaves of the trees. His features showed surprise and genuine concern. He untied the rope at his waist and stooping on his knees, placed the case on the ground. Then he sat down a few feet away from me.

"Aaraam, Aaraam," he said in Hindi, indicating for me to take rest. His face was dripping with perspiration, but his eyes contained an unmistakable light of kindness. In that moment, any fear or suspicion I had felt in the beginning was laid to rest. We sat together on the ground on the jungle path, both of us breathing heavily, then softer and softer until the rapid throbbing of our hearts returned to normal. I slowly stood up and he followed suit, lifting the case onto his stained brown jacket and bending low to shoulder the heavy burden.

He walked more slowly this time; he was obviously listening to make sure I was keeping pace with him. We traversed several zigzagging paths of hard gray rocks, broken and strewn like debris under our feet. Then he opened a rusting metal gate and we found ourselves in an orchard of flowering apple trees. Pink, white and rose-colored blossoms dangled weightlessly in the cool spring wind. Under the trees, the green grass was spread like a thick carpet. We made our way, up, up, up, about a quarter of a mile more, on a path made of earth. He leaned forward as he climbed, his strong legs moving with determined strides. Finally he stopped in front of a white building with a large window on the right side and three flat steps leading up to a glass-enclosed porch.

A door inside opened and a lama came out wearing a dark maroon dhoti and a beige woolen vest. It was Kunchen Lama, the monk I had met in the Buddhist Center in New Delhi!

"Namaste," he said, smiling when he saw me. "They told me in Delhi you were coming. Come in."

I went to pay the coolie and to thank him, but when I held out the ten-rupee note, he just frowned and turned away, refusing to even take it. Bewildered, I asked Kunchen what I should do. He said that what I had offered him was not enough and that was why he refused to take it. He advised me to pay him double the price. Gingerly, I searched for another ten rupees. When I found it, I went to the coolie and offered it to him, but he still refused it. He turned away with an angry look that made his features look darker, wilder, more severe. He untied the long brown turban from round his forehead and wiped his face and neck with it.

"What does he want?" I asked the lama who stood beside me, quietly watching.

"More money. He wants more rupees. Give him five more," he said simply; then he walked slowly inside.

I stood face to face with the coolie. He looked into my eyes with a piercing expression. I looked away, and then with my back turned to him, I unzipped my purse and took out a few more rupees in change. There were no five rupee notes; I only had two more ten-rupee notes. Turning back to face him, I held out the last payment I intended to give him: twenty-three rupees.

He counted it and stood still, glaring at me. Then he turned and walked away, slinging the thick brown rope carelessly over his left shoulder. The image of the anger and disappointment on the coolie's face lingered in my mind. *After all*, I thought, *what are a few extra rupees to me, but to him, it might be the difference between having a meal and not having one, having a roof over his head or sleeping out in the open, feeding his family or not...*

I walked inside the temple and gazed around at the small room. The walls were all wood-paneled, as was the ceiling. In the center was a large sculpture of a golden bell. Kunchen came out of the kitchen with a tray of tea and biscuits in his hands.

"Sit down; you are tired, yes?" He examined my face with gentle eyes, indicating for me to sit on a maroon cushion on the polished wood floor. Directly in front of us were five golden statues of the Buddha on lotus-shaped pedestals.

"So you have come to Manali. How long you will stay Manali?" the lama asked, pouring the tea and offering me the plate of biscuits.

"I don't know," I answered. "I must find a place to stay. Mr. Negi said he would help me find a place to stay."

"I will ask to Mr. Negi. I go call him." The lama got up and went out, pulling the door closed behind him.

An elderly Ladakhi was cleaning; then he sat down, fingering a rosary of shiny black prayer beads and muttering prayers from the yellowing pages of his Tibetan prayer book. He did not speak a word of English.

There was a creaking sound, followed by the patter of bare feet on the floor.

"Welcome to Manali!" Mr. Negi said, holding out his arms as he came into the room. "You are fine?" he asked, sitting cross-legged on the floor opposite me.

"Yes, the bus took much longer than I expected, but we finally made it. It was quite a walk to get up the mountain."

"You look tired," Mr. Negi said.

"Yes, I feel very tired."

"Good. Rest awhile. Everyone feels that way when they first come to the Himalayas. It takes a few days to get used to the altitude," he said.

"Oh, really? Now I realize why I am feeling like this. The walk was very difficult in my sandals..."

"You must get walking shoes. Did you bring any shoes? Then you can buy them in the market. No one uses chappals here. Take more tea. Relax – no hurry, we have time. I will go to tell my wife you are here." He got up with an effort, rubbing his knees with his hands, and left the room.

I sat alone. I looked at a statue of a Japanese holy man in the act of beating a drum. In front of him was a mound of biscuits, and to the side were two tall white candles. On the right side was the large drum used during the chanting of the prayers. I asked myself whether he would let me stay in his house, otherwise where was I going to live? How would I fare in this Himalayan abode with so little money left? I hoped that he would spontaneously offer me a suitable place. I gazed at the statues of the Buddha and my heart called out to Tashi far away in New Delhi. I wished that he, instead of Kunchen Lama had been assigned to the temple in Manali. Then I remembered Tashi's desire to go to America and I knew I had to help him accomplish his aim rather than focusing on mine.

Half an hour passed. It was dark outside. Then I heard the sound of voices at the door. Mr. Negi entered the room first, followed by his wife and Kunchen Lama. She appeared Chinese with her broad, flat cheeks and narrow, slanted eyes.

"Namaste," she said, smiling when she saw me. However, she did not sit down; she just stood next to Mr. Negi, staring at me curiously. Although the tone of her voice was warm, her body movements betrayed misgivings and distrust. I wondered what they had been discussing for such a long time.

Mr. Negi said, "We can offer you a room in an old lady's house, but it is tourist season, so she is asking two hundred rupees per night or we can help you find a room nearby in a few days. Manali is tourist place, especially these months, April, May, June. The season is short. In winter, it is cold and there is so much snow that no one wants to come. Life is very difficult here in the winter. However, during these three months, many tourists are coming, so prices go higher. Is it alright?"

I swallowed the lump rising in my throat. *Two hundred rupees a night! I will only have enough money for twenty nights at that price!* I thought to myself, but I only said, "I think I will look for a less-expensive place. It is too much. I cannot afford to stay there, but for tonight, I don't know..." My voice broke. Just then, a servant came in and told Mr. Negi that he had a telephone call. Mr. Negi and his wife left.

I looked helplessly at Kunchen and then said in a barely audible voice, "Would it be alright for me to stay here?"

"We are very busy... There are plans to build a large hall and then a stupa – much work. I'm sorry – here not possible – very busy."

Tears started trickling down my cheeks. Kunchen Lama noticed immediately. In a quiet voice, he said, "The temple has a room for two, three days. It's alright for you stay here." He picked up my suitcase, hoisted it onto his shoulder and carried it upstairs. I followed him up the polished wooden steps.

I wish I could live here! I thought as he opened the door to a medium-sized room with two very large windows. I could see the view of the mountains rising up to touch the soft, gray light of the evening sky and the dark green landscape below with its twinkling lamps in the village homes. On the wood-paneled walls hung colorful embroidered tapestries of Buddhas and bodhisattvas (highly evolved beings who are devoted to reaching enlightenment in order to free all living beings from the cycle of birth and death).

"Thank you very much, Lama-ji," I said, as I stood in the middle of the room in front of a polished wooden table with an ornate glass top.

"Take rest now," he answered, closing the door quietly behind him.

I sat down on one of the mats covered with maroon- and gold-colored felt fabric, which served as a decoration as well as a way of keeping the mattresses free of dust. The room felt cozy and warm as it was situated above the sitting room which had a wood-fired cast-iron stove burning in it.

I gazed out the window to the vast panorama of nature spread out on the horizon. *Here,* I reflected, *man has planted his towns and villages. Like many-petaled flowers, man's ideas have taken root assuming different shapes, colors, textures and forms. He has created his own landscape and embedded it within the greater wholeness of nature's perfect forms. However, in the manmade world, the song that arises from his villages and his towns is not always pleasing to the ear and heart, for many people are neither healthy nor happy nor at peace. But perhaps here, in this Himalayan abode, it will be different, more perfect, more peaceful, more joyous for to drink in beauty with every glance as those living here can do is to be healed and made whole.*

In the distance, the sound of drums broke my reverie. This sound was unlike the drum in the temple; it was a loud, gay, frivolous sound, which seemed to carry the laughter of many happy people as the wind carries the honeyed fragrance of wildflowers in the spring. The dancing rhythm was interspersed with the honking of horns and the faint whir of traffic far below. Overhead, the cawing of crows mingled with the songs of many unknown birds as the silken veil of evening floated down covering the sky with its soft gray wings.

Where will I go? What does the future hold? I must find a place... I have only four thousand rupees... I am on my own. What am I doing here? I love India, but WHY am I in Manali? These thoughts whirled round and round in my head like circling stars in the dark sky. I felt the burden of the unknown way that lay ahead bearing down upon me. The sight of the towering mountains that had just a moment ago painted a vision of joyous expectation now appeared so vast that I felt small, lost and insignificant in comparison. *Where am I to begin? It is dark – I must meditate*, I resolved finally. Sitting in lotus position, I leaned against a cushion and closed my eyes.

The outside world melted into a flowing sea of thoughts, images, dreams, desires and prayers. This inner sea moved, rippling, as it ran over stones and circling paths filled with mud, and along the shores of deserted houses, half-built houses, and tall palatial marble arches, balustrades decked with flags flying, thoughts masquerading in the circus of time, conjuring up worlds and watching them dissolve. As the sea flowed on, out toward the infinite expanse of the unbounded ocean, the depth of silence inundated the titillating world of sound, flooding the shores of the mind with a gentle light that stilled the yearning of the heart. Time was no more; the body a mere sheath, vaporous, transparent, no longer able to hinder or obstruct, without dimension. Silence merged with silence. Renewed inwardly by the taste of this reality, I slept soundly until dawn.

The next few days I just rested, meditated, ate and breathed-in the surroundings. Most of the day was spent alone as Kunchen Lama was very busy with his responsibilities and Mr. Negi was tending his large apple orchard as well as organizing the construction of a hotel in town.

On the third day, I ventured down the steep hill to go to town to buy a pair of shoes. I came upon blossoming apple orchards on carpets of lush green grass surrounding large and neat dwellings. But as I climbed further down the mountain, the "path" consisted of broken rocks and muddy lanes meandering through half-finished wood, brick and concrete houses. Some of the houses had only the foundation, others just the first floor, and still others everything but the roof. Around the dwellings lay piles of debris, plastic bags, scraps of food and other variegated types of garbage tossed in a heap beside the stream.

The trek down the mountainside was slow and arduous. A group of children ran behind me shouting, "Namaste! Namaste!" I greeted them and continued on my way. The mountain stream rushed down, cascading over rocks and splashing the earthen path in joyous abandon. Beside the stream, women squatted down, rubbing clothes on smooth, flat stones with a piece of wood. They pressed the soap into the fabric, rubbing it in deeper with the piece of wood. Then they beat the fabric with the wood. Soon the stone was hidden by frothy foam as the garments were alternately rubbed, pressed, beaten and squeezed clean. One woman looked up at me as I passed. She smiled and I smiled back at her.

On the way, I passed a row of wooden shacks selling knitted socks, sweaters and vests. The shopkeepers looked more Asian than Indian; I realized they were probably Tibetan refugees. Their simple, humble shops curved down the road leading to the river.

The Beas River swelled up, swirling over the round, white rocks jutting out of the water and lining its banks. On the dirt road on either side of the river, brown-skinned women with kerchiefs around their heads and a wooden hammer in their hand squatted beside large piles of rocks. I watched them lift the hammer high into the air and bring it down hard on the chunks of rock, breaking them into smaller and smaller pieces under the hot sun. Their faces were lined and their bodies thin. Many of them wore long, straight dresses tied at the back with a blouse underneath. Later I learned that this was the traditional Tibetan dress.

There was a traffic jam on the bridge. Three lorries, painted orange, were lined up behind each other, waiting to cross. I was standing at the side of the dirt road when I heard a low voice behind me.

"Baksheesh."

I turned and saw an aged man in dirty, torn clothes limping on his only leg, a wooden crutch under his arm. His body was as lean as the stick he held to keep from falling. He held out a wretchedly thin hand and gazed into my eyes.

"Rupee, madam."

I put my fingers in my purse, took out a few rupees, and dropped them into his open palm. Then, with a quiver, I turned back to the river. As I watched the waters cascading over the white rocks, I remembered Kalsang's words: *When you give a beggar food to eat, this is prayer. When someone who has no cloth comes to you and you give him your cloth, this is prayer.*

As I entered the town of Manali, I saw that most of the shops were crowded together in a flamboyant array along the main street; the rest were tucked into narrow alleyways. Every space was filled with antiques from Nepal and Tibet, Indian clothing, embroidered shawls, household items, sweets, restaurants, and travel agencies. Many open shop fronts displayed their wares so abundantly outside that one could buy all the things one needed without even stepping foot inside. Beside these shops, less-prosperous vendors set up impromptu stalls selling papadums, candy floss, peanuts and incense. The aroma of Indian sweets mingled with the hot, spicy fragrance of curry, peppers and cumin as dark-skinned boys labored over large, black iron woks, stirring, tossing and patting the sizzling delicacies.

At the market, I sampled some sweets, popped into several shoe shops and tried on bulky walking shoes with thick wavy soles. Many shopkeepers spoke to me in Hindi, thinking I was Indian. I finally found a pair of waterproof shoes with thick rubber soles – perfect for the mountains. They were not very expensive, so I bought them. Then, I headed up the main street.

As I wormed my way through the crowd, I saw a tall woman who looked like a Westerner. She was almost stately with thick dark shoulder-length hair. She was big boned, heavy but not fat. I went over to talk to her. She had a pretty face that reminded me of the silent-movie actresses of the twenties and thirties.

"Are you from Europe?" I asked her.

"Yes – Germany," she said. She had a square jaw and dark eyes. "What's your name?" she asked.

"Shantila. What's yours?"

"Margrit."

"I just arrived. I'm living at the Buddhist temple up on the mountainside for a few days. But I need to find another place to stay. Do you know of a place that isn't too expensive?"

"I may know a place. I will ask my friends. Why don't you come and meet them? I am having a lunch party on Thursday. Would you like to come?" Margrit asked with a smile.

"Yes, that sounds nice," I replied.

Margrit indicated that she lived on the opposite side of the valley, across the bridge over the Beas River, on the mountainside. She explained to me how to find it.

I continued my perambulation of the shops. I stopped in front of a Kashmir Emporium with beautiful, hand-embroidered woolen shawls in the window. Green, gold and pink flowers were embroidered on a pale cream-colored background. I could not resist entering. A tall, rather handsome man greeted me with a smile.

"Can I help you? You want to see shawl, sweater, Punjabi suit, jacket. What you like? I have all," he said, pulling out a dark brown pashmina shawl. "Feel. This shawl, finest quality, very soft, warm." He held it out for me to touch. It was the softest wool I had ever felt. "It is made from goat's hair – very fine. Kashmir is famous for these shawls," he said with undisguised pride.

"How much is it?" I asked.

"Two thousand rupees," he answered. "Very good price. This will last forever – hand wash, cold water."

"Too costly," I said quietly, "but it is very beautiful. Maybe later, another time. How much is the cream-colored one in the window?"

"Which? Show me."

I pointed to the shawl I liked.

"Six hundred rupees."

I thought, *I should go. I don't have the money for this.* However, all I said was, "Thank you very much. I will think about it."

"Why you have to think? Here, let me show it to you. Wait. I will get it." He went to the window and got the shawl and laid it on the counter, and started unfolding it.

I felt embarrassed. *I shouldn't have come in,* I thought sheepishly. I was wondering how I could gracefully disengage myself. I reached out and touched the embroidered flowers on it, then without thinking, I picked it up and draped it over my shoulders.

"Is there a mirror?" I glanced around the shop and spied a long mirror wedged between a stack of Punjabi suits and more shawls. I went up to it and smiled into it. The shawl was the perfect color. I had always wanted one like it. Reluctantly, I took it off and replaced it on the glass counter. "Very beautiful," I said, turning to go out.

"Why don't you take it? Only six hundred rupees! In Delhi, these shawls sell for one thousand rupees! How much you want to pay? Tell me!" he shouted, following me to the door.

"I will think about it," I said, stopping at the door. "I don't have so much money."

"Thinking! You're thinking too much! Thinking is very bad! Very bad. No thinking. If you want it, take it. Just feel. Otherwise blood pressure goes up and down. Thinking too much is no good for health. I will give it to you for a good price on my honor because I like you. What is money? Sometimes I have money, sometimes you have money. It comes, it goes. When I have money, then I give you, and then you give me some other time. Do Not Think. It is very bad." He walked to the back of the shop, shaking his head. When he returned, he said, "Would you like a cup of tea? You do not have to buy anything. You like chai?"

I fidgeted for a few minutes, then realized that I was feeling thirsty, so I said, "Yes." I followed him to a seat in the back of the shop. We sat side by side on a large metal trunk covered with a woolen blanket.

"Chai, do chai," he said to a boy who was busy folding women's suits at the counter. The boy went out and a few minutes later, he came back with two glasses of tea.

"You are from which country?" the shopkeeper asked me as we sat sipping the steaming-hot liquid from our glasses.

"I live in England," I answered, starting to relax and actually enjoy the experience.

"England – I have relatives there – in London. Good country. How long you will stay here?"

"A few months. I'm looking for a place to stay that isn't too expensive."

"Hotel? Guest house? Why you didn't say so? I can tell you. There is a place near Hadimba Temple way, not costly. Many foreigners are staying there. It is called Chandralal guest house. You want telephone number? I find for you." He stood up, walked toward the front of the shop, and pulled a brown book out from below the counter. He leafed quickly through it and scribbled something down on a loose scrap of paper.

"Here is the telephone number. You go there. Say Amar sent you." He handed me the paper, smiling. "You will come back, after?" he asked.

"Thank you very much," I said, taking the paper. "I will see. It was nice to meet you." I stood up and walked to the door. "Namaste," I said, waving to him as I left.

Once outside, I breathed a sigh of relief. *Nice man*, I thought, *but I'm glad I managed to escape.* Then I saw Tashi's face and immediately my heart filled with happiness. *If only he was here! If only we could be together!*

Quickly, I found a shop where there was a phone. I dialed the number and a man answered.

"Rooms? You need a room? Yes, we have. Please come. We are a few meters from the Hadimba Temple. Go straight – left side."

He hung up.

I decided to see what it was like. It was on the same side of the mountain as Margrit's house. I hopped into a rickshaw.

The rickshaw wound its way slowly through the bustling main street crammed with people. Finally, we reached the open road near the forest. The buzzing sound of the market became but a faint murmur and the pure, peaceful air of the mountains was tangible. Then the climb began: the road zigzagged upwards, past small hotels with big white billboards, past larger hotels built haphazardly on jagged cliffs with a breathtaking view of the valley, higher and higher up on the hard, dirt road, over pebbles and debris, through deep ruts and over bulging mounds of earth. On either side of the road stood massive deodar trees.

After a while, we reached a path lined with small restaurants on one side. On the other side, Tibetan-looking street vendors were selling their wares: Tibetan jackets, jewelry, gloves and belts. The spicy aroma of sizzling potato pancakes amid the loud laughter of children running across the road greeted us as we entered the area called Dhungri.

"Hadimba Temple – there." The rickshaw driver pointed to the forest. "Guest house, there." He pointed to the road opposite the gate leading into the forest. The guest house was five- or ten-minutes' walk from there. After the bustling marketplace in the center of town, it was a relief to be high up, near the thick forest.

I met the owner of the guest house outside. He was sitting on the veranda drinking a Coca-Cola.

"You called, madam?"

"Yes," I replied.

"Single? Double room? Someone is with you?"

"No, I am alone."

There was a row of doors leading off the wooden veranda of the guest house. The second floor of the house was still being constructed. He selected one key from the bunch of jingling keys attached to his leather belt. Then he thrust it into the rusty lock dangling from the bolt across the door. The door whined as it opened.

A few dirty dark green blankets were thrown across a bare mattress. The brown carpet was ragged at the edges. The bathroom was covered with water. My face fell.

"Hot water in bathroom," the owner said. "We give you good price." He smiled imploringly.

There was a shower in the bathroom, and even though the drains were blocked, the luxury of hot water was enough to make me decide to take it.

I moved in the next day. I tidied up the room as well as I could, but nearly froze the first night because, even though it was spring, the nights were still icy cold in the Himalayas. I did not dare to cover myself with the blankets; they were so dirty. However, I asked for cleaner blankets, and after about a week, I started to adjust to the place.

I wanted Tashi to know where I was. He had asked me to write to him, but letters to Delhi took a week or more. I phoned the Buddhist Center. Tashi was out. I left a message with the name and telephone number of the Chandralal guest house and asked that it be given specifically to Tashi.

Chapter Eight

Dear Tashi,

The mornings here have wings. I see them open wide at dawn, flying over the high peaks of the mountains, soaring, soaring, soaring and then melting into a sea of light. The sun pours its golden liquid into the vessel of the valley and the hills, bursting with life, drink deeply. The apple trees are in blossom. They sprinkle the green meadows with pink silken petals. I gather them up in my palms and offer them to you.

How are you? I wish you were here!

I have moved again. I could not stay in the temple more than a few days because Kunchen Lama was very busy. I decided to try to find a room in a guest house and with luck, I did.

It is on the other side of the mountain near a five-hundred-year-old temple in the forest called the Hadimba Temple. I like it better on this side as all the houses face the rising sun. The view from my room is magnificent. The mist rises over the valley and the light of the sun illumines the apple trees with their pale pink blossoms. Nearby, a small family temple sits perched on a high ledge of a house painted blue and white. The grandfather who lives with his son's family goes there in the early hours of the morning and again at noon to pray. They built the temple especially for him.

I met a German woman in the market who has lived here for ten years. We have become friends. There is a group of foreigners who meet regularly on this side of the mountain: an Iranian family, several Germans and an English woman who has been in Manali for twenty years. They invited me to have lunch with them.

I have written another letter to my brother. I will send the information to you as soon as I receive it. I hope you are well. I look forward to hearing from you soon.

Your friend, Shantila

It was the day of the lunch party. I decided to buy sweets for the party in the market. I also had to post the letter to Tashi.

I walked down the forest path. It was a cool morning and the sun shone through the branches of the trees. It took nearly half an hour to reach the town center. I asked a shopkeeper the directions to the post office. As I headed up the street, I saw a donkey standing in the middle of the road and a very thin baby donkey wobbled out from an alleyway and hid behind it. Nearby, a group of men sat in a room, with the door ajar, playing cards.

I entered the post office. It was a large dimly lit space with a long wooden counter and a glass pane separating the customers from the employees. Luckily, it was not crowded.

"Namaste," I said softly to the woman behind the counter, hoping she had heard me.

The woman looked momentarily annoyed. She continued vigorously stamping the pile of letters on the table, and pretended not to take any notice of me. I waited until she had finished.

"Can I buy some stamps here?" I asked.

"Which country?" she asked in a very serious tone of voice.

"New Delhi," I answered, with a smile.

She smiled slightly and looked away.

"What's your name?" I asked her.

She hesitated, wondering if she wanted to tell me, then said, "Swarma."

"Beautiful name – Swarma," I said.

She gave me the stamps and I walked around the corner to the sweetshop. As I was about to enter, I saw an old woman sitting on the sidewalk, with a bowl in front of her. She held up a hand without any fingers and looked sadly into my eyes. I shuddered involuntarily, then bent down and placed a few rupees in the palm of her hand.

In front of the sweetshop was a glass case filled with sweets. A huge cast-iron wok was used for deep frying kachoris. I had sampled these savory pastries filled with vegetables, nuts and raisins while on a previous trip to India. Now, I wanted to buy something for Margrit's lunch party. I lingered at the glass case for a long time. Some of the sweets were decorated with silver, some were rose-colored, some were filled with nuts or raisins. I mentally tasted all the sweets before deciding which ones to buy. Would it be the wide milk-based squares of almond or coconut burfi or balls of fresh cheese soaked in rose syrup, or laddus, the sweet round balls made of chickpea flour and pistachio nuts?

The boy behind the counter looked amused. He gave me a sample of one or two different sweets to taste. I finally bought half a kilo of almond burfi. On my way home, I paused and poked my head into a fabric shop to ask the price of a beautiful saffron-colored print.

"Eighty rupees a meter," came the reply.

"Is it silk?"

"No, polyester. No ironing needed."

"No, thank you." I was glad that it was polyester. I wouldn't have bought it even if I had the money. I continued on my way. The Tibetan shops were small and cheerful. Hanging on some of the doors were silk scarves and tie-dyed cotton shirts and trousers in bright colors. The shops catered to the tourist trade. Some of the shops also had the traditional Tibetan dress for women: long wrap-around dresses called chuppas. I passed the tourist office next. In front sat thin ragged-looking women from Bengal who made their children beg. One woman was breast-feeding her baby. She looked up as I passed and held out her open palm. I continued walking.

As I approached the foot of the mountain, the shops became smaller and more tightly crammed together. There were tiny dark restaurants with aluminum pots lined up outside on a wooden board with other tiny shops huddled beside it selling soap, cooking oil, biscuits and other household items. The unpaved road made of broken stones had deep ruts running through the gravel.

The previous evening, I had received a message from Tashi. Kunchen Lama called the Chandralal guest house to tell me that Tashi had called to make sure I was all right and had found a comfortable place to live. I felt more secure in the relationship, and awoke in the morning with my heart filled with love for him.

I was feeling light-hearted and happy as I walked toward Margrit's house for the lunch party. I had decided to wear my favorite saffron-colored Punjabi suit with a peach dupatta, a long graceful scarf, around my shoulders. I was the first to arrive. It was my habit to be on time – unlike the usual custom in India.

"Welcome! Come in, come in, Shantila! Oh, you brought something – so much! What! Sweets! Everyone will like this. I never have any time to go to the sweetshop. I'm too busy with the new baby." Margrit had a matronly air about her. Her skin-tight black leggings and long purple T-shirt made her appear younger than she was. Her house was comfortable by Manali standards. The walls were bright yellow. She told me she had painted them herself. Her cheerful yellow curtains turned brighter as the sun's rays lit up the room. A wooden bookcase contained many books. A bronze statue of the Buddha sat in the center of the bookcase with postcards of bodhisattvas on one side, and pictures of the Virgin Mary on the other. I glanced at a photograph of two children, both of whom looked Chinese.

"My children," Margrit said. "Norbu is almost five; he is still at school... And this is Aden," she said, swooping down and lifting the chubby infant from his wooden crib. He kicked his fat, round legs to free them from the blanket.

"Would you like to hold him?" She carefully placed him in my arms.

I struggled for a minute or two, unfamiliar with the wriggling, squirming of a two-month-old baby. Finally, I managed to rest his head upon my shoulder; I gently stroked his back.

"Your children are so beautiful, Margrit; they have an Oriental look." I hesitated, not wishing to pry.

"Oh, their father is Tibetan," she replied.

"Tibetan?" I repeated, not a little surprised.

"Yes. Norbu's father was a lama. He lived in Manali for a short time, and then he went away. I don't know where he is now. But Aden's father was not. I don't know where he is either."

"You don't?" I asked surprised.

"No. I really miss him. I don't know if he will—" Her voice broke. "I don't talk much about it..." She brushed away a tear. "We had a child, and then he didn't want me anymore. He said he didn't want any children, but how could I help getting pregnant? I was so upset when I realized I was pregnant that I didn't tell him for a long time. I hoped and prayed I would lose it, but I didn't. Now I love the child so much. I'm glad I didn't lose it. I'm glad I have them both." She sighed audibly and began arranging the sweets on a silver tray.

"His father, a lama?" I said quietly, looking at the sleeping baby I held in my arms.

Margrit cringed. "No, Aden's father was NOT a lama! His father was a friend of the lama I married. I really wanted to marry the second one. But it didn't happen. The second one has never even seen his child..." Her voice faded and she turned her face away so I could not see her. I wished I had not asked about the children.

"Maybe you WILL marry him...one day," I said softly. "Maybe he will come back."

We heard a knock on the door. With a sudden flurry, Margrit hurried into her bedroom. I heard her sob.

I opened the front door. A very thin woman entered. She had gray-blue eyes. Her yellow-white hair fell in a long straight line down the middle of her spine.

"Come in," I said. "I'm Shantila."

"I'm Agnes." She was wearing a gray pants suit with a pale blue scarf tied twice around her neck. She swept aside the toys that were cluttered on the low divan, and sat down, crossing her legs. She lit a cigarette.

"When did you come?" she asked, turning to me.

"About a week ago."

"How long do you plan to stay?" she asked, blowing the smoke over her head.

"Three or four months."

"Do come over for a visit. I live just up the road from the temple. The roses are almost out, beautiful pink ones, just like the ones we had in my parents' garden in England. A bit smaller, true, they aren't as big, but beautiful all the same. You're most welcome."

"Thank you."

"What do you plan to do here?" She stared at me.

"I'm a writer. I go into the forest every day and write."

"What are you writing?"

"A novel which is set in India," I replied.

"Have you been to India before?" Agnes asked, looking at me curiously.

"Yes, twice."

There was a pause, then she said, "So you are an artist. I am too." She told me she was a student of Tibetan tantric art. She had studied drawing with a lama in Manali for six years. She painted pictures of the Buddhist deities and sold them to her Western friends who came to visit her from time to time. She lived in a stone cottage with her Indian boyfriend.

Margrit came in, looking very composed. "Hello, Agnes. How is Amul? He didn't want to come?" Margrit asked.

"He doesn't like this sort of thing. He's gone off trekking in the jungle again," she said, inhaling deeply on the cigarette she held in her long, bony fingers.

"Oh, for how long this time?" Margrit asked, looking concerned.

"I didn't ask. I'm used to it by now. I don't care anymore – as long as he comes back." Her face flushed red momentarily. She uncrossed her legs and shifted nervously in her seat. Her ashen white skin was pulled like a tight mask over her face. Her eyes contained a sad, melancholy expression.

"Have you been painting, Agnes?" Margrit asked.

"A bit. I recently did a painting of Hanuman and I'm still touching up a big painting I started six years ago. I don't know when it will be finished. It seems to always need something added. Sometimes I think I'll go blind if I don't stop. My head and eyes sometimes ache so, but I am obsessed with getting every detail just right. I keep telling myself, 'Listen, Agnes, the hell with perfection! You want too much! Let go, you're wasting your time.' But then, my hand continues painting in spite of it. Last week, I was up until midnight working on one leaf of one bloody tree! And I still don't like it!" She ground the stub of her cigarette into the ashtray and stared blankly into space. Then, without warning, she covered her face with her hands.

The room suddenly became as silent as a tomb. Margrit was busy preparing lunch in the kitchen.

"What is it, Agnes?" I asked in a whisper, not wishing to enter uninvited so fragile a space.

"Oh, Shantila dear, it's nothing. The other week, Amul said, 'Please paint Hanuman for me.' So yesterday I showed him the painting. I'd worked on it for two weeks and all he said was, 'Mmmmh.' He'd forgotten he'd even asked for it." Her voice dropped as she frantically searched in her frayed green bag for another cigarette. "Now it feels like Amul is ready to give me his parting gift. I feel it. I see it in his eyes. He doesn't even look at me anymore. When I speak to him, he looks away or at his shoes, anywhere but at me."

I wondered how I could help her, but spontaneously I realized that each of us inhabited our own world and that world was unique to us. It contained our dreams, our fears, our hopes, and our loves, and no matter what we said about that world to anyone else, no one could inhabit that place except us because it was created by us alone. I also knew that our bondage to time would only dissolve when we gained our freedom from the past and the future, when we could witness the events and circumstances of our lives while fully aware of our divine nature as completely separate from it. I wanted to reach out, to comfort her for her body was quivering and I could feel a deep and undisguised anguish emanating from her.

"Don't worry. Whatever happens is for the best," I said.

"You are a dear. Don't be concerned. It's only – life. We live through it. The weight of memories, sometimes it feels unbearable. Sometimes, I try to forget, but the faces, they come when I least expect them. And I always hear their last words, again and again. If only I could put those words out of my mind – the goodbyes. The damned goodbyes..." Her last words trailed off. I could see she was on the verge of tears.

I moved nearer to her.

"It's nothing. Margrit knows it all. Our lives are similar in more ways than one." Agnes laughed wryly. "Two marriages and now Amul. But somehow one learns through failing; through failed relationships, that is. My marriages were both so similar. They had come full circle, finished, done, spent, annulled. So much the better! One must go on in spite of it..." She paused, gazing into space. "But the blasted last words! How they cut my heart!"

Margrit entered the room then, carrying a tray of tea and a loaf of newly baked German rye bread.

"Come on, you two. You must be hungry." She pulled a wooden bench up to the table and sat down. "Where are the others? Maybe they are not coming, you think?"

"Never mind, Margrit. The Iranians are busy with that child. He never sits still. What's he called? Firoz? He never stops asking for things. I went to visit them the other day and do you know, as soon as I walked in, he said, 'What did you bring me?' Luckily I had a bar of chocolate in my pocket or I would have been in trouble." She laughed. "What a child! Sometimes I'm glad I was spared the experience. Have you any children?" she asked, looking over at me as she bit into a slice of bread.

I still had the infant in my arms. He was asleep. I gazed at his peaceful face and without raising my eyes said, "No." My thoughts were elsewhere. I was thinking of the child I had lost so many years ago. I knew it had been a boy. When it was conceived, a great white light, like a shining star burst over my head. I knew then that a soul had entered my body. We had made love so intensely. It was the one thing in my life I still regretted, and yet on a deeper level I knew it had to happen the way it did. It too was part of the sacred dance, the ritual of offering back what had been given. It could not have been any other way; it was just another part of the role assigned to me in this lifetime.

Now as I gazed at Aden's angelic face and heard Agnes's cynical words, I wished that I was far away – by the river or on top of a mountain where life was simple, uncomplicated by problems, unmixed with chaotic human emotions.

"Children are gifts from nature. We don't know what kind of child we're destined to get. But they come with...with something to teach... Of course, we have to teach them so they don't become wild, but the truth is, they come and give us more than we give them." I paused, wondering if it was worth continuing. "I think they come to us to teach us how – to love."

Margrit, who was nibbling on a crust of bread stopped chewing and gazed up at me.

"Come sit over here, Shantila. You can put him in the crib, you know. He won't wake up now. He usually sleeps at this time every day."

I carefully laid the child on the patchwork quilt, and went to join them by the table.

"Tea?" Margrit asked, lifting the china teapot.

"Yes, thanks." I reached for the bread and cut a thin slice.

"What did you mean when you said – children come to teach us to love?" Margrit asked, tilting her head to one side, her wavy hair hanging over her left shoulder. She brushed her fringe away from her forehead and looked into my eyes.

"What I meant was, well, umm – there are two types – I mean, two kinds of love. Most of the time, when we say we love someone, we want something from them. We expect something, like companionship, marriage, financial help or some other preconceived object. We want someone to be there when we need them. It's one kind of love – based on need, a need to be loved. We have to compensate for something in ourselves so we look for someone to – to help us find fulfillment, or to make up for the loneliness we feel inside.

"But with a mother and child, it's different. The love is unconditional. The child is helpless at the beginning. What can it give? But the mother just keeps on giving to the child because she loves it; it's part of her. She doesn't ask why, she doesn't look for any reason. It's enough that it's her child; so she keeps on giving to it and this is how the child teaches her how to love unconditionally, without a reason." I paused, but the words continued as if by themselves. "This is true love, real love; it never asks the reason; it just loves and the love just continues without a break, up and down, OK, up and down, over hurdles, over bumps, but without a break, without a break in the overall flow. When I see a mother enjoying her child, I feel it's a blessing..." The last words came almost in a whisper.

"You can cuddle Aden as much as you want. He loves it," Margrit said, smiling. "You can even borrow him. No, better not, then I won't have anything to do." She laughed. "Norbu is so independent already."

"You're too serious," Agnes said, looking at me. "Why philosophize? We all have to learn the hard way – broken marriages, failed relationships. You think we need children to learn to love? What about all the nuns and lamas? Isn't their love unselfish?"

She lit a cigarette.

"Agnes, you promised not to smoke in the house. And weren't you intending to cut down?" Margrit asked, blowing the smoke away with her hand.

"Sorry, I'll put it out." Agnes crushed the cigarette onto the box and put the box in her bag.

"Maybe we should change the subject; I didn't mean to talk so much..." I said.

"No, go on, I'm interested in this kind of stuff," Margrit said. "That is, if Agnes doesn't mind."

"Not at all. It's time I found out what I'm doing wrong..."

"Well, I certainly don't have any answers. I'm also searching.... There is a Christian saint, Saint Julian of Norwich, who said there is only one thing we have to learn in life and that is how to love. I guess, it's why we're all here on this planet. The meaning of life is hidden in love. It's simple but we haven't grasped it. Look at the mess we've made of things in the world. The search for the Holy Grail... Wasn't that a search for pure love? Isn't everyone aiming for the same thing? What is it? To touch another person's heart is more important than all the money in the world or even fame or possessions... What's the meaning of all this? Why are we here? Isn't it to learn how to love?"

I stopped abruptly, embarrassed by the feelings which seemed to spill forth without any conscious thought. I didn't even know I felt this way until I heard the words echoing from deep inside.

Margrit said, "You make it all so, well – simple, but people spend their whole life trying to discover the meaning of life. I've tried Buddhist meditation, but it was very difficult. There are so many techniques for getting in touch with the inner self, the truth inside. Each master says: this is the way, this is the way to inner peace, happiness, and fulfillment. This is the way to reach the goal of life. But who knows? Some people are just masquerading. Like the beggars who knock at my door asking for money. One came yesterday morning and asked for water. I gave him a glass of water and then he asked for rupees. I said, no rupees, and he gave me such a look! I was afraid." Margrit made a face, mimicking the stern look in the beggar's eyes.

"That look! It's perfect, Margrit!" Agnes said, laughing loudly. "I agree! It's all a guessing game. I want, I TRY to believe in what everyone calls the path to perfection. But I just CAN'T! Not anymore! I WANT TO SO MUCH, but I've given up. How could there be a God who condones such misery in the world? Tell me that, Shantila! You seem to believe so strongly. I think those wretched scientists are right when they tell us everything is just a matter of chance, an accident, a coincidence! A cosmic accident, bang, bang, bang and here we are and here is the universe! Just look at what the cosmic womb ejected – US!" She laughed again, a cynical smile suffusing her wane features. Her eyes lit up momentarily and then she began to nervously twitch the end of the pale blue scarf around her neck.

"I guess I'm what you might call an atheist, but I would rather call myself agnostic. Sometimes the doubts get the upper hand, sometimes I manage to overcome them, and there are even times when I feel... Sometimes when I go to the Hadimba Temple, I feel, I can't really describe it, but I feel a kind of peace, a joy which lasts for hours..."

"Really? In the Hadimba Temple?" I asked, looking at her with surprise.

"Yes – really. It only happens sometimes, but it's unmistakable. It surprises me really. I'm not a Hindu, you know."

"Well, our lunch is still in the oven. Shall we eat it or do you think we should fast together?" Margrit asked, tossing her hair back and smiling at us.

Margrit brought in the rice, spinach and homemade cheese.

"Do you ever hear from Aden's dad, Margrit?" Agnes asked suddenly, looking up.

"No."

"Do you still love him?"

"Yes. One day he might come back. I hope so," Margrit said as she poured herself another cup of tea.

"What about the lama, Norbu's father? Have you heard anything about him?" Agnes asked.

"No, I think he's in Burma. He tried to go back to his monastery after our divorce. It was impossible to live with him. We were always fighting. He had a dreadful temper. A lama and such anger..."

"Lamas are usually so kind and gentle. I stayed in a Buddhist Center in Delhi and all the lamas there were wonderful," I said quietly.

Margrit interrupted me. "This one seemed like that at first, but later things changed. My husband had scars all over his body. They used to beat him in the monastery whenever he misbehaved. He had to study from eight in the morning until midnight and if they failed their exams, they got punished. I felt so sorry for him, but it was too late. The damage had already been done. He used to hit me, but once I surprised him. I fought back and then he left and that was it. Later we divorced."

"Can a lama get married and have a child, and then return to being a lama?" I asked her.

"Yes, they can," Margrit said stiffly.

"But I thought that once they took their vows, it was a decision for life." I was thinking of Tashi.

"They can go back. Usually, in Tibet, it is a lifelong vow. But, these days, lamas change their minds. Many marry. Let's change the subject, do you mind?" Margrit asked, obviously disturbed.

I had listened carefully to her words. I realized now that life in the monasteries was not always happy. Tashi's words reverberated in my mind: *"I want to go to a foreign country, in or out of the monastery, either way is alright. I no like life here... I want to live in America for many, many years until I am old. I won't come back for a long time."*

What was he escaping from? I wondered, perplexed. *What was it* really like to be given away at ten years old? And to go to Karnataka, in South India, a totally different environment from Ladakh, with four thousand monks? What did he feel? Could our relationship ever work or is it too doomed to failure?

We sat silently. As the afternoon light filtered through the sheer cotton curtains, casting shadows on the floor, I reflected:

How different our lives are and yet we are all striving, each of us in our own way to gain our wings, our freedom to live the truth. We have all suffered. We have created our destiny, but we also have the chance to go beyond it, to change it in the way we choose. What choice will I make now? What choice have I made in coming here? What choices am I making this very moment? Do we really choose or is everything predetermined? There's nothing to do. It's up to us to BE, to FEEL what is right, to FEEL what direction to take, to Feel each moment as it comes and to be guided by our inner voice, the voice of truth... What more can we do? My Guru says that we are made of divine bliss and we have only forgotten who we really are. We have only forgotten how to listen to the song of our innermost being, forgotten the melody of love, the melody of peace that sings silently, sings and sings and sings eternally deep within our heart.

Oh, Agnes! Oh, Margrit! I want to shout out loud: "We are free! We Are Free!" But I can't, not now, for I have not reached the other shore. I am still learning to fly...

Chapter Nine

The five-hundred-year-old temple dedicated to the Hindu goddess Hadimba was shaped like a huge Indian teepee. It had a three-tier triangular roof made of wood. Approaching it from a distance, it appeared archaic, simple, unassuming – as if fashioned by nature herself. I carried a few wildflowers as I walked alone at dawn down the long dirt road between the deodar trees.

Outside the temple was a sign which explained the origin of the temple. Hadimba was the wife of Bhima, one of the five heroic Pandava brothers who lived during the time of the great war described in the Mahabharata, an ancient record of Indian history. Pandu, the brother of the blind king Dhrishtarashtra, was managing his kingdom for him. When Pandu died, the one hundred evil-minded sons of the blind king attempted to usurp the kingdom and destroy the righteous sons of Pandu, called Pandavas. The mightiest warrior in the army of the Pandavas was Bhima. Hadimba was the daughter of a demon but as a reward for many years of rigorous austerities, she was transformed into a goddess. She was regarded as a manifestation of the goddess Kali, the goddess of destruction who annihilates all attachments on the path to liberation. Kali is said to destroy one's bondage to the realm of time and space, and one's clinging to the past and future. The word "Kali" is derived from the root "kal" which means time. She is said to devour all the fragments of time until we are able to live the eternal NOW.

The forest was deserted. Only a flock of crows circled the sky, parting the mist with their ebony wings. Remembering the tradition in all Indian temples, I perambulated the temple in the clockwise direction before leaving my shoes at the entrance. Then I reached up and rang the brass bells hanging from a beam above the stone steps. Each of the three bells chimed with a different tone. The sound rang out, mixing with the raucous cries of the crows in the still morning light. It was as if we both were announcing our arrival to the goddess.

Entering the temple was like entering a huge cave. Candles burned before bronze masks of the deity. A priest in white stood with prasad (a sacred offering) of small white sugar candy that he gave to the devotees before they departed. He also applied a small dot of red paste to their foreheads. The red paste was also prasad, as it had been offered to the goddess. The central altar was underneath a rock, hidden from view unless one knelt down and crawled into it. I crouched down as low as I could, lowering my head still further to keep from bumping it against the rock over my head. The regal goddess Hadimba was arrayed in a garland of marigold blossoms. A flame was alight beside her. Offerings of flowers and coins were placed at her feet. The earth around her was sprinkled with bright yellow petals with rupee notes spread like a carpet of leaves at her feet. Beside her were statues of Ganesh and the Buddha. Bending low before the image of the goddess, I prayed:

Dear God, grant that I may fulfill my mission on this earth and be a perfect instrument of Thy Divine Will. And that I may... The face of Tashi shifted beneath the sand strewn shores of my mind, then floated out to sea, further than words could reach. All became immersed in silence. I placed the purple wildflowers carefully around her feet, leaving one in her upraised arm. Before crawling out of the narrow space, I placed my palms over the flame beside her, then covered the top of my head three times so as to carry the blessing of her light within me.

When I emerged from the darkness of the temple, I once again rang the temple bells but this time a sense of triumph welled up. It was as if a victory had been won. How? Whose victory? I only know that my footsteps were lighter, more buoyant than before. It was not only my body, but also my mind that was less weighed down, more transparent. Maybe the act of bowing down to the goddess of destruction had been enough to erase a burden of sin, a load of karma. I do not know. I felt like a child again, innocent and free, moving without cares, without thinking, moving in a state of grace.

It was springtime in the Himalayas and the morning sun glittered through the branches of the trees. I sat in the forest, enjoying the stillness of the early-morning hours and the fresh mountain air. I sat down and started writing in my notebook. The words came quickly, tumbling over one another, like the rushing of a mountain stream. An hour later, standing up and stretching, I walked slowly out of the gate to the forest.

When I crossed the threshold of the Chandralal guest house, I met the lady who worked there.

"You take breakfast now? Chapatis? I make for you?" she asked.

I accepted as there was no cooking facility in my room.

"Is it possible to have lunch here too?" I asked her, thinking of the dark and dingy restaurants down the road.

"No lunch possible – only breakfast," she replied.

"Oh, alright, thank you," I answered, wondering where I would eat every day. Fortunately today, Margit had invited me for lunch. When I arrived at her cottage, she was busy preparing the food.

"I'm so glad to be having lunch with you," I said, "because the restaurants down the road don't look very clean."

"Why don't you come over every day?"

"Really?! That would be nice – but are you sure it isn't too much trouble for you?"

"No – making lunch for one more person isn't much trouble. You're welcome."

"Thank you. Maybe I should tell you that there are a few things I don't eat."

"What are they?" Margrit asked.

"Well... I don't eat onions, garlic, tomatoes, eggs, fish or meat.

I also try to avoid greasy deep-fried foods."

She was astonished.

"Then how will you manage in India?" she asked.

"I usually cook for myself," I said. Then I told her how, when I lived in Varanasi on my previous trip to India, I used a gas cylinder with one ring on top and lived on mostly rice, dhal and chapatis. I also told her about my rooftop kitchen which had only three walls and that sometimes when the electricity went off in the whole town, I had cooked by candlelight.

"It was a test but I survived," I said, smiling.

"Good for you!" Margrit said, laughing. "India is ALWAYS a test, ALWAYS, no matter where you are, on more levels than we expect."

"How do you mean?" I asked.

"I mean, it forces you to go beyond your limitations, to accept life as it is, rather than as you would like it to be. It strengthens you and yet it..." She paused, searching for the right words to express her feelings.

I finished the sentence instead, "... It opens your heart in spite of everything on the surface that is going on..." I said quietly, almost to myself.

"It is true, Shanti. I wouldn't have said it in those words, but it's true. I suppose that's why I keep coming back." She served the meal she had prepared and we ate together.

"Now I have to hurry to the clinic. Aden is scheduled to have his measles vaccinations today. Do you want to come?" she asked, lifting the baby from his crib.

"Yes, I'd like to come."

We set off down the mountain. Margrit carried Aden curled up in front of her in a sling tied around her shoulder. She walked with firm steps down the rocky path she knew so well. It was a steep, curving path lined with massive trees on either side. The trees provided a welcome shade from the hot afternoon sun. After twenty minutes, we reached the main dirt road and then she showed me the way to the clinic. It was an open square with small bungalows built around it. We went to a row of benches outside one of the buildings and sat down.

"Can you hold Aden for me?" Margrit asked, untying the knot in the sling.

"Yes, of course."

She handed me the baby who was still fast asleep. Then she walked into the building.

An Indian lady came up to the bench with a small boy in a stroller who was crying. She sat down next to me. She was wearing a pale green silk sari. Her long thick hair, parted in the middle and tied with a white ribbon behind her ears, fell in a long braid below her waist. In the parting, a flash of bright red chalk announced that she was married. I instinctively glanced down at her feet. She was also wearing the traditional toe rings: a silver ring on the second toe of each foot – another sign of marriage.

Leaning over, she lifted up her son and gently reprimanded him as she rocked him in her arms. Her golden bangles, three on each wrist, jingled as she swung him high up in the air, and from side to side. Obviously delighted, he started to laugh. Then she put him down on her lap and he immediately reached for her earrings and began to play with them. She started laughing and speaking to him lovingly in Hindi.

The sound of their laughter woke up Aden. He opened his eyes and looked at me. Then he started wriggling around on my lap. I held him up against my chest. The woman looked at me and smiled.

"Is he your baby?" she asked, looking at Aden.

Our eyes met.

"No, I'm – taking care of him for a friend," I replied quietly. I felt a sensation of happiness intermixed with a deep pang of regret that I didn't have any children. My eyes filled with tears. Embarrassed by the strong emotion, I bowed my head. A tear streamed down my face. I acknowledged the unwanted warm liquid as it trickled down to the corner of my mouth, then dropped onto the array of flowers stitched on my Punjabi blouse.

It's too late now – too late, I thought to myself. *If only I had the chance – if only, but...no time to mourn for what could have been.* I patted Aden gently on his back, then bounced him up and down on my lap. He looked into my eyes and gave me a big smile. We were smiling at each other when Margrit returned.

"He likes you," she said warmly as she took him in her arms. "Come now, Aden, it's your turn. Be a good boy." She carried him into the clinic.

As the weeks passed in Manali, I settled into a daily routine: morning walk to the Hadimba Temple, meditation, chapatis for breakfast, writing in the forest and lunch with Margrit.

One morning, when I came back from the temple, I met a stranger sitting on the veranda outside my room. He was tall with white hair and his bright red face was heavily tanned from the sun.

"Namaste," he said, in a rather husky voice. He was smoking. His quick glance seemed to swallow my face and figure in one flicker of his eye.

"Namaste," I replied, standing off to the side to avoid the smoke.

"Where are you coming from?" he asked, looking at me curiously.

"I'm American," I answered briskly.

"No, I mean – now. Where are you coming from – so early in the morning?" he asked.

"The Hadimba Temple. I go there every morning," I answered.

"Oh?" he mumbled. "You like going to temples, huh? You're a Hindu?" He eyed me suspiciously, over the steel rims of his round glasses.

"No. I just appreciate the sacredness of all religions. I like visiting temples."

"I see."

As I unlocked my door, he said, "I'm from Germany. We are neighbors. I live in the room next door to you."

I closed the door securely behind me. "You're a Hindu?!" I whispered. "Do I have to be a Hindu to go to a temple?! I wonder what he's doing here."

The room was in a disarray. I had dressed in a hurry; the faded wool blankets were on the floor and my shawls were scattered across the mattress. I made up the bed, and tidied the room as best I could. Then I sat down in lotus position to meditate. The irksome thoughts continued for several minutes: *Now I have someone smoking next door... I just hope he doesn't knock on the door while I'm meditating...* Gradually the waves of thought subsided and the mind was swept away in a rising sea of silence. The silence engulfed each individual wave of thought in one unanticipated motion and then peace, oneness, a stillness of breath, and all hung as if suspended beyond the touch of time. The songs of the birds like a far-distant melody did nothing to ruffle the abiding calm. The body was like a mere outline filled and surrounded by an all-pervading space; then even the outline almost faded. The inner space melted into the surroundings, melted into the ONE. In this state, I was able to taste the peace that passes understanding. I felt my lips touch the rim of the chalice that held the nectar of immortality. But I did not drink of the nectar. Nearly, but not quite. For even then a trace of the ego, a trace of difference remained. The mind was still holding on to the bare memory of time and space; it was not yet willing to let go. The individual ego was not yet able to surrender completely, to merge fully with the vast uncharted region of the ALL.

Of course, at this juncture, there was nothing I could do but take it as it comes. That was the well-guarded secret of successful meditation. Not doing, not interfering – just taking it as it comes.

This was the effortless path to perfection. The "pathless path" my Guru called it once. I had always savored that expression, and recalled it whenever I seemed held up – stuck – unable to advance any further in my meditations. I remembered his instructions: no anticipation, no expectation of any result. It was the right attitude no matter what did or did not happen. The Guru had said, *"We are not to aim for any particular experience. Everything that happens, happens for GOOD. Everything is guided by NATURE. Nature is all-knowing, all-good. Nature knows best how to organize, so from our side we only witness. We do not interfere with what is naturally happening. Just be a silent witness to the process. Allow it to go the way it must. Be innocent..."*

Finishing the mediation, I laid down to rest.

My Guru's words reverberated in my mind re-echoing from deep inside. Twenty years and I felt as if I was just beginning to fathom the depth of their meaning. For only now did I understand the aptness of his advice as a way of living life in freedom. Only now was I experiencing how to let go of all the incessant worries, imaginary fears, and doubts which interfered with feeling the wisdom of Nature guiding life forward, step by step, moment to moment. ALL-GOOD was guiding, so why worry, why doubt, why fear the future? Only now was I beginning to acknowledge an underlying pattern of perfection in the universe, in everything, an underlying reason for everything AS IT IS.

I remembered that once, long ago, an Indian holy man, told me: "When you gain enlightenment you will realize that the whole universe is perfect. Everything is the way it is meant to be and it is perfect."

I rebelled then: "How can it be so? Look at the suffering, the injustices, the wars, the cruelty – how can that be an image of a perfect world?" I was unable to accept his words, his vision of enlightenment. That was fifteen years ago, fifteen vanished years, another worldview, another dimension of time-space.

After my rest, I went to ask for chapatis for breakfast. Then I ventured down to the town to see if I had any mail. In the post office, I saw Swarma standing behind the counter. I greeted her with a smile. She looked up, her expression as serious as usual.

"Swarmaji," I said, adding the "ji", a term of respect used when addressing important people. "Is there any mail for me?"

She smiled at me. "No one has ever called me that before. I'll go and see."

She returned to the counter and handed me a letter. I examined the envelope. Was it from Tashi? No, or Mr. Rao? I opened it and quickly read it. It was a note which had been forwarded to me from Mr. Rao's office. A note from – Mr. Patel, the famous journalist! It said that he would be interested in meeting me. He had added his telephone number so I could call him. I was delighted. I jumped up and threw my arms up in the air.

Swarma started laughing.

"Good news?" she asked.

"Yes, it's about my book! I might get to have a newspaper article written about it."

"I'm happy for you," she said, resuming her work.

I immediately went to a shop to phone Mr. Patel. An Indian lady answered.

"May I speak to Mr. Patel please?"

"One minute please."

"Hello. This is Mr. Patel. May I help you?"

"This is Shantila Martin. I received your card. I would like very much to meet you."

"Yes, good. When can you come? Next week? No, I'm busy next week. Two weeks, is that alright?" His voice was kind and gentle, not at all what I had expected from what I had heard about him. He had been described as one of the most contro-versial journalists in India. He sometimes wrote such scathing columns about people that he had to have twenty-four-hour police protection.

"Yes, two weeks is fine," I said. Then added, "I also write poetry. Should I bring some poems as well?" I remembered that I had one hundred poems I wanted to have published.

"Poetry? Is it love poetry? I like LOVE poetry," he said, emphasizing the word "love".

"Yes, I'll bring some love poems and my instrument. I usually play tanpura to accompany the poems."

"Yes. Fine, fine, I'll expect you on the Monday." He hung up.

I walked up the mountain feeling elated and entered Margrit's charming cottage. When I walked in, she was breastfeeding Aden.

"Hello, Shanti. I'm very late today – up most of the night again. This is how it is with babies."

"Didn't you sleep at all?" I asked.

"I couldn't get back to sleep. I'm so tired. Would you mind cooking today? The rice is soaking in the kitchen. There is a cauli-flower in the fridge."

I loved Margrit's kitchen. She had had wooden shelves and cupboards built and there were colorful glass jars from Germany neatly arranged in rows. She had many different kinds of lentils as well as brown rice, white basmati rice, pasta, oat flakes, wheat porridge and dried figs, dates and raisins.

I took the cauliflower from the fridge. "How much should I use?"

"Oh, as much as you want. As much as you think we'll need," Margrit answered without looking up. She was very generous with the food. As I sat on the wooden bench, I broke the washed cauliflower into small pieces.

"How long have you lived in India?" I asked her.

"It will be eleven years this year."

"Do you ever consider going back to live in Germany?"

"No. Sometimes when I go to visit my mother in the winter, I feel so uncomfortable in Germany. There is so much stress and tension in the atmosphere and life there is so, so divided, fragmented. Nature seems so far away. It feels like nature is on one side, out there somewhere, and we human beings are on the other side. Life appears as if it is divided up into so many pieces. It doesn't feel right somehow. It's always the same. I can't wait to come back. This is a better place for the children to grow up, much better than Germany. I want them to grow up free and happy."

"You're lucky to be here, Margrit. I sometimes wonder where destiny will lead me. I've been on the road for so long."

"On the road? How do you mean – on the road?" Margrit asked looking confused.

"I better put the rice on. Then I'll explain what I meant." I went into the kitchen, put the rice into a large pot and added a few pinches of turmeric. On the way to the sitting room I stood in the doorway admiring the sweet picture of Margrit breastfeeding her child.

I sat down on the settee next to Margrit. Aden had fallen asleep in her arms. "I started traveling many years ago. I grew up in Harlem, a ghetto in New York City. Once when I was around sixteen years old, I had a very vivid dream: I saw myself living alone, high up in the mountains, far away from everyone and everything. It felt like a premonition. I told my younger sister about it and she started crying. She was afraid that I would leave and never come back." There was a long silence. Then I continued, "We were close then but I haven't seen her in nine years."

"Nine years?" Margrit asked, staring at me.

"Yes, nine years. I left America more than fifteen years ago because I felt suffocated by the materialistic values. People were so engrossed with getting and spending, buying more and more things – bigger houses, bigger cars, bigger television sets. Then some people started muscle building, building up bigger and bigger bodies! I couldn't stand it. It felt so strange. It was like living in a foreign country. People were so caught up in the physical value of life. I felt there must be more to life than this. I always knew I would leave America. Sometimes when I was growing up, I asked myself, 'What am I doing here?'

"I was searching for answers to the riddle of life and began to study comparative religion. I could see that every religion said basically the same thing: The kingdom of God is within you and love your neighbor as yourself. I read Krishnamurti in college, but I couldn't reach the thoughtless state he described in his books. It was so intellectually clear but it was the EXPERIENCE I was after. In the early seventies, I came to London to continue my studies, and not long afterwards, I learned to meditate. Finally, I began to have the experience that I was searching for. Then I went to live in a community where people meditate together in England."

"You meditate all together? That must be nice," Margrit said.

"Yes, it's OK. I expected the place to be better than it actually is. The British are polite but not very open on the level of the heart. I never really felt welcome there. Ten years ago, I came to India for the first time. I love it here. This is where I feel I truly belong. The Indian people are so open on the feeling level and they seem to be able to perceive the inner being of a person spontaneously. Most of the time, I live like a – a pilgrim, carrying my things from place to place, a bird without a nest. But I'm used to it now. I just accept it. I've given up trying to understand why things happen the way they do. I just want to live a simple life, a peaceful life, that's all."

"It's all karma," Margrit said. "Lord Buddha says everything is mind. Our thoughts create our reality. It's difficult to grasp. I studied Buddhist philosophy but I found it very difficult."

"You studied Buddhism?" I asked her.

"Yes. I have many books on Buddhism. Do you want to see them? They are on the bookshelf over there."

"Yes, I do." I was longing to learn more about Tashi's religion. I browsed through the books on the shelf, picked out a few and turned the pages. "Can I borrow a few of your books?" I asked her.

"Yes, of course," Margrit answered. "I've converted to Buddhism and even started learning the Tibetan language."

"Converted to Buddhism?" I said, a bit surprised. Then I thought, *Maybe I should learn Tibetan, then I can read the prayers with Tashi.*

I carried the tray of cauliflower into the kitchen and gathered together all the spices for the dish: cumin, coriander, peppercorns, and cinnamon. I roasted the seeds on the tava, a concave Indian frying pan, and ground them with the mortar and pestle, then sautéed the cauliflower with the spices in ghee (clarified butter). The sweet aroma of the rice and vegetables soon filled the kitchen. I was inundated by happiness. Outside, on a branch near the kitchen window, a robin sat chirping merrily while white and yellow butterflies danced in the tall green grass, chasing one another around and around in circles.

"A man has just moved in next door to me," I said, sticking my head into the sitting room.

"You mean Klaus? White hair, tall, sunburned?" Margrit asked.

"Yes. You know him?"

"Oh, yes. He comes to Manali every year. He's been all over India. He stays in Goa in South India in the winter, then comes up here in the spring."

"Really? What does he do here?"

"Just travels I guess. He enjoys himself since he doesn't have to think about money. He's retired."

"He's very rich? Independently wealthy?" I asked laying the table.

"I think so. Sometimes he comes to have dinner with me." Margrit put Aden in his crib. We started eating.

I was grateful for our friendship. She was one of the few foreigners I met who truly appreciated India.

When I returned to the guest house, Klaus was sitting outside smoking.

"Namaste," he said. "Sit down. You are always in such a hurry. You are too busy. This is India. Relax." He pulled out a plastic chair and motioned for me to sit on it.

I sat down trying to avoid the cigarette smoke.

"What are you going to do in Manali?" he asked.

"I like to visit holy places."

"Oh? I have been to them all, in India that is. No, that's not true. It's not possible to visit all the holy places in India in one lifetime. There are just too many. I've been to most of them though."

"You have?" I asked, becoming more alert.

"Yes. The ones in the South are the best, especially Chidambaram. They do pujas there all day and the atmosphere is very powerful. At least it felt powerful to me. It's a personal thing – how one feels in these places, I mean."

"Near Manali, are there any places which are – well, especially holy?"

"Yes. Vashishti Springs is good, or, what you say, special. Haven't you been there?" he asked, puffing on his cigarette.

"No, I haven't been anywhere yet." As I said it, the thought crossed my mind that it might be good to have a traveling companion for a little while. But I didn't say anything to this effect.

"I'll take you. We can go together." He grinned. "You want we go together?"

I looked at him in silence before answering. I said to myself: *He looks harmless enough. He's old. Margrit knows him. The people at the guest house all know him. Why should I be afraid?* I said aloud, "OK. When should we go?"

"Tomorrow," Klaus answered, his eyes traversing the whole of my body in one hungry glance.

The next morning the mist was slowly evaporating from the

peaks of the mountains, and between the white effervescent masses, patches of clear blue sky showed through. It looked like it would be a cool, pleasant day. I dressed quickly, drank a cup of warm milk, munched some sunflower seeds, ate a few chapatis and hurried out. Klaus was waiting outside smoking. I announced that I was ready.

"Did you have breakfast?" he asked.

"Yes."

"Why don't you take breakfast with me? I had a good breakfast, stuffed paratha, coffee and an omelet."

"Where did you eat?" I asked him.

"At one of the outdoor cafes down the road from the Hadimba Temple."

"I'd be afraid to eat in one of those places. They don't look, uh, very clean."

"They're fine. You'll have to get used to it. This is India, not America – or did you say you were from England? You shouldn't be so fussy." He started walking toward the gate. "Are you sure you're ready?"

"Yes."

"Then we go." He started off down the rocky path leading to the main road and I followed close behind with my knapsack strapped to my back. On the narrow road, rickshaws, jeeps and cars bounced along, maneuvering for space. The road was in the process of being repaired; gaping potholes ran through it like wide-open stitches in a cloth.

Klaus was used to going on long treks and was over six feet tall. I could barely keep up with him.

"Shall we take a rickshaw?" I asked, already feeling tired.

"Let's walk more. Are you tired already? You should have had a good breakfast like me." He turned back and grinned; then continued at the same pace down the sloping hill. By now the sun was out and my forehead was dripping with perspiration.

We cut across a forest path that led to stone steps which

descended in a downward spiral to the road leading to the market. The forest was cool and the dense shade of the deodar trees welcoming. I imbibed their silent serenity and immediately felt more at ease. Their branches were like fans suspended in the air, shielding us from the intense glare of the noonday sun. I stubbed my toes on protruding rocks as I gazed up at the towering trees.

After half an hour, we arrived at a concrete bridge. The road was very busy. Up ahead, army lorries lined the road. Mustached policemen in green khaki outfits with matching berets tried to keep the fast-moving traffic coming from one direction from colliding with the traffic advancing from the other direction. They were blowing a shrill whistle and waving their arms to make the cars stop.

What a job! I thought. *With all that smoke!* I plied my way slowly up the steep path. We had to walk up a very long dirt road and then climb a nearly vertical hill to reach the path leading to Vashishti Springs on the other side of the mountain. It was a forty-five-minute walk at the very least. There were heavy trucks loaded with bricks weaving their way between buses spewing black smoke. The trucks were trying to overtake racing rickshaw drivers and antiquated cars all moving at different speeds. They were whizzing past close to where we had to walk. Each time a car passed, dust blew up into my eyes and covered my face. I tried to walk as close as possible to the precipice overlooking the river without falling into it.

I was breathing heavily by now. I had my cardigan wrapped around my waist as it was too hot to wear it. Klaus was several feet ahead, still striding along at the same pace. Every once in a while, he turned back to see if I was still following, but he didn't slow down. My cotton top clung to my damp chest and the scarf I was wearing hung limp and creased around my neck as I was using it to wipe my face. The sun burned my forehead and my perspiration stung my eyes.

Damn it! I thought. *I don't intend to walk all the way in this heat! Why doesn't he stop?* I slowed down and found an iron railing and leaned wearily against it. In front of it, a young man was sitting on the ground selling slices of coconut. I stood staring at the coconut slices, trying to decide whether I should risk buying any. In my mind, I started weighing up the odds of whether it was hygienic because he was touching them and wondering how many dirty rupee notes he must have touched that day. Besides, he was sitting by a main road and with all the fumes, the food was probably polluted. I could almost taste the sweet juice of the fruit and I felt it would have helped revive me as I was ready to drop from the heat.

The young man looked at me curiously. Then with a friendly smile, he said in Hindi, "Eight rupees."

I stood there for a few minutes, totally bewildered, then dragged my feet up the path and away. By this time, Klaus was so far ahead I could only just barely see him. He was waving. I feebly returned the wave. Utterly exhausted, I decided to keep going. The sweat was pouring down my back. It felt like I was walking through an open oven.

After ten minutes and no sign of Klaus in the distance, I sat down on a large rock.

"That's it!" I said angrily to myself. "I give up. The first rickshaw that passes, I'm getting it."

The first rickshaw took a long time to arrive. I sat with my scarf tied around my head in the same way as the Indian women breaking rocks by the road had their kerchiefs tied. Finally I caught sight of a rickshaw and waved frantically until it stopped near me. I clambered gratefully into it.

"Vashishti Springs," I murmured to the lean driver who sat hunched over the wheel. In the front window of the rickshaw, there was a makeshift altar with three photos: one of Hanuman, one of Rama, and one of Laxmi. A dry, crumpled marigold garland was draped over the photos.

"Tik (OK)," he said. The engine sputtered and roared as he cranked it up with a strong jerk of his right arm. We sped up the road. On the way, I saw Klaus, still taking long, quick strides as if oblivious of the heat, his face even brighter red by now.

"Stop, stop!" I shouted to the driver.

He slowed down and turned around, looking quizzically at me. "What?"

I waved to Klaus. "I have a rickshaw! Klaus, I'm over here!"

The driver understood and pulled over to the side of the road, waiting until Klaus caught up with us. Klaus climbed in without a word and we continued on our way.

It was a long upward climb, and the mountain path was very steep, difficult even for the three wheeler to reach without sputtering. We skimmed the edges of cliffs and hung above deep gorges with only the sound of the rushing river dashing against the rocks far below.

"I could never have walked here," I said.

"It's only seven or eight kilometers. It's nothing," he answered without looking at me.

"In this heat, I would have fainted," I replied, annoyed at what I considered his insensitivity.

The rickshaw wound its way up the final stretch of the road toward the sulfur hot springs, famed for its ability to ease all the aches and pains that flesh is heir to.

An arched entranceway with a wrought-iron gate marked the dividing line between the outer world and the inner sacred ground. We crossed the threshold, leaving our shoes with an elderly woman who, for a few rupees, arranged them neatly in a corner of the courtyard and gave each of us a token with a number engraved on it. Just beyond the gate to the right was the hot sulfur bath for women. I gingerly peeked in.

Inside, a Tibetan woman was giving her small son a bath. She was busy lathering his hair with shampoo. After washing him, she started washing her clothes which she stacked on the edge of the bath. There was no one else there. I wondered whether to undress and bathe before visiting the temple.

Better to wash first, a little voice intoned inside. Meekly, I went into the bathing area and removed my Punjabi top, then off came the trousers. I dipped my feet into the warm green water, then slid down the side of the marble pool which was about eight by eight feet wide. The waters covered my shoulders like a cool shawl made of green silk. Its warmth soothed the body like a caress; I could feel the muscles in my arms relax and I couldn't resist smiling. It was worth the trouble. I was so thirsty I wished I could drink the water. The parched, heated sensation soon disappeared. The longer I stayed in the water, the lighter and happier I felt. Two more women came in. They stood looking at me for quite some time before they undressed and got in.

Reluctantly, I climbed out and only then did I realize that I hadn't brought a towel. I dried myself with my cotton scarf as best I could and dressed as discreetly as possible.

When I emerged, I saw two Hindu monks sitting in the courtyard in orange robes. They gestured to me, inviting me to sit with them. I felt peaceful and happy. One of them was very old with a long white beard and the other one had a shiny black beard. The young man's eyes were filled with light. I realized that he didn't speak English. I genuinely regretted not having learned enough Hindi to converse with him. We just looked into each other's eyes, an overflowing feeling of friendliness emanating from his heart to mine. Then I turned to go into the temple. I had to stoop down to enter as the doorway was quite low.

In the center of the temple was a small wooden shrine with a statue of Sage Vashishtha inside. On the inner walls of the temple were pictures of the Vedic deities: Hanuman, Rama, Lord Krishna, Saraswati and Laxmi. A priest in white sat at the door of the inner shrine with a bowl of prasad and the customary red paste which he dipped the ring finger of his right hand into before applying it to the foreheads of the devotees. I knelt in the queue behind several Indian couples. When I reached the door of the shrine, I bowed to the image and the priest placed the red dot on my forehead and sprinkled a handful of sugary sweets into my open palm. Circumambulating the shrine in a clockwise direction, I then sat, as inconspicuously as possible by the wall, and closed my eyes.

The deep silence of the space enveloped me immediately and the awareness of the body dissolved. In an ocean of silence, suspended in bliss and peace, time was no more. The individuality surrendered, letting go and merging in the ocean of pure existence. I don't know how long I stayed there. I only know I didn't want to leave. There was nothing I desired. Just the experience of BEING was enough, more than enough. It was sufficient; it bestowed more fullness than anything I could ever want or need.

When I stepped outside, the air vibrated with light. The light of inner happiness irradiated everything I saw. I felt like dancing as my bare feet touched the earth, but I restrained myself for there were many Indian people gathered together waiting to go in.

Outside the gate, I mounted the smooth stone steps which led to an older temple dedicated to Lord Rama. It had a red lintel adorned with garlands of dried flowers in yellow and lavender hues. On the walls, inscriptions in Sanskrit were carved. The temple was deserted. There was a large round bowl of sugar candy on the floor and beside it, a bowl of red paste. I knelt beside the central altar and prayed.

When I emerged, Klaus was sitting outside smoking.

"Did you bathe?" he asked.

"Yes, did you?"

"Yes."

"Wasn't it wonderful? This is a very powerful place."

Klaus just looked at me without answering. "Shall we go now?" he finally said.

"Yes, if you want."

We walked down the path together. There were many shops on the way selling Kashmiri shawls, jewelry and also other kinds of clothes reminiscent of the hippie generation. I peered into a window of antique jewelry.

"Do you mind if I go in?" I asked.

"Go in," Klaus answered blandly.

I entered a semi-dark room covered wall to wall with shelves of intricately patterned, hand-wrought silver necklaces, bracelets and rings. I picked up a bracelet, and was admiring the workmanship when an Indian man with a black beard and shoulder-length hair came up behind me and whispered in my ear.

"Hashish, madam? Fine quality, you want to buy?"

I veered around sharply and looked straight at him with undisguised distaste. "Excuse me. I want to go. No, I don't want anything from you," I said sternly, as I moved toward the door.

Klaus who had entered the shop with me stood in the semi-darkness huddled over, talking to the rough-looking person who had approached me. When he came out, I instinctively moved away from him.

"I can't bear this type of thing," I said.

"It's all over India, especially around Manali. It's part of life, Shantila. Don't look so upset."

"Why did you have to speak to him?" I blurted out.

"Just play. I wanted to see what he was selling. Bad-quality stuff. Everyone tries to sell whatever they can get."

"Shall we get a rickshaw?" I asked.

"You get one. I'll hang around here for a while. I want to go up into the mountains."

We parted. It was then I suspected that Klaus was taking drugs.

Chapter Ten

"If you really want to visit the holy places in India, then you must go to Manikaran," Klaus remarked one morning as we sat together having a cup of tea.

"Why is that?" I asked, turning to him.

"Because, it's...well – it's a very special place. Strong atmosphere. You have to experience it. It would be good for you."

I thought about it: Klaus was right about Vashishti Springs. It was really special.

"I want to go there," I said with conviction.

"I also want to go there," he replied, "we go together, yes?"

"How long should we stay? I must return to Delhi next week."

"Let's stay a few days, then you can catch a bus to Delhi and I can come back here. We can find a guest house for a hundred rupees."

The bus was scheduled to depart at ten o'clock. Klaus and I arrived as early as possible. The bus depot was hot and dirty with litter scattered in the alleyways. It was crowded with local people, some of whom sat, squatting on their knees, as they waited for their buses. Many of the men wore the traditional Kullu cap perched on their heads to protect them from the penetrating rays of the sun. Most had fair skin and aquiline features. Their faces expressed kindness and gentle forbearance. The older women wore the Manali dress consisting of one large square of checked woolen fabric with a red border. The cloth was draped around them and tied in a knot over each shoulder. They wore a blouse underneath. Many of the women also wore several gold rings in their earlobes; sometimes the entire ear lobe was covered with as many as eight or nine earrings. This was in addition to the nose ring which most of the elders wore. Their features expressed cheerfulness and inner fortitude. They had smooth skin except for the deep creases in their foreheads and around their eyes for many of them labored in the fields for hours under the hot sun, planting seeds, collecting fodder for the cows, and carrying baskets full of wood on their backs to feed the fire in their tandoors, the wood-burning stoves used by most families in this region.

We boarded the bus right away in order to avoid getting the seats in the back row which were the bumpiest. I chose a seat by the window in the middle of the bus and Klaus swung himself into the seat next to me. His six-foot frame had to hunch over in order not to hit the ceiling with his head. As soon as he sat down I wished I could move because his body reeked of cigarette smoke.

The bus swung from one side of the steep winding road to the other as it headed down to the Kullu Valley where the river gurgled and sang, flooding its shores with seething white foam. I peered out the window. The mountains seemed to sing and the hills to respond. The trees spread their flowering boughs, drinking in the light pouring down from the shimmering sky and the river gushed forth, rising and falling in sheer delight, for the joy of life surged and swelled weaving a tapestry of beauty from threads streaming with light. I marveled at the majesty of the mountains which soared heavenward and the deep flowing curves of the valleys, with their meandering brooks, streams and rivers intertwined between orchards of flowering apple trees and simple wooden dwellings perched on the summits of hills. The white stone cliffs etched by the heavy monsoon rains jutted out in sharp angular designs, carved by time and the inroads of human endeavor such as the endless lines of buses moving over it day after day. Yet even the stones were singing. The earth heaved beneath the grinding of the rubber tires, and yet it smiled as the human dance continued, and it wove its own rhythm from the combination of each heartbeat of each individual to the heartbeat of the plants and the trees, to the rhythmic flight of the winged ones, to the rise and fall of the waves of the river. The earth accepted all with an unfading smile, an inner rejoicing, which I inhaled as the bus swayed on the road, and inside, a seed of contentment grew.

The journey took several hours, but the resplendent scenes of beauty dispelled the notion of time. I watched spellbound as the earth revealed its own glory in a song of such great simplicity, innocence and uninhibited fullness. It was like stepping into the very heart of Mother Nature and bathing in the fresh springs of her divine creation. I took long slow drafts to quench the thirst that had accumulated over the years spent behind the closed doors of England. I wanted to plant the seeds of each scene deep within the soil of the subconscious. The bus hurtled over deep ruts in the road and up rocky ridges. The driver's body swerved all the way to the right and then all the way to the left as the bus reeled to and fro like a ship tossed by the wind at sea.

As we turned down a narrow dirt road, I stared awestruck at the new world unfolding before my gaze. Manikaran! The world I beheld was suspended in an ocean of divine music. Here, the very buildings were singing! What I saw first was an endless array of flags – pastel-colored flags, fluttering in the breeze. They danced, fanning out in all directions from atop a minaret on the tip of a temple; they flew gaily, spanning the length of the bridge above the churning waves of the Parvati River, then danced further out along the rooftops of the long white structure built on both sides of the river. At first glance, the scene evoked an idea of fairyland, a land more akin to heaven than earth, a place more ethereal than material. It was not just the pastel hues of the trian-gular-shaped flags on the temple or the frothing waves of the river which seemed ready to burst its banks, but the feeling of perceiving a world which existed apart, perhaps protected, shielded or nestled in a transparent bubble of silence, a bubble of bliss, a bubble of divine radiance.

"We're here," Klaus said.

"Manikaran!" the bus driver shouted as passengers filled the aisle, struggling toward the door with their luggage in tow. Klaus reached down, retrieved his case from under his feet, and headed for the door. I followed, making my way as best I could with my heavy shoulder bag.

Once outside, I collected my suitcase and stood to one side, letting the crowd disperse. For a few minutes, Klaus was nowhere to be seen. Then I caught sight of him, standing off to the side, conversing with an Indian man.

"I've been inquiring about guest houses," he said as I came up to him. "He said we can find a place down the road, near the Sikh gurudwara." (A place where spiritually minded people live together with their Guru or teacher). He headed off down the road without looking back.

I followed, struggling with my baggage, my back aching from the load. Under my breath, I muttered something about what a fool I was to travel with someone like him who never bothered to help me with my things or even to wait for me.

We reached the marketplace. The roads were old, as if unchanged for centuries. The taste of antiquity reminded me of Varanasi. It was as if time had stopped; we could have traveled the same narrow path in biblical times. We passed a large Hindu temple but didn't stop. We walked through a bazaar of narrow streets crammed with shops selling photos of Manikaran, as well as trinkets, clothes, and items used by the priests in the Hindu temples. There was also an array of fresh fruit and dried raisins, dates and figs.

Klaus paused at the end of a long alleyway. "I want to find the guest house I stayed in four years ago. I could bathe in the sulfur springs in that place. Some guest houses have the sulfur springs pumped in. I don't like going into the public places with the Indians." Then he turned and began walking. Finally, he stopped in front of an Indian restaurant and went in. When he emerged he was followed by a young Indian man who directed us to some rooms across from the restaurant. We ascended a narrow flight of stone steps leading onto a small terrace. Behind it we saw two rooms next door to each other. Each had a private toilet and shower.

This is fantastic! A shower, a toilet and clean! I was relieved. I slid the heavy bag from my shoulders and stretched out on the bed, opening and closing my red and taut fingers.

"I'm hungry," I said to Klaus. I glanced at my watch. It was nearly five-thirty in the evening.

"OK. Let's go to the gurudwara. They serve free meals there. Five minutes, then we go, yes?"

Ten minutes later, we stood at the threshold of one of the long white enclosures I had seen from the bridge. It was the first time I had entered a Sikh ashram or gurudwara. We descended the steps and passed through a long white cement tunnel. Then, we ascended a white stone staircase and found ourselves in a small vestibule. A man sat inside a room collecting shoes in exchange for a token of identification. He also instructed us to cover our heads before entering the large hall where the food was being served.

I put my scarf over my head while Klaus pulled a handkerchief out of his trouser pocket and balanced it on top of his hair. We entered the hall. A small group of Indians sat cross-legged on the floor in a row along one wall. We joined them. From the kitchen, which was in a far corner of the hall, a lean, rather tall Indian man with a long white beard and a white turban on his head entered, carrying a bucket. As soon as he saw us, he took two rounded stainless-steel plates and a spoon out of the bucket and placed them in front of us. Then he quickly went back to the kitchen and returned with a bucket full of steaming-hot moong dhal. He dished some onto our plates, then off he went back to the kitchen and returned with the rice. Again, he disappeared and reappeared with okra. He filled our plates with a smile.

I watched, overwhelmed with gratitude, my stomach growling with pleasure as the aromatic fragrance of the fresh, hot food filled my nostrils. I whispered a prayer thanking God for such a bountiful feast. Then I began to eat. As I was eating, the turbaned man returned with the dessert: a thick, brown sweet called halva; it was made of finely ground wheat and fried in ghee (clarified butter) and sugar. He dipped the ladle into the bucket and dropped a generous portion of the halva on the plate. We all ate in silence. Every once in a while, the turbaned man returned, asking if we wanted more food. I suppose I ate more than I needed to, but I was eating joy more than food.

As we sat there in our relatively neat, tailored clothes, an abjectly poor Indian family came in with four ragged children trailing behind them. They sat, heads covered opposite us, and waited quietly while the plates were brought and arranged in front of each of them. Then the turbaned, bearded man began the same ritual of offering them fresh, hot food, as much as they wanted, and water to drink. They hungrily dipped their cupped palms into the high mound of hot, white rice, mixing the dhal in with their fingers.

Tears welled up in my eyes. Here there was no distinction between rich or poor, Sikh, Hindu, Muslim, Christian or Jew. We were all hungry and all were fed in the same, simple spirit of service. Together, we ate our meal, covering our heads in the sacred shrine of the Divine where all needs are answered, all desires spontaneously fulfilled from the all-beneficent hand of God.

"When is breakfast?" I asked Klaus quietly.

"Anytime one comes, one can eat. Food is served here every day from morning until night, and there is singing and music every evening," Klaus said.

"I want to come!" I whispered eagerly.

"I want to come too. Baba Ramji, the head of the ashram will be speaking," Klaus said in a low voice.

That evening, we ascended another flight of stairs and found ourselves on the threshold of another world carved out of a glittering space with gold streamers hanging on the ceiling and pictures of deities and saints from all the major religions covering every inch of space on the walls and pillars of a large candlelit hall. In the center of the hall was an altar adorned with more golden streamers. On it were garlanded photographs of Guru Nanak, the founder of the Sikh religion, who was born in Manikaran. On the highest level was placed the Guru Granth Sahib, the revered Sikh scripture.

Klaus went to sit with the men on one side and I joined the women who sat directly in front of the altar on oriental carpets. Several of the women looked up and smiled at me. A bearded man with a turban was chanting. Then the sound of a harmonium was heard. I closed my eyes and my body rocked slowly back and forth in time with the melody. The music continued until a hush rippled through the space and everyone rose to their feet. I saw several of the women bow their heads in reverence.

Baba Ramji was entering the hall. He was a bearded man of medium height, dressed simply in a white dhoti and an orange turban. His face radiated kindness. As he passed clockwise around the altar, a tall, stately lady emerged from among us and knelt at his feet. He continued to his place, as if not minding, but not overtly concerned either with her unrestrained expression of devotion. He went to the place where the microphone was positioned and sat down cross-legged on the floor.

The silence in the room was almost audible. It was as if all of nature was poised for a moment, waiting for something.

It was his sermon. Moving closer to the microphone, he started to speak. His voice flowed like honey from his heart. Resonant, full and deep, it seemed to distill the very essence of sound from the soundless and it touched the heart. I did not understand all the words because his discourse was in Hindi but I knew that he was speaking about the virtues of Rama, the symbol of an ideal king. I did not mind not understanding many of the words, because just to feel the sounds of the words was like being massaged with bliss. After the discourse, he began to sing and then the outer world just melted away.

His voice, like an ocean of pure love, flooded the space and I swam in its midst without moving, drenched in tidal waves of sound. The singing reached a crescendo, then dipped suddenly into silence, paused, then re-ascended, rising even higher in waves of love and devotion. Instruments I had never seen before rattled and hummed, thrilling the air with a frenzied pitch of emotion, a song of jubilation stirred by the love of God.

The kirtan continued for about an hour. I felt that I would gladly have remained there all night and time would have been as nothing; my heart felt so full, so nourished, so flooded with love. At the end of the singing, with eyes still shut, I heard footsteps near me and a spattering sound as if some very moist morsel was being distributed nearby. Opening my eyes, I saw a rotund man with a white beard and a very gentle expression holding a silver bowl from which he was scooping out a brown glutinous mass of sweet pudding and dropping it into the cupped palms of all the people gathered there.

I held up my palms and smiling into my eyes, he filled my hands with a lump of the aromatic dessert which was oozing with ghee. It had the fragrance of roses. I said a prayer as I lifted the offering to my lips. The taste of the pudding added another layer of bliss to what I was already feeling; although it tasted like it was made of wheat, sugar and ghee, it might as well have fallen from heaven. The taste was exquisite. I learned later that it was called "the divine pudding"; it was the traditional prasad offered to devotees in the Sikh temples.

Early next morning I set out to find the hot sulfur baths attached to the gurudwara. The shops along the narrow alleyways were still shut, their corrugated iron gates securely fastened as it was just six o'clock. Near the entrance to the gurudwara, I discovered stone steps leading down and taking a different turning at the bottom, I found myself at the top of another flight of stairs. Peering down the steps, I saw steam rising up. Curious to know the origin of the hot white vapor, I started down the steps. There were a few sandals at the top of the staircase, so I followed suit and left mine there also. Descending the steps, the heat became more and more intense until at the bottom it felt like I was standing in a sauna turned up to the highest possible temperature. Stepping from the cool stone onto the flat surface at the foot of the steps, I had to lift my feet up and down to prevent them from getting burned by the scorching-hot floor. Boiling-hot steam rose like white clouds into the pink light of dawn, rose out of the gray-green waters which splashed against the white rocks in the Parvati River. Hot sulfur springs! I had read that Guru Nanak's disciples had cooked rotis, rice and dhal in it! The scorching liquid made of fire and light transformed the white rocks to a golden reddish-brown color that glowed. It felt like a primordial chasm of the gods, with water that burns issuing from the depths of the earth! As the clouds of steam parted, I beheld a temple to Lord Shiva who was said to have meditated here for eleven thousand years. The ground around the temple was adorned with garlands of roses and marigolds. Inside, bowls of Indian sweets were placed reverentially at the feet of a majestic bronze image of Lord Shiva. Circumambulating the temple, my face streaming wet from the heat, I entered and knelt at His feet. Reascending the steps, I walked down a long hall. Then I saw a white curtain. I heard women's voices and splashing sounds, and knew it was the bath for ladies. Here cool water from the river was intermingled with the boiling-hot liquid rising from the earth. There were two other ladies present. We all undressed in silence, covering ourselves as much as possible before sliding into the large square pool and letting the warm liquid embrace our bare bodies, simultaneously cooling and warming and soothing our world-worn limbs. It was a nurturing womb-like warmth that wrapped itself around me and I remained immersed much longer than anyone else.

Afterwards we chatted to each other, our former shyness having dispersed like morning mist from the mountains. We were like a family of friends, the mantle of strangeness having fallen from our shoulders.

After breakfast at the gurudwara, I noticed a small room opposite the dining room. Inside sat Baba Ramji; he was receiving visitors. I longed to meet him. I sat a few feet away from the open door, peering in as discreetly as possible. Then his secretary approached me. She said: "You can go in if you desire. Baba Ramji will happily receive you."

Her name was Jasmine. She was dressed in a saffron-colored Punjabi and a long saffron scarf covered her hair. She walked into the room and started to arrange books on a table next to Baba Ramji who was sitting cross-legged on the floor.

I covered my head with the pale peach dupatta which one usually drapes around the shoulders, then entered the small well-lit chamber.

As I entered the room, he looked up and smiled, motioning for me to come and sit beside him. I did. He then continued with his activities, writing notes on a pad. On the table was a round pile of rupee notes. I sat with closed eyes, tasting the tangible silence in the atmosphere. I felt welcome and was grateful for that welcome which was so freely and sincerely given. I was completely comfortable just sitting there, doing absolutely nothing. Time passed in silence unmeasured. When he had finished the work at hand, he turned to me, looked into my eyes and smiled.

"You are comfortable?" he asked quietly.

"Yes."

"Then just sit – please sit here."

"I wanted to ask you a question."

"Yes?" he asked.

"What is the most important thing for gaining liberation; jivan-mukti; enlightenment?"

He smiled warmly; his eyes kindled with inner radiance. Without speaking, he looked straight ahead. Then he spoke: "Seva and simran – selfless service and taking the name of God."

"Taking the name of God – you mean meditating?" I asked softly.

"Meditation or singing – that is, kirtan, chanting devotional songs like bhajans, whatever you like that brings you closer to Him."

"Thank you," I murmured, bowing my head with joined palms touching the forehead. I did not move to go, but remained sitting in silence, pondering his words.

Then I said, "I want to serve others but I live alone. How can I give selfless service when most of the time I am alone?"

"What do you do?"

"I am a writer."

"What kinds of books you are writing?"

"Spiritual subjects related to knowledge of the inner self..." I replied.

"Then this is your service, this is your offering. This is the way for you to give of yourself."

It was quiet in the room. He returned to his work. Not sure whether to stay or go, I shuffled in my position, as if preparing to leave. He turned to me and motioned for me to stay; an indescribable gentleness flowed in fullness from his eyes. I sat beside him in silence for two more hours.

He asked if I was hungry. Then Jasmine, his secretary, brought a tray of hot sweet milk and sweets and we ate together like friends. Before I left, he said simply, "Come again."

The following morning, I bathed again in the sulfur springs. After meditating, I ascended the stairs to the inner shrine. The priest was chanting the sacred texts of the Guru Granth Sahib. I learned that the chanting continued from early in the morning until sunset every day.

So that is why the atmosphere here is so sublime!! I thought. I covered my head and entered the wide carpeted hall. The gold streamers crisscrossing the ceiling glittered in the rays of the morning sun. The chanting seemed to bathe the air with a greater although invisible light. To enter the hall felt akin to entering the inner sanctuary of the human heart. The hall was empty except for the priest, the kind bearded man who sat beside the bowl of divine pudding.

A lady was sitting to the left of him. I recognized her face. She was the same lady who had knelt before Baba Ramji in the temple the day before. She wore a large beige shawl draped around her shoulders. She was following the chanting of the sacred text in the scripture which lay open before her.

Time was borne aloft on the silver wings of a hidden world deep within this one and yet far beyond it, far beyond the boundaries of matter. There was nothing I had to do, nothing to accomplish, no meetings to attend, no time schedules to keep. I dwelt in a region of pure freedom, swimming in the ocean of prayer as its waves carried me out, out, out, farther than the mind could follow.

After the midday meal, I decided to take a stroll outside to the bridge which joined the two halves of the gurudwara. All along the ramparts of the bridge, colorful flags waved in the wind and beneath the stone walkway, the Parvati River swirled, gushing, frothing, foaming, dancing in undulating rapture round smooth rocks, then heaving, swelling, rising, cascading endlessly forward, upward toward translucent skies vibrating in wonder. Standing above the teeming waves, I could feel the magnetic energy rise in the sky. It was as if the divine presence was immanent in everything.

Baba Ramji's door was ajar again in the afternoon. I stood hesitating outside for several minutes, then entered and sat beside him. He welcomed me with a smile. Devotees came and went. Some bowed and placed a few rupees on the table. He gave them a bag of sugar candy. Others came with questions or to share news; then there was a soft banter in Hindi. His eyes sparkled as he laughed and chatted with the parents that often accompanied their children. After some time, he turned to me and said, "When we are sleeping, the soul is in the heart. In dreams, the soul is in the throat. When we are awake, the soul is in the eyes. In the state of pure consciousness, the soul is in the third eye."

I listened to his words as he continued speaking, "We should not desire to remain in the pure consciousness. Life is to be enjoyed. We are meant to serve others, and life is a celebration. We are to sing and dance in love of God, not just sit in meditation. God wants us to be happy in our lives." He returned to the papers on his desk. After some time, he turned to me and asked, "What do you do here in India?"

"I am working on a book; I hope to finish it in India."

He opened a wide, flat hardcover book which lay on a shelf behind him. "Then read this. You may include this in your book."

I opened the book and saw that it was full of comments of the visitors who had come to the gurudwara.

I slowly read the handwritten notes:

It is indeed a blessing to have a place like this where God is honored and human beings are served. Serving humanity is the greatest "puja" to God and I am happy to have found such a place on the high mountains. I am honored by the hospitality these brothers have showered on me. With all my heart I wish this friendliness and this warmth will remain forever between the different religions and communities of this country. May God bless this institution with long life and prosperity. Coming from the southernmost part of India, Kerala, I am happy that my country and my people still value our tradition of brotherhood of all people.

Another person wrote: *God is a tree. All religions are its branches. Respect of any religion is the respect of God.*

And: *The wonder of the hot springs is equaled by the wonder of selfless service.*

And: *Such places represent ancient and real India... Once we remember that God is love, it will become easier for us all to emulate what is being done here in this temple – fostering fellowship and understanding, respecting people's differences yet seeing the universal essence that is within us all...*

Echoes of praise, like a bellowing chorus bouncing against the walls of an endless tunnel, resounded on each page. I added a few lines: *May the generosity of spirit that I have experienced here spread to the whole world family and bless the world with peace.*

The lady who had knelt in front of Baba Ramji in the main hall now entered the room. She was incredibly beautiful, tall and stately. Her oval-shaped face was reminiscent of a deer. Her features spoke of nobility, poise and grace. Her smooth skin was golden brown, her eyes dark and shining. She wore a large camel-colored shawl draped gracefully over her head and shoulders. Like a swan gliding down to the calm surface of a lake, she again bowed her head at Baba Ramji's feet, her forehead touching the floor. An air of serenity surrounded her like a pale pink halo. When she saw me, she smiled. I returned the smile. As we gazed at each other, it was as if the veil of time dissolved, and we became one.

Baba Ramji looked at me, then he said a few words to her in Hindi and she responded, nodding her head in agreement. Then she slowly reached out and offered me her hand. I placed my hand in hers and she held it to her heart and looked deeply into my eyes for a long time. A fountain of pure love flowed over us, and all I know is that at that moment I felt truly loved, truly nourished, truly appreciated and truly blessed.

"We have been together many, many times," she said, still holding my hand very gently in hers. "It is wonderful that you have come, that we could meet again. I am so happy to be here with you." Her voice was deep and resonant like a caress.

Tears welled up in my eyes. When had I last experienced a love so freely given? My whole life seemed to unravel like a scroll before her inner vision. It was as if all the pain, sorrow, frustration, disappointment and trials of life since we last met – in some distant past lifetime – were all understood, empathized with and transmuted in the brimming ocean of love flowing from her heart to mine.

Yes, it's true what they say. LOVE CAN HEAL, I thought quietly as I gratefully acknowledged and returned her love.

Baba Ramji just sat silently watching with a smile.

"You must come and spend the night here with us in the gurudwara," she said. "Stay here until you leave. Please come. Is it alright, Guruji?"

"Yes, of course." Baba Ramji seemed pleased. "We can prepare a nice room for you upstairs."

"No – downstairs. She can sleep with all of us together. Not alone."

"As you wish," Baba Ramji replied.

I moved my belongings to the gurudwara that evening, and said goodbye to Klaus who was returning to Manali. I learned that the lady who had invited me was called Vasundhara Auntie. She lived in Chandigarh in the Punjab with her husband who was in the Indian army. In India, "auntie" is an endearing term used for elderly friends who aren't part of one's immediate family. She had just arrived to spend a few weeks in Manikaran. She was known and respected by everyone in the gurudwara. I went with her to a room in the basement where all the ladies who had pledged their lives to the gurudwara slept. These ladies wore only saffron-colored clothes, a traditional color worn by those in India who have renounced the world.

Just outside the window, the waves of the river could be heard crashing against the white stone walls. We slept, with seven other ladies, on mats on the floor. One of them whispered to me, "Vasundhara Auntie is a very pious lady. She is very generous, she gives to the poor." Vasundhara slept next to me. I felt intertwined in a wholeness that transcended reason or the thought of bodily comforts. We were united in a love so simple as not to need words, a love without boundaries of language or culture. This love, as simple as breathing, enabled us to experience life as it truly is, one whole.

Vasundhara and I spent most of the following day together, re-enlivening our friendship after lifetimes apart. As we sat side by side on the cotton rugs spread out on the stone floor, she told me about her family. Both her son and daughter had emigrated to Canada. For six months each year, she went to Canada to be with them. Her daughter, a law student, had just had her first child, and Vasundhara was planning to care for the child while her daughter studied for her exams.

"She is a jewel, my daughter," Vasundhara said smiling. "We are very close."

"Do you like living in Canada?" I asked.

"Yes, it is a beautiful country. But I love India. India is my home. I could not stay anywhere else."

"I know how you feel. It feels like home for me too even though I was born in America. The first time I came to India ten years ago, it felt like coming home after so many years in exile."

"You must come and stay with me in Chandigarh for a few days. I will take care of you. I will give you so many things. I have a very comfortable house, everything I could want. But I like to come here and just live simply like these ladies who have almost nothing." She pointed to the seven ladies who sat in a circle on the floor chopping up vegetables for lunch. "They have given me a very nice room upstairs, but I don't want to stay there. I don't like to sleep alone. I want to be simple while I am here. I come every year for a few weeks, sometimes longer."

In the morning, I stood outside on the balcony watching the foaming waves crash against the white stone walls. Jasmine came and stood beside me. The long saffron scarf covering her hair lent her an ethereal air.

"Namaste" she said softly.

"Namaste."

"Why don't you come and live here with us?" she said very quietly.

"I would love to, but my destiny is – well, um, I - I - I cannot stay. You are very lucky. It is a great blessing to be in a place like this... How long have you been here?"

"Eight years." She paused. "I do not think of time anymore – I just enjoy."

"What if one day you decide you want to marry? Then what do you do?" I asked.

"We are free to go. If we decide to marry, Guruji takes care of everything for us. The entire wedding is paid for by the ashram. It is alright. Some ladies stay a few years, then they marry. I will stay my whole life."

"You are serving Baba Ramji?"

"Yes, for three years now I have been his secretary. He is like God to me. In India, the Guru is like God, the same. By serving the Guru, we reach God."

That afternoon, I was due to board the bus to New Delhi. I reluctantly packed my suitcase. Vasundhara Auntie and I ate lunch together. We spoke little. Words seemed extraneous. They could neither express the feelings that stirred within us then, nor was there anything to add that had not already been said. The golden thread between our hearts quivered, shimmering in the stillness.

Then the coolie arrived to carry my bags to the bus depot. Strapping the bags to his back with a wide and worn brown rope, he bent over, hoisted them up and began the long, uphill march across the bridge and up the steep dirt road. My body followed close on his heels.

However, my heart, mind and soul still lingered in the gurudwara, still hovered round the hall of the inner sanctuary, still dwelt with Vasundhara. I did not want to go. My body stepped up onto the gray, rattling bus, but I did not see anything because my eyes were blurred with tears. I turned my head to the window so that the person sitting next to me would not notice the tears streaming down my face.

The bus pulled out, roaring up the rocky path toward Mandi where I would catch the evening bus to Delhi. The forests above the churning river glided by in a nebulous array while I tried unsuccessfully to check the sobs rising from my throat. Soundlessly, tears streamed down my face and neck, soaking the pale yellow gossamer scarf I was wearing; they flowed ceaselessly as the distance increased between Manikaran and the body.

I cannot bear to leave. I cannot bear to leave! Never in my life have I known the love I experienced here. Oh why, why do I have to go? It is like falling from heaven back to earth. Take me back! Oh take me back! Don't force me to live in the world. Mother – Divine Mother – I don't want to leave your embrace! The world is too hard, too harsh, too cruel. I cannot bear to live outside Your Divine Embrace! Ma! Ma!

I was drowned in anguish as the bus hurtled on. One or two people on the bus stared at me curiously as I wiped away the onrushing tide of tears. But I was not concerned. I was only aware of the intense agony of leaving the divine nest and being flung again into the great unknown.

Chapter Eleven

As the bus wound its way toward Delhi, I bade farewell to the Himalayas which afforded silent protection. Without ever announcing their presence, the mountains were always there, changeless in their affection, ready to aid the hungering souls desirous of liberation. In those sacred mountains, even the most tenuous illusions crumbled to dust in the presence of those towering waves of silence reaching heavenward. The long descent to the plains was like returning to a storm-tossed world from the heights of a more-sheltered and humane existence. I bade the Himalayas goodbye as we rolled down, down, down to the flat plains of Haryana far below.

The trip was long and arduous, but I was gladdened by the thought of seeing Tashi. The seat next to mine was empty, so I was able to curl up on two seats and get a bit of rest.

We arrived in the steaming heat of the city at eight o'clock in the morning. The city aroused, but not yet fully awake, crawled into raucous activity, blinking its eyes almost painfully at the dazzling white light. Already the traffic had reared its gray head, eschewing smoke from its lungs and forcefully blowing its nose to clear the passageways of dust and dirt, all to no avail, for Delhi was old and sick like New York and Tokyo. It was on the list of the three most polluted cities in the world.

Still, there was a beauty about the royal path to Janpath road. The gardens were in bloom and the neat trim lawns of varied green flashing by as we drove past were a delight to the eye. My heart rejoiced as the bus turned the corner and came to a shrieking halt in front of a tall white concrete building, the last stop on the journey. I stretched my back in an arch and filed into the aisle with the other bleary-eyed passengers.

There were many rickshaws waiting eagerly outside, but it took almost half an hour to find a driver who was willing to charge a fair price for the trip to South Delhi. However I was determined and before long I was on the way to the Buddhist Center where dear Lama Tashi would be waiting.

I was anxious on the surface and yet calm deep within about our impending meeting. How did he feel now? We hadn't seen each other for three weeks and yet time was so meaningless. It might have been but a day. But how was it for him? Were his feelings still strong or had they waned like the shrinking moon? Would I be viewed as a distraction in his life or would he open his heart to mine in joy?

Thoughts raced past with the wheels of the rickshaw as we sped by the moving vehicles while stationary cows aimlessly sat in the middle of the road, and the colorfully attired pedestrians on their way to work waited for buses or rickshaws.

It was nearly nine o'clock. The same friendly Nepalese man opened the gate who had closed it behind me three weeks before. He smiled warmly, bowing his head. I greeted him and thanked him as he took my bags out of the rickshaw into the empty lobby of the World Buddhist Center. Quietly removing my sandals, I ascended the polished wood staircase to the sitting room. My heart began pounding as my foot touched the last step. As I turned to go in, Tashi came out of the dining room. He stopped in the doorway. Neither one of us spoke. Our feelings overflowed in silence from our hearts into our eyes.

"Ah, Shantila Martin, you have come," he said softly. "You will take tea?"

I couldn't speak. All I wanted was to sit beside him, to feel the quiet strength of his presence, to let the deep silence of his being fill the space between us until we no longer recognized ourselves as two separate entities.

"Yes – I mean, just water is fine," I murmured.

"Please sit down – you must be tired," he said, motioning for me to sit on the divan in the sitting room.

I sat facing the statue of the Tibetan Buddha that I had

admired so much on my first visit. Tashi went to the kitchen and returned with a stainless-steel pitcher of water and a glass which he placed before me. Then he sat down.

There are moments in one's life when words only clutter the innocent realm of pure emotion. Sometimes it is better to just witness the flowing waves that gather rippling round the rocks and eddies in the river of life... Sometimes it is enough just to know that silence contains its own language. But to hear and heed this inner language one must put the thinking mind to rest. This was one of those moments.

Tashi leaned forward on the divan and I felt his touch though we did not touch. He opened his lips as if to speak. No sound came forth, yet I heard the voiceless voice of his soul echo in the stillness. We sat wed to silence for some time and as ordained by the gods, no one entered that space during our communion.

Then suddenly the moment ended. The wooden door adjacent to the sitting room opened and the Japanese monk called Tashi's name and he was gone. Kalsang entered and showed me to my room. I rested there until noon.

When I entered the dining room for lunch, a lady came to sit beside me. She had a boy of about five years old with her.

"Hello," I said.

"Jullay," she replied.

"Jullay," I repeated. Tashi had told me that the word "jullay" was used to say hello and goodbye in Tibetan. "Are you from Ladakh?' I asked her.

"Yes. Have you been to Ladakh?"

"No," I answered, admiring her son, who was cheerful and composed at the same time. They both had clear, bright eyes and shining skin. They looked strong and healthy.

"My name is Rinchen. I am a school teacher. I live in Nubra Valley. My son," she stroked her son's head, "is in school in Delhi. I came to visit him."

"Don't they have schools in Nubra Valley?" I asked her.

"Yes, but education is better here. He is my only son. I have three daughters. I want my son to have a good education. If you come to Ladakh, please come to visit me. The road to Nubra was closed to tourists, but it is open now. You can stay in my house." She smiled warmly.

The lamas took their seats around the table. Tashi was not there but it was as if nature orchestrated that the place opposite me be left vacant. None of the other monks took that seat. Perhaps, being lamas, they intuited the golden thread that joined our hearts. When Tashi came in and took the seat opposite me, my heart rose up to greet him. My heart swelled as the tide rises beneath the moon and stars. When the waves subsided, I felt completely content and settled inside. He smiled discreetly at me as he bowed his head in prayer before beginning the meal. Without looking up, I appreciated his every movement, so filled with grace were his hands, long and slender with infinitely perceptive fingertips. His arms, too, were long like mine, yet very strong. His was a silent strength that didn't blare out, a natural fullness in the curves of his muscles and the roundness of his chest, like the arching curve of a sacred mountain and the graceful lines of the deodar trees that emitted the sweet fragrance of spirituality. The meal was enriched by his presence. I did not want it to end.

Rinchen and her son and the three other lamas left us sitting alone at the long dining-room table. The bright afternoon sun lit up the dark mahogany surface.

"How long you will stay here?" Tashi asked.

"One week," I answered.

"Short time. You enjoy Manali?"

"Yes, I love the forests. But I must tell you about Manikaran. Have you been to Manikaran?"

"No. What is that place?" Tashi asked.

"It is so incredible. There are boiling-hot springs rising from the ground. The river is flowing so fast and steam rises from the side of the river. In the Sikh gurudwara, the atmosphere is divine. They feed all the people, everyone and anyone that comes, all day long. They serve everyone with such love and devotion. I never knew a place like that existed. It was so beautiful to see."

Tashi did not say anything, he just looked at me. Then he nodded his head. "The Sikh religion is a good religion. There is a gurudwara in my village in Ladakh. There they also feed the poor people and people can stay there without payment. The Sikhs are very good people."

"Would you like to see some of the photos?" I asked him.

"It's alright – if you want. You have them with you?"

"In my room upstairs."

"Then, later, later... I will see them later. Take rest. I will go now." He got up to go. I followed him to the landing at the top of the stairs, and then he descended the steps to the monks' quarters.

I could not rest. I stared up at the ceiling in my room. Then flicked through the pages of my diary. Tomorrow I had the interview with Mr. Patel, the famous newspaper columnist. I jotted down some notes about the things I had to bring: poems, tanpura... But all I could think of was Tashi: *Why do we have to be separated? Will the gods consent to allow our paths to conjoin?* Questions flew like swallows in the wind through the wide-open fluttering pages of the mind.

The next morning I dressed carefully for the interview. Taking my new jade and cream-colored sari out of the closet, I redid the pleats at the waist three times until I got them perfect. Then I went to retrieve my tanpura from the room where it had been kept during my absence. I selected ten poems and put them in my bag. I hired a rickshaw and set off to Mr. Patel's house. It was a modern terraced apartment complex built in a semi-circle around a trim, well-kept garden. I rang the bell and a female voice answered on the intercom.

"Who is it?"

"My name is Shantila Martin. I have an appointment with Mr. Patel for an interview."

The buzzer sounded and I pushed open the heavy outside door. Then I rang the bell.

A very thin elderly lady opened the door. She was dressed in a gray silk Punjabi.

"Come in. Mr. Patel is in there," she said softly, directing me to the living room. Then she went away.

Mr. Patel sat slouched in a big armchair near a white marble mantelpiece. He was an elderly man with a small round figure, and a gray beard and mustache.

"Come in, Miss Martin. It is nice to see you." He extended his hand and shook mine warmly. "Ah, you have brought an instrument! You will play on it for me. I love music. Yes and poetry! You said you were a poet? Love poems, is that it?" he asked, leaning forward to get a closer look at me.

"Mrs. Martin, you look just like an Indian!" he exclaimed, leaning back in his chair and chuckling. His protruding belly shook under the large silk shirt.

"It is Miss Martin. I'm not married," I said quietly. *So this is the great Mr. Patel!* I thought to myself. *So kind, so gentle, so unassuming!*

"Not married? How can that be? You are very attractive. You have beautiful eyes. You have spiritual eyes. Yes, that's it. Surely you must have had many proposals, haven't you?"

"I had some – yes," I said, a little embarrassed. I had not expected him to ask me about my private life.

"Now then, what are you here for? Some book you want me to help you sell? I am always being asked by new authors to review their books. OK. What is yours about? Tell me in a few sentences." He reluctantly put on his spectacles, and picked up a pen and a notepad.

"Creativity – the creative process in man...and perception. The source of creativity is the deepest level of life; it is a field of pure intelligence." I gestured with my hands as I tried to describe the deepest, most abstract level of life. Mr. Patel seemed to enjoy the movements. I thought he was following my train of thought when suddenly he interrupted me.

"Wait! This sounds like a description of God. Is pure intelligence the same as God? I am an atheist. I don't believe in God." He leaned forward and removed his spectacles. Then he said, "Can you prove to me that God exists?"

I was stunned. As the sunlight streamed in through the white lace curtains, I searched for the right words.

"You're right. The deepest level of life IS divine; it is infinitely pure, whole and all-good. This is what pure consciousness or pure intelligence is – a field of wholeness. This is what God is. Like pure intelligence, God is everywhere, in everything and in everyone. Pure intelligence is lively in every grain of creation." I paused.

"Have you experienced this – this, what you call pure intelligence or pure consciousness?" Mr. Patel asked, in a tone of genuine curiosity mixed with hopeful expectation.

"Yes, many times, sometimes more clearly – sometimes less clearly," I replied gently.

"And you are SURE God exists?"

"Yes. I am sure." I smiled and looked into his eyes. Then I said in a more quiet voice, "God is love."

A silence enveloped both of us then. I felt utterly relaxed, and intuitively I knew that he felt the same. It was as if an imaginary wall had dissolved and we were communicating on a deeper level.

"I'm not really an atheist. I'm an agnostic. Sometimes I believe, sometimes not. I would like to believe in God... What you said is beautiful... Now play for me. I want to hear you play." He slouched back in the cushions of the armchair and dangled his arms over the sides.

I took out my tanpura and placed it upright on my lap. Then

I took out the poems I had brought. I recited some poems about nature. At the end, I read a few love poems.

He clapped his hands. "I liked that last one! May I have a copy? I will print it."

I handed him the poem.

"Now I must return to my work, Miss Martin. It was very nice to have met you." He showed me the way out.

I was overjoyed when I left. I hired a rickshaw and went straight to Mr. Rao's office.

"Shantila. How are you?" Mr. Rao looked up from his desk as I walked in.

"Fantastic! The interview with Mr. Patel went great! It lasted for over one hour!" I said excitedly.

"One hour? You talked to him for one hour? All about your book?" he asked, looking very surprised.

"About my book and about other things. We spoke about God."

"About God?! With Mr. Patel?" Mr. Rao said in undisguised amazement.

"Yes, we had a good talk. He's a wonderful person – so kind and caring," I said.

"Hmmmm – yes. I've never met him," Mr. Rao said, clearing his throat.

Just then, a youngish man with a mustache, who was dressed smartly in a suit and tie, entered the office. He said something to Mr. Rao in Hindi and Mr. Rao nodded his head. Then the man walked out.

"My younger son," Mr. Rao said proudly. "He also works in the company."

"Oh, you have two sons?" I asked.

"Yes, but only one is married." He paused. Then he looked at me. His gaze moved slowly over my sari, over my arms and hands, and then to my face. Then with his head tilted to one side, he said, "How old are you, Shantila?"

I was shocked, then indignant and finally amused. "In my forties," I replied.

"Oh," he said in a surprised tone. He returned to the papers on his desk. "What more do you have to tell me?" he muttered without looking up.

"Would it be possible to have an – an advance payment?" I said hesitatingly.

"Advance payment? We don't give advances," he said flatly.

"I'm almost out of money. I didn't expect to have to be in India for so long."

"I'll think about it. I'll let you know. How would I get it to you?" Mr. Rao asked. There was a glint of concern in his eyes.

"One of the lamas can bring it when they go home for their holiday. They usually stop in Manali on their way to Ladakh."

"Alright, we'll see. Write to me from Manali and I'll consider it."

I returned to the Buddhist guest house. I was scheduled to leave Delhi in two days. Tashi was absorbed in a tedious paperwork project assigned to him by the Japanese monk. He was older than the other lamas and the task had been entrusted to him alone. We had had hardly any time together except for exchanging a few words at mealtime. In the late afternoon, I came and sat on the floor beside him as he stapled a pile of papers together. His eyes were downcast and a shadow veiled his features. He was far away and though I sat beside him, I could feel the distance. He had retreated deep within himself, and seemed to be brooding in his cave. Without speaking, he acknowledged my presence and continued working.

"Can I help you?" I asked, so softly that at first he did not hear me.

"What did you say?" he asked, looking up at me.

It was then I noticed the sadness in his eyes. *Oh, Tashi. Dearest Tashi!* my heart cried out in silence. *How I love you. What is it? Tell me, Tashi, what is troubling you?* But I only said, "Do you want me to help you?"

"No, it's OK. I am supposed to do it alone." He paused. "When will you go Manali?"

"The day after tomorrow."

"Very soon," he said, holding the bundle of papers poised momentarily in the air. He appeared lost in thought. "Have you any letter from your brother in America?"

"No, not yet, Tashi. No reply. Did you receive the list of Buddhist monasteries in America that I sent to you from Manali?"

"Yes, I got it. Thank you."

"Do you think it will help?" I asked quietly.

"I don't think so. I need an invitation letter from someone so my visa will be firm. I must go from here. The Japanese is getting very angry; some days he is shouting at us. I not feel good here. I must go from here soon. Maybe I not return after my holiday in July or August."

"You have a holiday in July?" I asked.

"Yes – one month. Two lamas go, two remain, then two more go to Ladakh for one month."

"When will you go to Ladakh?"

"In July, end July or August I think. If I get information from America, then I don't come back here. Just go to Ladakh for maybe two weeks, and then America or I may stay in the New Tibetan Colony with my friend until I go to America."

"I would like to visit Ladakh," I said quietly. The thought of being in Tashi's homeland with him filled my heart with joyous anticipation. I knew that Ladakh was called "The Last Shangri-La." It was a place remote enough to be unspoiled by the follies of modern technology and the subsequent pollution of the environment.

"Maybe you can come there, maybe we go together," Tashi said slowly. Then he lifted his head and smiled into my eyes. It was the first time in several days that our hearts met and touched and we both felt a simultaneous upsurge of happiness.

The next afternoon was intensely hot. All the lamas and servants retired to their rooms almost immediately after lunch. I now understood the logic behind the siesta which is so common in hot climates. Sleeping was the only way to survive the fierce heat; it was so debilitating. I lay on the bed with the fan swirling around above me. The cotton suit clung to my body. I decided to take a shower. Even the cold water was warm. As I lowered my head under the nozzle, the cool drops trickled through my hair. How deliciously welcome it felt! I threw my hair back, shaking water all around and like a thirsty camel finding an oasis in the desert, a sense of exhilaration rose unexpectedly.

I must see Tashi! The thought came uninvited. *I must.* I dressed carefully, choosing the soft gold Punjabi, his favorite color. Then I tiptoed down the stairs and slid open the glass door of the temple where the five golden Buddhas were enthroned on lotus petals. Tashi's narrow room was adjacent to the temple. I had to enter the temple to reach it. *I don't want to wake him,* I thought, sliding the glass door closed behind me. Then I saw a light in his room. I went to his door and knocked lightly.

"Yes?" His voice was gentle.

"It's me – Shantila."

"Come in," he said.

I opened the door. Tashi was sitting on his bed reading.

"Come. Sit down." He gestured with his right hand indicating that I should sit on the bed.

"I, uh, I – wanted to see how you, I mean, I—" I hesitated, feeling embarrassed.

He didn't answer.

"This is a nice bedspread," I said, pointing to the mandala design on the yellow and gold cotton bedspread.

He didn't answer. Instead he reached into a small wooden box beside his bed and took out a silver spoon inset with a pink coral stone.

"This is for you," he said, handing it to me. "You can use it when you are in England – for sugar."

I took it, not knowing how to respond to his words. "Thank you, it's beautiful," I said.

Then Tashi rummaged through a few more boxes and pulled out a mala, a necklace of round, shiny, black prayer beads. "These are for you," he said. "Prayer beads for when we make a sin. Then we pray for forgiveness with these beads. These are my beads," he said, holding up a string of small brown beads.

"Oh, thank you," I said, cradling the beads in my cupped palms. *I will keep them always*, I thought as I touched the beads to my forehead as a sign of respect. "Do they have any special effect on the body?" I asked, thinking of the rudraksha and tulsi beads I always wore as a protection against illness.

"No, no special effect – just for praying." We sat in silence side by side. The river of time glided by as we sat watching the invisible waves, motionless and yet moving on, carried by the tide.

"Do you have any photos of your family?" I asked.

"Photos – yes. I show you," Tashi replied, smiling.

He reached under the bed and took out three small photograph albums. "This is my family," he said, pointing to a photo of a lama standing in front of a Tibetan monastery. "He is my mother and my father. He is my Guru. I went there to Karnataka when I was ten years old. He took care of all the Ladakhi boys."

His mother and his father... I repeated his words in my mind as I gazed at the photos. Then I remembered Charlotte's words: *"They beat him in the monastery..."* But the lama in the photo looked kind and wise.

"Was he strict?"

"Strict?" He didn't understand the word at first. Then he grasped it and replied, "Sometimes strict, sometimes..." He stroked the air with his hand as if caressing someone.

"Sometimes gentle," I added.

"Yes." He flicked open the pages, one after the other. On every page were photos of lamas. Some were photos of Karnataka, some of his pilgrimage to Bodhgaya and Varanasi, and some photos were of Sarnath and Rewalsar Lake near Mandi. He had visited all the sacred Buddhist places of pilgrimage in India. There was not a single photo of his earthly mother or father or any other of his blood relations, except for one brother who had been sent to the monastery with Tashi, but who had given up his robes and returned to the world.

"He is no more a lama," Tashi said when I asked about him.

As I sat there, I felt the hopes for our life together crumble and fade. *This is his life, his destiny.* In silence I knew it. When I was finally able to speak, I softly said, "I feel my life is the same as yours, Tashi. Even though I am not in a monastery, I feel our lives are the same. The path we are on is the same path. I want enlightenment more than anything else." I continued to sit there though inwardly I knew it was time to go. Then a suppressed sob rose in my throat and I murmured, "When I return to England, will you write to me?"

He shifted as if he was becoming uncomfortable. "Give me your address, and then I will write."

"I will."

"Now go – it is better." His voice was quiet but firm.

I turned and walked out leaving my dreams suspended in mid-air.

The following day was our last before the journey to Manali. In the morning, the dining room was empty. As I walked in, I saw Tashi on the balcony, leaning over the railing, peering into the courtyard down below. I wanted to go and stand beside him, but the cook walked in and looked at him strangely. I took two steps forward and then I could go no further. My feet were riveted to the spot. Just as I stopped, Tashi turned around, saw me and walked quietly out of the room. He was obviously disturbed. Perhaps his heart was in turmoil. Perhaps I was to blame; I didn't know.

No matter how close two people are, it is impossible to enter another person's thoughts or feelings. The door to the inner sanctuary is guarded. Only God can enter, can know all. I have often found that if I try to guess the reason for someone's actions, especially someone I love, I tend to misconstrue it due to my own doubts and fears. The quivering of the small ego clouds the pure seeing into the spirit of things.

Later, as I sat alone in the dining room reading a book on Buddhist philosophy, Tashi walked in and turned on the fan above me.

"It's too hot," he said and left the room.

A tear trickled down my cheek, but I ignored it and continued reading. The passage said:

... Holding the visualization of our root master in enlightening form clearly before us, we request that he come and inspire us to achieve actual attainments. O my glorious and precious root teacher, come take your lotus and moon seat placed here upon my head. Take care of me always through your bountiful kindness and bestow on me please the actual attainments of your enlightening body, speech and mind...

The master in front accepts and radiates inspiration in the form of rays of light. These enter our heart and, filling our body, eliminate the darkness of unreceptive attitudes...

I prostrate before you, O (my root mentor) complete amalgam of every source of safe direction. Like the precious, clear evolved, you are my peerless teacher; like the precious hallowed measures, my peerless protector; like the precious intent community, you are my peerless guide.

I present you all offerings, both these set before me and those sent from my mind... I dedicate my own and others' positive deeds for the greatest purified growth (of all limited beings).

Yes, what I said to Tashi is true. I reflected. *Our lives are the same. I recognize myself in him. Something in him calls awake my inner being.*

I want to run into his arms but this is part of the illusion. This I know, and yet the feeling continues... We have met and our hearts have commingled in the heart of God where the body is as wind, a golden breath on the lake of pure consciousness. There, in the shrine of the Infinite Being, there are no arms or legs or bodies to touch. There is only one eternal melody shimmering in the ocean of pure love.

The next day, at twilight, we stood together on the doorstep of the Buddhist Center, awaiting the rickshaw which was to take me to the bus. Tashi spoke to me.

He said, "Shantila, I feel you should go to Dharamsala, where the Dalai Lama is. Become a nun. Nuns and monks, they live separately, but the study is the same. In two or three years, you will be able to speak and read Tibetan. You will be happy there." A gentle light shone in his eyes as he gazed long at my face.

I didn't answer. I just looked into his eyes for a long time. I couldn't speak. Finally I bent my head as the tears began silently falling.

Then the gatekeeper's footsteps were at the door. He looked embarrassed when he saw us and gingerly reached for my bags, hurrying back outside as fast as he could.

"I will think about what you said," I whispered.

"Write to me." Tashi's voice was so faint, as soft as a caress.

"I will."

"You must go now or you will miss the bus. Jullay," he said, opening the door. We stepped out into the sunshine together.

The bags were already crammed into the three wheeler. As I stepped in, Tashi arranged a fair price with the driver.

"He asked for fifty, but I got for forty," he said, smiling.

"Thank you, Tashi."

The rickshaw zoomed forward. I lifted the flap behind my head in order to see him once more. We waved to each other. Then I saw him turn to go back into the temple. Then the river of New Delhi flowed between us, carrying me further and further away, upstream, up, up, up to the high mountains. Impulsively, I sought to stem the onrushing tide, to turn back, to resist the momentum of destiny, but I knew it could not be done. Inwardly, I knew all was as it was meant to be. I HAD to keep going. By the time the bus pulled out, leaving the heat of the city in the distance, I was at peace.

As we rolled through town after town under the cover of darkness, the voice of the inner self echoed in the hollow cavern of my heart:

Did not the same Divine Being who fashioned the sun, the moon and the stars and the wide, flowering earth, and soaring mountain glades, and silver streams descending like songs from the high hills – also design the intricate interwoven pattern of my life? And does He not know what will bring me most happiness and the deepest peace and fulfillment in life? And is He not all-good, and infinitely compassionate and merciful? Like a Father-Mother of all beings, HE-She is guiding life to perfection. THY Will Be Done! Surely, Thou knowest what is best for me! O make me Thy instrument, O Lord. Make me an instrument of Thy peace. Where there is suffering that I may bring joy, where there is darkness that I may bring light, where there is despair, that I may bring hope, where there is doubt that I may bring faith.

The familiar words of the prayer of Saint Francis watered the desert of loneliness which threatened to engulf me, lighting a flame which burned in stillness at the hidden altar throughout the long night which had yet to be traversed.

Chapter Twelve

The sun shone, illuminating the lavender hills on the stage of dawn. The song of morning awakening created a chorus of birdsong more perfect than any instrument. The hands of God strummed the lute of infinity and the melody sparkled like morning dew on the rich green carpet of grass woven on the blue-gray mountainside.

"Manali! Ah, Manali, Manali, I'm back!" It was with a light heart that I stepped onto the Himalayan soil once more. This time I had arranged to live with Margrit's Iranian friends. They had rented a two-bedroom house up in the mountains, but were content to live in only one room. They had agreed to rent the other room to me. The place was high up on the mountainside near a fast-flowing stream. The stream ran down to the flat plain on which stood a Tibetan Buddhist monastery. I quickly engaged a rickshaw to take us to the foot of the mountain path, and a coolie to carry my baggage up.

The rickshaw chugged along on the bumpy road from the crowded bus station through the narrow winding lanes leading to the Tibetan colony. Here, many of the shops were mere storefronts made of wood. In front of the shops were tables on which all kinds of different items were displayed from Tibetan woolens and jewelry to shawls and even footwear. Some items, like skirts and trousers, hung from hooks on the door. Because each shop was so small, every inch of space had to be put to good use.

Most of the Tibetan women were slender, of medium height with smooth fair skin and straight hair tied behind their ears. They had wide cheekbones and slightly slanted, smiling eyes. Some women were wearing the traditional Tibetan dress. The married ladies also wore aprons.

Across from the stream stood the Tibetan monastery, a silent symbol of a life apart. It was painted white and maroon and had a bright yellow roof. At the entrance were two white pillars with round stupa-shaped domes on top. Above the monastery, pastel-colored prayer flags flew in a row in the wind. It looked exactly like the photograph Tashi had shown me of the monastery or gompa in Karnataka where he had lived for ten years.

The coolie lifted my bags out of the rickshaw and strapped them to his back. He was a young fellow with a sweet smile. When he saw me take a small bag which was very heavy, he shook his head as if to say: *Let me do it. I can manage that as well.* He smiled as he took the bag from my hand. I was in awe of his strength. He strode forward with quick, sure steps, pointing with his hand to ascertain that the direction was correct.

At the foot of the mountain, a herd of gray donkeys waited while two men piled red bricks into burlap sacks and hung them across their backs. The donkeys came to drink water from the stream before beginning their arduous task. Using donkeys was the only way to transport the materials needed to build a house on the heights. The coolie and I began our ascent up the steep hill.

It was early in the morning and the mountains were wrapped in a soft, gray mist which served to shield us from the heat. The mountain path curved straight up at a ninety-degree angle. I had to walk slowly and carefully to keep from sliding backwards on the sandy dirt road. The walk was grueling. Beside us, the stream flowed over rocks and patches of green grass dotted with white and yellow wildflowers in the midst of piles of rotting garbage thrown haphazardly, in profusion, along the path. An endless array of plastic bags, in every imaginable color, spilled forth litter which floated downstream or sunk into the mud on the edge of the once-clear stream. Like a contagious sore, the garbage spread itself shamelessly out along the rocks and eddies. I held my breath as we passed a particularly sullied patch of earth; but the coolie simply walked on, as if it was all part of life. Every now and then, he looked at me and smiled.

The house of the Iranians was small, square and made of

concrete. In front were two doors. Neda came out to greet me. She had long thick auburn hair which was fastened behind her ears with shiny metal hair clips. With her tight blue jeans and vibrant red lipstick, one would not have guessed she was a Muslim.

"Welcome! Welcome!" she said, waving her hand above her head as she came up the path to meet me. "Are you tired? It's a steep path, isn't it?"

I paid the coolie. Then she showed me to my room. The first thing I noticed when she opened the door was the smell.

"Oh," I said, "what is that smell?"

"Don't worry," Neda replied with a smile. "It's only the concrete. The house was just built, and it hasn't been aired for some time. We can open the windows now."

She undid the latch over the windows and a fresh breeze blew in. I breathed a sigh of relief. The walls were painted yellow and there was a wooden bed in the middle, and a pine wardrobe which Neda used for her clothes. Other than that, it was empty. There were no curtains, but I was grateful for the woven cotton mats on the cold concrete floor. They had asked for one thousand rupees per month and I was allowed to share their kitchen. I also met her husband Hamid and their son Firoz.

They had emigrated to India over one year ago. At first, they had stayed in Hyderabad, but found the heat too oppressive. Hamid had been raised in the mountainous region of Iran, so they decided to try to find a place in the Himalayas.

Hamid, who was thirty-six years, had accumulated enough money to live self-sufficiently in India for several years. He had earned the money through much hard work and exceedingly long hours in the import-export business in Tehran. He had left his homeland because of the fanatical political leaders who were training terrorists. He had no intention of returning until the present government was overthrown.

Neda would have preferred to live in Iran. But she accepted it as her wifely duty to obey her husband and to follow wherever he led her. Neda, who was twenty-five years old, was trained as a midwife. She confided in me that she never attended the mosque even in Iran. She would have nothing to do with any organized form of religion. She simply desired to live in the way she wanted, without any interference or restrictions on her dress, lifestyle or beliefs. In India, she finally had the freedom she wanted.

I only expected to stay for one month and then to go to Ladakh with Tashi. I was looking forward to visiting the Tibetan Buddhist monastery that so closely resembled the place in Karnataka where Tashi had lived. A few days later, on the way home from the vegetable market, I ventured across the threshold of the Tibetan monastery. I felt elated as I drew nearer to Tashi's world, and his tradition.

Entering the gateway, I passed through a courtyard with a large white stupa to the left and on the opposite side a small garden with colorful flowers arranged around its borders. From the outer courtyard, I passed through two large arched doors into an inner courtyard. On the right side of the courtyard stood the temple. Looking up, I saw the lamas' living quarters arranged in a square on three levels. Beside the stone steps leading into the temple was a sign which said: Temple Open: 6 am - 7 pm. Please leave your shoes here.

I placed my shoes neatly by the bottom step. Then touching the step with my right hand as a sign of respect, I entered the temple. The heavy wooden doors at the entrance were painted a rich red hue embroidered with a black and gold design. The temple was carved of wood and evoked a sensation of entering a living, breathing space as wooden dwellings have the capacity to do. An invisible curtain fell on the outside world as the divine space unfolded its treasures before my awestruck gaze. It was square with four round pillars, two on either side, draped with turquoise and gold cloth and painted red. The ceiling was azure blue with red beams. Colorful murals were painted on the walls depicting the Buddha and bodhisattvas and great lamas in the Tibetan lineage. The feeling of inner liveliness was magnified a hundredfold by the glittering statues of the Tibetan deities enthroned on the altar. As one entered the inner sanctuary of the temple, one immediately came within the aura of their benevolently smiling gaze. Slowly moving toward the altar, I came to stand before a large golden statue of Lord Buddha, draped with white silk scarves. On either side of the Buddha were statues revered in the Buddhist tradition. Most majestic of all was the statue of the Buddha of compassion, the patron deity of Tibet, called Avalokateshwara. Rays of light emanated from him in the shape of a golden lotus. He is a symbol of infinity and is said to have a thousand heads and a thousand arms. Indeed, the statue had many heads and many arms. His expression was one of benevolent watchfulness. In His cupped palms, he held a shining azure object that looked to me like he was cradling the world with infinite compassion.

I had only intended to stay for a few minutes just to have a look inside. But now it was hard to leave. *I want to meditate here*, I thought. I sat cross-legged on one of the maroon mats and closed my eyes and was immediately enveloped in a sweet and nourishing nest of deep silence. The inner space of the temple was already saturated with silence. It was only a matter of bathing in the ocean of peace already present. The body seemed to dissolve in a soundless stream. Time disappeared. All that remained was bliss.

Then I heard the shuffle of bare feet on the floor and the rustle of robes close by. The room was filling up! But I did not move or open my eyes. It would have required too much effort. All sounds then ceased. Time seemed to stand still.

And then the prayers of the lamas emerged. Like an echo resounding from within a deep cave carved out of the primordial elements of earth, wind and fire, interlacing melodies of sound wove in and out of each other creating a tapestry of pure harmony. The voices of the lamas rose and fell in waves and as they chanted, I was carried out, out, out – far beyond the limits of time and space. The low, deep and warm sound of their voices was infinitely soothing to my heart. The chanting of the prayers continued for a long time. I heard the ringing of bells and the beating of drums all around me. I was sitting in the midst of the lamas of the Tibetan monastery! Opening one eye slightly, I saw that there were lamas sitting on the maroon mat in front of me, beside me and also behind me. I didn't dare to get up or move while the prayers were being sung; it felt too awkward. I slowly opened my eyes, and saw that the lamas were sitting facing each other. They all wore maroon robes, and had shaved heads; most were aged. The lama opposite me was swaying back and forth in rhythm with the prayers as he bent over the unbound pages of the long, horizontal prayer book in front of him. I noticed several prayer books stacked on the window ledge in long narrow boxes, wrapped in bright yellow cloth and tied with a red string.

Photographs of His Holiness the Dalai Lama, the spiritual head of the Buddhist order, and the Panchen Lama, another high lama, were placed on separate altars. The altars were adorned with white silk scarves, which, I realized, were like the flower garlands offered to the deities. A row of round brass bowls filled with water stood in front of the main altar, fourteen on the lower and fourteen on the upper ledge. I had read that these are emptied and refilled everyday as an offering to the deities.

After what seemed like an hour, I shifted my position to increase the circulation in my legs and then as discreetly as possible, lifted up my knapsack and tiptoed out of the temple. I couldn't wait to return the next day.

The following afternoon, I went to the post office to check the mail. Would there be a letter from Tashi? I wondered. Now that I had visited the gompa in Manali, I understood why Tashi was so unhappy in the Buddhist Center in New Delhi. The atmosphere in the two places was totally different. The peaceful atmosphere in the center in New Delhi could not compare to the lively deep silence in the temple here. And here, in Manali, the prayers were sung in the Tibetan language, Tashi's mother tongue! Of course, he missed this life. Even I, as a stranger to the Tibetan Buddhist tradition, felt an unmistakable pull.

When I arrived at the post office, I found a letter from Mr. Rao. Opening the envelope, I saw a newspaper clipping. I hurriedly unfolded it. It was the article by Mr. Patel! In the center of the page was a photograph of me playing the tanpura. I started laughing. The article was sweet and funny, and at the end of it was the love poem he had liked the best:

I will catch rainbows if you promise to catch the wind for me
if you promise to hold it until I may come
until I may breathe of that world and drink of that sea
and be able to see the splendor of this earth
and the splendor of your face clothed in the sun's light
naked as the dawning fires
I will catch rainbows if you promise to catch the silence of wakening
and hold it before the waters until I may see it reflected
in the pathways of my soul.

I was so happy that I decided to celebrate by going to the sweetshop around the corner. I stopped in front of the glass case containing all the mouthwatering delicacies, and then the long deliberation began. I finally chose the gulab jamuns – the sweet round balls soaked in rose syrup. I went in, sat down and opened the letter from Mr. Rao. He was pleased with the article and sent his best regards.

On the way home, I crossed the threshold of the temple again. This time I was greeted at the entrance by a youthful lama. I tried to find out what time the prayers would be chanted. He spoke only a few words of English, and did not understand the question. As I was about to give up, another lama – who was obviously revered – entered and answered my question. He said that the lamas would be chanting for four hours every day during the next weeks because it was an especially auspicious time preceding the full-moon day. I immediately resolved to attend every day.

"At what times during the day?" I asked him.

"At nine o'clock in the morning until eleven o'clock and from two to four in the afternoon," he said, smiling. "Are you interested in Buddhism?"

"Yes, very much. I would like to know more about the figures on the altar."

"Come with me," he said. He bowed three times as he entered the temple. First, he touched his joined palms to his forehead, then to his throat, then to his heart.

"I do not know what this Buddha represents," I said, standing in front of a luminous statue of a Buddha with a gold crown whose expression radiated poised detachment.

"This is the Buddha one prays to for a long life. He is called Amitabha Buddha."

"Who is this lady?" I asked, indicating the smaller statue below Amitabha Buddha.

"This is the guardian of health – Tara Devi."

I saw that her left arm was upraised, palm outwards. It looked as if she was saying: Have No Fear.

The lama continued: "This is Maitreya Buddha, the future Buddha, the divine symbol of Loving-kindness."

As I gazed up at the towering figure, I felt irresistibly drawn inward. From the hands of Maitreya Buddha, a white silk scarf fell like a wave of pure light. The figure radiated inner silence and unselfish love. The lama explained that this altruistic love is the love which desires only the fulfillment of the desires of the beloved, irrespective of whether one gains or loses in the process. The wish of the beloved is foremost. As I gazed at the figure of

Maitreya, I prayed inwardly to be granted that type of love in my relationship with Tashi. The golden smiling countenance of the Buddha filled my heart with peace and the glittering wings fanning out from him lifted me towards the Divine.

The lama continued, moving to the next figure. "This is Lama Tsongkapa who was a great scholar of Buddhist philosophy. He first systematized the rules and regulations governing the life of a monk."

I looked at the simple figure of the lama in a yellow robe. One of the books I had borrowed from Margrit had been written by him.

"He was the founder of the Gelugpa branch – our branch – of Tibetan Buddhism."

"What is the difference between the four branches?" I asked.

"Each branch has practices which differ. The Gelugpa branch is regarded as the strictest of the four orders."

This is Tashi's branch... I thought.

"And this is the great lama from Bangladesh who brought Buddhism to Tibet. His name was Atisha."

The figure radiated the sweetness of spiritual peace.

As we passed the grand statue of the golden Buddha in the center of the altar, the lama bowed his head. Then we stood in front of a fierce-looking statue with a wide face and big teeth.

"This is the founder of the Nyingpa branch of Tibetan Buddhism, Guru Padmasambhava, a great yogi."

I found him a bit frightening to look at, but noticed that behind him was a statue of a beautiful meek-faced lama in gold-colored robes with a staff in his right hand.

"May I ask you something?" I asked.

"Yes, please come. Sit." He motioned for me to sit on a mat. Then he said, "What is it?"

"I would really like to learn Tibetan. Is there anyone here who could teach me?"

"Very good." He paused. "The lamas are very busy, but there

is a lama coming from Nepal... He is a very good teacher. He is coming to visit his brother who lives here. He plans to stay here for one month for his holiday. I will speak to him. Perhaps he can teach you."

"Thank you very much." I was happy.

"There is something else I would like to ask you about. I am reading a book by Tsongkapa that says that on the path to liberation, the wish to gain enlightenment is not enough. But isn't this wish very important?"

The lama's eyes glowed. "Yes, yes, it is very important but," he paused, "one has to understand that one's wish will only be fulfilled if one cultivates this desire for enlightenment, not just for one's own sake, but in order to remove the suffering of ALL living beings. Only then is the wish worthy of being fulfilled."

"Oh I see..."

The lama smiled. Then he continued, "The way to cultivate this caring, compassionate feeling for ALL living beings is to realize that due to our innumerable lifetimes, every human being on this earth has at some time or other been our mother. As a mother, she has nurtured us, suckled us, and endured numerous hardships and privations for our sake. Thus, we owe our love to ALL living beings, no matter who they are, or how they treat us. We owe them love and kindness and respect and most of all, compassion."

We sat together in silence for some time more.

We are all ONE, I thought. *All humanity is ONE INTERCONNECTED FAMILY and just – just as a mother nourishes her children, it behooves us to open our hearts to nourish each other on the path to liberation.*

The following day, there were several Tibetan men and women sitting under the window near the wall on the right side of the temple. They had brought cushions or blankets to sit on. As I had nothing with me, I decided to sit on a vacant space on the maroon mat.

The lamas entered the temple in their long, maroon robes. After bowing to the Buddha, they came and sat on the mats, in two long rows facing each other. They glanced at me, then bowed their heads. I closed my eyes; I did not want to look directly at the lamas sitting opposite me while they were praying.

The sounds flowed forth. It was as if they didn't begin anywhere; instead they arose from the depths of silence and surfaced in low, sonorous waves which just melted into and rose out of a boundless sea of silence. The waves were shaped, formed, composed of silence asserting itself. Their deep voices circled around each other, embellishing the monosyllabic melodies as they issued forth from one voice, then another and another, blending into one inseparable whole, a harmony of differences, an interplay of silence and sound.

As I listened, I gradually became aware of one particular voice which stirred my heart very deeply. Out of partly closed eyes, I peered out and saw the lama, whose voice reverberated with incredible power, sitting directly opposite me. He appeared younger than most of the others. His strong features reminded me a little of Tashi. The prayers rolled effortlessly from his heart and his head was tilted upwards as he prayed. He looked like he was far away from the world.

What a beautiful soul! I reflected, gazing at his face. It was obvious that the world of prayer was everything for him – his shining path to heaven. *He is chanting from the level of pure consciousness!* As I listened, my body was transformed into light and my heart flooded with bliss. Wave after wave of energy spontaneously rippled up my spine and rays of light expanded, like fireworks inside my head. My whole body vibrated as the light shot upwards; at times I was unaware of the body at all.

Visiting the monastery day after day was like entering a new domain, a world woven of a finer texture than that of the earth. It was a world humming with resonant melodies, woven of golden threads of kindness and compassion. The sounds of their prayers went straight to the heart, inundating the central altar of one's being with unspeakable bliss.

At the beginning and end of each ritual, a long horn was blown whose sound seemed to herald the unlocking of the gates of heaven to welcome the gods to earth. During the prayers, the deep, low voices of the lamas were punctuated with the ringing of bells, the tapping of small drums and the soft swishing of cymbals. The lama whose voice had so moved me also played the cymbals in a way unlike I had ever heard before. It was so powerful, so sublime in its gentle intensity. It was as if I was cradled by the sounds, healed, protected and made whole in love. At times, the sounds melted into total silence. Only then did one realize how immovable the silence had become. Every moment was like a precious jewel strung on the necklace of infinity.

During the prayers, we were served butter tea. Its smooth, slightly salty taste warmed the body. We sipped the tea, as did the lamas, at intervals between the prayers. On the third day, a kind Tibetan lady told me to come and sit beside her as the maroon mats were only for the lamas to sit on. I smiled inwardly at the thought that I had been sitting there and the lamas had never said a single word to me about it. My immersion in the Tibetan Buddhist tradition began in utter innocence. I gladly joined the Tibetans under the window.

Each day as I neared the monastery, or gompa as it is called in Tibetan, my heart ran ahead up the stone steps into the serene atmosphere of purity and peace. As I listened with closed eyes, I was immersed in a glowing stillness. I felt the deities descend from heaven and fill the temple with their divine presence. In an inner vision, I beheld the glowing form of Maitreya Buddha with wings outspread and golden rays emanating from a translucent form. It hovered in the air, radiating infinite kindness and love to all. I had prayed to Maitreya Buddha for pure love in my relationship with Tashi and now this love inundated every pore of my being. I instinctively bowed my head to the form.

One day the rains came thundering down in a torrential downpour. The soil outside our house was transformed into thick mud which oozed from the ground. The leaves hung limp from the trees, and the fields of wheat turned from bright yellow to a soggy brown hue. It was almost time to descend the mountain to go to the prayers. I listened to the pitter-patter of the falling drops and the rushing of the wind washing through the trees. Donning a white wool jacket I had recently had stitched in the market and pulling on a knitted beret, I opened the door of my room, a smile of rugged determination rising inside. Then I bolted the door and turned the key in the lock.

When did rain ever stop me? I thought, descending the wooden staircase and stepping out into the pouring rain.

A rushing stream separated our house from the path down the mountainside. Two flat stones placed in it were used by us as a bridge whenever we came and went to the market. As I threaded my way through the overgrown hedges lining the muddy stream, I suddenly stopped short. The stream was flooded! The two stones were nowhere to be seen. All one could see was water, water, water; thick, brown, gushing, full and fast in a swelling, heaving, thundering mass over the rocks, with full force down, down, down the mountainside.

Should I risk it? I asked myself. *One wrong step and down I go, with the current, dashed against the rocks... Is it worth it? Dare I do it?* I wondered if I could remember where the stones had been and could risk placing my foot there now in the hope that they were only submerged and not washed away. I did not dare.

But I want to go! I must reach the gompa! My mind raced back and forth in a quandary. Finally I resolved to try an alternative route.

There was a sloping hill in front of the house leading to a narrow dirt road which wound its way between half-built houses and through grassy meadows. Hamid and Neda often took that road to the market. I had never walked it alone. Retracing my steps back to the house, I stood peering down the sloping hill at the tall grass blowing wildly in the fierce and driving rain. Putting one foot down the side of the hill, I slipped and slid down on my back. Exasperated and ashamed of the feeble attempt, I caught hold of a branch of a tree and managed to clamber back up to level ground. *Maybe I can cross the stream further down*, I thought, returning to the rushing water. As I stood on the bank of the stream, watching the swelling waves crashing over the rocks, I heard footsteps approach from behind. Turning around, I saw Neda in her red boots.

"Shanti, you want to go to the monastery? You can go. Come on. I will help you. Come this way." She led the way down through some hedges until we reached a small clearing which jutted out over the stream so that if one jumped carefully, one could just clear the rushing water. Neda led the way to the best spot for the jump across.

"I'll go first," she said, "then you come." She jumped across and leaning out over the water, extended her hand to me.

I looked at Neda standing there in the pouring rain, with her hand extended toward me – helping me get to the prayers which she knew I loved so much. *This is true friendship*, the thought flashed through my mind.

"Oh, Neda, thank you so much! I REALLY appreciate your helping me like this. Alright, I'm ready!" I leaped across and except for a quick dip of one shoe into the water, I made it without falling in.

"Thanks again! I'm off now. I'd better hurry or I'll be late." I ran over the slippery rocks lining the path. I was elated by a sense of victory as I neared the gompa. I remembered a saying I had jotted down in my notebook long ago which said: *I will always be happy. Nothing can hinder me.* I was laughing as the rain fell, dripping from the umbrella I held poised above me, not really caring whether I got wet or not. *Almost there.* A voice inside beat out the sweet rhythm of victory.

I nearly ran the last few meters to the outer courtyard. At last, I stood before the doors of the temple. I looked in. There was no one there! In bewilderment, I stood gazing at the statue of the golden Buddha on the altar. How long did I stand there? Eventually the familiar face of a lama greeted me.

"Prayers?" I asked, trying to make myself understood in English.

"Nay, today, no." He shook his head and smiled.

"But I came all the way down the mountain," I said quietly, looking down at my wet trousers. "I came all the way in the rain."

He only shook his head and smiled. Then he was gone and I was alone. Tiptoeing through the illuminated world vibrant with color, I knelt before each one of the deities. *At least this I can do, now that I am here,* I thought. Last of all, I bowed before Avalokateshwara, the Buddha of compassion. Having made obeisance, I departed, entering again into the pouring rain which somehow felt wetter, colder, and more dismal than before.

Slowly, I started the long, tedious climb back up the steep, slippery slope of the hill. My heartbeat quickened as I picked up speed, hoping to reach the fording place where I had crossed over the stream before it was flooded. Already the rising water had covered rocks which were still visible on the way down. Clambering over stones jutting out of the water, where previously the path had been, my feet slipped into the gushing stream, soaking my shoes through and through. I continued marching upwards with firm strides until eventually I saw the place Neda had shown me half an hour before. The water nearly covered the ground. I stood peering at the mounds of debris which had been cast up on the grass. Then I heard someone call out to me. Turning I saw an old man coming up the path.

"Nay, nay!" he said, pointing to the stream and then at me.

He is warning me not to try to cross here, I thought, *he knows this path. I shouldn't do it.* An inner voice confirmed the feeling. While I was wondering how to get home, a young Manali man came down the path. Gazing at the flooded stream, he realized my predicament, and beckoned me to follow him. I followed, and together we climbed the rocks a bit further up and then he leaped across and extended his arm to me.

"Ow!" I moaned painfully as my foot hit the ground. "I think I've sprained my ankle!" I sank down on the wet ground, removed my wet shoe and dipped the agonizingly painful ankle in the icy cold water.

"What a pity!" the man said, bending over me. "Let me help you. Where do you live?"

"Just there," I said, pointing to the house.

He helped me to the house.

Chapter Thirteen

In the field in front of the house where I lived, women were cutting stalks of wheat under the boiling-hot sun. Bending over, a sickle in their hand, they swung it rhythmically, forward and back, forward and back. The golden sheaves of grain made a crackling sound as they fell. The women wiped the sweat from their faces. I sat on the terrace with a book on my lap but I could not keep my attention on it. After cutting the wheat, they squatted on their knees as they collected the stalks into bundles, tied them together and laid them in the sun. They had been working without a break.

I got up and went into the kitchen and filled a large pitcher with water. My ankle was still swollen and painful, but I didn't mind. I brought the water and offered it to them. They came and stood by the terrace, drinking the water and smiling at me. They didn't speak any English. We smiled at each other for awhile, then they went back to their work.

Sitting on the terrace, I glanced down at my swollen ankle. The doctor at the clinic told me it would be alright if I stayed off my feet. He had wrapped a tight bandage around it and told me to keep my leg raised. *How boring!* I thought with exasperation.

Neda had been very helpful. She brought a chair into the kitchen so I could sit down while we prepared our separate meals for, unlike me, she was not a vegetarian. As I rinsed the moong dhal several times under running water, and then poured the basmati rice into a stainless-steel pot with the dhal and lit the stove, Neda stood cutting up small pieces of red meat on the cutting board.

"Why you don't stay in India? You are more like Indian than Westerner," she remarked, glancing up from the board.

"Maybe I will," I answered, thinking of Tashi. "It is in God's hands. I just take each day as it comes. Maybe I stay, maybe go.

I'll just see what happens."

"But it's your decision. You could teach English at Firoz's school. They have no good English teachers. They come for a few months from Delhi, and then go back. There is nothing for them to do here; they miss the city life. So the teachers, they always leave. You could live in Manali."

"I suppose I could. Margrit told me life is very difficult here in winter, especially up on the mountain. It is hard to get down to the market. It is very cold and I have no one to help me. The village ladies – they collect wood from the forest every day. They work so hard carrying wood on their back. But I couldn't do that. I'm not built for that kind of work," I replied, adjusting the flame under the rice and dhal which looked like it would boil over any minute.

"But you could live at the school. The teachers from Delhi live at the school. The rooms have heating in the winter; I heard they were nice rooms," Neda said.

I didn't answer.

"What are you thinking of, Shantila? Is something bothering you?"

"It's well – you know what it's like around the school – the type of people who are there; it's obvious they are on drugs. I don't like to go to Agnes's house – mainly because I have to pass through there. It's such a pity that they hang around the houses near the school."

Neda nodded, her eyes downcast. "That's why Hamid and I take turns taking Firoz to school and back. We don't want him to walk around there alone. It's not safe. I saw a woman who looked like she was mad. Her hair was matted and she was wearing a bathing suit! In the street!"

We both burst out laughing.

"You need to get an Indian boyfriend like Margrit and Agnes, and then you'll have help in winter," Neda said, still laughing. "Why don't you get someone?"

"Because I'm not interested in having a boyfriend. I don't want to live that way, with just anyone. It's not my way. I don't believe in living like this. If I meet someone and we love each other, then we may marry. If he doesn't love me enough to marry me, then I don't want to live with him," I said, lowering my voice as my inner feelings were being revealed to her for the first time.

Neda put the lid on the potatoes and turned to me, a surprised look on her face. "But you – you are different. You are like the Eastern people, Shantila. I thought everyone, all the foreigners want to live like this, having boyfriends, no marriage, no commitment, just taking someone for awhile, then another and another. How come you think different?" she asked, with a perplexed look on her face as she sat down facing me.

"I have been meditating for over twenty years. Maybe that is the reason. One's values change. I would rather live alone than be in a relationship without meaning, without devotion or commitment. These relationships that come and go, I don't believe in living like this. Many times, the woman becomes pregnant and the father leaves her alone with the child. This kind of relationship is so painful in the end. Why do you think the world is in such a mess? So many children are being born from these type of relationships and they grow up without fathers, feeling afraid and insecure emotionally. What's the point of living like that, adding to the misery in the world?"

I reflected on the years that stretched far back into the distant past. My early love life had been dotted with great hopes and shattering disappointments which inevitably jolted one up and down like the broken wheels of a carriage, dragging one over deep ruts on the road of love. To come to someone now meant letting go of all the pain that went before and beginning anew, innocently opening wide the heart's windows with trust and faith.

I looked over at Neda.

"Was Hamid the only man in your life?" I asked her quietly.

"Yes, Shantila. I wasn't interested in men at all. My mother got worried. She thought maybe I would not marry. Hamid was a friend of the family. At first, I didn't like him. He is eleven years older than me. When I was eighteen, he spoke to me. I felt, he has a good heart – I will marry him. This was what happened to me. His heart mattered more to me than how he looked or anything like that. I told my mother, 'I will marry Hamid.' She was surprised. 'He doesn't look so nice,' she said. 'He isn't very handsome. My daughter should get someone better.' But I would not change my mind. Finally, my mother agreed." Neda paused. Then she said, "I am happy with Hamid."

Yes, I felt she was lucky in a way. She was spared so many complications, doubts and misgivings on the feeling level because she only had had to adjust to one man. She only had to attune herself to his moods, his thoughts, his feelings and gradually over the seven years of their marriage, their commitment had naturally deepened.

Neda continued speaking, "It was hard to leave my family and my country. But if Hamid wants to live in India, then I am happy to live here. In Iran, the men are very aggressive. One cannot walk outside alone at night without feeling afraid. In India, the people are gentle, even the men; one doesn't feel fear here. Maybe because they are mostly vegetarians, it makes them gentle like this."

"Maybe you will become vegetarian after living in India for some time," I said. "I've read somewhere that eating meat does make one more aggressive."

"In Iran, people eat so much meat. I don't mind not eating meat but Hamid and Firoz, they want meat. They ask for meat so I must cook it for them," Neda said softly.

"It doesn't matter. If one says a prayer of thanks before eating, it purifies the food. The purity of the heart is more important than the food one eats," I replied.

"Hamid is not aggressive, he is a good man. Once when we

were riding home on his motorcycle in Hyderabad, we saw a very old man, a very poor man walking in the rain with a bag over his head. He looked like he had had nothing to eat for a long time. Hamid stopped the bike and offered him three hundred rupees. The man looked at the money and then took only one hundred rupees. He refused to take any more money than that although Hamid wanted to give him all of it. I think he was a spiritual man. Most Indian people are always cheating to try to get more money, but that man would not take all the money we offered him and he was very poor."

"He was not poor; he had his dignity," I replied firmly. "That was more important to him than the money. Money isn't everything. He took just what he needed, no more, no less. If everyone took only what they needed, think how much simpler life would be! No one would be starving in the world because no one would be taking more food or hoarding more money than they needed. There would be enough food for everyone if we all shared what we have and took only what we need." I paused. "That man was poor on the surface, but on a deeper level, he was rich. That's why he didn't take any more of the money."

"I don't understand. I know he needed the money. Why you say he didn't take all the three hundred rupees?" Neda asked with questioning eyes.

"There are two kinds of wealth – spiritual wealth and material wealth; and two kinds of poverty – spiritual poverty and material poverty. That old man may not have had many rupees, but he was spiritually wealthy. Spiritual wealth is more important because with spiritual wealth, money comes when you need it. With spiritual wealth, nature takes care of one's needs. Without asking, whatever one needs just comes at the right time – just like the money came to that man, through you and Hamid. In the West, many people are very rich, but spiritually poor. They are constantly searching for ways to make their life meaningful."

Neda smiled at me. "I don't believe everything you say, but I know a Sufi story that expresses the same meaning. The story teaches us not to worry about money. You should stay in India, Shantila. You think like us in the East."

"We will see," I said, smiling.

Placing our food on a tray, we carried it out to the wooden table on the terrace where we usually ate.

Neda said, "A friend of ours is interested in reading your book."

"Who?" I asked.

"His name is Ralph. He is an elderly man. He lives with his servant Sudesh in a house not far from here. He is Australian."

"Australian?" My curiosity was aroused. "He's interested in meditation?"

"I don't know. All I know is that he likes to read spiritual-type books. Would you loan it to him?"

"Yes, of course. I'll give it to you," I replied, sitting with my sprained ankle balanced on the edge of the wall of the terrace. The pain had subsided but I still couldn't walk without limping.

While we were eating, a young man came to collect the bundles of wheat. He stacked all the separate bundles into one big pile, and sat on the ground with his legs stretched out in front of him. Tying a thick rope around his waist, he tossed the rest of the rope over the pile of wheat behind him. Then, in a very quick agile movement, he arched his back and hoisted the wheat onto it. He slowly stood up, but the bundle of wheat was so heavy that he had to walk with his back bent far over.

"What a job!" Neda said, sighing. "They have to work so hard."

"Yes," I nodded. "That was an amazing sight."

Neda looked at her watch. "I better go to get Firoz. School is out." She stood up and stretched. "Shall I take your dishes in?"

"Yes, thank you."

Neda put all the dishes on the tray and went into the house. She waved to me before leaving. "See you later, Shanti."

"See you," I called after her.

Thick white clouds of mist were moving across the face of the mountains, alternately hiding and revealing the dark green hills abounding in thick green forests of deodar trees. Through the mist, the dark silhouettes of crows in flight pierced the whiteness with their black wings. From my seat on the terrace, I could hear the music of the mountain stream rushing over the rocks and far below, in the village, I heard the sound of drumbeats proclaiming the beginning of a wedding ceremony. Quite often, these drums resounded through the night until the early hours of dawn, for wedding ceremonies here continued for seven, sometimes even eight hours. *What kind of ceremony would I—?* The thought stopped in mid-air.

I lived with Hamid and Neda for about one month. One day, quite unexpectedly, Neda told me her mother was coming to visit and they needed the spare room. It was such short notice. I didn't know where to go. I knew that I couldn't afford a hotel now as it was high season in Manali and my finances were ebbing. But an inner voice said, *Remember everything that happens, happens for the best.* This was an echo of my mother's salutary advice. She often repeated these words as I was growing up to give me confidence when I had to face disappointment, rejection, or disheartening circumstances which I found difficult to understand or accept. She was always there whenever I needed her, so strong in the face of any odds. In spite of having to endure many hardships in her life, she always retained her inner joy.

A few days later, I went to collect my book from Ralph, the Australian man. His house was built halfway up the mountainside. It was a large stone house, one of the most comfortable-looking houses in Manali. As we sat drinking tea on the veranda, I marveled at the panoramic view he had of the towering snow-capped mountains in the distance and the endless miles of forests across the valley.

"When did you build this house?" I asked my tall, white-haired host.

"Over eleven years ago," he said. "I retired and came here on holiday. I was so taken with the beauty of this place that I decided to come back. I have a small pension so I can live the kind of simple life I want, and it's so peaceful here."

I learned from Neda that Ralph had never married and he was very reclusive by nature. He lived a quiet life with Sudesh, his Indian servant, who was having tea with us.

Sudesh was about forty years old. He was a handsome man who had an air of nobility about him. He was married with one son and one daughter. He had been a farmer in Mandi, but farming didn't provide enough money to offer his family the kind of life he wanted to give them, so he went to look for work in Manali. Sudesh was very grateful when Ralph hired him five years ago as a doorkeeper to look after the house at night and to cook, clean and manage the garden. But during the time they were together, their friendship had developed and now Ralph treated Sudesh as an equal.

"If Sudesh is working, I can't just sit and watch," Ralph said to me laughing. "I have to work too."

"First I only like Indian food," Sudesh said, "but now I always eat with Ralph. I eat the same food as Ralph. We eat together. Only fish I do not eat because my Guru says my luck will be better during the next few years if I do not eat fish."

Ralph asked Sudesh to go to his bedroom to bring the book. Sudesh returned a few minutes later. Ralph handed me my book. "I read some of it, different sections of it. I liked it," he said.

Then I mentioned that I had nowhere to stay.

"Neda just told me that her mother is coming and I must move out. I don't know where to go..."

Without a moment's hesitation, Sudesh said, "Why don't you come here and stay with us? You can sleep in my room."

"How long do you need a place for?" Ralph asked.

"A few weeks. I'm planning to go to Ladakh as soon as the

road opens in July."

"Then it's alright – a few weeks, that is," Ralph said slowly.

I was overwhelmed. It was too good to be true. Holding my breath, I asked, "How much should I pay you for the room?"

Ralph replied, "There are three rules in my house: no charge to stay here, no television and no pressure cooker."

I could hardly believe it. Tears spontaneously welled up in my eyes. I was able to stay for free!

Sudesh saw the tears and spoke softly to me, saying, "Why you cry? This is India. This is natural. No problem in you coming. I sleep out here." He pointed to a little room on the veranda. "Why you feel like this? We help. It is natural."

"I just didn't expect it. Thank you so much." I said a silent thank you to God. Again my mother's wisdom re-echoed, *Everything that happens, happens for the best.*

Sudesh showed me to my new room, which was his bedroom. It was just as large, comfortable and well-furnished as Ralph's. They treated each other like brothers. Sudesh said that whenever he or his son or daughter needed to see a private doctor, Ralph gladly paid the bill. Ralph had even financed the repair of Sudesh's ancient family home in Mandi.

"I hope you will be happy here," Sudesh said. "If you need anything, just tell me."

"There is such a good feeling in the house," I said.

"Yes," Sudesh replied. "Ralph is a good man. I am happy with him, very happy."

We walked back outside to the veranda. Ralph was sitting gazing at the mountains. "I don't know what will happen if I get sick or have to go back to Australia," he said softly.

Sudesh, who overheard, replied quickly, "If Ralph gets sick, I will care for him. Wherever he goes, I will go. He has been so good to me and my family. I stay with Ralph always."

One evening soon after my arrival, Sudesh cooked potato parathas out on the veranda. Ralph and I sat cross-legged on the wooden porch as the hot frying pan hissed and the air was saturated with the tantalizing aroma of fresh bread and fried potatoes. I felt like part of a family. We laughed together as we ate until we could eat no more. Afterwards Sudesh went to visit a friend. Ralph and I remained sitting, talking softly as we gazed at the starlit sky above the mountain range in the distance.

"Of one thing I am sure," Ralph said, "and that is if one becomes attached to anything in the world, it will only bring sorrow. This is one lesson I have learned in my life."

I didn't reply. In the past few days I had been experiencing the pain of separation from Tashi.

"But, Ralph, is it alright? I mean – I agree with you, but still there is attachment to friends. I want to be with my friends. Must one give up all attachments, even these?" I was speaking to him as I would to a wise man because I had come to realize that knowledge comes to us in many forms, through many different people. It comes when we need it and are ready to assimilate it. Everyone and anyone can be our teacher for all beings are but reflections of the One Intelligence that governs life everywhere. It is really only Pure Being that speaks to us through his own expressions. If we are open enough to listen, we can learn from everyone and from every experience.

Ralph thought for a while before he answered me. "Attachment to friends is alright if it is an unselfish friendship. If it is unselfish, it will continue without clinging because our friends will want to be with us. The Buddha says: right thought, right speech, and right action. If all these are right, the friendship will continue. We won't lose our friends, so this attachment may not bring pain. How we approach our relationships is up to us."

I sat quietly allowing his words to settle deep into my awareness.

How true, I reflected. *How many times we want to achieve some particular aim in a friendship and when that particular thing doesn't materialize, we are disappointed. How beautiful it would be just to love, just to be, and not to expect anything, just to be able to flow with the current of life.* I remembered the words of Kahlil Gibran: *And think not that you can direct the course of love, for love, if it finds you worthy, directs your course... When you love you should not say, "God is in my heart," but rather, "I am in the heart of God."*

I stayed with Ralph and Sudesh for two weeks. I missed Tashi very much; he had been in my mind and heart almost constantly. Each day I traveled the long route down the mountain to the post office to see if a letter had arrived. The weather in Manali was getting hotter and more humid every day. Still the road to Ladakh remained closed due to a heavy snowfall which blocked the pass through the mountains.

One day when I arrived at the post office, a mother and baby donkey were standing in front of it. Entering, I saw Swarma. She waved to me, then she went to see if I had any mail. When she returned, she was holding a letter in her hand.

"A letter for you," she said, smiling.

I took it. It was from Tashi! I was so happy that I jumped up and down. The people in the post office did not even try to contain their amusement.

"Your boyfriend?" Swarma asked.

I just smiled. *If only they knew he is a monk!* I thought, holding the precious letter to my heart. I walked to the sweetshop and found a quiet seat near the back. Then, very carefully, I opened the letter. The letter read:

Dear Shantila,

I hope you are comfortable there in Manali. Here I have much work. Two lamas have left for Ladakh. I come later. We can go together on bus 450 kilometers to Leh. Did you receive a reply from your brother? I wait for your letter. Write soon.

Best wishes, Tashi

I held the letter in my hands, and then I ran my fingers over the

185

paper. I closed my eyes... *We go together the 450 kilometers to Leh!*
Oh, my beloved, please come soon, dearest Tashi. Please come soon!

When I returned to Ralph's house, Sudesh told me he needed
his room as his son was coming from Mandi to visit him.
Inwardly, I knew it was time to move on. Sudesh told me about a
guest house further down the mountain. I went there and spoke
to the owner who showed me a room on the second floor. It had
a balcony with a magnificent view of the mountains and the
green, rolling valley in the distance. Adjacent to the guest house
was his family dwelling. It was a quaint wooden cottage painted
blue. Outside was a large courtyard in which two brown cows
stood, munching grass. It was such a serene setting in our
mountainside retreat.

I asked the owner the price. He gave me a quote which was far
too much. I explained to him my situation, and he said he would
discuss it with his family. When I returned later in the week, the
grandfather was there. He willingly consented to give me the
room for the same price he charged his Indian guests, which was
a big difference from the owner's original offer.

At Ralph's house, I had been able to cook for myself on his
electric hotplate. I wanted to continue cooking for myself, but I
didn't have anything to cook on. I went to Margrit's house to see
if she had a spare hotplate, but she didn't. She thought that Agnes
might. Luckily, she did.

I was happy to be living on my own again. Every evening, I
carried my empty jug to a farm up the mountain, where it was
filled with fresh milk. A young Indian lady who had just had her
first child sat on her terrace breastfeeding her baby. Sometimes I
sat with her on the wooden terrace while her brother milked the
cow.

"You are married?" she asked, looking at me.

"No," I replied.

"You no want to marry?" she said, with a puzzled look.

"Yes, but – I'm happy anyway..." I shrugged my shoulders. I

felt a little bit uncomfortable.

She looked into my eyes with great tenderness. Then she said, "Marriage is a good thing. Remember this when he comes to ask you to marry him. Marriage is a good thing," she said again, emphasizing her words.

Her brother came with my jug filled to the brim.

"I'll remember," I said, as I smiled and waved goodbye.

It felt great to be self-sufficient, not having to rely on anyone else for a roof over my head or for food, not having to talk when I felt like being silent, not having to postpone my meditation in order to be sociable. But the idea of self-sufficiency didn't last long. Inevitably, I found myself forced to depend on others to meet my daily needs.

I learned to accept this reality when a few days later, I returned to my room at lunchtime with a knapsack full of vegetables. After the long walk to the market, I was hot, tired and ravenous. Hurriedly I washed the rice and dhal and cut up some of the vegetables. I put it all in the pot together and thought of turning the heat up to maximum. I was so hungry!

I placed the pot on the electric ring and switched on the knob. But nothing happened! The ring remained stone cold! Usually, it turned red-hot within minutes.

"Oh, please – no!" I sighed aloud. I tried talking to the electric cooker to coax it to heat up, but it was to no avail. It remained totally oblivious to my sighs of frustration and desperation.

Suddenly a thought occurred to me: *This is my chance!* I had wanted to sample the kachoris in the sweetshop. Here was my excuse. I picked up my straw hat, slung my cotton shoulder bag over my shoulder and walked out, heading nonchalantly down the long, winding road to the market. My mind toyed with the idea of a typical Indian lunch: potato parathas, or two kachoris (a pastry stuffed with vegetables, nuts and raisins) with dhal. Anything I chose would be a welcome change from the usual rice and dhal soup I cooked every day, or maybe I would order channa, spicy chickpeas with a yogurt sauce poured over it with samosas, fried pastry stuffed with vegetables...

I entered the sweetshop and gazed around. Dark-skinned men with wiry, lean bodies sat together, four or six at a table, bent over plates of steaming-hot channa, eating, chatting and smoking cheap tobacco leaves rolled up in what resembled a faded bay leaf. A handsome lad of about eighteen came to my table and took my order: two kachoris, one rasgullah and one coconut burfi. He brought me some water. Looking around, I realized that I was the only woman there. I started to feel a bit uncomfortable. I realized that several men in the shop were staring at me. I quickly shifted my gaze, pretending not to notice.

They are probably wondering who I am, with my big straw hat and simple Indian clothes. If they only knew the whole story of this "wandering pilgrim," who is practically living on air and a few rupees... I laughed inwardly.

My stomach was rumbling. It was a very late lunch. As I whispered the grace before meals, my mouth watered. Breaking the flaky pastry in half with my hands, I bit hungrily into it. The dry vegetables crumbled out onto the plate. I poured some of the yogurt sauce from a side dish onto the two open halves. After finishing the meal, I sat listening to the notes of the Indian singer on the radio fill the humid room. As I did not want to look at the men, I stared at a picture of the snow-covered peaks of Manali. Then I shifted my gaze to a large photo of a white dove with outspread wings hanging on the wall.

Then, a young woman entered the shop dressed in the traditional maroon robes of the lamas. She had very close-cropped dark hair and beautiful soft features reminiscent of the Buddha. She sat at the table in front of me.

A nun, a Buddhist nun, I thought. *Tashi suggested I become a nun... Is she happy?* I asked myself. *Is she fulfilled as a woman? Perhaps not as a "woman" but as a spiritual being. Yes – she looks happy, even serene. What is primary?* I asked myself. *What is more significant – our "womanness" or our "spirituality"? Who are we, in essence? What are we, in truth, fundamentally? From where does our real fulfillment arise?*

The nun ordered tea and two gulab jamun. She was sitting with her back to me. I debated with the idea of approaching her and asking if I could join her at her table. I wondered whether she spoke English. I decided to try. Gingerly, I went over to her table.

"Do you speak English?" I asked her softly.

"Yes," she said, warmth emanating from her eyes.

"Could you tell me something about – ummm, about what it is like to be a nun?"

"Yes. You are welcome to join me," she said, gesturing for me to take the seat opposite her. "What do you want to know?"

"What do you do during the day? I love the sound of the prayers, the chanting..." I said.

"It is a simple life. We pray three times a day. We study the teachings of the Buddha."

"Do you live in a monastery?"

"Yes, there are lamas and nuns living there, in separate buildings. Why don't you come for a visit? You can stay in my room for a few days. It would be nice if you come." She smiled.

"I am planning to go to Ladakh soon, and then when I come back, maybe I will come."

She wrote down the directions of how to reach her monastery. I said goodbye to her, thanking her for her kind invitation.

What a lovely person! I thought, still sitting in the chair after she had left. *But do I really WANT to become a nun? Or do I – want something else?* I remembered the words of the young mother at the farm where I got my milk: *"Marriage is a good thing."*

On the way up the hill, two Indian ladies passing on the road greeted me very warmly. They asked me in Hindi where I was going. I pointed up. As we were all going the same way, we walked together. One lady turned off on a side path and the other told me in English that her name was Ama and that she had been born in Manali. Her English was good enough for us to converse easily.

"I have a friend from England. She lived in our house when my father was alive. She sent letter to me from Singapore. She helped me learn English. She's teaching English in Singapore now."

Ama was heavyset. She had light brown skin and a round, moon-like face framed by thick dark shoulder-length hair which she wore parted in the middle. Her weight made her slow movements seem labored, but she appeared healthy nonetheless.

"Don't go so fast, Shanti," she said. We were both breathing heavily as we climbed the steep slope. "Go slowly, easily – better for you. My son always runs down the mountain, then he gets headache."

"It's probably the altitude," I said.

When we reached Ama's house, she insisted that I come in for tea. She was so warm and friendly that I decided to accept the invitation.

She swung open the iron gate leading onto the small patch of land in front of her house. Once inside, she went up to a cot where an old woman with white hair wearing a simple cotton Punjabi suit was sitting. Ama called her "Mataji" and explained that the woman was her mother-in-law. She and her husband were visiting them for the summer months. The old woman didn't speak any English, but she made me feel welcome. Then she went away to pray. Ama said her mother-in-law prayed several times a day, and she didn't touch meat, fish or eggs.

"Chai? Shanti, I make chai. One minute."

Despite her weight, Ama was not without grace and the soft pastel colors of her clothes were a perfect complement to her gentle maternal nature. A few minutes later, she reappeared, carrying a tray of tea and biscuits.

"Market? You market?" Ama asked.

"Yes. No electricity today – so I had to eat in the market," I answered.

"You take food in market? Oh, no, not good. Why you no come my house? I make food for you. You no have to go market. You come my house for dinner," she said. "You like rice, dhal, chapati? I make for you."

As we sat together sipping tea, she began telling me about her marriage. "My husband is from Punjab. The men from Punjab are very good. They never take other women. They have only one woman. I am lucky," she said, smiling broadly.

I was happy for her. She was so easy to talk to that I decided to mention to her the experience I had with Mr. Rao's wife.

"Sometimes I feel that some women in India dislike Western women. Why should Indian women feel that way?"

"Oh, that's an easy question, Shanti. Some Indian mens, they are not faithful to the wife. Western peoples, they divorce many times. My friend from England – she divorced twice. Now she lives in Singapore alone. Indian ladies, they do not want to be left alone. In India, divorce is disgrace." She paused, shaking her head. "If divorce comes, it is hard for us to marry again. I lucky. I never divorce. I have two sons. My husband loves me TOO much!" She laughed contentedly.

When I left, Ama invited me to come again for a meal with the whole family.

"You come my house!" she called after me as I opened the iron gate. "You no have to go market. I have a big heart. I no small heart – I BIG HEART!!!"

Chapter Fourteen

It was a beautiful bright sunny day. I sat inside the entrance to the temple awaiting Lama Lobsang, because today I was scheduled to begin learning the Tibetan language! At precisely the appointed time, I saw him walk briskly across the courtyard of the monastery. He was of medium height with broad muscular shoulders and arms. His features were even and strong. He moved with a sense of purpose. He was on holiday for one month and had come to visit his younger brother who was a lama here. He entered the temple.

"Good. Today you will begin learning Tibetan," he said, peering deeply into my eyes. "We will go to my brother's room upstairs." He turned and walked down the stone steps. His long maroon robes rustled in the wind as I followed him across the courtyard to a wooden door on the ground floor. He left his sandals outside and I did the same.

It was the first time I'd entered a lama's room in a monastery. A feeling of grateful anticipation welled up inside as I crossed the threshold. The first thing I noticed was the altar opposite the door. An ornate thanka of the Buddha (a painting on silk fabric) hung in the center of the altar. There was a faded painting of Maitreya Buddha on one side of the altar and a Tibetan Buddhist calendar on the other side. A row of small round stainless-steel bowls filled with water were arranged in front of the thanka.

"What a beautiful room," I whispered softly as I came in.

"Please sit down." Lama Lobsang motioned for me to sit on one of the maroon cloth-covered cots.

Walking over the faded ochre-colored straw matting on the floor, I sat down. On the cot were two cushions covered with gold fabric. I gazed at the small hand-carved shelves on either side of the altar. On one side, he had placed his collection of audiotapes and a tape recorder and on the other side, there were thick volumes written in Tibetan. On a ledge under the altar, I saw the familiar Tibetan prayer books wrapped in bright yellow cloth and tied with a red string.

"Would you like a cup of tea?" Lama Lobsang asked.

"Yes, thank you," I replied.

He picked up one of the traditional large oriental flasks decorated with flowers, and pouring a cup of Tibetan butter tea into a cup, he offered it to me. Then folding together his long robes, he sat down next to me.

"Now we begin. Today I will teach you the sounds of the alphabet. I will pronounce and you please pronounce after me. In Tibetan, the sound is very important. Now repeat. I go slowly. Listen carefully."

He pronounced the first letter slowly three times. Then I repeated. I felt a deep sense of comfort in his presence. It was as if the simple purity of his being covered me with an invisible mantle of protection. When the lesson was over, I thanked him and gave him a donation.

As I was leaving, I met a very pretty Japanese girl in the courtyard. She looked like a Japanese doll. Her name was Yuki. She was very open and friendly. She told me that she was staying at the gompa until she left for Ladakh with a lama friend. She invited me up to the lama's room where she was staying.

We had to ascend two flights of old wooden stairs to the second-floor balcony. After removing her shoes, Yuki drew aside a thick white curtain embroidered with an oriental design which hung over the dark red wooden door. We entered a small maroon-colored room and sat together on one of the cots.

"Do you like staying here?" I asked Yuki.

"Yes. I sleep very well here. The lama whose room this is, sleeps there." She pointed to a long vertical cot covered with maroon-colored fabric. "He insisted I stay in his room until my friend comes from Dharamsala."

"You sleep in the same room with the lama?" I asked, not

trying to hide my surprise.

"Yes. The Abbot knows. For a few days, it is allowed," Yuki replied. "First it felt strange but now it is OK." She smiled.

Yuki and I became friends immediately. We soon discovered that we were in a similar situation. We were both traveling alone in India with very little money. We were both single and we both had high ideals. There was something similar that drew us to India, a nameless 'something' which was guiding us in the direction of a truth we could only feel.

"I don't know where I will go next," I said to her as we sat together in the little wooden room.

"I don't know either. Don't try to plan, Shanti. It will become clear when the time comes to leave. Just be simple. We must learn to become simpler and to trust. The future will take care of itself."

After saying goodbye to Yuki, I walked through the Tibetan colony into the forest behind the monastery. Stepping into the forest, I closed the gate behind me. I took a deep breath. The cool fragrance of the majestic cedars filled my heart with bliss. I took off my sandals, walking barefoot along the dirt paths. There were very few people around. Above me, birds flew gaily through the curving outspread branches of the fir trees. In the distance, the rushing torrent of the river sang as it gurgled, running over white stones, glistening in the sun. My heart soared into the sunlight, rising with the birds on the currents of the wind high into the treetops. I came to a clearing in the woods and stopped.

Oh, what is this? I asked myself.

I walked over to a ladder erected against the massive trunk of a tree; it was one of four huge trees which had grown close together, almost in a square. I ascended the steps of the ladder, my heart beating with joyous anticipation. At the top was a wooden board, fastened securely between the trunks of the four trees. It was a tree house!

How fantastic! What a perfect place to write! I thought, as I stepped onto the wooden platform. Sitting cross-legged, I had a wonderful view through the trees of the snow-capped mountains in the distance. I closed my eyes, feeling the air caress my skin. *Never have I felt so happy!* I thought as I sat enveloped in stillness. After awhile, I decided to write a letter. I took a pen and a pad of paper from my knapsack and started writing.

Dear Mr. Rao,

How are you? I am really enjoying Manali, especially the forest. I write in the forest every day. The only problem is that I have almost no money left. Please can you send me an advance for the book? Lama Tashi will stop here in Manali on his way to Ladakh when he takes his holiday. Would it be possible to give the money to him? He can then bring it to me. I would appreciate this very much.

Best regards, Shantila

I carefully climbed down the rickety steps of the ladder and headed towards the post office to mail the letter. On the way up the path through the Tibetan market, I waved to the lady standing at the entrance to a tiny doorless Tibetan restaurant. Then I went in and bought a loaf of Tibetan bread. It was round and flat and crisp around the edges, perfect for breakfast or dinner with a mug of hot milk.

"I'm learning Tibetan!" I told her as she wrapped the bread in paper.

"You learn Tibetan?" She nodded her head vigorously. She was always cheerful, although her life was far from easy. She worked from early morning until ten at night, in the heat, in the rain, in the cold over her cooking pots.

Then I saw the tailor perched in an open stall, hunched over his sewing machine. He nodded and smiled at me as I passed, and I waved. I walked up the road past more shop fronts crammed together; their wares were colorfully displayed on tables or hanging up on the doors. I passed the photography shop and the shoe shop, the Indian restaurant on the corner and the place on the path where the donkeys usually stood, but they were not there. I walked down the road toward the sweetshop. The beggar lady without fingers was sitting outside as usual. I smiled at her and placed a few rupees in her palm. She nodded her head in gratitude.

Bless you, I said silently as I passed on.

Then I entered Tenzin's shop. Tenzin was Tibetan. His family owned a few shops in Manali. In his shop, he sold Tibetan cards, jewelry and clothing.

"Hello, Tenzin," I said, peeking in from the doorway.

"Shantila! Come in. What's been happening with you? Why I haven't seen you for so many days?" he asked, leaning forward over the glass counter.

I entered the shop.

"I've been busy as usual, writing. And guess what? I've started learning Tibetan! A lama at the monastery is teaching me. I had my first lesson today."

"I'm glad you are learning Tibetan," he said in his deep voice. "I will test you."

"I've only learned the letters of the alphabet." I paused. "I'm leaving soon for Ladakh. A lama friend of mine is coming and we will go together on the bus."

"A lama?" Tenzin asked, a little surprised. "I know about the life of lamas."

"Oh tell me, Tenzin! I love going to the prayers at the gompa. Please tell me what you know about their life," I asked eagerly.

"For a lama, a simple life is all. I know a lama in my village that just lived on nettles. For a lama, I think three things are important: no sex, no jealousy or greed and not too much sleeping. We believe that when someone who is very pure dies, when they are cremated, something white remains. It looks like pearls or small crystals, this white thing."

"Really? But what is it?"

"I never saw it, but my grandfather saw it and he told me it is true. This is what the old people say: something white remains. They also say that the body doesn't smell. It doesn't decay, at least not for two or three days after the person dies."

"I've heard that this is true of saints..." I said.

"In Tibet, my country, bodies are usually not burned like in India. They are given to the vultures. But even the vultures won't eat the body if the person was very sinful in his life. They won't go near it until a puja is performed. Only then they eat it.

"A pure heart, being kind to others, is more important than how much one prays or reads the scriptures. We say in Tibet: 'The heart is more important.' If anyone reads the scriptures but is unkind, then it is not good. He is not a good man. But if there is both – a pure heart and reading the scriptures and praying, then very good."

I always enjoyed talking to Tenzin, but I had to reach the post office before it closed. Finally, I arrived and mailed the letter to Mr. Rao. There was a letter for me from Tashi telling me that he would take his vacation at the end of July, and that he would meet me in Manali and we would travel up to Ladakh together. It was already the middle of July!

As I bounded up the steep mountain path, I felt as carefree as a child. I didn't keep my attention on the stones jutting out from the grass. Suddenly, a group of children emerged from around a bend, racing down the hill. When they saw me, they yelled out.

"Chocolate! Chocolate!" and held out their hands.

I tripped and fell.

"My ankle!" I moaned, sinking down on the grass. "Not again!" I pulled myself to my feet, but I could barely walk. Removing my sandal, I dipped my foot into the rushing stream cascading down the mountainside. My green knapsack lay in the grass. The scorching-hot sun poured down liquid rays of molten fire. I put my hands into the cold water and rubbed my forehead and the back of my neck to cool off. I still had some distance to go before reaching the guest house.

Limping, I picked up my knapsack and with slow, painful steps started up the path, careful not to slip on the slick wet stones beside the gushing stream.

As I lay on my hard wooden bed with my ankle propped up against the wall, I thought, *How will I be able to climb the mountain path now? Perhaps it's time to move down from the mountain. I can't continue spraining my ankle like this.* I closed my eyes, letting my thoughts drift. Like clouds passing in the wind, the thoughts came and went. *Where shall I go? All the hotels in the market are hugely expensive and much too noisy.* Then suddenly, the idea flashed: *The gompa!*

I remembered Yuki's words now as I lay on the bed. I decided to ask the lamas if I could stay in the gompa for ten days until I left for Ladakh. The next time I limped into the gompa for my Tibetan lesson with a bandage tied around my ankle, I asked if I could come and stay for ten days. A few days later, I received the answer from the Abbot of the monastery.

I was welcome to stay for ten days! He allocated me a large room on the ground floor which usually was reserved for families visiting from Tibet. The nightly charge was usually ten rupees.

Lama Lochen came to show me the room. It was adjacent to the temple. When he opened the padlock on the door, I saw a large room with blue walls and a long wooden platform which served as a bed. The wood had rotted away in some places. The wooden platform was covered with a few very old dirty dark woolen blankets which were torn, ragged and threadbare at the edges. As I entered the room, a large spider crawled over the bed. On part of the floor was an old linoleum mat and some rotting straw matting. The rest was bare stone. From the ceiling a naked light bulb hung from a twisted wire. Other than that, the room was empty.

Lama Lochen revealed to me that the Abbot had said, "Do not take any money from her."

I did not know how to express my gratitude, so I simply closed my eyes and touched my joined palms to my forehead instead. The lama understood. The next ten days in the gompa were the happiest days of the entire three months I spent in Manali. I moved in the next day.

A coolie brought my suitcase down from the mountain the next morning. As I entered the gompa, my heart rejoiced. Walking clockwise around the large white stupa to the left of the entrance as a sign of respect, I led the coolie to the door of my room adjacent to the temple.

After I paid the coolie, Lama Lochen came in and swept the dusty floor. The room had been closed for a long time.

"I thought you were coming in the afternoon," he said, apologetically.

"I could only get a coolie in the morning," I explained. "Thank you so much."

Lama Lochen lifted my suitcase and tucked it securely into one of the shelves inset in the wall. Then he handed me the key to the padlock. Before departing, he told me that today was a very holy day in the Tibetan calendar and that the lamas would be chanting the prayers three times: from six to seven-thirty and from nine to eleven o'clock in the morning and again in the afternoon from two to four o'clock.

The rise and fall of the prayers was like the murmur of a gentle river, bringing with it a sense of calm and tranquil happiness. Crossing the threshold of the temple, I bowed down three times. Entering the sacred space made fragrant with the sweet breath of dedicated lives was like coming home. I felt infinitely safe, protected by so many fathers who had created a circle of light here at the foot of the mountain. Here was a peace which transcended speech, a deep ancient wellspring of silent renewal, as if one was nearer to the heart of God.

That night when I retired to my room, I decided not to use the torn dusty blankets. Covered with a piece of white silk from an old sari and a thick green woolen shawl bought in Varanasi several years before, I slept soundly that night, my first night in the home of the lamas.

At dawn, the faint tinkling of bells stirred the air. First from above, the sound came. Then again, in the courtyard opposite, the bells tinkled softly in the velvet darkness before sunrise. Sitting up in bed, I listened intently. There was a rustling on the floor above me. The sound was muffled and deep, like a whisper on the wind; a lama's voice rose slowly as the bells punctuated the sonorous echo. Like silver wings opening to the light, the murmur of voices praying hovered on the breath of morning. I could feel the air grow brighter as the lamas prayed. As the bells faded, the sun rose.

Slipping quietly out of my room, I tiptoed up the side staircase to the third floor where there was a shower Yuki had used when she was living in the monastery. I tried to remain as invisible and discreet as possible so as not to meet any of the lamas with my dressing gown on. I never did.

The temple drum resounded at a quarter to six, in slow notes, calling, calling, calling the lamas to the temple for the morning prayers. I was just about to begin my meditation or yoga exercises at that time, but I decided to go to the prayers first and meditate afterwards. I saw the maroon-robed figures with shaved heads descend the wooden steps. Most of the lamas were nearly sixty years old or more and some walked slowly, laboriously. Some moved more easily, though without haste. There were perhaps six lamas in their twenties and a few novices of maybe sixteen, seventeen or eighteen. They all moved with an inner quietude; a sense of purpose; a simple unquestioning devotion. With a soft patter of slippers on the wooden balcony and a rustle of robes, they filed down the stairs, one after another into the sacred shrine where the deities waited, and sat on their mats on the floor. The water bowls had been filled to the brim by two humble lamas who attended to the temple offerings to the deities.

After fifteen minutes of prayers, one of the youngest novices brought warm bread, and butter tea from the monastery kitchen to the temple. The lamas had ten minutes to sip their steaming-hot butter tea, dipping their bread into the round bowls. They ate in silence. Then the prayers continued, filling the hall with sonorous waves of silence.

Their voices rose in stillness as the statue of the Buddha and the deities adorning the altar smiled down at them. As I listened to the chiming of the bells and the swish of the cymbals, the outer world was washed away and I was transported to a vast unbounded shrine of inner peace. Here was a place where one hungered not for anything, for the heart was inundated with a rising sense of inner fullness that became more and more immovable. There was no sense of time – only a benediction of pure unalloyed happiness.

As I listened to the lamas praying, I was drawn to a special figure whose voice cast a spell which seemed to be woven of threads of golden light. I glanced up and saw that he was praying with his hands. Sometimes the lamas would translate certain passages of prayer into specific movements of their hands called mudras. I was spellbound by what I saw. The lama was deep inside the cave of his being. Although his eyes were open, he was not looking outside at all. His hands moved in gestures of unearthly tenderness, not like hands, but rather like petals, like the petals of a lotus unfolding, curving round and opening, giving, offering, blessing, creating, revealing and returning inward to his God. I was mesmerized by the beauty of the movements. It was as if the voice of love was speaking, telling its own story in silence, in a song without words, yet far more powerful.

As I gazed at him, tears welled up in my eyes. Never had I beheld such gentleness in anyone's hands. This was a language reserved for the devotee and his God, more beautiful than even the sound of which it was a symbol. The tears overflowed, poured forth from my heart like the torrent of a waterfall. I could not stop them. I cried and cried, bowing my head on my chest so as not to be noticed. The lamas continued praying as my unburdened heart lay at rest at the feet of the Infinite. All boundaries of time and space were washed away. In this way, I came to know the way of life of a lama. In the gompa, each day unfolded in silence like a prayer, in an unspoken language, known, well-known to every lama, a ritual which required no thinking, only calm obedience, a silent way of flowing with the current of the river. After the early-morning prayer, a loud gong resounded. The sound was a summons. The lamas descended the steps to the kitchen to fill their thermos flasks with tea or water. The prayers in the temple resumed from nine until eleven. Again at noon, a gong sounded thrice. The lamas brought their bowls to the kitchen and took their lunch back to their rooms where they ate in silence or with a few others. After lunch, they rested. At two o'clock, the gong sounded, summoning the lamas to the temple for the afternoon prayers which lasted until four or four-thirty. The day was punctuated by the sound of the gong and each individual part of the day was part of a larger ritual in which life unfolded in peace, almost moving without movement. It was a dance that required no thought, only simplicity, acceptance, a letting go, a giving in to the almost imperceptible flow of the river.

Between prayers, there were the flowers growing in pots on the roof above the kitchen to be watered, robes to be washed, walks in the forest and to the market to be taken, and friendships between members of the brotherhood to be nurtured. These were like the quiet melodies that rippled between the chiming of the gongs, the soundless sounds that bound together the fabric of a lama's life into one integrated whole, a wholeness fragrant with inner joy.

The days ebbed and flowed with the rising and falling of the prayers and I was as if baptized in the sacred waters of primordial sound. Inside, I could feel that the time of saying farewell to these mountains and this blessed hall of the Gelugpa Monastery was fast approaching. In a way, I prepared myself in advance for departure.

As I walked down the path from the monastery to the market, I gazed with more affection at all the faces which had become so familiar during the last three months in Manali. There was the beggar lady who sat outside on the path near the sweetshop, who had no fingers, into whose palm I often dropped a few rupees whenever I passed. There were the boys who worked in the sweetshop who smiled whenever they saw me enter the shop. There was Swarma, who worked behind the counter in the post office who always looked so serious, except when I called her "Swarmaji." Then she had to smile.

When she saw me come in, she held up a letter in her hand.

"For you," she said.

It was from Tashi! I went to my usual seat in the sweetshop and opened it. The letter said that the Japanese monk had asked Tashi to stay on in Delhi for a few more weeks! I was stunned. I stared at the letter in anguish. I felt an uncomfortable pressure build up in the center of my chest.

"Oh no." I sighed, slumping back against the chair. *If I wait for Tashi, I will miss all the special festivals in Ladakh where the lamas dance in the gompas. Should I wait for him or should I go alone?...* I sat still in dismay, without thinking at all. Finally the answer came: *I must go ahead alone.*

I went to see Sanjay, the travel agent. I had visited his office several times to inquire about when the road to Leh would be open. He had given me a beautiful brochure describing the festivals at the gompas. He had been there the previous year and he really wanted me to go. When he asked me about booking a ticket, I didn't say anything. How could I say anything when I knew I couldn't afford to go on a decent bus? Yet I wanted so much to reach the Takthog Gompa in time for the festival.

"What's wrong?" he asked, concerned.

"I don't have the money," I replied in a totally dejected tone of voice.

He looked at me for awhile. Then he said: "Don't worry. I'll take care of it. Leave it to me. Come back tomorrow evening."

When I returned the next day, he told me he had telephoned a Tibetan friend's travel agency, and organized a free seat for me on his bus!

The last day before my journey to Ladakh came. On that same day, the lamas were also leaving for their holiday in Rohtang Pass. It was a holy day in the Buddhist calendar. I awoke to the faint tinkling of bells, and washed and dressed in time for the sounding of the first gong summoning the lamas to the temple. In the shadow of their footsteps, I entered the temple, the only lay person among ten or fifteen ancient fathers. Sitting in my usual place, I closed my eyes, listening to the murmur of the first prayer songs as they filled the morning air. After an interval, the butter tea was poured and the round sweet bread passed to each lama. I knew the ritual and remained sitting with my eyes closed. I heard the soft rattle of a teacup being placed before me and the tea being poured, all with eyes closed. I bowed my head in gratitude. When I opened my eyes, I saw, to my surprise, a piece of the special bread resting on top of the cup of butter tea. I was having breakfast with the lamas for the first time, as one of them, as one family! Again, the tears welled up from my heart. The lamas would never know how much that simple repast in their company meant to me.

I spent nearly the entire day with the lamas as they prayed three times. Their voices became one with the innermost threads of my being and the lute which joined my limbs together reverberated with the sound as with the rhythm of my breath. I walked above the earth and breathed air that mingled with sweet milk and saffron water and exuded the cedar-like fragrance of a Tibetan temple.

Chapter Fifteen

On the morning of my departure, I awoke with a sense of exhilaration. Today I was setting out for Ladakh, the little Tibet at the top of the world, The Last Shangri-La! This was the journey I had heard so much about, had thought about and waited for. The bus was scheduled to leave at five-thirty in the morning. My suitcase was packed and ready. I glanced at my watch. It was five o'clock. I had arranged for a man from a nearby hotel to take me to the bus station. He had said that he would come at five o'clock. But when I looked outside, there was no sign of him. The only sound was the faint murmuring of the prayers of the lamas.

Suddenly, a crack of thunder rent the air. The sky divided and a torrential downpour flooded the street. The rain beat against the windowpane in an unrelenting rhythm. It was fifteen minutes past five. I didn't even have an umbrella. In desperation, I threw open the door and ran outside into the pouring rain. Luckily, he had showed me where he lived the day before. The hotel was still locked. I went around to the back door and knocked loudly. Groggy-eyed, he came to the door. He was still in his pajamas!

"It's almost time for the bus to leave! Hurry! Hurry! Please hurry! I have to make the bus on time!" I shouted.

"Your suitcases? Where are they?! I'm so sorry. I overslept," he said apologetically.

"They are in my room at the monastery! Hurry!" I shouted frantically.

He ducked back into his room and quickly changed his clothes. Then he emerged with an umbrella. We jumped into his car and raced back to the monastery.

"Don't worry," he said over and over again, trying to help me calm down.

My heart was racing as we sped down the narrow, winding road to the bus station. He loaded my suitcase onto the bus and I climbed in. The only seat left vacant was in the front, in a cabin next to the bus driver.

But it is perfect! What a fantastic view! I thought, peering through the large window. It was perfect until, much to my chagrin, five more passengers squeezed into the front cabin with me. *But I made the bus. That's all that matters!* I relaxed into the seat. And with a grinding of wheels and a roar of the robust engine, the bus set off for Ladakh.

I sat gazing out the window as the bus hurtled forward through the thick fog, moving slowly up the mountain pass. Thick fir trees shrouded in morning mist hung like Japanese painted scrolls on the vast canvas of the sky. Huge gray boulders clung to heaving mountains and narrow mountain streams fell in long thin threads, weaving a path between massive rocks and crumbling stones. Wooden shanties grew up out of the rocky terrain, and green-textured meadows breathed wide in valleys cradled between soaring mountain glades. We passed billboards with signs which said: Whispering Rocks Resort and Dove's Nest. And as the scene changed, the curtain of fog opened, revealing a gushing waterfall cascading from an invisible height into a bubbling foaming pool at whose feet was a simple sign in broad brush strokes which said: **LOVE.** *So this is LOVE,* I thought, gazing wistfully at the gushing waterfall as the bus charged up the dirt path, up, up, up. As we scaled the heights of the Himalayas, the inner exhilaration increased. The mist hiding the face of the mountains gradually cleared, revealing a crystal blue sky. Through the patches of mist, two white stallions emerged, wandering over the plains. Wild horses grazed on the barren sand-strewn hills where tufts of grass grew in patches between miles of crumbled stones the color of sand.

As we traveled on, the bus slid from side to side through the soft mud-filled roads. The mountainside was dotted, as if by a painter's loving hand, with tiny wild flowers, yellow and white, which resembled daisies. Further up were manmade walls, arranged on the edge of huge precipices to stop falling rocks from crashing into vehicles passing on the winding road. Deep ruts in the road, filled with rain water, caused the bus to swerve precariously from side to side, leaning heavily over the edge of deep gorges whose depths could not be gaged. We passed an eight- to nine-meter glacier frozen like an ancient mound clinging to the side of a mountain, surrounded by frozen rivers of snow.

Ascending higher still, I saw a sign which said: In the Land of the Lamas, Take It Easy. At 3,978 meters, we passed the source of the Beas River in Rohtang.

We entered La Haul, the land that stretched to the very gateway to Leh, the capital of Ladakh. We saw white snow-covered mountains gleaming under a clear blue sky. Deep green velvet-covered mountains rose amidst jagged rocks, white, glittering like scintillating pieces of cut glass, with upturned faces illuminated by the sun. Heaving rivers of rock littered the mountainside like jewels. Here bright purple and iridescent blue wildflowers grew in clumps between crumbled stones, vibrant, alive, irrepressible, even in the midst of the sand-strewn landscape.

On the way, we passed dark-faced laborers with scarves tied around their heads to allay the searing heat of the sun. They worked on the roads, filling in the deep pools of water with small stones collected from the mountainside. Others were working in the fields.

A man sitting next to me said, "Here, the main source of income is growing crops. Peas, potatoes and hops are sent from La Haul to the rest of India. The best potatoes in India are said to be from La Haul."

Small villages nestled in the valleys, while here and there, isolated houses clung to the sides of the mountain. Beyond the tree line, the soil turned gray-white. Sculptured gray and gold boulders pointed skyward with faces of fossilized textures carved by rain and wind and snow. In the mid-afternoon light, it looked even brighter. Wild gushing silver streams cascaded over the road as the wheels of the bus waded through the water, veering sharply to the left. The driver's body swayed with the motion of the wheels, sharply to the left side, then to the right and left again; he moved ably to avoid the edge of the narrow road and the deep gorges down below.

A herd of white long-haired goats wandered by. We halted in La Haul beside the Chandra River. There was a profusion of wildflowers robed in orchid, yellow, white, blue, purple and pink, sprinkled like luminous gems upon the hills. The Chandra River flowed past. Here the Bhaga River flowed into it.

"The sangam, the meeting place of the two rivers is regarded as a sacred place. After a cremation, the ashes of the dead are thrown into it," the man sitting next to me said. He pointed to a monastery on the hill and another one on top of a mountain. Then he said, "Kardung monastery is the most famous monastery in La Haul. It was built in the thirteenth century."

We pulled onto the side of the road and the bus came to a halt. Soldiers with rifles strapped to their backs stood in front of black triangular tents. They ordered all foreigners off the bus with their passports. I turned to the man next to me.

"But this is still India, isn't it?" I asked perplexed.

"Yes, this is for safety. There is still fighting in Kashmir, you know. There has been much trouble near the borders." He paused, and then added, "This is just a routine passport check."

After marching single file through the tent and inscribing our names and our countries in a logbook, I and the rest of the foreigners, boarded the bus. We set off at a faster pace as if attempting to reclaim the time we had lost. Dust swirled up from the road as the bus wound its way forward. Then it stopped with a jolt.

Just in front of the bus, in the middle of the road was a huge boulder. It looked like a big chunk of the mountain had fallen away. The muscular driver stood up with a gesture of impatience and several hefty men followed him outside. Standing with their full weight pressed against the rock, they pushed hard. Nothing happened. They pushed again; the veins on some of their foreheads were bulging out. Then I saw the rock move; first it moved slowly. Then they gave it a big shove. It tottered and fell over the edge of the precipice, crashing down into a rocky ravine far below.

The wheels ground forward through the hard broken stones that lay in the path. Driving the bus seemed to me to be like attempting to train a wild bucking bronco as it reared its head, galloping wildly over the rolling hills. The bus driver drove the bus with aggression. His face was lined like the path, but his eyes, wide open, dared the landscape to deter him in his upward movement. Undaunted by the danger looming at every turn in the narrow mountain passes, he cast fear to the wind, even revved up the engine, making the wheels of the bus rotate fiercely, cutting his way through stone-filled ruts in the road. Faster, faster, he plowed his way forward. He refused to be slowed down by heavier, less-agile vehicles on the road. With his hand pressing down on the horn, the sound blared out loudly in the air. Drivers moved over to the side to let us pass.

Gazing out the window, I saw a lorry in front of us lumbering forward, ever so slowly. The driver of our bus impatiently honked his horn. Just ahead of us, the lorry moved as fast as it could. But for our driver, it wasn't fast enough. I covered my ears with my hands to muffle the blast of the horn. But the sound didn't stop. He pressed down on the horn, again and again. The lorry refused to move to the side. Our driver continued to blow his horn, unremittingly.

Finally the lorry driver allowed us to pass, and we were ahead again. Suddenly our bus churned to a grinding standstill. The driver jumped out. Several of his friends followed.

"What is going on? Why are we stopping?" I asked the passenger sitting next to me. "Where are they all going?"

"They are fighting," he said.

"What?! Fighting? I – uh – why?" I asked, alarmed.

"Because our driver always has to be first. He thinks he owns the road."

Voices were shouting. A group of tall, bearded Sikhs rushed out of the lorry, waving heavy sticks and iron clubs. They surrounded our bus driver. I stared out of the window, terrified.

"What if they kill him!? Then we'll be stuck high up in the mountains without a driver! Why, oh, why did he have to get out? Why didn't he just drive on when the road was clear!?"

The Sikhs stood over our bus driver with their fists in the air. They hurled insults at each other, shouting at the top of their voices. The air vibrated with frenzy for ten, maybe fifteen minutes. Then our driver returned, followed by his cronies. They tumbled into their seats, cursing and sweating. The engine roared, the wheels rotated wildly as we set off again up the winding path.

"Thank God." I breathed a sigh of relief.

But it was too early. Shortly afterwards we were halted again by a boulder in the road. A jeep ahead of us waited as several men pondered over how to move it. The bus pulled in behind the jeep and we were allowed to disembark for a while. I walked to the edge of a cliff and peered down, down, down into the valley far below.

Suddenly I heard the sound of angry voices rising behind me. Turning around with a start, I saw the same lorry driven by the Sikhs parked behind our bus. The bearded Sikh drivers and their comrades quickly jumped out. They were running toward our bus brandishing knives and clubs in their hands.

"Oh my God!" I lifted my hand to my mouth. "Oh God, please! No!" I shouted. I grabbed the back of a Tibetan man. "Do something! Do anything; please, I do not want anyone to be hurt!"

The Sikhs entered the bus and menaced the driver and his

friends. Angry voices rose making a hissing sound. A crowd of passengers gathered round, hiding them from our view, while the rest of us clambered out of the bus. Their angry voices rose.

"Do something, anything! Let's pray!" I said hoarsely to the Tibetan man.

"Nothing will happen," the Tibetan man said quietly, comforting me.

An elderly Indian man in a white dhoti came forward out of the crowd. It looked as if he was counseling both sides. He parted the main adversaries in the group and reprimanded them. It seemed as if they were listening to him. Slowly, one Sikh after another moved back down the road to their lorry. As I entered the bus, our driver was slumped forward over the steering wheel, totally exhausted. We waited until finally the boulder was shifted and we traveled on.

Be Gentle on My Curves, a sign said. It was painted on the face of a flat rock. I wished they had been.

Many sharp drops and blind curves caused the bus to veer from side to side as it resumed its upward climb. The rumbling sound of an approaching lorry roared. Ahead of us, I saw a large lumbering vehicle carrying highly inflammable oil. On the rear fender, there was a sign which said: ILU with a little heart on either side of it. *I LOVE YOU,* I thought, smiling. We passed through small villages surrounded by bare rock faces of a gray, green and copper hue. The vegetation was sparse. A herd of donkeys grazed among the sandy hills. Threads of snow trickled down. The mountains resembled huge waves frozen in stillness, carved by the Almighty Hand of an invisible artist, tinted with luminous brush strokes of pink, salmon, deep purple, gray, copper, peach, brown and pale yellow. They spoke of worlds as yet undiscovered, awash with the pure and brilliant energy of life.

The mountains flowed down in long, smooth graceful curves. Mountain streams, frozen with snow, ran like veins through the sides of the breathing mountain peaks. Grains of sand blew in through the open window. I pulled my long cotton shawl up over my mouth and nose as I gazed out at the vast horizon. Bald rock faces and bald hills like the shaved heads of the lamas looked in through the glass as we churned our way forward. Their copper-colored summits gave way to dark gray ridges. The vista cleared under azure skies, aglow with light as evening descended.

The narrow road wound its way slowly upwards. There were no more trees. Only massive hills of multicolored rock with pink wildflowers and gray-colored peaks pointing heavenward. I felt as if I was entering the very womb of creation and beholding the naked flesh of the earth: raw, unadorned. It was as if I was standing in the mixing bowl of creation, seeing the beginning of the world taking shape. The sight of nature unmasked in all its singular beauty, so primitive, so full of energy, was utterly capti-vating. The primal colors of creation were glowing like the flesh and bones and skin of Mother Earth. It appeared like a picture of the skeletal structure of the earth, or rather more like the very body of God, and the pure, vast, unbounded dimensions of His Divine Mind. All the lines of His thought were so radiant and so grand. Could it be the flow of His Divine Mind? The whole creation – a mirror image of that flow? I felt as if I was seeing all the convolutions, lines and textures which had instantaneously been created when the earth first breathed...beholding the bulging muscles of Mother Earth as Her body grew big with life...beholding the Divine Mother, naked with innumerable bellies, and breasts full with milk, flowing pools of milk, streaming from the rounded summits of the mountains. Every curve of Her Divine Body was simple, rounded and pregnant with mystery. It was as if She spoke, saying: *Take Me as I Am – free, naked, simple, and unadorned. Through the fullness of emptiness, enter the inner shrine of My Being and discover the fullness of Fullness.*

There was water: deep blue mountain pools and ribbons of silver shimmering in the twilight air. But no human habitation for miles and miles and miles. It was as if we were alone with God's thoughts – alone in the vast abyss of creation. Ochre-colored mountains sculpted of sand with patches of white snow rose up on the backdrop of the sky.

We were approaching tents – white triangular tents. The landscape was hidden by darkness. The bus drew to a halt in Sarcu, 251 kilometers from Leh. Here we rested for the night. Colorful mats were strewn on the ground inside the tents. Packages of snacks awaited our hungering eyes. The air was cold, fresh and pure. Some slept in the tents with sleeping bags; others huddled in their seats under blankets and shawls for the night. I slept crouched up in the seat of the bus. We passed 4800 meters today. Tomorrow we would traverse mountains as high as 5200 meters.

At dawn, I awoke with limbs stiff from the cold. As I cleared the mist from the window, I stared out, stunned. The terrain was more akin to the surface of the moon than that of the earth. I stared awestruck at cascading silhouettes of mountains etched in sand. The sublime majesty of each line, each curve, and the subtlety of the pastel hues, all mingled together to form a scene of quiet splendor, a symphony of nature's pure forms bathed in the pristine light of dawn.

Walking outside, I found a stream just above us on a hill where I washed my face and hands. I also picked a few blue wildflowers for Tashi which I gently placed between the pages of a book in my knapsack.

I didn't intend to eat anything other than the fruit I had brought with me from Manali. Then I noticed people coming out of one of the tents.

"Have you had breakfast?" someone called out to me. "Breakfast is in the tent."

I opened the flap of a white tent and went inside. Our bus driver was seated before a plate piled high with chapatis. When he saw me, he whispered something to the man in charge and he glanced over at me.

"You take breakfast with us. No charge for you. You like chapatis?" The man looked at me and smiled warmly. "How many chapatis you like?" He told the cook to make more chapatis and then he poured a cup of tea and handed it to me.

"Thank you very much." I was overwhelmed with gratitude.

After everyone had eaten, the bus pulled out, leaving the lone white tents in the distance.

We seemed to have reached the very summit of the earth. It looked like the inside of a volcano; primordial substances were etched into the basin of the earth. Rich tones of gold and peach arose like vapor from the depths of the cauldron of life. There was only sand and sky.

"This is the highest mountain. It is 16,600 feet," the man sitting next to me remarked. Like a mirage in the desert, whole Tibetan villages, and regal palaces appeared carved out of sand, hanging suspended from towering mountains resembling huge sand dunes.

We paused for a tea break in white tents pitched on an endless ocean of sand. The road to Tanglangla was completely flat. Empty oil cylinders lined either side of the road. Small clumps of vegetation were still visible at this altitude. Salmon-colored hills loomed on the horizon. The landscape was totally dry. Huge sand dunes and stone-filled desert plains mixed with white snow-covered peaks. The road was bleached white from the sun. Even the streams had dried up. My mouth felt parched as I gazed at the dismal gray hills totally bereft of plant life. The bus swayed. We soared over huge plummeting slopes framed by high mountain ridges. Frozen glaciers clung to the sides of mountains. On the way, we passed dark-skinned men in long khaki jackets. Their skin looked as black as the boiling tar which they used to pour over the ruts in the road. Their heads were swathed in scarves which also covered their mouths. Clouds of black smoke and searing flames swirled up from red-hot cylinders. We hurriedly shut the windows of the bus as the acrid smell filled the air outside, burning our nostrils.

As we approached the last stretch of the journey, we left behind the vast stretches of uninhabitable land and entered a new domain. Here the land was blessed with rippling streams which fed lush fields of green grass. A herd of ibex grazed in meadows radiant with sunlight. Here, I saw the first cows grazing! Here, there was a fresh palette: each vista was washed with ultraviolet light. The rivers, the rose-tinted mountains and fertile fields, all seemed to sparkle.

Am I entering paradise? I asked myself. *So pure and bright is the light.* My heart rejoiced.

Onward through a passage lined with soaring mountains sloping down to grassy meadows where crystal rivers ran over gleaming white rocks, onward toward white stupas rising, glowing, welcoming us as we crossed the threshold into Ladakh, the land of the lamas, the land at the summit of the earth, The Last Shangri-La!

Chapter Sixteen

We entered Leh as the sun set behind the mountains. The bus scorched the sandy road with its wheels. Then it halted in a field where we proceeded to unload our luggage from the roof of the bus. I couldn't get mine down; it was too heavy. I stood in front of the bus wondering what to do. A man who looked Tibetan helped me lift my suitcase. It fell from the roof with a thud onto the dry, hard ground. With an effort, I stood it upright and peered around. Darkness was setting in. Milling around us were young men who offered to help us find accommodation in Leh. I asked one of them where I could find a room for twenty rupees a night. I had only five hundred rupees left.

"Impossible!" Their answers echoed from one to another. "Impossible to find in Leh."

The sky turned dark purple. I gazed around at all the faces as a feeling of quiet desperation constricted my chest. *Where should I go?*

Then I remembered Kalsang's house. A flash of hope! He had told me it was close to the Shanti Stupa. I approached a handsome Ladakhi man who was standing near a white jeep.

"Do you know 'Japanese Kalsang'?" I asked. "I want to go to his house. I know him and his daughter. Maybe I can stay with them."

"Japanese Kalsang? No, I don't know him." He looked at me curiously.

"But Kalsang said everyone would know if I just said 'Japanese Kalsang'. He works in the Buddhist Center in Delhi. He works for the monk who built the Shanti Stupa. I can't afford to stay in a hotel."

The young man peered at me, and then he smiled. He decided to help me. He thought for a few minutes. Finally he said: "I'll take you up to the Shanti Stupa. Maybe they will know where his

216

house is. Is this your suitcase?"

"Yes." I sighed, with obvious relief, as I climbed into the comfortable front seat of the jeep.

"You are alone?" the man asked as he pushed on the ignition key, propelling the car forward with a jolt.

"Yes," I said quietly.

"You are very beautiful," he said. I did not answer. He jerked the car forward again as we turned toward the mountain pass leading up to the Shanti Stupa.

"I came to Ladakh so I could attend the Takthog Festival, the last religious festival this summer at the gompa."

"You want to go with me? People sleep overnight in tents when they go to the festival."

"In a tent? Then where will you sleep? In the tent with me?" I asked, laughing slightly. "No, I will go on the bus."

He did not say anything after that for some time.

"You have a boyfriend?" he asked.

"There is someone – a very good friend. I'm waiting for him. He'll come to Ladakh in a few weeks."

"A boyfriend or a friend?" he persisted.

"A friend, but maybe more – maybe it will become something more..." I answered. I didn't want to hurt his feelings.

Finally he pulled up in front of a small Japanese-looking stupa-shaped temple. He got out and knocked at the door of a house adjacent to the temple. An elderly lama opened the door, and pointed to a house down the hill.

"It is there," the driver of the jeep pointed as he entered the car.

"Can I have a look at the temple?" I asked.

"Some other time. I have things to do." He pulled the clutch, and backed out of the narrow dirt road. As we headed down the circular mountain road, he seemed to be driving even faster than before. The wheels of the car bounced up and down as it veered around blind curves and over rocky ruts in the road.

"Could you slow down a little please?" I asked timidly, glancing at him out of the corner of my eye.

"We're almost there," he said, as we tore onto the flat path near the village down below.

Night had set in and I could see the outline of trees as we headed up a winding path.

"Here it is," he said, slowing down in front of a small dwelling.

He got out and opened a corrugated iron gate and called out to someone inside. A small girl came out.

"Yes?" she asked.

I came into the front yard and stood in front of her. "Please, is your sister here? I met her in Delhi at the Buddhist Center. Could I stay here for a few days? I cannot afford a hotel. Can you ask your sister to come?" I asked the girl.

"Yes, my sister is here. Ani! Ani!" she shouted.

A few minutes later, the wooden door opened and a beautiful girl with long dark hair came out. She came over to me. "Oh come in! Come in! It's great to see you," she said, taking my hand and leading me inside.

I thanked the man who had given me the lift, and he drove off. Then I went inside. The house was dark and it smelled like the earth. Ani led me into a small sitting room.

"Tea?" Ani asked, motioning for me to sit on a bench under the window.

"Yes, alright, thank you," I replied, smiling.

I looked at a large wooden cupboard decorated with painted flowers like one sometimes sees on Swiss chalets. The wooden shelves covered the wall from the floor to the ceiling; they contained an array of copper and stainless-steel pots and pans and a small collection of china, arranged in neat rows. Everything looked clean and polished. Ani was cooking water on a cast-iron stove with a long pipe which went up into the ceiling. In a corner of the room was a television set, a tape recorder and a box of audiotapes. The room was dimly lit by one solitary light bulb suspended from a wire in the middle of the ceiling.

"What is that?" I asked pointing to a decorated cylindrical implement with a long rod.

Ani told me it was used to churn the butter for the traditional Ladakhi salted butter tea.

I told her that I needed a place to stay for a few days as I had come especially to attend the religious festival at Takthog Gompa. After that, I planned to visit a friend of mine called Rinchen in Nubra Valley.

"Is it possible to stay here? Is there space for me for a few days?" I asked softly.

"Yes, we do have space. You stay here," Ani replied happily.

I was very relieved when she led me upstairs to a large bedroom with mats covered with rugs along the wall and low wooden tables. Metal trunks were piled in the corner near the bed. On the walls were pages from a Japanese calendar depicting Japanese ladies in fancy kimonos.

"You sleep here. Sometimes I sleep here, but I go to another room," Ani said, pulling back the quilt on the bed.

On a hook near the window were Ani's clothes: several Indian Punjabi pants suits in dark blue, green and a red checkered design. On the table were a pile of magazines and school notebooks.

"But I don't want to take your bed," I said. "I can sleep on a mat over there."

"No, no, I sleep somewhere else. You can sleep here. It's OK for you?" she asked, indicating the blankets at the foot of the bed.

"Yes. Thank you very much." I took some of my things out of my suitcase which was too heavy to carry upstairs.

That night, I slept soundly. The journey from Manali had been physically demanding and my body sank heavily into the thick cotton sheets, grateful for the chance to stretch out after two days of sitting crouched in the seat of a bus.

The next morning, when I awoke, I pulled back the cotton curtains over the window and peered out. The dark blue outline of the mountains beckoned in the distance. Gazing down into the yard below, I saw a large brown cow ensconced between two calves. The mother cow was licking the coat of her small black calf. The other calf was pale beige. It was a scene of such tenderness; my heart rejoiced. I slid the curtain back over the iron pole and sat up in bed to meditate.

The outside world melted away like a mirage in the desert. I was aware of a deep silence drawing me down, down, down into an inner world, far beyond images, thoughts and the constant play of emotions. In the silence, the wings of the heart spontaneously unfolded, spreading wide into the inner firmament, a world finer than thought, lighter than air. "I" was no more. Only "Thee", only "Thee" – only a peace which could not be named, only a time which could not be measured, a space which breathed life without moving. THAT was I – THAT was all.

After some time, the body dozed off. I lay half-awake on the bed, thoughts returning tumbled one after another; vague thoughts wrapped in fog, gathered like mist on the top of a mountain, then faded into thin air.

As I opened my eyes, I looked up at the painting of Green Tara, the deity one prayed to for good health. It hung in one corner of the room, a frayed and yellowing page taken from a Tibetan Buddhist calendar. I noticed some itching feeling in my arm, but did not pay much attention to it.

I wandered outside. There was no running water in the house. The toilet consisted of a narrow slit in the earth with a pit underneath it. I saw Ani across the road, filling a bucket with water from a metal pipe from which spring water gushed forth. The stream from which it came was used for washing one's clothes.

"You wash? Here is water," she said simply. She then led me upstairs to a square space of earth in the house which was surrounded by stones on the floor. Above it hung a piece of fabric which was rolled up. "You wash here. Take water. I pull curtain." The water felt tinglingly cold and fresh. I sprinkled it over my body and scrubbed my skin with a cotton cloth until it glowed with warmth. It felt so good to be clean again!

Afterwards, I climbed up the staircase outside my room which led to the roof. It was nearly noon and the sun gleamed on the open meadows. From the roof, I could see the Ladakhi landscape stretched out far and wide in the distance. Around the house, vegetable gardens were planted, row upon row of round green leaves, bursting with vigor, and beyond the vegetables, apple trees and apricot trees glistened in the strong rays of sunlight. In the distance lay golden hills of sand, and beyond the hills, blue-gray mountains rose, in a majestic array, surrounding the green fields on every side, like a protective armor.

The very air seemed to shimmer with light. There was a freshness as of newborn life, a pristine beauty which reveled in the colors of the earth, the fields, the hills, the mountains. It was as if the air was singing; the land alive with the sound of an inner music pregnant with joy. Gazing around, I saw the simply constructed houses, two stories high, made of stone and sand, with square flat roofs stacked along the edges with green grass turning golden in the sun. I looked at the trees, not very many, with their thin pale leaves and the glistening streams coursing through rocky fields like silver threads interwoven into the soft earth tones of the landscape. It was a sight that lifted the heart up to God.

The most unique feature of the landscape were the stupas. They were white, step-like structures built in layers with a wide base at the bottom. Each layer became smaller and smaller until it reached the top. As I gazed at them, I wondered what the stupas symbolized. After some time, I heard footsteps on the stairs and a young Japanese student joined me on the roof.

"Oh hello," he said, "have you just arrived?"

"Yes," I replied. "This is my first time in Ladakh."

"Oh, you will enjoy it. This is my third visit. I am a medical student in Japan, but I come here for my holidays."

"Do you know what the stupas symbolize?" I asked him.

"Yes, yes. The stupas are holy..." he paused, "...because each one contains a relic of the Buddha, a tooth or a hair. There is a relic in each stupa."

"Really?" I asked surprised.

"Yes, and the layers of the stupa symbolize the layers of the human being: the body, senses, mind, intellect and the inner Self. At the top of the stupa, all the qualities are unified. We as human beings must develop gradually and become like the Buddha. The aim of human life is to reach the top, to find inner peace like the Buddha did."

"Oh, how amazing. I didn't know that. Thank you very much," I said.

We sat in silence for awhile. I looked at the stupas dotting the hills and perched at the summit of the mountains. The sun dazzled my eyes; I started to feel a little dizzy. I touched my forehead with the back of my hand. I realized it was hot.

"I'm not feeling well," I said quietly, looking at the young man. "I think I have a fever."

He looked at me and then, with a knowing nod, he said, "You must go inside and rest. It is the altitude. It takes two or three days to adjust. It is better not to sit in the sun or walk around too much. Drink as much water as you can. Your headache will pass. It happens to everyone when they first arrive in Ladakh."

I became aware of an aching throbbing in my head. It was an effort to move. I steadied myself as I stood up.

"I'll go in now," I said. I made my way into the house and stretched out flat on the bed. My head ached. I could not eat very much. I felt weak and exhausted. Green Tara, the protector of health, spread her benevolent aura into the room. She looked down from the yellowing page of the Tibetan Buddhist calendar in the corner of the room. A once-white silk scarf was draped around the borders of the picture. As I lay in bed, I became intermittently aware of tiny insects crawling around under me. The fever lasted for two days.

On the third day, I had to leave the house at six o'clock in the morning in order to catch the bus to the Takthog Monastery. I was determined to arrive on time to see the last of the festivals during the summer season. I slept uneasily that night. It felt as though there were insects in the bed, but I was too tired to turn on the light to investigate. At five o'clock, I dragged myself out of bed and tiptoed downstairs and out to the stream to wash my face and rinse my mouth. Then I quietly dressed and slipped out of the house with my knapsack on my back and a few extra clothes in a bag so that I could stay overnight for the duration of the two-day festival.

As I walked down the winding dirt road, the sun rose, illumining the green fields. The earth appeared as if clothed in a raiment of pure light, soft as white silk. It spread its gossamer threads over the silver seam of mountains, over the translucent green leaves of the trees and over the flat roofs of the houses. The air sparkled like crystal, and the soft murmur of the stream blended with the songs of the birds to create a tapestry of gentle music.

"Jullay!" An elderly man's face creased into a smile as I passed.

"Jullay!" A child called out to me from an open window.

The sound of this simple greeting echoed in the stillness of the morning air, then floated in waves before disappearing into the silence of the newborn day.

The road curved round a small pool filled with reeds, and then onto the main road leading down to the market. Small colorful shops, still boarded up for the night, stood in a long line with signs which read: Ladakhi Gems, Leh General Store, German Bakery. As I hurried down the path, I saw young men with straw brooms sweeping the dust and debris from the road.

The streets were remarkably clean.

Having just arrived, I wasn't sure how to reach the bus depot. The streets were empty except for the sweepers and a few shopkeepers who were in the process of unlocking the corrugated-iron shutters of their shops. I stopped a dark-haired man in a white dhoti to ask for directions.

"You wait here. I will get a ride for you. It is not far. But better you get a ride. Then you are sure to make it." He stood in the middle of the road and flagged down a jeep driving past. Then he beckoned to me. The Tibetan driver smiled as I climbed into the front seat.

"You go bus station? Yes, I can take you." He started the motor and zipped down the road. "Where are you from?" he asked.

"I live in England."

"You look like Indian," he said, turning toward me.

"Many people say this. On the inside, I feel India is my home. I'm going to Takthog today for the festival."

"Good place. Festival – very beautiful – lamas dancing."

He pulled into the bus depot where several Westerners were sitting on stone steps, eating rolls and drinking water from clear plastic bottles. There were also a few lamas there, in their long maroon robes, standing together talking. I asked a lady when the bus was due to arrive.

"Seven or seven-thirty – maybe earlier. It is not a fixed time. Just wait. It is coming here."

I gazed into her smiling face. Like all Ladakhis, she had fair skin, broad cheeks and slightly slanted eyes. Her nose was small and pointed and her lips gently curved. Like many of the women, she wore the traditional Ladakhi attire, which was a woolen dress in either dark blue, black or gray with long sleeves, a tight-fitting bodice and a full skirt gathered at the waist, falling to the ankles. Underneath their dresses, they wore trousers for additional warmth.

The bus arrived fifteen minutes later. Nearly thirty people

filed in, filling all the seats. As we waited to depart, ten more Ladakhis arrived. They stood up in the aisles or sat on the edges of the full seats. They were all very polite.

I met the eyes of a beautiful woman with long dark hair. She was dressed in navy blue. As we looked into each other's eyes, a warmth of feeling flowed between our hearts; her look was full of innocence and openness. There was no trace of fear or suspicion or distrust, just a simple invitation of friendship.

As the bus approached Thikse, a young boy of about ten years old boarded the bus and held onto the metal pole near my seat. He stared at me, first at my hair, unusual because of its curls, and then at the bulging knapsack on my lap. Then he smiled. In his eyes, there was such a feeling of love that I immediately felt very close to him. He stood beside my seat, smiling into my eyes for a long time. As the bus moved slowly down the dirt road to Takthog, many Ladakhi passengers boarded and I was aware over and over again, of the same joyous pattern in their eyes and gestures. There was a natural ease, warmth, joy and openness in their nature which made the two-hour trip feel much more comfortable in spite of the cramped conditions.

The landscape mirrored the feeling I found expressed in the Ladakhi people, or perhaps it was the people whose natures unfolded in the same way as the landscape. The quality I noticed most was their softness, the ease expressed in their spontaneous smiles and the simple gesture of touching their right hand to the center of their forehead whenever they greeted each other. The land, much of which was made of desert sand, was open, and flat, with simple dwellings surrounded by towering mountains which rose like mighty waves; eternal symbols of silence, strength and an almost austere beauty. Dotting miles and miles of parched sand were glowing white stupas, sacred emblems of the Buddhist religion, so deeply embedded in the culture of Ladakh. Like the landscape, the men and women wore the strength of the mountains and the simplicity of the desert in their features; they carried the silence and peace of the stupas in their eyes and hearts, so gentle and welcoming and full of light.

When the bus finally arrived in Takthog, the young boy motioned to me to let him carry my knapsack. I gave it to him and he proudly flung it over his back and marched ahead of me toward the monastery. He had come alone from the village of Thikse to attend the religious festival.

The festival was to be held in the square courtyard outside the monastery. In the center of the courtyard was a tall pole bearing the prayer flags. On a table around it, the puja offerings were being prepared. Opposite the door of the gompa was a platform decorated with colorful silk brocade cloths. It was the place reserved for the high lama who was to address the gathering. I sat on the stone steps outside the gompa opposite the platform.

Many tourists had come laden with their cameras and other equipment. They crowded around the entrance to the gompa until a lama came out and told them that the middle of the stairs had to be kept clear so that the lamas could enter and exit during the festive dances.

There was a hush in the square as two lamas entered the center of the courtyard. They blew two long thin twelve-foot horns signaling the beginning of the ritual. The deep low tones of the horns carried me away from the everyday world, inward toward the silence of antiquity and timeless offerings in sacred shrines.

A line of lamas descended the steps of the gompa, arrayed in elaborate silk brocade robes, intricately woven in blue, turquoise, maroon and yellow with gold embroidery on the borders. They wore crowns on their heads, and in their hands they carried small round drums and brass bells. Slowly, they circled the sacred ground, whirling round and round, their outstretched arms moving gracefully like the gliding of bird's wings in the windless air. They circled the central pole in the middle of the courtyard.

As I gazed at their mask-like faces, I could see that, although their eyes were open, their vision was directed inwards. It was as if they were dancing alone before God, before the Buddha. They never even glanced at the people, but remained wrapped in a circle of inner peace, draped in a mantle of solemnity, poise and reverence. Some of the lamas wore masks which looked very fierce with long teeth; others wore masks with peaceful expressions; others wore masks of young Buddhist monks; others masks of the Buddha. There were many different dances. All consisted of slow whirling movements with characteristic gestures or mudras, and small leaps. Their movements were accompanied by the swish of cymbals, the boom of drums, the melodious sound of a pipe, and the deep resonance of the twelve-foot horns.

Each dance began with an invocation to the gods and guardians of the four quarters. The gods were invoked to witness the holy ritual with offerings of sacred water and food. The elaborately decorated masks represented different divinities. The dances depicted stories of both the fierce and the sublime, the divine interplay between the earth and heaven. I felt as if we were being allowed to enter a region known only to the lamas. They unveiled a landscape inhabited by spiritual beings that protected the earth from immemorial times.

At the close of the two-day ritual, the head lama blessed us, touching each of us gently on our heads as he moved along the row of bowed heads before our departure.

I was wondering where to spend the night when a lama from the gompa asked me if I needed a place to stay and then offered me his sitting room. I gratefully accepted and left my bags there. He told me that the founder of the Takthog gompa was said to have meditated in a cave on a hill nearby. His name was Guru Padmasambhava, the founder of the Nyingpa branch of Tibetan Buddhism. The lama told me about the very old gompa that had been built over his cave in the wall of the mountain.

I climbed up the hill. A minimal entrance fee was requested as is usual at the gompas in Ladakh. But I hadn't remembered to bring my purse. A Ladakhi guide really wanted me to go into the cave and kindly offered to pay the fee for me. As soon as I descended the steps into the darkened cave, I felt immense power emanating from it. The consciousness of a great being permeated the space. Spontaneously, my awareness was pulled inward. Kneeling before the image of the saintly lama, I prayed for liberation in order to become capable of helping to relieve the suffering of all living beings.

After some time, I returned to the little room I shared with the lama. It was highly decorous and covered from wall to wall with red woven rugs. The walls were painted maroon with a Tibetan border of yellow, green, red and blue. On a tall wooden mantle stood framed photographs of His Holiness the Dalai Lama and other high lamas. Each photo was garlanded with white silk scarves.

I sat on a maroon-covered mat as the lama placed tea and biscuits on the central table. There were photographs of him in a bookcase containing many books in Tibetan. He was forty years old and had entered the monastery at eighteen. He was a gentle, generous soul, but I felt somehow that he was not really happy inside. We spoke quietly together until evening fell and the stars shone through the open curtains. In silence, he reached toward me but he soon realized that the bridge was not destined to be built.

On the last day of the festival, I was searching for him in order to return the key to his room. I didn't want to miss the bus. I went to the monastery where the lamas were having lunch and scanned the room. Several of the young lamas looked up at me and smiled, but the lama I was looking for was not there. I quickly went to look outside. The sun was extremely bright.

As I was hurriedly trying to make my way through the crowd, I tripped. The strap on my sandal broke, and my foot slipped into the dust. I picked up the now-useless sandal and hobbled over the stone path. The ankle I had sprained in Manali ached miserably. I stood on the side of the road as people folded up their tents, packed up their makeshift restaurants and closed their display cases containing Ladakhi jewelry and handicrafts. The lama I had been searching for finally appeared. I gave him his key.

"Are there any more buses to Leh?" I asked him.

"No, the last bus has already left," he said kindly, walking away.

What am I going to do? I asked myself in desperation. *How will I ever get back?*

Bewildered, hot and tired, I stood in the scorching sun, feeling like a wilting plant in the desert.

A Ladakhi man came up to me. He looked friendly. "Where do you need to go?" he asked me in a comforting voice.

"To Leh," I said.

"You can come with us; we'll take you to Leh."

I got in his car with three other men. He drove me back to Leh. When we arrived, I asked him how much he wanted me to pay.

"Whatever you can afford," was his reply.

I gave him fifty rupees.

In the marketplace, a shoemaker fixed the strap on my sandal. As I climbed the hill to Ani's house, I felt exhausted but elated. The memory of the ritual dance of the lamas was still swirling in my head, and the kindness of the driver filled my heart with happiness.

Chapter Seventeen

When I woke up the next day, my right arm ached terribly. It was swollen and covered with a rash. I jumped out of the bed and examined the sheets. There were little black dots all over it. I finally realized what they were: bedbugs! I had been bitten so badly that I knew I could not stay at Ani's house any longer.

I thought of Rinchen, the teacher I had met at the Buddhist Center. She had invited me to visit her house in Nubra Valley. I decided to go to the tourist information office to inquire about how to get there.

The tourist office was an imposing square brick building near the polo ground. To reach it, I had to walk for a long time. It was on the opposite side of Leh. It was a hot, dry day. But the thought of Rinchen, and her warm invitation, gave me strength. When I finally reached my destination, a man in the tourist office politely informed me that Nubra Valley was one hundred and twenty kilometers from Leh and to reach it, one had to travel over the highest motorable road in the world, the Khardung La. He warned me that the road was in very bad condition.

I listened to his words, but my inner resolve remained unshaken. "I am determined to go – I must go," I replied softly, but firmly.

"But who are you going with?" the man asked.

"Alone. I am going alone."

"But it is not possible to go to Nubra Valley alone. Nubra Valley has only recently been opened to foreigners. To go there, you have to go in a group of at least four people," he said, with a gentle look in his eyes.

"I don't know anyone in Leh that could go with me," I said in a despondent tone of voice.

"How long do you want to stay there?" the man inquired.

"For at least ten days," I said.

"Foreigners are only allowed to stay for a maximum of one week," he informed me.

I dropped my head in anguish. My brilliant plan of where to stay until Tashi arrived was rapidly crumbling and to pay for a hotel in Leh was impossible.

"I'll go for one week then," I said in a hoarse voice.

"You need a permit in order to go because..." He seemed reluctant to continue because he could see that I was upset. Then he added, "... It is close to the Chinese border. The permit costs one hundred rupees."

"One hundred rupees?!" I burst out. "One hundred rupees? For a permit! I can't afford one hundred rupees. OK – thank you. Goodbye."

I walked out; I was in utter despair. I felt as if the ground had been pulled away from under my feet. Slowly I walked to the edge of the polo ground and slumped down on the stone wall. As I gazed out over the wide, empty arena, life felt gray and joyless. *Why did I come here? I should have waited for Tashi. Here I am in the middle of nowhere, with no money and nowhere to go. What am I going to do? I can't afford a hotel and I can't afford to go to Nubra Valley.* Feeling totally dejected, I burst into tears.

A Ladakhi man came up to me and asked me what the matter was. He advised me to go to another tourist office and to ask for the man in charge. When I arrived, I explained my predicament to him. He said that he owned a hotel.

"You can stay there for free until you can organize the permit for Nubra Valley," he said warmly. "And I know a travel agent who can arrange it for you. Don't worry. I send many people to him."

He took me to his hotel which was, in fact a small guest house. He even arranged for me to receive free meals. I was so grateful to him, but he would not allow me to thank him too much.

"I am glad to be able to help you," was all he said.

When I met the travel agent and asked him about the permit,

he offered to process all the papers and to give me the permit free of charge. In case I still needed a place to stay, he said I could stay at his house with his family. I remained at the guest house for two days while the paperwork was completed.

Finally the morning of the journey came. The bus was scheduled to leave at six in the morning, so it was still pitch black outside when I had to leave for the bus depot. When I opened the door, I couldn't see anything. *How can I walk one kilometer in total darkness when I can barely see the steps leading to the main road?*

I heard someone stirring on a cot outside the hotel. I realized it was the security guard. He sat up.

"Taxi?" I asked timidly.

"No taxi. Why you didn't say so last night? Too late to get taxi now." He lay back down on the cot.

"I can't see anything," I whispered. I moved out, feeling my way over the steps and crossing the path as best I could into the deserted street. The knapsack strapped to my back was heavy and I held a full bag in one hand and a thermos flask in the other. *I pray I make it to the bus.* I lifted up each foot to avoid tripping on the stones in the road.

Passing a police station, I approached a guard.

"Bus station – Nubra Valley – six o'clock," I said.

He didn't speak any English. Desperate, I tried gesturing, imploring his aid for a lift to the depot.

A very tall Westerner passed by with a flashlight strapped on his forehead.

"Are you going to the bus station?" I shouted.

"Yes," he answered without stopping.

"Can I come with you please?"

"Yes," he said in a low gruff voice, with a thick German accent. "I know a shortcut."

I followed as best I could. He walked with very long strides which were natural for his height of six feet or more. Luckily, the torch on his forehead was very bright.

"I'm going to Nubra Valley," I said.

"Me also," he replied stiffly. "I'm not feeling so well. I just stayed in a house where I got over one hundred bedbug bites. The poison was so strong that I had to go to a doctor to get allergy medicine."

"Oh, how awful. I know how you feel. I had a similar experience. I'm still recovering. My arm was nearly twice its size..."

He had moved too far ahead of me to hear me so I stopped talking. We walked on in silence. The dark narrow road was shrouded in shadows. Then the path disappeared and we climbed over piles of stones beside a barbed-wire fence. I was afraid to walk too fast as my ankle was still not healed completely.

Finally the path opened out to the main road and in the distance we saw the faint outline of the buses standing in rows in front of a beige brick building with wood-trimmed windows. The bus to Nubra was small; it could only seat thirty-four passengers. Several Westerners were waiting with huge knapsacks on the ground beside them. Some Ladakhis were also waiting. They stood together chatting. We boarded the bus.

The bus pulled out of the depot at six-fifteen, turning toward the upward pass leading to Khardung La, the highest road in the world. It climbed up over sleeping villages of sun-baked houses and countless hills of beige sand, then higher, higher, where the hills grew into mountains, sun-baked mountains in the dry, desert landscape, mountains carved of wind and earth and silent songs, rising into towering slopes, rising and then descending like waves of the ocean. There was no water supply, only sand, endless golden grains of sand.

We climbed up narrow twisting roads, over dangerously high gorges; the bus constantly swayed back and forth, up and down over the rough terrain that was not tamed for the use of modern vehicles. The road rose up before us like a serpent, hissing fiercely and then wriggling out of sight into the fiery heat. We sat crammed into our seats, our clothes clinging to our moist backs with perspiration dripping from our temples and dotting our foreheads as we peered out of the windows into the cascading valleys far below. Sometimes I shut my eyes tight as the bus hovered precariously close to the edge of a precipice. It was a long hard climb over a very stony road.

The bus ground to a halt. A pile of rocks was blocking the road. It had slid down from the mountain into the middle of the road. The driver got out of the bus with a shovel and cleared it away. Several teenage boys walking on the road came over and helped him. They picked up the rocks and tossed them down the mountainside.

We continued up the narrow mountain pass until we had to stop at an army check-post. The soldiers were dressed in khaki uniforms. We foreigners had to give our names and passport numbers which were listed in a logbook. We were examined with curiosity by the soldiers. The multifarious costumes of shorts and torn blue jeans worn by some of the foreigners was very alien to their culture.

We saw tents pitched on the flat plain. A thin river flowed past a stretch of grass. Black and white cows grazed lazily on the plateau in the distance.

We drove on and on and after a few more hours, we reached the top of Khardung La. The bus stopped so that we could get out. I saw a sign posted on a small building which said: The World's Highest Temple. Outside it, colorful Tibetan prayer flags waved in the wind. I slipped off my shoes and entered. On the walls inside were pictures of the saints and gods and goddesses of all the different religions. From Buddhism, there was the Buddha and the Dalai Lama; from the Sikh religion, there was Guru Nanak; from the Hindu tradition, there was Krishna, Shiva, Vishnu and the goddesses Durga, Saraswati, Parvati and Laxmi, and from Christianity, there was Jesus Christ.

In the center of the room, three large bronze bells hung from the ceiling. I rang them. In the inner shrine, just beyond the outer room was a statue of Lord Ganesh and Lord Shiva. There was also a Shiva linga. On the walls surrounding the linga were more pictures of the deities. I knew that Lord Shiva, a symbol of eternal silence, was regarded as the presiding deity of the Himalayan heights. I knelt before the linga and said a prayer. Then I placed ten rupees at the feet of Lord Ganesh. Before departing, I gently rang the bells again.

We boarded the bus and slowly began the descent into the valley leading to Nubra. The journey was long and arduous. When the bus finally pulled into Diskit seven hours later, we were relieved to be able to stretch our sore, aching bodies.

How will I find Rinchen's house? I asked myself as I looked around for help. A Ladakhi man who was getting off the bus told me I could come with him. He worked in Leh but he was going home to visit his wife for three days in Nubra. His wife taught at the same middle school as Rinchen, so they knew where she lived.

As I came up to the house, I saw that it was still in the process of being built. The outer layer of sand was being mixed and applied to the stone walls. The hallways were filled with clay and buckets of water. Rinchen, who was supervising the builders, welcomed me heartily and showed me around the house. The new house was to be much larger as Rinchen had three daughters and one son.

She led me to a very comfortable room which contained a large wooden bed and a sofa. In one corner of the room was a small altar with a photograph of the Dalai Lama adorned with a white silk scarf. Rinchen brought a tray with sweet tea. This was followed by salt tea, biscuits and raisins, as is the custom in Ladakh. Then she left me to rest as I was very tired.

The next day, she told me a puja was about to be performed for the happiness and welfare of the family. It was going to last a whole day. When four lamas arrived from the main monastery, she told me to go and sit with them, so I climbed a wooden ladder leading to the upper floor in which there was a sanctuary.

On the earthen walls hung very old thankas (embroidered tapestries of the Buddhist deities) and in front of the altar was a row of brass bowls filled with water. Butter lamps were alight before the photograph of His Holiness the Dalai Lama and the statues of Maitreya Buddha and Tsongkapa, the founder of the Gelugpa order of Tibetan Buddhism.

When I arrived, the four lamas were already sitting on the maroon-covered mats on the floor in front a large bowl of flour and a jug of water. They were busy shaping the elaborate items used in the puja: small triangular-shaped objects made from a mixture of flour and water. One lama chanted in a soft whisper as he mixed soft butter into circular designs and pasted it onto the triangular shapes. Another lama handed me a pair of scissors and some fabric on which Tibetan prayers were inscribed. He showed me how to cut the fabric into long vertical strips which were then tied around the triangular shapes. Rinchen's mother brought tea for us as we sat in the sanctuary together. I was so happy to be able to help prepare for the puja, a timeless ritual in which every detail was so intricate, and which was the very "life" of a lama's life.

After at least an hour of preparation, all the items which were to be used in the puja were lined up in front of the altar. The lamas took their seats. Then slowly, with a ringing of bells, the puja began. The head lama sat nearest the altar. During the chanting of the prayers, he offered a plant with long green leaves as well as many other items.

The voices of the lamas resounded gently in the small room. I closed my eyes and listened as their voices blended, echoing each other like threads intertwined in one endless melody.

After one hour, Rinchen's mother brought thick Ladakhi chapatis and puris for us to eat. The butter tea was poured and we sat together and ate our breakfast. Ten minutes was all the time allowed. The lamas drank their tea, ate one puri and left their chapatis stacked up on a plate under the wooden table in front of them. As I was very hungry, I attempted to eat all the puris and chapatis in front of me. Little did I know that two hours later, soup would be served followed by a full lunch. When the lamas come to perform a puja, they are always well fed.

We had a short break, and then the puja resumed for two more hours. I sat in the temple for nearly the entire day. By the end, it was as if time had closed its eyes and fallen fast asleep. A divine dimension of inner beauty and peace had been born in the little room hidden away from the bustle and cares of the outside world. Stepping outside was like opening my eyes after a very long meditation. I was uplifted and refreshed. I also felt very close to the four lamas. With a warm farewell, we said goodbye. The smile from their eyes entered my heart and nourished the finest level of feeling.

On the following day, it was very hot. In the afternoon. I gazed up at Diskit gompa perched high on the mountain overlooking the village. I was debating whether I had the strength to climb the two kilometers to the summit to visit the solitary white building surrounded by stupas.

I started climbing. The dirt road wound round and round, up, up, up the steep mountainside. On the way, very old stupas, with crumbling tops, white under the glowing sun, beckoned me on. The path was strewn with gray slate-like crumbling stones and the heat bit into the straw hat I was wearing. A scintillating white light was pouring forth from the unveiled face of the sun.

Slowly, slowly, pausing to drink from the bottle of water I carried, I made my way up the long winding mountain path. Standing on the edge of the path, I saw the valley – green fields amidst blue lavender hills with the desert sand like a mandala radiating outward far below. The mountains, dark gray, blue and salmon-pink surrounded the valley like an illuminated fortress built by the gods. It was a vista sketched in luminous colors, pure pastels, glowing in the light of the afternoon sun.

Panting for breath, I continued, pausing here and there, as I gazed up at the stone steps leading to the gompa; I was almost there. I could hear the voices of young lamas just ahead.

At the entrance to the gompa stood a large colorfully painted Tibetan prayer wheel. I turned it thrice, walking clockwise around it until the tiny bells attached to the wheel chimed. Then I saw a row of small wooden prayer wheels; I turned them also before ascending the steps to the main hall where the lamas were praying together. Young boys dressed in red robes ran ahead of me, carrying empty stainless-steel bowls. It was lunchtime and they had just finished their meal.

Climbing up a staircase made of white stone, I saw small enclosures perched on cliffs, embedded in walls of rock, and small wooden doors painted red and tiny windows and twisting tunnels hidden in the crevices of the mountain.

The main prayer hall was adorned with beautiful thankas. From the entrance, a golden statue of the Buddha was seated, smiling. It was encased in a large glass altar. On the mats near the altar sat a few lamas, their voices blending softly together. I took a seat on a mat near the wall behind them and closed my eyes. Like waves washing away the fatigue of the journey, the prayers, muted and soft, were like a balm, healing the heart and soothing the mind. As I sat listening, I saw the familiar faces of two of the lamas who had come to Rinchen's house. One of them offered me a cup of butter tea. When the prayers were over, with a rustle of their long robes, they disappeared. When I descended the mountain, it was with renewed vigor, bathed in a sea of calm which was like nectar to the soul.

One day I walked to the outskirts of Rinchen's village. On that day, the air was crystal clear. I saw very simple, yet beautiful dwellings made of earth with rooftops covered with hay to be used for the cattle during the long hard winter. In front of some of the houses were small gardens with flowers trailing over the gateway at the entrance.

Afterwards I returned to my room to meditate. As soon as I closed my eyes, the body dissolved into space and the circle of awareness expanded outward to infinity. I became one with the farthest reaches of the universe. The awareness of the body was gone; only consciousness, like a radiant orb of light with countless rays of golden threads, spread out to touch the hem of the Infinite. It was as if I had no end or beginning. Consciousness was a pure mirror of life in which the whole of existence breathed in ever-expanding waves of joy and peace. Never before had I felt so unbounded, so full, so complete. Old habits of thinking were ground to dust in this moment of coming face to face with the eternal truth of life. The bonds of ignorance, the pangs of separation, the illusion of fear, doubt and distrust all momentarily melted away in the sunlight of pure consciousness. When I opened my eyes, I thanked God for having brought me so far on the road to freedom.

Chapter Eighteen

One week later, when I boarded the bus back to Leh, I met Emma, a lady from Belgium. She was blonde and appeared to be about fifty.

"How did you like Ladakh?" I asked her.

"This is my fourth time in Ladakh. For some reason, I keep coming back."

"Why?"

"I don't know. It does something to me, deep inside. I long to come here every year. Something draws me back. I can't explain it."

When the bus arrived in Leh, she asked me where I was staying.

"I don't know," I said.

"Why don't you come with me to my guest house? They might have a spare room for you."

The owner had a single room available which he agreed to let me have for only fifty rupees a night. I only expected to stay for two nights. I thought Tashi would arrive on the tenth, but the tenth day came and went with no sign of Tashi; no message – nothing! I was becoming desperate: *What should I do?! I can't afford to pay for the room much longer. Is he coming or not?* My mind was tossed about like a ship at sea in a storm.

I decided to telephone him even though it was an expensive call. I dialed the number and Tashi answered.

"Shantila. Jullay. How are you?" he said in a casual tone.

"Tashi, when are you coming to Leh? I've been waiting for you—"

He interrupted me. "I'm sorry, Shantila. I have to wait for my holidays because the Japanese is going to Japan on business. He said I should take care of the center until he returns." He sounded apologetic. "In one week or ten days, I can come."

"But, Tashi, I have almost no money left. I've been waiting for you, because, I mean – I asked Mr. Rao, my publisher, to send me an advance of two thousand rupees and he said he would give it to you. Now that your holiday is postponed, I won't get the money in time. I won't have any money at all."

There was silence on the other end. I waited. There was nothing else I could say.

Then Tashi spoke. He said, "I am coming to Leh and I will stay for one month. I am surely coming to Leh."

"Alright, Tashi. I'll be alright somehow." I was anxious to hang up. The phone call had already been much longer than I had planned.

"Don't worry," Tashi said firmly. "I will arrange for you to get the money from a lama at the Shanti stupa. He's returning to Leh very soon." Then he hung up.

I walked out of the telephone exchange disappointed. I had already waited over two weeks and now our time together was delayed yet again. When I returned to the guest house, I confided in Emma.

"Perhaps I should go back to Manali. Maybe we're not destined to see each other."

"You must wait for him," Emma replied.

"I know. If I don't wait, how will I ever know what it feels like to be with him outside the Buddhist Center? There's a slight chance that we may want to stay together. I must give it a chance or how will I ever know what might have been between us?" I decided to wait no matter how long it took for him to come. Tashi's words echoed and re-echoed in my heart: *"I am coming to Leh and I will stay for one month. I am surely coming to Leh."*

I constructed a picture in my mind: In the picture, we were so overjoyed to see each other that he opened his arms and enfolded me in a long and tender embrace. There were no words, only a feeling of deep love rising in waves of joy, and then the time we had been apart dissolved into mist and we held each other and quietly, very quietly we knew we were destined to be together forever. It was a dream I planted and tended and watched over in the days and weeks I waited for him to come.

Tashi arranged for me to meet a lama at a temple near the Shanti stupa and collect the money sent by my publisher. To reach it, I had to walk up at least one hundred stairs built into the mountainside, from the base of the mountain to the summit. Luckily, I started out at sunset and there was a slight breeze in the air.

When I finally reached the top, I slowly opened the door to the temple. It was a very small, but highly decorated room with a big bell and candles and many photos of the Japanese monk adorning the walls. But it didn't feel like a holy place.

I looked around for the lama. I hoped the money had arrived safely. It was a large amount to put in an envelope. Would it all be there? Could I go to a restaurant and have a proper meal instead of just eating Ladakhi bread with jam and apples? Would there be a letter from Tashi in it?

I heard a door open quietly. A lama walked in. He held a letter in his hand.

"You are Shantila Martin?"

"Yes," I nodded.

"Tashi asked me to give this to you. He knew I was flying to Leh and he said you needed this right away." He handed me the envelope.

"Thank you very much."

I walked outside. The sky glowed as the last bright rays of light disappeared. I couldn't stop smiling. I walked to the top of the steps and opened the letter. In the envelope, there were a few letters and the money was there, all of it. There was also a letter from Tashi.

Dearest Shanti,

I am coming. Wait for me. Here is the money. Take it. I will meet you soon.

Jullay, Tashi

It was the first time he had written a letter to me with the word dearest. I pressed the envelope to my heart. Descending the steps of the mountain, I felt as if I had touched the feet of my beloved. I counted the few remaining days until I would see the face I had held within my heart for so long. I paused halfway down the mountain, lost in my dream. Perhaps I would touch the shaved head of my beloved, perhaps I would be blessed with his caress, and his gentle whispers. Perhaps... I hoped, I believed it could be... Elated, I returned to the guest house.

The envelope also contained a letter from Mr. Rao which I opened when I returned to my room. It contained a photocopy. I wondered what it could be. It was from the Federation of Indian Publishers. I read the script. It said: *The Federation of Indian Publishers – Awards for Excellence in Publishing.* Under it was mentioned the name of my publisher. He had been given the FIRST prize for my book! He had won the prize for the best English-language publication of the year. I was thrilled. I thought: *India has really appreciated my book! I'm glad it was published here.*

I opened Mr. Rao's letter and read it.

Dear Shantila,

We snagged the first prize for your book. Well done. Here is the advance as you requested.

All the best, Mr. Rao

I couldn't wait to tell Emma. I knocked on her door.

"Emma! Guess what? My book got the first prize for the best English-language publication of the year!"

"What book? Calm down and tell me what you're talking about," Emma said, inviting me in.

"I'm so happy, Emma. My first book was published in India in the spring and the Federation of Indian Publishers liked it. The publication won first prize for the best English publication of the year." I showed her the photocopy.

She read it. "That's great, Shantila! Well, how should we celebrate?" She paused. "Have you been to Shey Palace?" she asked.

"No. Is it especially beautiful?"

"Yes, I think so. It's the ancient palace of the ruler of Ladakh. There is a lovely route we can take by the river. We have to walk about three and a half kilometers. Do you want to go?"

"Yes."

We set out the following morning. On the way, we passed a beautiful monastery built on top of a high mountain peak. I stopped to gaze at it.

"That is Thikse gompa," Emma said.

"Oh, I want to visit that place," I said eagerly.

"I've been there twice. I don't feel like climbing up there in this heat. You go ahead. It's worth seeing. It's a very famous monastery. I'll get something cool to drink in the restaurant at the foot of the hill."

I began the climb up to the gompa. Innumerable steps zigzagged up, up, up until the end of the path was no longer visible. I pressed on, motivated by an inner drive to reach the top. The blessed summit beckoned. Like the Diskit gompa, most of the gompas in Ladakh are built on the summits of mountain peaks. A young boyish lama charged down the steps. He looked happy. I imbibed his joy as I climbed higher and higher. Having started, I knew I would not turn back. An inner calling urged me on, as if to place my foot on that high ground would be tantamount to soaring beyond the bondage of fear, attachment and anger combined.

It was a typical Ladakhi Summer day: dry and hot. A water bottle dangled from my hand and my knapsack was tossed casually over my shoulder. I passed three boy lamas of a tender age playing together on a landing just below the main hall of the monastery. Finally I stood outside the main hall where several pairs of shoes were placed in rows.

Two lamas, carrying very long horns came out. I followed them up to the roof. From there, I could see for miles. The landscape spread out before me like a painting. The lamas stood, facing the quiet grandeur of the scene. Placing the horns to their mouths, they blew, creating deep sonorous notes which shook the air. It was a call to prayer. Then they descended the steps to the main hall.

Opposite the entrance, I saw a large kalachakra, a mural of the eternal wheel of life. There was also a mural of the Buddha painted in vibrant hues as well as a mural of Guru Padmasambhava. Slipping off my shoes, and bowing three times at the entrance, I entered the semi-lit hall where the lamas were seated in long rows. They were about to begin their prayers.

Their voices washed away the awareness of the outer world and I sat immersed in the silent echoes of prayer until the holy veil between this world and the outer was hastily parted by a large crowd of tourists who noisily entered, speaking loudly and clicking their cameras. I slipped out and tiptoed over to an adjacent temple where a famous statue of Maitreya Buddha had been erected. As I crossed the threshold of the temple, I was spell-bound by the beauty of the 45-foot-high statue of the future Buddha, Maitreya Buddha, the Buddha of Loving-kindness. Crowned with a golden diadem, the Buddha was two floors high, poised in a meditation posture, blessing the world. The eyes of the Buddha were transfixed in an inward-looking gaze which was not of this world; the eyes emanated peace and love. The stainless luminosity of the colors of Maitreya Buddha's robe and crown surpassed the beauty of anything I had seen thus far. I circumambulated the towering statue several times, marveling at the workmanship of the artist. Then, kneeling before the butter lamp lit before the Buddha, I prayed that my heart be filled with all that the Buddha symbolized. Spontaneously, the prayer of Saint Francis of Assisi found its way to my lips and soundlessly, the words formed themselves:

Dear God, make me an instrument of Thy peace,
Where there is darkness that I may bring light,
Where there is suffering that I may bring joy,
Where there is doubt that I may bring faith,
Where there is despair that I may bring hope,
Grant that I may not so much seek to be loved as to give love,
Not so much seek to be understood as to understand,
For it is in giving that we receive
It is in pardoning that we are pardoned
It is in dying that we are born to eternal life.

I wanted to sit there and meditate but already, outside the door, I could hear the voices of the crowd approaching, so I reluctantly departed. Descending the stairs, there were tears trickling down my cheeks. *Why oh why must I leave this place filled with such a beatific image of love? Can I not stay and worship here and enjoy life in this peaceful place? It is so hard to tear myself away. Yet I know I must go, again yet again, out into the world...*

Through a mist of tears, I found the road down to the restaurant. Emma had already left for Shey Palace. I had been at the temple much longer than I had anticipated. I asked the manager of the restaurant where to find the path beside the river and started on my way.

I followed a stream until it opened out to the river. The river was overflowing its banks, soaking the ground all around, running over white rocks where pink, purple and yellow wildflowers grew in clumps, pressing their stems out of the cracks in the earth. Beside the streaming waters I walked, enjoying the cool moist touch of the water as it oozed through the soles of my shoes, making my socks damp. Delighted by the sheer majesty of the mountains which glowed in gleaming purples, blues and silvery-whites, luminous in the distance, my heart rejoiced. The vibrant green of the fields stretched joyous wings over the flat plain and as I moved forward, I felt I could have been in heaven, so exquisitely beautiful was the scene painted before me, around me, above and below me, so vibrant with color, so alive, yet so peaceful, pure and unsullied. The very earth seemed to be rejoicing in a voice overflowing with fullness. Like the river, the hills, the fields, and the mountains sang in golden mellifluous notes, sang a song which told a story of innocent life, born and reborn, in a spirit of eternal joy. I felt like this was a place where the gates of heaven were always open. Like the hearts of the people who greeted me as I moved through their land, here the gates of life were flung wide, and one could move freely along the paths, meeting only the freshness and innocence of life greeting life. Here, the air was luminous and pure and the wings of my heart skimmed over golden passageways where time and eternity were one.

I drank in draft after draft of beauty, never tiring of the splendor of the colors, shapes and images rising up on the horizon. The white stupas glowed in the sun, bestowing their own messages of silence; they were soundless notes in a timeless symphony. Villages sprang up, vestibules of gentleness, a succor to the spirit, along the route. Above the simple dwellings, pastel-colored prayer flags waved in the wind.

Shey Palace, an ancient monument embedded in the mountain, appeared on the horizon, a row of golden stupas adorning its topmost walls. I had heard that one hundred golden statues of the Buddha were housed within its walls. Elated, my footsteps quickened as the sun was soon to set. I wanted to return home before darkness set in. Mounting an upward slanting path to the palace, I saw a huge prayer wheel; I turned it. I crossed a narrow passageway and entered a small courtyard leading to the gompa. It was about to close but the high lama saw me and a few others and he invited us in.

They were a small group of Buddhist devotees from Chile. The lama was showing them around the inner room of the temple and explaining the meaning of the paintings on the walls. Spontaneously, I knelt before a very grand golden statue of the Buddha enshrined in the center of the room. There was a feeling of deep peace and stillness enveloping the room.

When we stepped outside, ready to depart, the high lama asked us to wait. He went into a room in the palace. When he returned he had four white silk scarves draped over his arm.

He came and stood in front of us and said: "Each of you bowed before the Buddha upon entering the temple. Because you showed respect for the Buddha, I will garland you." He stepped forward and gently garlanded each of us with a white silk scarf.

I felt so humble, protected and blessed. There were no words in my mind – just a silent ocean of gratitude moving in my heart.

I waited for a bus back to the guest house. It was almost dark when I arrived. Emma was sitting outside on the terrace having supper.

"What happened to you?" she asked, looking up from her meal. "I waited at the restaurant and when you didn't come, I walked to Shey alone. Did you go to Shey Palace?"

"Oh, yes," I said. "The chanting of the prayers was so beautiful at Thikse that I couldn't leave in the middle of it. Then I went to see the statue of Maitreya Buddha. At first, the room was crowded, so I waited until most of the people had left, then I went in. I'm sorry, Emma. I hope you didn't mind going to Shey alone." I sat down next to her.

She laughed. "Of course not, Shanti. I understand. The monasteries here are like that. I know. It's always hard to leave. That's why I keep coming back." She stopped and stared at the silk scarf around my neck.

"Where did you get that?" she asked.

I told her how I had received it.

She nodded knowingly. "It's right for you to be here. This is an important time for you, Shantila. I can feel it." She looked as if she was thinking about something. "You should visit Alchi gompa. Alchi is my favorite place. I always have my strongest experiences at Alchi. Of course, everyone is different, but I think you will like it."

"How do I get there?" I asked her. "Is it far from here?"

"Not that far, about one hour on the bus. She sipped some tea and munched on a roll. "Why don't you join me, Shanti?"

In the short time since we had met, we had become good friends.

"Do you want something to eat?"

"Yes. Maybe some hot milk and some bread."

"I'll treat you. Here's the man." She waved to the owner who was coming up the stairs. "Alchi is close to Likir, and at Likir, there is a ten-foot-high statue of Maitreya Buddha, the future Buddha. It is incredible. You have to see it."

"Where are you going tomorrow, Emma?" I asked her.

"I think I'll go to Lamayuru. It's the oldest monastery in Ladakh. It's a long journey on the bus, six hours I think."

The following morning, she was gone before I finished my meditation. I did not see her again until one week later. She was due to leave for Belgium the following day.

We sat together on the terrace enjoying the vision of the sky awash with stars. Never before had I seen so many stars! I thought of Tashi. I remembered his remark at the bus station in Delhi: *"In Ladakh, there are so many stars..."* Ten days had passed and still he had not arrived. The money Mr. Rao had sent me was rapidly diminishing. I had had to pay Ani for the week at her house more than I had anticipated and there was the money for traveling back and forth to the monasteries, as well as the money I had to put aside for my return ticket to Manali and onward to Delhi. Of course, I also had to take into account the money needed to buy food.

"What are you thinking of, Shanti? You look kind of sad," Emma said softly, turning to me.

"Oh nothing... I'm just wondering when Tashi will come. It's been ten days already. Maybe I should just leave before my money runs out. "

Emma sat upright in her chair and looked straight at me.

"No, don't leave, Shanti. Wait for him, otherwise you'll always regret it. Don't worry about the money. If you need money, I have enough. Besides I'm leaving tomorrow. You can have whatever rupees I have left. So now you can wait for him."

I whispered a silent thank you to God. Then I said softly to Emma: "That's very kind of you, Emma. I appreciate it very much."

We sat looking up at the sky, oblivious of time, floating on the wings of our desires, hopes and dreams.

"How was Lamayuru?" I asked.

Emma didn't respond. It seemed as if she hadn't heard me. I was about to repeat the question.

"Fine," she said, "it was great – really special – the best this year. The lamas are in the middle of a twelve-day puja. They have made a special sand mandala. If you leave tomorrow, you could be there for the last few days of the puja." She paused.

I felt as if her mind was preoccupied with something else. Then she sighed audibly.

"Oh, Shanti, I must tell you something. I can't hold it in any longer."

"What is it, Emma?" I asked, looking at her.

"I'm in love," she said smiling.

I knew Emma had been divorced for over fifteen years.

"Oh, how wonderful!" I said smiling.

There was a long silence. It was as if she was wrestling with the strength of her feelings.

"It happened so quickly. I haven't felt like this for years. I really feel like – like a woman again. I don't care what happens. It's my – my tour guide. He's such a beautiful person – so strong and so – I don't know what it is about him that attracts me so much..." Her words drifted off.

"That's great, Emma! But what is the matter?"

"He's twenty – I mean I think twenty-five years old... That's half my age."

"Oh, um – well, well – that's a pity," I said quietly.

"We were together all the time at Lamayuru. We went for walks and he told me about his family. His father is in the army so he hardly sees him. He's the only son. I think he's lonely. I have invited him to come to visit me in Belgium," Emma said. "I was afraid he would not accept, but he said he will come! I'm so happy!" She smiled as she gazed out over the treetops.

"Be careful, Emma," I said quietly. "You must be careful. He's very innocent and he trusts you as a friend."

"What do you mean?" she retorted, looking a little disturbed.

"I mean, what you feel for him...you must be careful; he's coming as a friend. You'll be responsible if anything happens, because you are so much older than him."

"Happens? Like what? For the first time in so long, I feel like a woman when I'm with him. I know we cannot marry because of our ages, but I love him!"

"Love is a beautiful thing." I said quietly. "When we truly love, the other person's happiness is our main concern. Love is unselfish. It desires only what is good for the beloved. Love him, but don't ask anything of him. Let him remain friends with you. Be happy with the relationship as it is." I felt constrained to say these things because I knew she could easily be led astray by her unrestrained emotions. "If you have an affair, you may sacrifice the friendship."

She was silent. We both gazed up at the stars, wondering what the future held in store. Before she went to catch her plane the following morning, she left one thousand rupees.

"I know you will use it well," Emma said, handing me the brand-new folded rupee notes. "Is it enough for you to wait for Tashi and to go to Lamayuru, or do you think you will need more?"

"More than enough," I said. "Thank you, Emma."

"I'm glad to be able to help you," she said.

I waved goodbye to her until her taxi turned the corner and was out of sight.

I went inside to meditate, and then went to a restaurant and ordered a big meal. For the first time in weeks, I didn't have to add up the bill in my mind beforehand.

Afterwards, I went to buy a ticket to Lamayuru.

"What time does the bus leave?" I asked the man behind the counter.

"Five thirty-five," he replied without looking up.

"In the morning or the evening?" I asked as I tried to get his attention.

"Morning," he said flatly.

I paid for the ticket and went home to pack my things. I was in bed early so that I could reach the bus station on time, but when I arrived at the counter, there weren't any buses in the Lamayuru lane.

"Where is the bus to Lamayuru?" I asked the ticket officer.

"It just left," he said.

"Left?! When did it leave?!" I asked alarmed.

"Three minutes ago. I saw it pull out," he said casually.

"But I am on time!!! The man at the counter said the bus was leaving at five thirty-five. Its five thirty-six now! I was here at five thirty-five!" I shouted.

"There is another bus tomorrow," he said, stepping back. "Why do you have to leave today?" He looked at me quizzically.

"I must leave TODAY," I said firmly, pulling myself together, "because I want to be on time for the special puja at Lamayuru gompa."

"If you have to leave today, the only other option is taking the bus to Khaltse which is twenty kilometers from Lamayuru. You can hitch by truck from there." He paused, and then added, "Oh, I forgot, the trucks only leave very early in the morning and very late at night. Your bus will arrive in Khaltse at noon, so you will need a place to wait – for the truck, I mean." He shuffled his feet and looked at his watch.

I was becoming desperate. I was determined to leave today and to arrive today. Frantically, I went from driver to driver, inquiring as to the best way to reach my destination. Finally, a kindly bus driver came up with a solution. He asked the Khaltse bus driver to let me off at the police check-post and to ask if a police officer would be willing to drive me to Lamayuru. Satisfied with that solution, I boarded the bus to Khaltse.

Miles and miles of desert tracts stretched as far as the eye could see, parched, dry land without a sign of human habitation. Flat plains rose into mountains of sand, outlined in beige silhouettes against a crystal blue sky. The ground shimmered with heat as we drove over the seamless landscape, mile after mile after mile, hour after hour after hour. The journey seemed endless.

At Khaltse, the bus driver let me out at the police check-post. Two police officers sat in a tent, playing cards.

"I need to reach Lamayuru," I said, looking into the tent.

"You can hitch from here. We are busy." They resumed their game.

I went back to the road and stood there. A passing car slowed down and stopped in front of me.

"Do you need a lift?" a man asked.

"Yes, I want to go to Lamayuru gompa."

"I'm going past there. I'll take you," he said warmly.

"Oh, thank you very much," I said, hopping in. *Fantastic!* I thought. *Thank you!*

"Is something special going on there?" the driver asked.

"Yes, the twelve-day puja. There is a special sand mandala.

The puja is almost over," I replied.

"Oh yes, I've heard about that. Are you interested in Buddhism?"

"Yes. I am."

"Well, I'll tell you something about a very special place I visited last month. It was a retreat where some lamas go, to be in silence, for three years, three months and three days. They don't see anyone during this time. Someone puts a little food outside their hut once a day, that's all."

"Really? All that time? Alone?" I asked, my interest aroused.

"Yes, it is a hard retreat. It is only for the lamas who are advanced – only then they can do it. Otherwise, one could go mad – being alone all that time."

I listened, intrigued by the idea. Three years, three months and three days, alone in the Himalayas in a hut.

"I would like to do something like that," I said. "Can ladies do it too?"

The man looked over at me with a surprised expression.

"You want to be a nun?" he asked.

"I don't know, but I would like to go on a retreat like that."

"Oh," he said, "I didn't see any ladies there. Maybe they can do it. I don't know."

The car pulled into a deserted plain with one or two isolated shops which looked like ships stranded on an island of sand.

"This is where you get off. Gompa down there." The driver opened the door of the car and I stepped out, into the middle of nowhere. I began walking down a hill of sand, in the direction in which the driver had pointed.

Suddenly from out of the sky, the gompa emerged, stupas and all, perched between the peaks of two mountains, 3600 meters high. It stood out against the sky, austere, like an ancient fortress, etched out of the silence of the mountains surrounding it, suspended between earth and heaven, beckoning, beckoning, beckoning in silence.

"What will I find here?" I asked myself as I moved slowly down the steep path. At the foot of the hill was a prayer wheel. An old woman, clad in the traditional dark-colored Ladakhi robe, wrinkled with age, sat beside it. She smiled up at me as I passed. I touched my right hand to my forehead in greeting.

Then I traversed the last stretch of the path which led into the courtyard of the monastery. As I crossed the threshold, it was as if I stepped back in time. There were large stupas, still white, but crumbling with age, adorning the dirt path up the winding road to the gompa which stood high on the hilltop. White buildings in need of repair lined the path. On the mountainside were small huts, the lamas' dwellings. Three or four lamas stood together in the courtyard. They looked up as I entered tired and bedraggled with my knapsack flung over my shoulders.

"Welcome to Lamayuru," one of the lamas said, coming up to me.

"Thank you. This is the oldest monastery in Ladakh, isn't it?" I asked him.

"Yes this is a very old gompa. It was built in the twelfth century. It is named after a gompa in Tibet. This spot – it is very sacred."

"Is this a Gelugpa order?" I asked, thinking of Tashi. He was part of that order.

"No, this is a Digumba branch of the Kagyuga order. It originated with the tantric master Tilopa, and his disciple Naropa..." He turned as if he had to go.

"When will the prayers start?" I asked him.

"In one hour, we start," the lama answered, turning back to the others.

I went into the gompa guest house and asked for a room for one or two nights. A young man led me to a room; I had to climb a ladder to reach it. It was bare except for two beds. He explained that we had to wash and go to the toilet outside.

An hour later, after resting and washing, I mounted the steps to the gompa. The view from the landing was magnificent! The mountains breathed wide, rising majestically toward the sky, then spreading voluminous wings upwards, they seemed to express the soaring of the human spirit toward God. I stood in awe of the creation of a scene so vast and mighty and as I continued gazing at it, my heart seemed to expand, opening wide to embrace the blessed vision with the entirety of my being. Then I turned and entered the inner courtyard of the gompa which led to the main hall of the temple.

Leaving my shoes outside, I crossed the threshold into a darkened hall lit by the inner light of devotion and the vibrant shimmer of countless invocations. A lama beckoned to me; he seemed to want to show me something. I came over to where he was standing.

"This is the special cave where the great saint Naropa meditated," he whispered. He opened a window in a wall of the main hall and showed me the cave. The vibration coming from the cave was so powerful that my body shook as I peered into the darkened space. Spontaneously I bowed down before the invisible presence which emanated from there.

I went to look at the exquisite sand mandala, symbolic of the sun, which was on display in the main hall. In two days, when the puja ended, it would be consigned to the river; it was a "meditation" on the impermanence of the ever-changing relative world. As beautiful as it was, it would be poured into the water where it would dissolve into the flowing waves. This was a reminder not to unduly attach oneself to anything in the impermanent, ever-changing realm of the material world.

Finding a seat on a wooden platform covered with a rug, I closed my eyes as the lamas' voices rose in prayer. The deep inner silence of their life reverberated in deep sonorous tones that filled the hall. They prayed, not only with their voices but with their hands, in mudras that unfolded like the petals of a lotus blooming, and the sight ignited unimaginable bliss. Their faces reflected profound dedication and purity. Most of the lamas appeared to be over fifty years old, but there were also many young boys between ten and fifteen years old. They were playful and full of mischief; yet when they prayed their faces shone with the light of maturity. The older lamas exuded an aura of peace and piety intertwined with gentleness and compassion. I felt totally at home in this place.

The monastery was totally devoid of any luxuries. Life was stripped bare of all but the most basic necessities and yet there was more fullness of heart in their overflowing generosity here than I had experienced anywhere else in Ladakh. From the very first evening, the lamas invited me to come and eat with them. We sat together like a family on a long wooden bench in the big friendly kitchen and ate our meals in a spirit of total ease and simplicity. It was as if they knew on a subtle level that I did not have much money. I never had to say anything. They just extended an open invitation from the beginning that touched my heart deeply. When the time came to depart, it was with tears in my eyes that I bid them farewell.

One evening as I sat outside in the courtyard, two lamas spontaneously began to dance. They extended their arms outwards on either side and whirled round and round like two stars orbiting in the sky. I could feel the upsurge of joy in their innocent movements. Like children, all sense of inhibition was abandoned and they moved freely in tune with the music of their soaring spirits.

On the last day of the puja, the lamas assembled in the courtyard of the gompa, arrayed in regal shawls and headdresses. Many held instruments such as drums, cymbals and very long horns. The ceremony began with the lamas standing in a circle chanting and playing their instruments. Then they marched gallantly out of the gompa in a long procession, winding their way rapidly down a narrow mountain path. I longed to see them throw the mandala into the river. I had to run to keep up with them. They climbed effortlessly over stony cliffs and precipitous banks with the sound of their instruments and their voices ringing in the air. The path they took to the river looked dangerous. I wasn't used to scaling cliffs at such a height, but I was determined to make it to the river. I tried not to lose sight of the last lama in the procession. They were far ahead of me; they climbed the steep rocky paths as nimbly as mountain goats. I was running so fast that I got out of breath.

At last, I saw them stop. They sat on a grassy mound by the river and continued chanting. I came and joined them. I was so exhilarated; I felt such fulfillment.

A high lama went to the shore and cast the exquisite mandala which they had carried in a vessel into the flowing water. I was so happy. The words of my Guru floated into my awareness: *From fullness to fullness and what remains is eternal fullness...*

Many people had come from the village to view the colorful procession. After consigning the mandala to the water, the lamas took tea together and then joined in the festive mood of the local people who were playing drums. Some of the lamas began to dance on the shores of the river; it was a dance of joy.

The lama who had shown me Naropa's cave in the gompa came over to talk to me. He said, "Once this entire valley was under water. An arahat, liberated one, prayed for a monastery to be founded. He made an offering of grains of corn to the water spirits. The grains of corn caused the water to drain and the corn grew into the shape of a sacred swastika. The gompa was built in this place. It is a very holy spot."

"How amazing," I said. "It feels very powerful here." Then I thought that maybe I could ask this lama about the thing I was really curious about. I hesitated, then said, "Is it true that there are lamas who can fly?"

He smiled knowingly at me. "Yes, it is true. They meditate on their veins, and afterwards, some of them can fly. We do not practice that kind of meditation here. It belongs to a different order."

A nun came and stood nearby. She was dressed like a traditional Buddhist nun; the only difference was she looked European.

"Jullay," she said, as she sat down beside me.

"Jullay," I replied. "Where are you from?"

"Austria," she said.

"How long have you been a nun?"

"I have been a nun for ten years." She smiled. "I left my country and everything. This is the path I always wanted to take."

I looked at her eyes; they were radiant.

"Oh, that's wonderful. I can see that you are happy."

"I am about to fulfill the greatest desire of my life. I am going into silence for three years, three months and three days. My hut is almost complete. I will begin my retreat in a few months."

I stared at her. *Her retreat! Three years, three… ! I WANT TO DO THAT!*

"Really? You're going into silence – all alone?"

"Yes," she said. Her eyes were filled with joy.

"What made you decide to do it?" I asked in a quiet voice.

She paused and looked into the distance. The river flowed past, murmuring quietly as it ran over the stones and pebbles in its path. Above us, a soft breeze blew through the trees, and in the distance, I heard the songs of the birds mingle with the staccato rhythm of the drums.

"It is something I have wanted for a long time. It is really the silence which I long for – the chance to go deep within myself, free from all the usual distractions. It is the chance I have waited for and prayed for. I guess this is part of the reason I became a nun: to devote my life to reaching the Buddha-mind and then from there to be able to help remove the suffering of all living beings." She paused, and then added in a soft voice, "One must purify oneself or how can one help others? That's right, isn't it?"

She looked deeply into my eyes.

"Yes, I agree with you," I said.

"I want to go beyond duality, to reach the state which is beyond thoughts, beyond the opposites. We suffer because we live in the field of duality and we identify with that field which is always changing. Identifying with the field of change means we are constantly tossed about, between gain and loss, pleasure and pain, victory and defeat. The only way to find lasting peace is to go beyond all change – to experience Nirvana, the great emptiness, the state beyond suffering. This retreat is a step away from the world – a necessary one – so I can come back and give more in the future."

"That's so beautiful," I whispered. I thought, *It is the same thing we do when we meditate – letting go of everything twice a day...we enter the cave within our heart.*

"I've spent every penny I have on building the hut and collecting firewood for the winter. I have to pay someone to leave food outside for three years, but it's worth every penny. I'm so happy to be going into the hut."

"Was it hard to get permission from your order?"

"At first, they wondered about it, but I was so persistent that they finally agreed. More and more nuns are asking to be allowed to follow the traditional path just like the lamas."

I gazed at her. We sat side by side in silence looking at the river. On one side of me was a nun; on the other side, a lama. The idea of the retreat fascinated me. I was irresistibly drawn to it. Then I caught myself. *I want to be with Tashi – but Tashi suggested I become a – I don't know. I don't think that becoming a nun is my path in this lifetime.*

Chapter Nineteen

Tashi was due to arrive in a few days. I wondered whether to wait in Leh or to visit Alchi, Emma's favorite monastery, alone. I decided to go to the bus station and if the bus was there, I would go to the monastery.

The Alchi bus stood at the depot; it was only half-full. I climbed in. As the bus pulled out, leaving Leh behind, I thought again about the Austrian nun.

Should I do what she is about to do? On a level beyond words, the answer came, clearly forming in the silence in which both mind and heart are one: *This is Her path, Shantila – not Your path. You have been meditating for twenty years, you have your Guru. If I become a Buddhist nun, will I be able to do my meditation? Furthermore, I don't know the language, or the tradition or the prayers. It is better to follow my own path. It will open out in time... Besides my heart is longing...*

By the time we reached Alchi, I had made up my mind.

I stepped out of the bus at Alchi into the bright light of the midday sun. Beside the road were small wooden cottages half-hidden behind overgrown hedges.

"Monastery – down there," the bus driver pointed to a gate.

I opened the gate and walked down a narrow, paved road that curved round and round like a spiral. Near the road were a few open-air shops selling jewelry, scarves and Ladakhi handicrafts. Whenever I thought the road would end, it curved around in another loop until eventually I entered a small courtyard surrounded by trees. As I crossed the courtyard, I saw a lama.

"Please can you tell me where the monastery is? I came to see the special paintings."

"Oh, yes," the lama said, smiling. "I'll take you. I have to unlock the doors."

A bunch of keys dangled from his waist; they jingled as he

walked. We walked down a dirt road together until we came to another courtyard; inside were three or four small, white buildings arranged in a semi-circle. The lama went to the door of the first building and unlocked it.

"It will take a few minutes for your eyes to adjust," he said, stepping to the side.

I crossed the threshold into a cool dark space. At first, I couldn't see anything. After a few minutes, my eyes made out images painted on the curved walls of the room. Moving close to the wall, I saw that it was covered with hundreds of tiny images of lamas sitting cross-legged. At first glance, each image looked alike, but after a closer examination, I saw that the hands of each lama was shaped in a different mudra.

Here, in this ancient monastery, every detail of the mudras was painted on the walls so long ago..., I thought, admiring the precision of each painting.

"Where did the different hand movements originate?" I asked the lama.

"The Buddha taught them to his disciples," the lama answered. "We must keep the rooms dark because the sunlight makes the colors fade," the lama explained as we walked out.

He opened the door to the next building. It was dimly lit by a skylight. Inside were four huge carvings of the Buddha, each detail painted in vibrant tones. As I moved in a circle around the room, I could feel a silent power emanating from the statues.

The next building contained even more elaborate wall paintings, reminiscent of monastic life, but the colors had almost disappeared in many places.

As it was very hot and I was hungry, I retraced my steps up the winding road. On the way I stopped to admire a jewelry display. A lady dressed in Western clothes came and stood near me.

"Those are beautiful earrings," she said, glancing at the amber earrings I was holding up to my ears.

"Yes, amber is so lovely. I like the way it catches the light."

"Are you going to buy them?" she asked.

"No. I don't really need them," I said, putting them back on the table.

"Where are you from?" the lady asked. "You sound American."

"I am American. Where are you from?" I asked her.

"Oh, we're – that is my husband over there." She pointed to a tall, good-looking man who was examining the leather belts. "We're Indian. We live in Nainital in the Himalayas. Are you alone?"

"Yes," I replied. "I am in India working on a book."

"Oh, you're a writer?" she said enthusiastically.

"Yes, my first book was published in March in New Delhi."

"Oh, how wonderful! Congratulations! What was it about?" she asked.

"Creativity and um – meditation and perception..."

She interrupted. "Oh, do you meditate?"

"Yes. "

"So do we! We have been meditating for fifteen years. Rajan! I want to introduce you to someone!" She beckoned to her husband. "Rajan, this lady is practicing meditation, just like us! She's a writer. Her first book was published in Delhi in March," she said excitedly.

Rajan extended his hand. "Very nice to meet you. What is your name?"

"Shantila Martin," I said, shaking his hand.

"Will you join us for lunch or have you already eaten?" Rajan asked politely.

"I'd love to join you," I replied.

After lunch, they offered me a lift to Leh in their very comfortable jeep. While we were driving, I mentioned that there was one more monastery I wanted to visit: Likir monastery. According to what Emma had told me, I thought it would be in the same vicinity as Alchi. I asked Rajan if he knew where it was.

"Not exactly, but it should be close by. I can let you off at the next turning. It should be easy to find from there."

I happily agreed. Likir was famous for its huge golden statue of Maitreya Buddha, the Buddha of Loving-kindness.

They let me out near a path off the main road that led up a hill. I waved goodbye to them until their car was out of sight. Then I flung my knapsack over my shoulder, and carrying my almost-empty thermos flask in my other hand, I started up the path. On either side were vast stretches of sand. I stopped to remove my cardigan. I continued walking but the scenery remained the same. In every direction, there was sand, bleached white by the sun. I hurried to the top of the hill, expecting that at any moment, the towering figure of the golden Buddha would appear. But there was only silence, a silence made of sand. There was nothing else on the landscape. The only sound was the whisper of my footsteps sinking into the sand.

"I wonder where the monastery is," I asked myself. I was starting to feel a little anxious. "Maybe I'm going the wrong way."

I turned and headed down the hill in another direction. I walked and walked until I saw a man in the distance. I increased my pace until I reached him.

"Where is Likir monastery?" I asked him.

He didn't speak any English, so I had to repeat the question. "Gompa – Likir gompa"

He pointed up the hill with his hand. It was the same direction in which I had been walking before.

"How far is it?" I asked him desperately.

But he didn't understand what I was saying and continued on his way.

Oh my God! I better keep going! I lifted up my feet and tried to run up the hill through the sand. But I soon slowed down; I was panting and out of breath. The air in my lungs was dry; my forehead was hot and dripping with perspiration. I kept walking until I reached a path on top of a hill. On an incline just off the dirt road were two half-withered trees. Still, they offered shade! I made my way to the shade and laid down on a thin stretch of parched grass, totally exhausted. I opened my knapsack and saw that I had a few biscuits left. I ate one. Then I unscrewed my flask. There was only one cup of water left.

"Oh, why didn't I refill my flask at the restaurant?! I knew I should have done it!" I muttered to myself in exasperation. *What am I going to do? ... Get up, you fool! You have to make it to the monastery!*

I looked around. There was not a sound. I sipped half of the water and poured the rest back. Then I got up.

The dirt road wound up a steep hill. As I ascended the hill, more trees appeared on the side of the road. I kept going. Further up, the grass was greener, still very dry, but more alive. I kept going.

The monastery is probably at the top, I thought with renewed vigor. *Just a bit more to go – a bit more, a bit more.* I talked to myself on the way. *You can do it, Shantila. This is a test. You've got to make it!*

At the top of the hill, I heard the gurgling sound of a river. Walking to the edge of a steep bank, I saw water rushing at a great speed through a ravine. On either side of the river, more trees grew, hanging their leafy boughs into the running water. But no matter in what direction I looked, there was no sign of the golden Buddha.

I saw an old man coming down the path, leaning on a walking stick. He seemed to have appeared out of nowhere.

"Likir gompa," I said, walking up to him. I felt like I was going to collapse.

He pointed across the river and up a mountain. Then he walked away.

Across the river! Up the mountain! I looked across the river and saw a few tiny buildings far in the distance.

But how can I reach it? I asked myself. I sank down on the dirt road, opened my flask and drank the last of the water. I gazed down the steep bank at the rushing river far below. Thoughts tumbled through my mind one after another: *Now I know why monasteries are built high up – on top of mountains... This is how it is: We are all pilgrims on the path to God...and we must – keep going – no matter what. It doesn't matter what obstacles come – what disappoint-ments...we just have to keep going. The spiritual path is always up. My mother – she used to say: 'Life only gives us what we can handle.' So I can handle THIS! It's just a test like all the others! I made it to Nubra and to Lamayuru and I will make it to Likir! Tashi! Tashi! Please come, I feel like I'm dying, please...* I closed my eyes and laid down on the road, my legs stretched out. I wasn't aware of time. I felt so weak I could barely move. I thought, *If I die here, no one will know.* I prayed: *Oh God! Oh Ganesh, Ganesh, remove the obstacles – help me make it to the TOP!*

I took several deep breaths, then I pulled myself to my feet and started walking. At the end of the road, the path curved sharply back again. There was no straight path across the river to the top. Whenever I reached the end of one road, I found another one. My feet felt like lead; I could hardly lift them up. I stumbled over small pebbles in the road. I thought of leaving my knapsack and cardigan, and continuing on, empty-handed – just to lighten the load. My eyes itched and burned from the sun.

Bleary-eyed, I gazed up the mountain. Then I stopped, totally transfixed. Looming large on the summit of the mountain stood a huge golden statue of Maitreya Buddha. His hand was upraised in a gesture of blessing. He seemed to call me, to beckon me onward. Beside the Buddha, bathed in the light of the setting sun, stood Likir monastery, in all its solitary glory. I drank deeply of the vision, for it seemed to appease the gnawing thirst within my body.

From that moment on, the journey was easy. The road rolled

by under my feet until finally I crossed the threshold of Likir monastery. When I arrived, I was invited to have dinner with the lamas and was given a comfortable room where I stayed for two days. Most of the temples in the gompa were closed, but a lama gave me the key and I saw the highly decorous interiors of some of the temples. I also visited a room where a lama was painting a large mural on the wall. In the evening, I stood with the lamas watching the sun set over the vast tracts of forests surrounding the monastery.

The lamas also showed me a place, just outside the monastery, where I could catch the bus to Leh. When I returned to Leh, it felt as if I had been away for a long time. Tashi was due to arrive any day and my heart beat expectantly, counting the hours until we would meet again after so long.

I went to lunch at a restaurant near the path leading to the market. Seated at the table near mine was an Irish lady who invited me to join her. Her name was Karen. She was fairly tall, stocky and strong. She had straight dark hair which fell just below her shoulders. We sat together for quite some time, waiting for our meals to arrive.

"How long have you been in Ladakh?" she asked.

"For almost a month," I replied.

"That's a long time. This is my second visit to Ladakh. I was here about three years ago for the first time."

After the food arrived, she told me she had traveled alone in India, China and Tibet. She worked as a gardener in Dublin and had never married.

"I am waiting for a special friend to come, so we can go to the gompas together," I confided in her.

"Sometimes," she said thoughtfully, "when two people have waited a long time to see each other again, the atmosphere between them becomes as if charged with electricity. It is like two magnets being pulled together. I have had that experience..." she said, gazing straight ahead. "I once met a lama from Assam and fell in love with him."

"Really?" I said.

"Yes, we were together for a short time, then he left me. I cried and cried for forty-eight hours. Afterwards there was a faint knock at the door. When I opened it, he was standing outside. He said, 'I have come back for you.' That was all." Karen smiled.

"You must have been so happy to see him," I said softly.

"We remained together, traveling in the Himalayas for three months. Then we agreed to go our separate ways." Karen gazed into the distance. There was a long pause. Then she added, "I wish you well."

After the meal, we parted; I did not expect to see her again.

The day that Tashi was to come finally arrived. I telephoned New Delhi to find out if he had left yet. They told me that he had taken a plane to Leh that very morning. By the time I telephoned, he should have been in Leh already! I literally jumped for joy in the telephone exchange! I hurried back to the guest house lest he should call me. I showered, washed my hair and changed my clothes. Then I waited. I postponed going out for lunch until after two o'clock. But the phone did not ring. Finally I decided to go down to the market for lunch. When I returned, there was still no message. So I went out again, trying to remain busy so as not to think about why he hadn't called. When I returned to my room, the proprietor said he had called while I was out, but had left no message. A few hours later, he called again.

"Hello, I called you a few hours ago but they told me you were in the market." Tashi's voice sounded deep. There was a slight edge of severity in his tone.

"Yes, I went out for half an hour or so. It is so good to hear from you, Tashi. Where are you?"

"I'm in Leh."

"Oh!" I was so happy that I started to laugh.

"What is it? Why are you laughing?" Tashi asked, sounding a

little annoyed.

"I'm so glad you're here," I replied. "When will you come?"

"Tomorrow. In the morning."

"What time?"

"Between eleven and twelve." His voice was serious. "OK. Goodbye." He hung up.

I put the phone down and slowly ascended the stairs to my room. *Tomorrow. Tomorrow. Not today...* The voices started quietly – like the slow ticking of a clock in my head. *Tomorrow. I've waited so long. And now he is here. He won't come – now. He's tired from the trip... But the flight from Delhi is only thirty-five minutes. How can he be tired? He wants to visit his family first. Of course. That's it. He hasn't seen his family in over a year.* I consoled myself with the thought that it was in less than one day I would see him.

There was no avoiding the feeling of disappointment. I wondered if he would have come today if I hadn't missed the first phone call at four o'clock. I undressed and prepared to start my meditation. When I closed my eyes, my heart was inundated with a flood of inner happiness and love for Tashi. Time passed quickly, unnoticed, and when I lay down to rest afterwards, all anxiety had disappeared. I decided to go to sleep early so as to be well-rested...

The next morning, I took longer than usual with my morning routine. I did a long massage with coconut oil and washed my hair, filed my nails and dressed very carefully. I decided to wear the gold-colored Punjabi suit because I knew gold was his favorite color.

The hours slid by, too slowly for comfort. Finally the hands of the clock told me eleven o'clock had come. I resisted spending my time peering over the balcony. Instead I decided to read *Shankara's Crest Jewel of Discrimination*. Shankara gives a clear warning about the danger of becoming overly attached to anything in the changing sphere of life, so it was very apt.

After nearly an hour had passed, I heard the brush of

footsteps on the staircase and then a lady's voice said, "She lives here." I saw the wife of the proprietor first. Only afterwards did I see Tashi following close behind her. I was seated on the veranda. I stood up and went to meet him. He was dressed in the maroon robes of the Buddhist monks.

He's wearing his monk's robes, I thought.

He placed his palms together as if in prayer as he approached me.

Will he embrace me? I wondered.

Then we stood face to face. He smiled warmly, keeping his palms closed in front of him. I realized he didn't want to touch me. Then he joined me at the table, taking the seat opposite mine.

"I brought your mail." He fumbled in his monk's bag which was draped over his right shoulder. Then he took out a medium-sized brown manila envelope. From the envelope, he took out several letters. He spread the contents out on the table.

I picked up the letters; all were from England. I had no desire to read them now as we had only just met.

I looked across at Tashi's face. He looked different and yet the same. In my mind, he was handsomer, his eyes brighter, his smile warmer. He looked older, more tired and less at ease. He looked at me. I was thinner than when I had left Delhi three months before; perhaps even older-looking. I wondered what he saw – what he was feeling. Then he spoke.

"Is there any letter from America?" he asked.

"No – all are from England," I answered.

"Nothing? No letter from your brother?"

"No."

"I think your brother did not get your letter or maybe he moved," he said. "Can you telephone your brother?"

All he cares about is the letter from my brother... He doesn't even seem happy to see me. It is only his desire to go to America that really matters – and all this time, I thought he—

"No, Tashi. That would be very expensive. I'm sure he

received the letters. I wrote to him twice. I don't know what is happening in his life. Sometimes my brothers and sisters don't write for a long time. They are very busy with their own lives."

"I told someone I would go to America. If I don't go now it will be a lie in my mouth," Tashi replied.

I remembered that he had told me that, in Buddhism, lying is regarded as a principle sin. A small lie is alright, but if a lama tells a big lie, he is no longer considered a lama.

"I have done all I can, Tashi. From Manali, I sent you three pages with the addresses and telephone numbers of Buddhist centers all over America. I wrote out a sample letter for you to send them. I gave you the address of the American Embassy. I don't know how I can do more. You could go to America as a tourist and then find a monastery and see if they will invite you to join them." I looked at him. I had never seen him in his monk's robe before as they were not allowed to wear them at the Japanese Buddhist Center in Delhi.

"You visited the gompas?" he asked me.

"Yes, some of them – not all. I loved going to the gompas. It was such a beautiful experience. I want to visit a few more of the main ones but I was waiting for you so we could go together."

"OK." He sat without saying anything for a while, then he said, "Let's go. You can leave suitcase here."

"But I'm going to stay with your family, isn't that what you said? I can't afford to stay here any longer," I said quietly.

"My village is about twenty-five kilometers from Leh. I feel boring there. I want to stay in Leh with my older brother."

"But, Tashi, I—" I stopped speaking. I didn't know what to say. He obviously didn't understand that I had barely enough money left for food. I had waited two more weeks for him with the hope that finally, when he arrived, I could move out of the guest house and stay with his family as he had said in his letter. Then I would be able to remain in Ladakh a little longer with him. Now my dream was starting to crumble.

"You stay here for a few more days. I have some business in Leh," Tashi said, "then we go to Hemis Gompa for three days. I have a lama friend there that I want to visit. It's OK?" he asked, shifting uneasily in his chair. He appeared anxious to leave.

"I'm sorry, Tashi. I'd love to go to Hemis with you, but I have no more money left to pay for this place. I can't stay here. You said I could stay with your family when you came to Ladakh."

He was getting impatient. "Alright, let's go. Take a few things with you, but leave suitcase here. It's OK? We go to my family tonight. My place is Nimmu village. We take bus at four o'clock."

"Alright." I unzipped my bulky suitcase and took out a change of clothes, a towel and some toiletries. I asked the owner of the guest house if he could store my suitcase. He agreed. I did not ask him to save my room. Then we left the guest house.

As we walked down the hill to the market, I was distinctly aware of walking beside a monk. Tashi kept a fair distance between us and seemed preoccupied with his own thoughts.

When we reached the main road, he turned up a side alleyway and then climbed a stony path between two rather dilapidated buildings, not far from the polo ground. I followed behind him as best as I could. He never turned around. Finally, he stopped in front of a wooden door and began scraping under a stone in the dirt. After a few minutes, he held up the door key and unlocked the door to his brother's room. It was a small rather gloomy room. There was a disheveled mat with blankets piled on top of it. On the floor was a gas cylinder with a few aluminum pots and a tava for cooking chapatis, and on the table was a bowl with old wrinkled apples in it. The curtains were dirty and worn and the rug on the floor was old and ragged. Tashi motioned for me to sit down on the mat. He stood uncomfortably by the gas cylinder.

"You will take tea?" he asked.

"Yes, alright."

He removed a lid from a large red plastic bucket and scooped out some water with a plastic cup. Then he poured the water into a pot, searched for some matches and lit the fire. As the water began to heat up, he continued searching for something. Finally he said, "I'll be back in a minute." Then he opened the door and went out.

A few minutes later, he reappeared with two packets of biscuits. He opened one packet and shook some of the biscuits onto a flat metal plate. Then he finished preparing the tea. When the tea was ready he offered me the biscuits.

He sat down on the edge of the mat, as far away from me as he could. We drank tea and nibbled our biscuits in silence. Then he got up.

"We go now. OK?" he said.

"Yes. Fine."

I stood up. He looked at my Punjabi suit. I could feel his eyes on my breasts. He stood still. Then he paced back and forth in the room like a tiger, nervously stalking its prey in the jungle. Then he slowly moved off to the door.

"Why you wear Indian suit? You're not Indian," he said stiffly.

"But in India, I always wear Indian clothes. What else should I wear here?" I asked, surprised and a little hurt.

"You should wear Western dress."

I stood up, tying my shoelaces as he buried the key in the sand by the door. He looked down at my shoes.

"Those shoes are rubber. Why you not get leather shoes?" he asked. "Leather shoes are better."

"I like these shoes," I replied. "They have lasted for three months and they're still in good condition. I bought them in Manali when I first arrived." I was peeved. I looked down at his shoes. He was wearing thick leather boots; they looked practically new. *So what?!* I thought. *I don't really like wearing leather anyway!*

We walked back to the main road. It was nearly time for lunch. We decided to eat at a newly built Tibetan restaurant. I ordered a vegetable noodle soup while he ordered the non-vegetarian variation of the same soup.

As we ate, I realized that Tashi was not the same person I had waited for. I had waited for someone else, someone I had constructed out of my imagination – a dream body, a dream image – not the man who was sitting at the table across from me. This man had little in common with the man I had held in my mind, offered my love to, and waited for. This man was someone new to me, someone I could barely even relate to. As I swallowed the salty soup, I also had to swallow hard in order to accept the reality of the situation. We hardly even knew what to say to one another.

At four o'clock, we boarded the bus to go to his village in Nimmu. The bus was almost empty. I slid into a seat by the window near the back of the bus. Tashi stood next to my seat looking at it, as if considering something, then he walked to the last seat in the last row of the bus across the aisle from me and sat there.

The bus filled up with passengers. An old man who smelled badly took the seat next to me. I recoiled inwardly but there was nowhere else to sit. As the bus pulled out of the depot, the anguish became almost unbearable. I felt as if my heart would burst with pain. I turned and looked over my shoulder at Tashi. He was staring straight ahead. I turned to face the window. The landscape rushed past but I did not see it through my tears. It was all an indistinguishable blur. *Here we are – together – after so long and he doesn't even want to sit next to me in the bus...* My thoughts tumbled, one after another, trying to make sense out of what was happening.

It took nearly two hours to reach Nimmu. We got out and I followed as Tashi began climbing a steep hill covered with stones. A young man who met us at the bus accompanied us up the hill. Tashi, who was carrying one of my bags, gave it to the young man, who slung it casually over his shoulder. The climb was long and difficult. At one point, the wind began to blow fiercely. I covered my eyes to shield them from the sand and suddenly my straw hat was lifted off my head. It started sailing down the mountain in the wind.

"Tashi! Tashi!" I shouted.

He turned around and hastily clambered over the rocks to fetch my hat which had landed on the stones beneath a tree. He picked it up and climbing up to meet me, handed it to me.

"The bus used to go all the way to my house. But now the road is broken so we have to walk. I'm sorry if it is uncomfortable for you," he said.

"I'm alright. Thank you for getting my hat for me."

Tashi looked into my eyes for a moment. In that instant, his heart touched mine and I felt an upsurge of joy. Renewed, I followed him over the stones, beginning to enjoy the challenge.

It took about fifteen minutes to reach the house. It stood alone on the top of a high hill overlooking the river. It was large house made of earth and stone. In front of it was an old row of five stupas. Below the stairs was a small yard in which a cow was sitting on a bed of straw. A little gray kitten greeted us on the path. There were rooms downstairs, but we climbed a stone staircase until we reached a small earthen rooftop with three rooms built around it.

Tashi led me into an empty room with pale blue walls. He told me to leave my bags there and he also put his knapsack inside. Then he went into the kitchen, a large dark room with a few pots beside a black cast-iron stove. Except for a few worn mats on the floor it was bare.

"This is my house. I feel ashamed. We are very poor," Tashi said, his eyes downcast.

"I like your house, Tashi. It has a beautiful feeling. It is a nice house." I really did like the house. Certainly it was a very simple dwelling without any luxuries. But the placement of it, high up overlooking the river, was perfect. It was a peaceful place, away from the rest of the village, and I especially liked the row of stupas in front of it.

He took a loaf of sweet bread out of his monk's shoulder bag.

"Have some bread," he said, breaking off a piece and giving it to me.

"Thank you." I ate it.

Then two children, a boy and a girl, entered the room. They smiled shyly at me from a corner of the room.

"These are my brother's children," Tashi said. The girl came up to Tashi, and he put his arm around her. Afterwards the boy followed and sat next to Tashi on the worn brown mat. They were barefoot. Tashi offered them the bread, but they shyly refused to take it.

A few minutes later, a very old man entered. He looked at Tashi and Tashi looked at him. There were no words spoken, just a silent acknowledgement of each other's presence. The young man who had carried my bag up the hill was also there.

"Chai," Tashi said, and the young man responded by preparing tea for us.

"Who is that man?" I asked Tashi.

"He's my younger brother," Tashi said.

"Is this your father?" I asked, indicating the old man who sat by the wall near the two children.

"Yes."

We had tea and as we sipped the boiling-hot liquid, Tashi exchanged a few words in the Ladakhi language with his father. I listened as the wind blew outside the windows. Twilight was falling over the mountains. A lady entered the room dressed in the full dark skirt of Ladakh. With her came a small boy of perhaps four or five years. The lady had two long braids which fell below her waist. Her face was chiseled in the classical mode. As soon as I saw her, I thought, *How beautiful she is*. But there was a shadow clouding her features as if a dark curtain had been drawn over the natural light which should have shone forth from her eyes.

"This is my sister," Tashi said.

"She's beautiful," I said.

"Not beautiful," Tashi said. "Her husband is dead. She was living in her own house with her son, but she could not live alone, so now she stays here with my brother's family and my father."

I didn't know what to say. I felt so sorry for her. How awful it must have been to lose her husband when she was so young and had recently had a son.

"Can she re-marry?" I whispered to Tashi.

"Not possible," he replied firmly.

We drank our tea in silence in the dark room. Night fell and we got up and I followed Tashi across the rooftop to another room.

Across from the door was a long wooden table with a stack of quilts and blankets neatly folded on top. Inside, I saw a single bed covered with an oriental cotton bedspread, and a beautiful red-velvet pillow with embroidery on it. The floor was covered with a simple straw mat.

"You sit here," Tashi said, motioning to a few plastic deck chairs similar to those found on the sun deck of a ship. In front of the chairs was a simple wooden table. "I will help prepare dinner," he said, leaving me alone in the room.

I sat on a chair, closed my eyes and began to meditate. The room faded; the trip on the bus dissolved. I was alone. The waves in the sea of consciousness slowly subsided and the ocean of unbounded awareness was all. The silence deepened. I was far away from all that I had ever known, far away from the world of forms, colors, and shapes, from the rise and fall of the sea of emotions, from the rippling stream of thoughts, ideas, dreams, and fancies. I was alone in the shrine – hidden away – in the depths of the forest of Being. I felt free. I felt at peace. There was no need for anything – not words, not people, not food, just peace and freedom – just pure Being – without craving.

Tashi came in, but when he saw me meditating, he went back out. His sister came in to change the sheets on the bed. She moved very quietly so as not to disturb me. The children came in and sat next to me, not speaking, just feeling. I was happy. I did not move or speak. I was feeling the bliss of the pure mountain air in the silence of Tashi's abode. When I opened my eyes, one hour later, it was dark outside.

Tashi came in again. "You will eat?" he asked me.

"Yes, alright – a little," I replied. I was very hungry, but I wondered whether I would be able to eat a full meal so late at night.

Tashi disappeared and returned with a full plate of boiled white rice, lentils and cabbage. He handed it to me.

"Is this enough?" he asked quietly.

"Yes, more than enough." I closed my eyes and thanked God for the food. Tashi returned a few minutes later with his own plate mounted high with food. When he came to sit down, he chose a seat not next to mine. He left an empty seat between us. We ate in silence.

"More dhal? Rice?" Tashi asked.

"I've had enough rice – just dhal – thank you."

He called one of the children, who took my plate and added more dhal in the kitchen. I tried to finish everything, but Tashi had given me too much rice. A few hard balls of rice remained on my plate when he took it back to the kitchen. From his expression, I could see that he was displeased. I had read that Ladakhis never wasted anything. I remembered watching the lamas from Ladakh at the center in Delhi cleaning their plates of every last morsel of food at every meal. I regretted not being able to eat everything that he had offered to me.

After dinner, he said, "Tomorrow we will take early bus to Leh."

"Alright. Do you want to go to the festival?" I asked, smiling.

"Maybe, I don't know. I must do something. I have some

business in Leh." There was a note of irritation in his voice. "You can go to the festival if you want. You will enjoy it." He stood up abruptly. "Now you sleep, alright?"

"Yes."

"You sleep here," Tashi said, pointing to the bed. They had changed the sheets while I was meditating, and put a thick quilt on the bed.

"May I sleep in here?" Tashi asked, pointing to the opposite side of the room.

"Yes – as you wish," I answered.

"No – outside is better," he said. "I will sleep outside." He took a few blankets and a quilt outside.

"Don't get cold," I said to him. "If you feel cold, just come in."

He didn't reply. When I went outside to go to the toilet which was a hole in the earthen floor, I saw Tashi lying on the ground, the quilt nearly covering his head. Looking up, I saw the sky shining with innumerable stars. *You have the better place to sleep, Tashi*, I thought as I passed by. *I wish I could sleep with you under the stars.* Then I remembered what he had told me in Delhi: *"Here one doesn't see many stars. But in Ladakh, there are so many stars."*

I stood still, not far from where he slept and looked up at the sky for several minutes. Before he came to Leh, I had dreamed of sitting close to him gazing up at the stars. Slowly I returned to my room and crept under the quilt, but I could not fall asleep for a long time. My heart reached out to Tashi in the silence. I wished he had slept in the same room with me. I wished and wished, and silently wished until my eyelids grew heavy with fatigue and the night drew in becoming colder with every passing hour.

At about six o'clock, I awoke and donning Punjabi trousers and a cardigan, I collected soap, toothbrush and toothpaste. Tashi came in soon after and we went down to the river to wash together. There was something exhilarating about washing my face in the icy cold water in the early hours of the morning. I felt so close to Mother Nature, so simple and innocent, as I squatted down on my heels on a large smooth stone and dipped my hands into the cold water. Tashi squatted behind me. Once as I turned around, I realized that he was busy relieving himself using nature's "outdoor" toilet. I hurriedly turned back to face the river.

Having brushed his teeth and washed his face, Tashi hastily returned to the house while I lingered for some time, watching the waves dash against the stones and flow rapidly downstream, out of sight, into the valley below. I collected Tashi's toothbrush, which he had left on a stone, on the way back to the house.

We had breakfast in a different, much cozier kitchen downstairs. Tashi's sister-in-law, the mother of the two children, cooked chapatis, deep-fried in oil for Tashi and I. She also served us generous portions of freshly made yogurt, and steaming-hot cups of Ladakhi butter tea. It was a sumptuous breakfast after the sparse meals I had ordered for myself at the guest house.

"This is the best breakfast I have had since I came to Ladakh," I said to Tashi.

"It's a simple meal," he answered.

After we had each eaten four or five chapatis, she offered us more.

"We can take them with us, to eat later," I said, stuffing them into my bag. Then we thanked her and said goodbye. She was very warm, friendly and generous and I knew that if we would have had more time together, we would have become good friends. Feeling full and happy, I sailed over the stones as I followed Tashi down the steep hill.

"I'm feeling really happy today!" I shouted as I ran down the hill to catch up with him.

"Be careful coming down," he said, turning to look at me. He smiled. I felt like the ice had broken that morning, and we would have fun together at the Ladakhi cultural festival which was scheduled to begin that very morning.

The bus was standing at the foot of the hill – empty. Even the driver was nowhere to be seen. Tashi went in and put his knapsack in the last row of the bus.

"Can I sit with you?" I asked in a soft voice, bringing my bag near his place.

"No – you sit there." He pointed to a seat a few rows down, in the opposite aisle. I just stood there in the aisle. My mind went blank and my heart sank into the soles of my feet. Then I slowly picked up my bag and moved it away from his. I found it impossible to reconcile his present behavior with the last letter I had received from him and which I had pressed to my heart in joy.

Slowly the passengers arrived and when we finally set off down the road, the bus was half full. I was relieved that the seat next to me was still empty. But not for long. A tall man with a mustache who looked like a Muslim from Kashmir got on and sat in the seat opposite me and proceeded to nonchalantly stare at me without a break. I felt so uncomfortable that finally I got up and moved to the last row of the bus, on the opposite end from where Tashi was sitting. Much to my chagrin, the Muslim man came and followed me and sat down squeezing himself into the seat next to me in the last row. It was all I could take. The morning had begun on such a high note, and already a tidal wave of despair threatened to engulf me. I turned to face the window and this time, the tears came, uncontrollably rushing down like a silent waterfall. I didn't even try to stop them. I covered my face with my shawl and closed my eyes as the bus hurtled along the road to Leh.

When we got out of the bus, Tashi looked at me but didn't say anything. He knew I had been crying. We trudged up the hill toward the polo ground where the festival was to be held. When we reached the main road, he stopped and turned to face me.

"I meet one lama friend today. You go guest house. I will see you this evening or tomorrow morning."

I was incredulous. "But I can't stay in the guest house. I don't have a room there anymore."

"Then where you will stay?" he asked.

"I don't know."

"Then I go now. I meet my lama friend today."

"But, Tashi, I may not see you again. I may have to go back to Manali if I have nowhere to stay in Ladakh."

"OK. I see you in Delhi. Goodbye." He shifted uncomfortably in place, obviously eager to leave. "I must go now."

"Goodbye, Tashi," I said. I watched him as he walked off down the road without looking back.

The world turned upside down for me then. For a moment, nothing made sense anymore. I could not decipher anything. The writing on the wall was all in hieroglyphics. I tried to discern a pattern in the chain of events, but the chain broke and the pattern was irretrievable. All I saw was the empty spot beside me where Tashi had been but a moment before. All I saw was a figure draped in the maroon lama's robe disappearing like a dot in the crowd. I stood there for – I don't know how long – wondering why I had waited – why I had lived in expectation of so much and now – this.

Slowly, with heavy steps, my arms aching from the load I was carrying, I headed up the hill toward the guest house. I barely saw who I was passing on the road. My eyes were open but unseeing. My heart was shrouded in a gloom which dimmed my vision. It was a long slow walk.

Chapter Twenty

As I neared the guest house where my suitcase was stored, someone came toward me. Then I heard a voice, calling my name.

"Hello! Shanti! It's Karen. How was your meeting?"

It was the Irish lady I had met in the restaurant the day before. I looked up at her and as we stood together, face to face, my body crumbled in a fit of sobs and I fell into her open arms.

"What's the matter? What happened?" Karen asked, enfolding me in a warm embrace. "What is it?"

"It was all an illusion. It's over – finished." I could barely form the words, but she quickly grasped the meaning.

"But why? Did you meet him? What happened?" Karen looked at me. "Why not come up to my room and have a cup of tea?" She led the way to her guest house which was only a few steps away.

The guest house where she was staying had a beautiful garden filled with roses, sunflowers, daisies and many other colorful varieties of flowers. Behind the small house was an orchard of apricot and apple trees. Karen led me upstairs to her room; then she ordered a pot of tea. We sat by the open window overlooking the garden.

"Now tell me, Shanti, what happened? Wasn't he happy to see you?"

I leaned back in the chair, wiped my eyes and blew my nose. Then I took a deep breath to regain my composure.

"It just vanished into thin air. The whole thing dissolved. It was just an illusion. It was a mirage. I conjured it up in my mind. When we met, it felt like I had just woken up from a dream. I realized the whole thing was wrong. He had asked me to wait for him and so I waited. I thought: let me give it a chance, let me give the relationship a chance. I waited until all my money ran out... He finally arrived. I expected to be able to stay with his family but he told me he was bored staying there. He only told me this after he came. He knew I was hoping to stay there for a little while. And then he simply told me to go back to the guest house because he wanted to be with his lama friend. When I told him I had no money to go back, he just said goodbye. Goodbye! That was it! Where was I supposed to go? What could I do? How could he just say goodbye? Just like that. I simply can't believe it. I don't understand it. I loved him so much... I must be going crazy."

Karen sat still in the chair gazing out at the garden. She sipped tea from her cup and poured another cup of tea for me.

"No, Shantila, not crazy, just – well, um, innocent perhaps. You expected too much of him. Maybe you forgot that he was a lama. You say he wore his robes?"

"Yes, he was wearing them. It was the first time I saw him in them."

"That was a sign, Shantila. Don't doubt him...his love, I mean..." Karen said the last words slowly.

"But he just walked off and left me. Anything could have happened... He walked away when I needed him most."

"I know. But it still doesn't mean he didn't love you," Karen said firmly.

"But he didn't even want to sit near me on the bus when we went to visit his house. On the way there and on the way back, he chose a seat far away from me. It was so painful."

"It doesn't mean he didn't care. Maybe he cared too much. Maybe that caring was uncomfortable for him. What could he do under those circumstances? Perhaps, I'm just saying that, perhaps he felt that he had to protect himself...and you...from getting hurt. Don't be too hard on him, Shantila, because how do you know what he was really feeling?"

"What do you mean – he had to protect himself and me?"

"I mean this: he is a lama, right? He had made a choice, had taken his vows. He stuck by them, right? If you'd sat next to him, it would only have made it harder for him and more painful. It isn't easy for a man to be near a woman he loves and not be able to share his feelings with her, even if he desperately wants to... I must say one thing to you, Shantila: I think you expected too much of him."

"I gave my heart to him. I trusted him."

"I know. But one must learn not to expect anything in return. Just give, be happy you had the chance to give him your love. Accept what he was able to give you. We can't expect men to give in the same way, to the same extent. It's a rare thing – this process of opening the heart completely. Some men aren't willing or able to respond like that or maybe they can, but it takes them much longer..."

I listened carefully to her words. Gradually it dawned on me that she was right. From childhood, I had aimed for perfection, so much so that whilst a student at university, a close friend from Africa, once felt obliged to say to me, "You can't change the world. It isn't perfect. You must accept things as they are." And before my mother died, she said, "Shanti, don't ask for too much."

Echoes from the past floated by on the stream of consciousness. As Karen spoke, I remembered Tashi's words: *"There are four rules for a lama... I cannot marry... Become a nun... We live separately, but the study is the same.* Then Ralph's words floated past: *"If the friendship is unselfish, it will continue. All attachments bring sorrow..."* Then I saw the glowing visage of Maitreya Buddha, the Buddha of Loving Kindness, the symbol of that love that desires the good of the beloved above all else. Then I heard my voice as I spoke to Emma but a few weeks before: *"Enjoy the friendship as it is but don't try to make it into something it is not destined to be..."* I hung my head in shame. When I lifted my head I saw through the open window a lavender horizon of mountains washed by sunlight. It was quiet in the room. Only the sound of birds chirping could be heard amidst the occasional rattle of our teacups. I smiled.

"I'm glad it's over. I'm glad I realized it was all an illusion. Now I'm free. I can forget and move on. No more waiting and wondering what will be in the future. No more longing. I can just be simple now – just live my life, just be and whatever comes, comes. I'm glad I found out. It only took one day to see that it was not meant to be."

"You can stay here with me if you want," Karen said. "Sleep in the bed over there. I just changed to this room with two beds yesterday because I wanted a room overlooking the garden. I don't mind if you stay here."

I was so relieved that I didn't know how to respond. It felt like a huge weight had been lifted from my shoulders.

"Thank you very much."

"You must stay for the festival which starts today! Shall we go to the polo ground and have a look?" Karen asked, getting up and stretching her back in an arch.

"Yes, let's go!" I exclaimed.

It was nearly eleven o'clock when we reached the main road of the bazaar. There were crowds gathering in the street and in the background, I could hear the sound of music. I saw banners waving and brightly costumed ladies riding on horseback in a parade. I craned my neck, peering over the heads of the people in front of me in order to see the regal fanfare. A herd of shaggy-haired yaks were being led down the street by long-haired men wearing fur-trimmed hats and long woolen coats. Behind the yaks there were beautifully adorned ladies in silk embroidered outfits riding on the backs of camels. The camels looked totally unconcerned with all the people standing along the path. They moved regally through the crowd, their necks held up, poised with moist rounded noses and sweet smiles on their broad lips. I wanted to reach out and hug them but had to be content with a quick pat on the back of one camel as it passed.

Karen and I made our way to the polo ground which was already filled. The stone tiers surrounding the arena were hot from the sun. We climbed up to a seat and watched as children dressed in a variety of colorful school uniforms paraded in front of the audience in step with the beating of drums. It soon became unbearably hot; it was high noon and there was not a cloud in the sky. Since we both were very thirsty and hungry, we decided to leave and have lunch.

In the Tibetan restaurant that was still empty, we continued our conversation. Karen looked into my eyes with compassion as she spoke.

"It is better not to want anything – just to let things be as they are...to know that everything is as it should be. We are so used to craving for things, to expecting things, to attempting to control things, to trying to make things happen the way we want them to happen. We have forgotten how to trust – how to let go..."

"I know, but even with the knowledge, it's not always easy to practice."

"It's really true that everything is happening in the way it should. I see it in the gardens where I work. Things grow the way they are meant to. The buds open at just the right time. They bloom in time. Everything does, you know. If we could only enjoy the process and stop trying to interfere with things, stop trying to manipulate, we could see the pattern unfolding... We would see that it is right – it is always perfect. All we could ever want is on its way to us. The river is flowing all the time. There is no need to worry, to be afraid or to doubt the future. The only thing is love, to love. That's all. Just continue to love and everything else will take care of itself..."

"You say to love. It's like taking the risk of being hurt all the time," I interrupted her.

Karen ignored my words and continued. "Thinking, planning, deciding – just leave it all by the wayside. Just keep one thing: keep your heart open – keep loving – keep trusting. Know that your love will carry you wherever you are meant to go. It's enough. The flow of love is strong enough. Just trust...trust the flow. Sometimes it's hard, I know that. When we feel hurt or disappointed or lonely, we sometimes get scared and lose our balance. But it comes back. It will come back." She paused.

Her words were so reassuring. She had a calm confidence that seemed to be born from experience.

She continued, "Balance always comes back, Shantila. So don't be afraid to fall in love again. Just keep giving... You'll realize one day that you don't need anyone to make the experience of life full. It is already full. We think we need people. We only need to return to our center. There is an ocean of love inside us that is always full, always flowing. We can drink from that ocean at any time – with or without a person – with or without a 'someone' to love."

"How?" I asked Karen.

"By accepting things, people, events as they are. By bowing your head to the river and taking up the water in your hands. By immersing yourself in the ocean all around you...accepting the flow and becoming one with the rhythm of the waves..."

A vision of a scene I had witnessed many years ago at dawn on the banks of the Ganges surfaced in my mind: I saw a man standing knee-deep in the river with open palms raised upwards to the sun. He took up the glowing water, sprinkled with sunlight, in his hands and offered it up to the sun as it rose on the horizon, then he let the drops fall from his hands back into the river, their source. An inner voice translated the vision: *Accept whatever comes unasked and offer it back to its source – with love.*

I looked at Karen and for a moment, I thought maybe she was there, maybe she had crossed over into the world from which there is no more rebirth, crossed the threshold dividing the immortal, never-changing and the mortal ever-changing realms of life.

"I am no different than you are," Karen said, as if reading my thought. "I am only here where you are. We are swimming in the same water... Only you are thirsting and I am full – for now.

Tomorrow I may imagine I am thirsting too."

"You won't really be thirsting then?" I asked her.

"No, I will only imagine that I am. How can I be thirsting when I am swimming – perpetually swimming in the ocean. It must be only my imagination playing tricks on me – fooling me. How can I be thirsting? It's not possible with water all around, is it?" She smiled.

"I guess not," I replied. "But then most of the world is lost in an illusion – an illusion of sorrow, pain, hunger and loneliness. Then why is everyone behaving in this way? Tell me that."

"You must discover that. Keep asking yourself until the answer comes, Shanti. Keep asking and the answer WILL come. It may not come in words; it may not come today or tomorrow. It may just be a feeling, a knowing – without speech – but one day you'll understand. You'll realize what I have been talking about. Then you'll always be happy, always, no matter what happens. You'll be able to accept whatever comes without losing your balance."

The restaurant was now full. A sweet Tibetan song, distilled in quiet tones of joy, swelled and ebbed, swelled and ebbed as we sat in stillness together.

I had only just met Karen but now I realized that she had come into my life just at the right time. Her words sank into my heart and resonated with the frequency of my own thoughts and feelings. I looked into her eyes and saw only peace, and a kind of abandon, a freedom from care. She had traveled in the East for many years. She had fallen in love with a lama and many more experiences came on her journeys. She digested them all and simply collected her bags and traveled on. Now our paths had crossed. We were destined to part a few days later, but her words remained printed indelibly in my heart.

Before she left for Lamayuru Gompa, she gave me one thousand rupees.

"Here, take it. I know you need it. Someone did the same thing for me in Tibet when I had almost nothing left." She handed me ten one-hundred rupee notes. I quietly accepted.

"There is no need to pay it back. I know you will make it go far," she added, pouring me a cup of tea.

"Where are you going after Lamayuru?" I asked her.

"Oh, probably Alchi Gompa. I don't know. I'll just relax and see how I feel after I get there. I want to sketch a bit and just enjoy each place without keeping to any schedule. It's my holiday you know. Just another ten days, and then back to Ireland."

"Thank you, Karen, for everything. I'm going back to Manali soon. I just want to see a few more places, and go to the polo match which should be fun. I've never seen a polo match in my life and I do love horses."

"I've seen them. It can be a bit violent. In Ireland, they play polo but it is the polite version."

The morning drifted slowly by like clouds in the wind, as we sat and chatted quietly, sipping tea together. The book I was writing was nearly finished and I felt that my journey to India was drawing to a close. I had one more stop, Manali, or rather two, Manali, then New Delhi, before the plane to England would lift off and India would be left behind, a precious memory fading into the distance.

The bus to Manali was scheduled to leave very early, so I had arranged for a taxi at three-thirty in the morning. I found the taxi parked beside the stream next to the guest house. The taxi driver was fast asleep in the back seat.

"Dorje! Dorje!" I called to him, tapping on the window.

He stirred, then tossed back the blanket which covered his head. When he saw me, he quickly sat up and opened the door. He climbed into the front seat of the old Ambassador. Dorje had decided to sleep in the taxi near my guest house. He wanted to be sure he would wake up in time to take me to the bus which was scheduled to leave Leh for Manali at four o'clock in the morning.

Quietly, I swung open the corrugated-iron gate to the guest

house and led Dorje to the dark hallway where my suitcase lay; thirty kilograms of possessions. He picked it up and carried it to the car, his short frame leaning over at an angle so as not to scrape it on the ground. Then he lifted it into the back seat, and started the engine.

The town of Leh was still fast asleep; the sun still hidden behind the blue-gray mountains. In the dawning hours, we heard dogs barking, and saw the shadows of street cleaners gathering their brooms to clear the road of debris before the shopkeepers opened their doors. But most of all, there was just a silent feeling of saying goodbye in the darkness before dawn.

The bus pulled out of the depot at four-thirty, with the luggage piled high on the roof, tied down with ropes, and covered with a green tarpaulin. I had bought the cheapest ticket available and the seats were far from comfortable. The bus was carrying mostly Tibetan passengers and the seats were numbered.

The seat I got was next to a man who was quite stout and I had to be content with being crammed against the window with the heat of his right leg creasing the trousers of my Punjabi. My only consolation was that two lamas sat behind me, praying.

In the evening, a storm broke out. Rain lashed the windows of the bus. The wind howled, shaking the trees. The dirt roads became like muddy pools and the bus rocked precariously. I was looking out the window when suddenly a thought flashed through my mind: *My manuscript! It's on top of the bus! In my cloth suitcase! Oh, no! If it gets wet, all my work is lost!*

I stood up. Climbing over the other passengers, I rushed to the front of the bus.

"Stop the bus! Please stop the bus!" I pleaded frantically with the bus driver.

"What is it?" he asked, staring at the road, but glancing at me out of the corner of his eye.

"My book! It's raining and my book is on top of the bus! My

suitcase isn't waterproof. Please, please can I get my suitcase down and bring it inside?"

The bus driver pulled over to the side of the road and opened the door. I ran outside into the pouring rain and attempted to climb up the ladder in the back of the bus. A man got out to help me.

"I'll get your suitcase down for you," he said. I described my suitcase to him and he brought it into the bus.

My hands were trembling as I unzipped it. Inside I found my manuscript wrapped securely in a plastic bag. I sighed audibly and whispered a silent thank you to God.

It was very dark when we reached Keylong where we were to spend the night. I had decided beforehand to sleep in the bus, but when we arrived, everyone got out and the bus was taken to the workshop overnight for repairs. The sleeping arrangements turned out to be quite dismal. The only accommodation available were dormitory rooms in which men and ladies slept in single beds in the same room. When I discovered that some of the men in the rooms were drinking liquor, I refused to take a bed.

I went outside and sat on the steps, gazing at the dark silhouettes of the trees. *What should I do?* I asked myself. *Should I go outside and sleep in the forest? The forest would be better than this!*

Totally exhausted from the sixteen-hour trip, I broke down and sat sobbing outside the guest house. A young Tibetan girl came and sat beside me.

"What is the matter? Please don't cry. Can I help you?" she asked.

"I can't sleep in the same room with men I don't even know, and some of them are drunk. I'm thinking of sleeping in the forest," I said between sobs.

"No, you mustn't sleep in the forest. I will sleep next to you. I will protect you during the night. I know a large room with only one lama in it. Shall we go there together?"

I followed her into the room, deeply relieved to see that there was only a lama there. Even so, I spent half the night crying. At six in the morning, the bus was ready to complete the remaining seven hours of the journey to Manali.

When we finally reached Manali at about twelve-thirty in the afternoon, I was lucky to find a coolie who strapped my suitcase to his back and carried it to the Tibetan gompa, where I hoped to be able to stay, but the room was occupied by two monks from Karnataka who had recently returned from Ladakh. Suddenly I was stranded. But a voice inside me said, *Don't worry. You'll find a place – if not here, then somewhere else.*

Leaving my suitcase by the door of the room in the gompa where I had stayed before, I walked outside, and greeted the shopkeepers whom I had become friends with during my three months in Manali. At one shop, I mentioned to the proprietor that I was a writer and that I was looking for a place to stay until the room at the monastery was vacated. He made me tell him all about my book.

Then he said, "I have a hotel. You can stay there for nothing." He smiled at the solution which he had found.

"Really?" I asked, surprised.

"Yes, really. When are you coming?"

"I'll come this afternoon," I answered. "Can you show me the room?"

"Yes. Come with me."

I followed him up the road until it curved round. We stood in front of a small three-story building painted pink. A sign across the front of the building said: The Sunbeam.

"You only pay the tax – eighteen rupees per day," he said. Then he paused. "No, you don't have to pay anything. You stay for free." He seemed to be very pleased with his final decision.

This morning when the lama told me that the room was not available, I said to myself: "Don't worry. Everything that happens, happens for the best." I felt God would organize everything. So I didn't worry. I just trusted and now this. "Thank you so much. I am very grateful," I said in a soft voice.

"It's nothing. I'm glad to be able to help you," he said, smiling as we walked up the stairs to the room.

It was a simply decorated hotel with all the basic amenities, no frills attached. But at least it was clean and everything, including the water heater, electric lights and toilet, worked. I moved in that same day.

When I returned to the gompa, I discovered that the lamas had begun a special puja which lasted two weeks. This meant that they would be praying three times a day. I was overjoyed at the news and decided to attend in the early morning and again in the afternoon.

Early the next morning, I entered the temple of the monastery. It was like coming home. The dear faces of the lamas I had shared so many precious moments with were all there bowed over their prayer books, their auras painted in gentle colors, with shaved heads, voluminous robes and soft voices. I bowed three times before the golden Buddha and took my seat on the right side of the hall under the window.

Closing my eyes, the outside world melted away. Once again, I sailed out on a silver sea of silence – out, out, farther than the mind could reach – into the boundless region of pure being – a land of softness, silence and compassion. Above me, Maitreya Buddha – the future Buddha – the Buddha of Loving-kindness spread his golden wings, his crown glowing above his head like the rays of the sun. I saw him in my inner vision – luminous, transparent, His Body filling the universe – His Being, the Being of all beings. It was as if the Divine Father-Mother held the world within Himself, sheltering, nourishing, and protecting every living being within His omnipresent Body, which was transparent, invisible to mortal eyes. And coming as I did, on the wings of prayer of the lamas, carried on the wings of their shining raft of silence, I could feel the Divine Presence of the Father-Mother of Creation. In that silence, undisturbed by thoughts, undiminished by fears or doubts, I saw within it, the perfection of life unfolding. In a moment of truth, I felt that all was as it was designed to be. I heard the music of the birds, the rattle of the lamas' prayer beads, the clash of the cymbals, the beating of the drum, the lamas' voices rising and falling like waves, deathless, serene, and the ringing of the bells, and it was PERFECT. Every sound, every pause, every moment so sublime, so deeply RIGHT it felt. I could not want anything. I could not move or open my eyes. I simply swayed back and forth like a comely branch of a tree, swaying in the wind. My body knew only peace, only peace, only peace and wave upon wave of happiness, wave upon wave upon wave.

Each day I returned and the experience I had added to itself ever-new layers of happiness and peace. A divine fulfillment began to flow like a swelling river, from deep within my heart. The river rose. Even as I awoke each morning, a new wave of bliss inundated my heart; even as I opened my eyes and looked upon a world, ever the same and yet ever new, ever fresh. Sometimes, when I walked outside after many hours of prayers with the lamas, I felt as if my individuality had merged with the unbounded grandeur of the Father-Mother God. It was as if my awareness overspread the universe, and contained within it every living thing. Every being that moved within my range of vision, I found I could hold in an invisible embrace, and nurtured by the silence of the Infinite, we breathed as one interwoven whole.

In that moment of truth, I realized that so many times we look outside, searching for a perfection which already exists inside all the time. We search for the perfect companion, the perfect piece of music, the perfect cloth to wear, the perfect house, the perfect meal. But the perfection is already everywhere. Omnipresent, it evades our gaze. Like the musk deer who carries the most heavenly fragrance within itself, who wanders in search of that divine fragrance, covering countless miles of hills and forests, roaming, roaming far and wide until it finds that the fragrance is created by itself. Like that deer are we – in search of the fulfillment which will never wane, and which exists eternally deep within our own heart. But where can we find it? Unseen is That, unmeasured by time or space, unheard except in silence, undigested except when cooked by the inner fire deep within the temple of the heart.

We find It only by becoming one with It. By leaning inward toward the music – the dance and the dancer become one. In the silence between the lamas' prayers, I realized that there was nowhere to go and nothing to do. I realized that each moment contained all we could ever seek to know, to feel and to believe. Each moment contained perfection.

I remembered who I was: a simple child, an aged pilgrim, a Mother of Creation, a human being made in the image of the Eternal Being, That One, unbreathed upon, ever giving life to all, ever reborn, ever the same. The lamas' prayers re-awakened something in me which had forgotten the interwoven fabric of love of which all that is, is made.

The voices of the lamas, filled with kindness and compassion, gently lifted aside the veil from my eyes and heart. In their message of unspoken love, my heart succeeded in surrendering the cover of darkness which had shielded my eyes from the luminous rays of the sun. Now, in freedom, I could look upon the world without fear, without doubt, without sorrow, and without regret. My life, unchanged on the surface, carried within it, a new level of peace. I walked home on the same road, but there was no sense of coming or going. All resided in the Eternal Now. The moment was pregnant with renewed meaning. I tasted the nectar of a love which came, not from people, not from outside, but from an ever-flowing fullness deep within. This love nourished my heart and enabled me to nourish others without losing anything or feeling I was doing anything. It was just a sense of Being – just a natural flow – an outpouring of the spirit.

One day, while walking in the forest, not far from the monastery, I found again the ladder leading up to the tree house. Someone had painted the ladder bright blue! I climbed the blue wooden steps, holding onto the broken, rickety banister, part of which had fallen away. Once inside, I spread my green woolen shawl on the wooden boards and sat down, cross-legged, gazing out at the silver-rimmed mountains across the river on the horizon. I was so happy to be there with only the sound of the rushing waves of the river to distill the silence of the forest.

A wave of fatigue washed over me, and I lay down on the shawl and was soon fast asleep. Nothing disturbed the gentle slumber which my body craved. Only the sound of the crows flying overhead punctuated the stillness which enfolded me in nature's mantle of serenity and peace. When the need for sleep had been fulfilled, I opened my eyes. I was unaware of how much time had passed, nor did I care. I felt completely happy. There was nothing more I desired, nowhere I longed to be, nothing I lacked. In that moment of utter simplicity, I felt as if I had all I could ever need or want. As I gazed out at the trees, the perfection of God's creation shone out from every fiber of every tree, stitched with care and precision. All I saw, from the fan-like leaves of the deodars, to the green-velvet grass, to the lavender hue of the mountains, to the azure sky, to the white froth on the river, all contained a vision of divine grace. That vision melted into me and filled me as I merged with a happiness I knew could never be erased completely.

Today, I am preparing to depart, to leave Manali for New Delhi. But where I go, from where to where, no longer has much significance. The journey I had to take has been taken. The pilgrimage I sought to complete has been completed, not to the temples of Rishikesh, Haridwar, Badrinath or Gangotri, but to the omnipresent God, to the temple hidden within every human heart. I discovered on my journey that God is everywhere, in the forest, upon the summit of the mountains, beside the silver streams – everywhere. I found the temple of His love in the people I met on the way, in the help I received all along the way. He came and stood near, guiding and protecting me, through each of them. What was it, if not His Love, that carried me?

To that Temple of Love, I offer all I am, each thought, each word, every action, may it be as a petal placed at the feet of God.

Praise for: *The Contribution of Maharishi's Vedic Science to Complete Fulfillment in Life* **by Barbara Ann Briggs**

"Knowledge for Complete Fulfillment in Life"

This compact book is a must read for those who seek clear and basic understanding of the main concepts of Maharishi's Vedic Science. The author masterfully accomplishes this in an easy-to-read format with key concepts succinctly extracted and condensed from the vast volume of Maharishi's works. The presentation cites over 100 direct quotes of Maharishi in substantiating each concept. Here is timeless knowledge derived from delving into the heart of the science of consciousness, the Self of everyone. This astute and concise compilation of Maharishi's Vedic Science gifts us with a book worthy to keep, refer to and cherish.

Teresa Meyers, MS

"A Feast of Absolute Wisdom"

Barbara Briggs' book is an excellent and compact source for this supreme practical Vedic wisdom as presented by Maharishi – the "Genius of Consciousness". It is faithful to Maharishi's exposition, being replete with well-chosen quotes from Maharishi's works. Sources are given. It makes what used to be a highly specialized field of knowledge easily accessible to today's reader, wherever they are starting from, and points the way to how one can achieve the timeless goal of full personal development and a comprehensive understanding of oneself and of life.

Charles Cunningham, BSC(hons) Psychology, MSC, Health Promotion

"Brilliant Reference Book for Maharishi's Vedic Science"

I found this a brilliant reference book for Maharishi's Vedic

Science. Here is a map of the territory of higher consciousness, its development through all the seven states of consciousness to unity and the fundamental principles that underpin each one. With copious referenced quotes of Maharishi, the book does not seek to re-interpret the path but simply highlight the landmarks that Maharishi brought back to light for all future generations to find their way.

Henry Brighouse, Graduate, AA School of Architecture, London

"Excellent Introduction to Vedic Wisdom"

Barbara Briggs has written an excellent introduction to Vedic wisdom. Her book does justice to the depth of the material and at the same time is easy to understand. It won't make you enlightened, but it will make you want to get enlightened.

William T. Hathaway, author of *Wellsprings: A Fable of Consciousness*

Roundfire

FICTION

Put simply, we publish great stories. Whether it's literary or popular, a gentle tale or a pulsating thriller, the connecting theme in all Roundfire fiction titles is that once you pick them up you won't want to put them down.

If you have enjoyed this book, why not tell other readers by posting a review on your preferred book site. Recent bestsellers from Roundfire are:

The Bookseller's Sonnets
Andi Rosenthal

The Bookseller's Sonnets intertwines three love stories with a tale of religious identity and mystery spanning five hundred years and three countries.

Paperback: 978-1-84694-342-3 ebook: 978-184694-626-4

Birds of the Nile
An Egyptian Adventure
N.E. David

Ex-diplomat Michael Blake wanted a quiet birding trip up the Nile – he wasn't expecting a revolution.

Paperback: 978-1-78279-158-4 ebook: 978-1-78279-157-7

Blood Profit$
The Lithium Conspiracy
J. Victor Tomaszek, James N. Patrick, Sr

The blood of the many for the profits of the few... *Blood Profit$*
will take you into the cigar-smoke-filled room where American
policy and laws are really made.
Paperback: 978-1-78279-483-7 ebook: 978-1-78279-277-2

The Burden
A Family Saga
N.E. David

Frank will do anything to keep his mother and father apart. But
he's carrying baggage - and it might just weigh him down...
Paperback: 978-1-78279-936-8 ebook: 978-1-78279-937-5

The Cause
Roderick Vincent

The second American Revolution will be a fire lit from an
internal spark.
Paperback: 978-1-78279-763-0 ebook: 978-1-78279-762-3

Don't Drink and Fly
The Story of Bernice O'Hanlon Part One
Cathie Devitt

Bernice is a witch living in Glasgow. She loses her way in her
life and wanders off the beaten track looking for the garden of
enlightenment.
Paperback: 978-1-78279-016-7 ebook: 978-1-78279-015-0

Gag
Melissa Unger

One rainy afternoon in a Brooklyn diner, Peter Howland
punctures an egg with his fork. Repulsed, Peter pushes the plate
away and never eats again.
Paperback: 978-1-78279-564-3 ebook: 978-1-78279-563-6

The Master Yeshua
The Undiscovered Gospel of Joseph
Joyce Luck

Jesus is not who you think he is. The year is 75 CE. Joseph ben
Jude is frail and ailing, but he has a prophecy to fulfil...
Paperback: 978-1-78279-974-0 ebook: 978-1-78279-975-7

On the Far Side, There's a Boy
Paula Coston

Martine Haslett, a thirty-something 1980s woman, plays hard on
the fringes of the London drag club scene until one night which
prompts her to sign up to a charity. She writes to a young Sri
Lankan boy, with consequences far and long.
Paperback: 978-1-78279-574-2 ebook: 978-1-78279-573-5

Tuareg
Alberto Vazquez-Figueroa

With over 5 million copies sold worldwide, *Tuareg* is a classic
adventure story from best-selling author Alberto Vazquez-
Figueroa, about honour, revenge and a clash of cultures.
Paperback: 978-1-84694-192-4

Readers of ebooks can buy or view any of these bestsellers by clicking on the live link in the title. Most titles are published in paperback and as an ebook. Paperbacks are available in traditional bookshops. Both print and ebook formats are available online.

Find more titles and sign up to our readers' newsletter at http://www.johnhuntpublishing.com/fiction. Follow us on Facebook at https://www.facebook.com/JHPfiction and Twitter at https://twitter.com/JHPFiction.